Saving the Queen

WILLIAM F. BUCKLEY, JR.

Saving the Queen

Doubleday & Company, Inc.
GARDEN CITY, NEW YORK
1976

ISBN: 0-385-03800-3
Library of Congress Catalog Card Number 75-17405
Copyright © 1976 by William F. Buckley, Jr.
Printed in the United States of America
First Edition

FOR F. REID BUCKLEY

Exculpa me quod minxi in formam quam magnifice perfecisti

Acknowledgments

I don't yet know whether I—let alone the world of letters—am indebted to Mr. Samuel Vaughan of Doubleday for his mischievous suggestion that I write a novel in the first place; but I am certainly indebted to him, and to his associates, Betty Prashker and Hugh O'Neill, for their acute criticisms and fine suggestions. My thanks also to my friend and aide Frances Bronson for her help with the manuscript; to Robin Wu for his research; and to someone who prefers to remain anonymous for critical help in the research. And, finally, my thanks yet again to Joseph Isola for reading the galleys with his incomparable eye.

Saving the Queen

Prologue

HIS THREE FRIENDS, *his closest professional friends, were there at dinner in part because they weren't the type of people you have to tell it is time to leave. They could have stayed on to discuss the business at hand indefinitely, but, really, it would have been repetitious. Sometimes it doesn't matter if you say the same thing again and again in three or four different ways: It is a subtle technique for advancing a position—dangling it high, so that you can look at it from different angles, letting all the facets shine. But there were objections to doing so tonight. For one thing, he was right up against the deadline, and had to save those final hours to make his own decision. For another, the alternatives had not been raised at the dinner table for the first time. They had been the center of conversation among the highest officials of the Central Intelligence Agency ever since it had been resolved that a special panel, headed by the Vice-president, would interrogate them deeply about the kind of thing the CIA had been doing.*

For a while it was expected, within the organization, that a party line would be laid down by the director. But as the days went on, it became clear that he was not intending to do anything of the sort.

Perhaps in other days. But Watergate had just come and was not by any means yet gone. There a party line had been laid down, and it was only a matter of months before the people on the other side seized on the contradictions, charted them, computerized them, gloated over them: And

1

then, almost every day in the right-hand column of the morning paper, someone else was indicted. At the opposite end of the paper, the headline reported the conviction of the poor wretch indicted six months earlier—for following the party line.

Besides, no one in the Agency was going to urge him (*a*) to take an oath, and then (*b*) to tell a lie. If he wanted to, he could always plead the Fifth Amendment.

"I'm sorry, Mr. Vice-president, but I must decline to answer your question on the grounds that by doing so I might incriminate myself."

"That," Anthony Trust had remarked around the little dinner table in the handsomely appointed dining room, "is a pretty elegant solution, you know. They can have you fired. But would they? And what if the rest of us did it? Right down the line? We'd be roasted by the press. But there's something of a corporate nobility in our all doing it. . . ."

"Anthony"—his host smiled—"you have a wonderful way of glamourizing things, which is one reason, I suppose, why you are a successful veteran in this accursed profession into which you corrupted me as an innocent twenty-four-year-old. . . ."

Trust spoke with straight face: "Could we, please, cut the crap?"

He smiled at his oldest friend—still a bachelor, and at forty-six quickly becoming the most eligible one in town, tall, slim, with the dark glamour and bright, sudden smile, and the mysterious affinity for his work to which, indeed, he was married, as they say routinely of priests who are "married" to Mother Church.

It wasn't known whether Anthony would be summoned before the panel. The Agency (the top people had long since ceased calling it "the Company"—that was for recruits, middle-echelon bureaucrats, and popular novelists) had distributed a directive announcing that it was the wish of the Rockefeller Panel that witnesses should not consult with one another either to co-ordinate strategy or to compare notes. It could not seriously be expected that such an order would be observed: No force on earth, that spring evening in 1975, at 3025 P Street, Northwest, could have kept him,

2

and Anthony Trust, and King Harman, and Singer Callaway, from discussing the subject that quite naturally preoccupied them, so much so that he had sent his wife and youngest son to spend the week at the cottage at Martha's Vineyard. He had been told he should make no other appointments during the entire *week, suggesting the possibility that he would be on the stand during the whole period, allowing for the lengthy recesses a panel of such eminence permitted itself, for the discharge of other duties. Still, the staff was always on duty.*

It had been different with the director. He had testified the preceding week rather briefly (presumably, the panel intended to recall him after listening to his subordinates). His associates assumed they would hear the gist of his testimony. Even if it failed to come in to them obliquely, through an intermediary, at least they could reasonably expect to read about it in the New York Times, *to which, surely, one of the Rockefeller Panel would leak it.*

But there had been nothing.

Nothing at all; and now, suddenly, it was his turn, and he had no knowledge of what his responsibilities were. When the original announcement of an investigating panel was made, he had gone straight to the director.

"What's the line, chum?" He tended to become increasingly idiomatic as tension increased. This had become something of a trademark, though he remained, really, without affectation, with the possible exception that he never labored to conceal his intelligence, which is so much the accepted thing to do that, acting naturally, intelligence sometimes becomes suspect as affectation. The director was not so much hostile as protective.

"Look," he began. "There's a Hanging Party out there. Never mind who it is—let's stay professional, as we are trained to do, and keep our emotions out of it. They want the Rockefeller Panel to report that we have been"—he began to slur—". . . lying, stealing, killing, bribing, forging . . . fornicating . . . as a matter of official foreign policy for twenty-five years. They're not interested in what takes up ninety-nine per

3

cent of our time, which is studying the rainfall in the Ukraine. We're about to be examined by a political body. When a political body is convened, it has to satisfy political appetites. How to do that and do minimum damage to the country is something I-can't-write-a-directive-about. For one thing I am expressly forbidden to do so. For another, each of us has slightly different responsibilities and, predictably, a different way of explaining them to anybody who asks us to explain them.

"And, finally"—he walked away from his desk—"I am not going to suggest to anybody, let alone order him, to say something that will cause him to end up spending five years in jail as a reward for risking his life for his country."

He paused; distracted a moment ago, he now looked wizened, and cynical.

"There's no feeling anymore for the kind of thing we're doing, and there's no way, overnight, to stimulate that kind of feeling. I sometimes feel if the Washington Post's next edition revealed that at midnight I called the President and tipped him off that the entire first-strike resources of the Soviet Union were programmed to launch against us at 6 A.M., and the President persuaded Brezhnev against it after three hot hours on the hotline, the investigative reporter would give it out that the Agency had nearly triggered a nuclear war. Go away . . . by God, I'll be interested in how you handle them. I'll have the advantage of reading your transcript. Probably you'll never see mine. I don't know whether things will ever be the same after the hearings. Maybe we can use our remaining contact in Turkey and get jobs as eunuchs in the baths the congressmen patronize on counterpart funds. . . . Say, I wonder where I got that information. Take a note. Find out the name of the agent who gave me that information, and fire him. No, better still . . ." The director was now playing Ronald Colman, and flicked his fingers as if discarding an ash from a cigarette holder. "Better still, get rid of him." But he permitted himself a smile as he shot out his trigger finger to the door, which was the director's way of saying, "Out"— to which there was no known demurral.

After saying good night, his guests walked down the street toward Anthony's car. Singer said, "You know, I don't have any idea what he's going to do. I mean, I just can't guess what he's going to do. If they set aside a whole week for him, they've obviously decided to go over his entire period of service, to find out what one man, beginning at the bottom, and going up just about all the way, actually did."

Anthony Trust said, "They've picked on a man who got off to one hell of a start."

There was no comment. Harman, for one, knew nothing about the first assignment. Anthony knew more than he let on, but he didn't know it all, by any means. And it would greatly have surprised Singer Callaway to discover that not even he, who had been intimately involved in the operation, knew exactly how far the young man had got in, in the course of saving the Queen.

One

BLACKFORD OAKES was a good listener, but he had also developed skills at guiding any conversation in the direction he wanted to take it, including termination. Still, despite almost four years of practice with John Liebman, the skill tonight was offset by his roommate's lamentable condition: Though only 10:30, Johnny was quite drunk, and quite determined to tell Blacky in very considerable detail why, after all, he had decided *not* to marry Joan, the sufficient explanation of which Blackford knew but was careful not to reveal, namely Joan's antecedent decision not to marry John. Then Johnny, opening the window to reach for another can of beer sitting on the sill overlooking Davenport College Court-yard, discovered with horror that there were none left; and reaching into the cigarette box to dampen his frustration, discovered that he had simultaneously run out of cigarettes.

He turned to Blackford. "You and your goddamn . . . continence. I guess after graduation you'll go into training for the Graduate Engineering School lacrosse team and inflict on the next guy the necessity to go out into the wild night, in search of a normal room, with normal people, and normal supplies of the normal vices of this world."

Johnny got orotund when he was tight, and Blackford smiled at the familiar chiding, but, mostly, at the prospect of Johnny's going out. It was safe to assume, in his present condition, that he'd be gone at least a couple of hours, and that would give Blackford the time to open and study the sealed envelope passed to him that afternoon by the assistant registrar, after receiving in the morning mail the unheard-of summons *Please report Wednesday,*

March 14, at 4 P.M. (At Yale, mere registrars don't summon students thus peremptorily.) Out of sheer curiosity, Blackford had complied with the summons, rather than ignore it and wait for a conciliatory telephone call. Freshly returned from the war four years earlier, before Yale's bureaucracy became adjusted to dealing with war veterans, he once had been summoned—by the engineering dean himself—for missing a morning class. Engineering students were allowed no cuts. He appeared before the huge apple-cheeked, egg-bald bachelor who was rumored not to have left the Yale campus in forty years, except to take the baths in Germany during the summer.

"Mr. Oakes, why did you miss your chemistry class last Tuesday?"

"Diarrhea, sir," Oakes replied, with great gravity. Even as he said it, he winced at the memory of Greyburn College, where he had tested the limits of insolence as a fifteen-year-old, and lost, very heavily. But he was twenty-one now, a freshman, a war veteran, something, in fact, of a minor ace, and in an instant, he knew he would win this one. The dean paused just long enough to divulge, helplessly, his despair at framing an appropriate reply. He mumbled something about the necessity for maintaining rigid attendance records in the engineering school, and Oakes left, and cut as many classes thereafter as he was in the mood to do, without ever laying eyes again on the dean, except when the vast old man led the academic parades, carrying the huge mace, and looking neither to the right nor to the left, nor ever, under any circumstances, in the direction of Blackford Oakes, 1951.

Now, at the registrar's, he was put through to the assistant who had summoned him. Blackford was given a large envelope, with instructions to open it there and then. Inside was a typewritten note, attached by paper clip to a second, bulky envelope. The note said: *The person who has handed you this package is cleared. The attached envelope is to be opened when there is no possibility of your being seen or interrupted. Take the note you are now reading, detach it from the envelope, and return it to the person who gave you the package. Further instructions will be given to you in due course."* Blackford looked up at the registrar's assistant, a freckled man in his thirties, probably a failed graduate student who had eased into the educational bureaucracy and had acquired one of those special clearances Anthony had told him about. There was nothing more to say, so he returned the note folded, thinking to himself that he was off to a good start by folding it so as to conceal the printed matter.

"Thanks," he said, and walked out past the secretary, and the four bookkeepers. He wondered vaguely which of them had written on his March bill: "Mr. Oakes: Your account is three months past due." His stepfather paid all Blackford's bills promptly, once they were ninety days overdue. Sometimes, when he wanted a bill paid on time (his stepfather gave him fifty dollars a month and paid all his bills unflinchingly), he would type, or write in disguised hand over the face of the bill: PLEASE REMIT. NINETY DAYS OVERDUE. He mentioned this to Anthony Trust, at one of their frequent meetings in New York, and was faintly surprised to hear Anthony, so urbane in all matters, say, "Avoid petty deceptions." To which Blackford had answered, "Avoid saying 'Avoid' anything," and Anthony flashed that total smile, so specially appealing for its rarity.

"When I ran out of money at Yale"—Trust had graduated a year earlier—"I bought a stamp: DECEASED. RETURN TO SENDER. It obviously didn't work at places like Mory's, where they would see me night after night—for them it was just a post office error. But it did work with lots of odd-lot accounts. Yet you see, Black, that was a *major* deception, and that's all right. And besides," he said, "when I get money"—this euphemism was standard for "when my mother dies"—"I'll pay everyone back through a lawyer who will announce that young Trust, who died while a student at Yale, is the posthumous beneficiary of a legacy, part of which has been reserved for paying bills outstanding at the time of his death."

Anthony Trust was Blackford's oldest friend. Blackford recognized that chronological seniority is an unreliable fix on friendship. He was surrounded by classmates who were fonder of classmates they had not known longer than a few months or years than they were of their own brothers or sisters, or of friends they had come upon as classmates at kindergarten, or grammar school, or high school. There is no correspondence between length of service as friend and intensity of friendship. But there with Anthony,

9

the friendship had been both of long standing and of intensity. They had met as schoolboys during a period, in England, that had a gruesome climax. But that climax, although no doubt it annealed their friendship, did not bring it about. Black found himself situated to recognize, in Anthony, a quality he did not describe. But once or twice, in free-wheeling conversations with Sally, he ventured to say that, when all was said and done, there were those students at Yale who cared primarily about themselves, even if you interpreted this widely enough to include girls, grades, dogs, wives, children natural and unnatural, and dependent grandmothers—the whole lot. And others, who—somehow—felt, as automatically as anyone starting a long motor trip would feel the necessity to check the fuel gauge, the necessity to meditate regularly on the human condition. Anthony did this in a most natural way—rather like St. Theresa, with her worldly, workaday concern for the comfort of the sick sow and the dangers to the immortal soul of the King of Spain. ("Black! How *dare* you come out in favor of the Mundt-Nixon Act without asking yourself what its likely consequences are for lambs in the State Department who have strayed?") Anthony, for one thing, though formal of speech, was incapable of pomposity. Besides, he cared more about effective relief for those who suffered than about bombastic relief for those who formed committees. Often, the main purpose of "humanitarian" groups was to relieve themselves of effective concern for those who suffered. Anthony shrank from any form of reductionism: If you made the mistake, after the sixth beer at Mory's, of asking him to identify the principal source of evil in the modern world, he would pretend he didn't understand you. He disliked theoretical formulations. But, increasingly, those who knew him came to know what it was that principally horrified him. He said to Black, late one night at a beer joint on Park Street, "After Hitler, and Stalin, you *had* to say to yourself: Things have got to get better."

Trust influenced Blackford—more than that, had something of a hold on him—from the time they were at school together in England just before the war, and Trust was in the fifth form and Blackford a callow third-former. And now Trust had talked him into chucking plans for graduate school and, instead, applying for an altogether different line of work. Blackford's reasoning, at first, had been straightforwardly self-serving: The Korean War was beginning to go badly, he had received a note instructing him not to leave the country, his reserve unit was on stand-by notice. Unless he entered the FBI or a paramilitary research institute, or developed a sudden, gratifying disability, he might very well go from graduation to a quick refresher course in the latest fighter planes, with which he was dangerously current, having spent a month last summer mastering the new jet, and from there to Korea.

"Korea!" Trust said. "You thought *France* was a dull place to return to after a mission." Blackford had arrived in France in December 1944, fought several rather spectacular missions (he contacted, and destroyed, three Kraut ME109s) out of Rheims, contracted, and did not defeat, hepatitis in January, and celebrated V-E Day, at the hospital in Maxwell Field.

"I have been to Korea," said Anthony. "Unlike MacArthur, I shall not return."

Blackford knew that of course Anthony would return, if told to do so. Either that, or he would quit. But he would not be likely to quit, at such a time, an organization he was selling to Blackford, even if he stressed, in their early conversations, only the advantages of the CIA over the United States Air Force in Korea. Blackford sensed the other factor on the following Saturday. They had been ushers at a wedding and were driving together to New York with that bleary after-party feeling that makes ritual conversation unbearably irrelevant, inducing great bouts of deep-talk. Soon he realized that Anthony felt himself a member of a brotherhood. His distinctive individualism had been already conspicuous at seventeen, at Greyburn College: Though a prefect, Anthony was never a member of the prefecture. In the naval air force, he would contrive to go to a movie whenever there was a squadron social function, or a threat of one. At Yale he was asked to join, and declined: a fraternity, an honor society, a secret society, and a literary society. His only apparent extracurricular involvements were an occasional letter to the *Yale Daily News*, acerbic, polished, and conclusive in the sense of unfailingly suggesting that any contrary opinion should not presume to expect from him any rebuttal, and membership in the Political Union and debating team, whose meetings he generally missed.

11

But in those letters there was a strain of idealism. He did not believe in cheating, which wasn't that unusual; but it was awfully unusual to say so, in public: and rarer still to combine moralism with a debonair style. He thought the coup in Czechoslovakia the most devastating development in European history since Hitler's march on the Sudetenland, and he was savage in his destruction of the local fellow traveler in the History Department who had dismissed it at a college forum as a natural pre-emptive Soviet maneuver against a fascist resurgence. The candidacy of Henry Wallace aroused his supreme scorn, and he actually tabulated the Communist fronts to which Wallace's most conspicuous backers had belonged, and on one occasion even defended, at a formal debate, the proposition: *"Resolved, fellow travelers are worse than the real thing and should go to jail until they are old and gray."* Sarah Lawrence won, defending the negative, and everyone cheered, and Anthony remained unimpressed. Although he was studying as an exchange student at Oxford when the Wallace movement realized its fiasco in November, he was amused by the virtually unanimous pleasure that defeat had given to campus spokesmen for liberalism—Blackford had sent him a copy of the *Yale Daily News.* "They caught up with me," he told Black.

Blackford tore open the envelope. He fingered then the longest form he had ever seen. Forty pages. Leafing through it, he realized it would take him a full dull day's work to complete. The questions were of a dogged thoroughness that made the comprehensive form for flight school in 1943 look like a driver's license application.

Blackford was methodical, and neatly put away in a file case a foot from his typewriter, all the necessary autobiographical documents reposed: birth certificate, draft card, discharge papers, curriculum and grades dating back to early childhood. He had neatly recorded the date of his mother's birth in Buffalo, and of his father's in Akron, and even the basic figures on his stepfather. He could see that he would have to explain in some detail the reason he spent the night in jail in Cambridge, but he thought the circumstances innocent enough—or was the CIA made up only of people who never attended a bachelor party? He had never belonged to any political organization of any sort, though he would certainly have joined America First if they had accepted fourteen-year-olds; and other than the air force reserve, there was only the fraternity at Yale, and the senior society, in response to any mention of which, he smiled, he would dutifully leave the room, as tradition prescribed. He knew how many countries he had visited, how long he had spent there, even if some of these countries he could not remember—he had been too young. Anyway, his father junketing about the world to exhibit and sell airplanes, it was natural, until the divorce, that Black should have jogged about with the family. He knew exactly whose names to give as references, though he would not give the name of Dr. Chase at Greyburn or of Mr. Simon, but—yes, he would give the name of Mr. Long, the athletic director, with whom, in the last ten years, he had exchanged discreetly worded Christmas cards. Filling out the form would be an ordeal, but Blackford had an engineer's aptitude for recognizing the necessity of painstaking detail: All progress, someone had written, is made by the taking of careful measurements. He realized about himself that he could become an accountant without any great strain on his spirit—provided, of course, there was plenty of after-hours activity.

Within three days he managed to complete the form by carefully synchronizing his work on it with Johnny's frequent absences from their little suite, and then he stuffed it into the envelope (plain) addressed to someone he had never heard of, in Chevy Chase, Maryland.

Two months later he became anxious and called Anthony, who said that there was no way he could help him, that it was altogether possible that he would never officially know whether Black had been accepted: that there was literally nothing to be done, inasmuch as the CIA people already knew from the covering letter that if it didn't act before the United States Air Force did, they would either lose Blackford to the air force or face the intricate job of extricating him from his unit without, so to speak, anybody noticing. This the CIA knew how to do, but since it was always something of an operation, it was preferable to act quickly, pre-emptively.

"If they turn me down, how will they do it?" he asked Anthony.

"You'll never hear from anybody again."

So Blackford completed his application for graduate school rather listlessly; convinced, correctly, that he would never matriculate during this bellicose season—they were eating up fighter pilots in Korea. He felt rather bad about asking the two professors to write long enthusiastic letters of recommendation, but after all he was an honor student, with very high scores on the aptitude tests. Perhaps when it was all over he would go back to engineering. He found it especially vexing that he couldn't *talk* to anyone, except Anthony, about the application: The terms were laid out matter-of-factly. *Any leak would disqualify him.* Conversations with Sally about his future became wooden, and once, late on a Friday afternoon, before he took the seven o'clock train to New York, with Johnny safely departed for Poughkeepsie, she said to him, slouching on the sofa listening to the new phonograph that played 33 rpm, that he was beginning to sound like an Erector Set. On which remark Blackford made a ribald pun, naturally, and Sally, who was nicely spontaneous, eased up her skirt, a bare but unmistakable inch, which was her signal for encouraging his ardor. Even then, blissfully distracted, he found himself wondering, *in medias res:* Would his future duties require him to . . . seduce women routinely? He had been reading intensively in the general literature of intelligence and remarked that the old melodramatic idea of the spy whose achievements were done mostly through sexual manipulations and passenger pigeons had gone through a generation's literary disparagement. The subject came up these days only for the purpose of poking fun at it ("Spy work consists in eight hours a day with a dictionary and a basketful of foreign-language newspapers and magazines available at any cosmopolitan newsstand," one ex-OSS graduate student had told him). But his blood had quickened when Anthony said one day that that was only *largely* true, that the other stuff was also true, and that a month didn't go by that someone, "one of ours, one of theirs," didn't get—"eliminated."

"Or seduced?" Blackford asked.

Anthony looked disgusted and changed the subject.

Blackford had whispered to Sally, audaciously, that she was *such* an accomplished seductress, "you ought to become a foreign spy." Sally replied unnervingly, How did he know she wasn't one?

"I admit," she said later, her eyes sparkling, an unlit cigarette in her mouth, "my accent is so American you wouldn't be expected to guess what my real country is. . . ."

He took her cigarette, lit it clumsily, and said in the accents of Humphrey Bogart, "All right, baby. The game's up. Don't try anything, because the police are outside." Then he inhaled deeply, but spoiled the intended effect by coughing convulsively for ten minutes. It was the first ingestion of tobacco smoke since the vow he took along with the freshmen swimmers four years ago, hope-to-die, he said looking the coach in the eye, no cigarettes as long as I swim.

Later he sat down in the dining car and, textbook in front of him, gave his order—frankfurters and beans. He could not charge this dinner to his stepfather. A flannel-suited type sat down opposite him, and Blackford raised his eyes briefly, hoping it wasn't a college friend who would interrupt the hour-and-a-half New Haven–New York run he coveted for his book. It was nobody he knew, and in any case the bulky man was obviously as anxious to read his *Journal-American* as Blackford was to read his book. Neither engaged in any way a third man who was slowly eating his cheese, washing it down with red wine and complaining to the waiter that it had been chilled. After the main course was removed, dessert rejected, the dinner paid for, and the disgruntled cheese-taster finally gone, lecturing the porter on the way out, the flannel man leaned over and passed the sugar, which Blackford had not requested. He said in a quiet monotone:

"Mr. Oakes, your application has been acted on. We are familiar with your schedule, and you should not have any problem in coming in to see us tomorrow morning at 10:06. Press the button with the name Lawrence Dickering, at 23 West Twenty-fourth Street. You will need to put aside about two hours. You are to advise no one that you have been approached." He folded his paper, stood up, and said, "Good night."

Blackford took the subway and headed straight to Anthony's apartment.

"That's a bit goddamn much! How long have you creeps been following me around? *I* wasn't sure what train I'd take till *this* afternoon. No wonder they're recruiting all over America. They must need *millions* of people. Now I know what my job's going to be—to ride the rails until I see through my special prismatic lenses the invisible ink on somebody's lapel, and sit down and tell him to go to 23 West Twenty-fourth Street and ring old Larry Dicky's number, so that we can get one more guy to ride another railroad and keep Dicky—"

"Dickering."

Black paused. "How did you know?"

"Forget it," said Anthony. "Remember, other people's rituals always seem strange. We'll talk about it later, a lot later, and you can tell me then what happens and how you would run things if you were head of CIA." He rose and left, saying good night mechanically. Though the door to the hallway stayed open, and the elevator took a full minute to come, he said nothing else, nor did Anthony.

Blackford walked to the party, a dozen blocks away, down Park Avenue in waning June light, the spring song of the trapped little islands soothing his spirits. He passed the Soviet legation on Sixty-seventh Street, and stopped. As he looked through the iron rails into the courtyard, he thought of the time, three years before, when a Soviet schoolteacher had landed there after leaping. He looked up at the great vertical distance between the stories of the old mansion—to the third floor, where she had been detained. The police and ambulance arrived and she protested her imminent deportation to Russia, where, she said, she was destined for liquidation because she had inadvertently revealed her disillusionment with communism to her boyfriend, who turned out to be an MGB agent. Moments after arriving at the hospital, Soviet musclemen materialized, guarding her room. The Soviet ambassador announced flatly to the press that Madame Kosenkina would fly to Moscow immediately on being released from the hospital, that she was a Soviet civil servant whose behavior was none of America's business. An ingenious New York attorney woke up a judge and got a court order giving her a habeas corpus authority over her own movements, and she limped out of the hospital, under the glare of her immobilized captors, to an undisclosed haven causing, it was somewhere reported, a splendid storm of outrage late at night when the news was timidly given to Stalin himself. Blackford wondered if the CIA had been involved in any way. Then a policeman approached him. "You'll have to move on. No loitering here."

Blackford did as he was told, but—the habit was ingrained in him—only after that slight hesitation that causes doubt, and not a little apprehension. The policeman was relieved when the young man suddenly strode off, because his build, though slim, was pronouncedly athletic, and deep in his eyes there was an anarchic stubbornness, which policemen detailed to guarding the Soviet legation were experienced enough to spot, and, as necessary, make provision for.

Two

HE HAD INTENDED to ask Anthony whether "10:06" was an affectation, but forgot, and accordingly took pains to be punctual. This required him, it being Saturday and the subways uncrowded, to walk at an exaggeratedly slow speed, having arrived at the Twenty-third Street and Sixth Avenue subway station at 9:48 (the last thing he did before bunking down at Aunt Alice's apartment was dial ME 7-1212 and set his watch exactly). There was a newsstand on the corner and he lingered there, wondering whether, in the CIA, they teach you the art of lingering unselfconsciously. He remembered the story his father had told him when he was a little boy about the old man with the beard who was asked one day did he go to sleep with the beard under the covers or outside them, and the man said, You know, I don't remember, and that night he tried it first with his beard under, then over the covers, couldn't sleep, and in due course died of fatigue. (How Blackford had mused on that!) It occurred to him now that all his life he had loitered at book shops and newsstands without the least self-consciousness, but now he was absolutely convinced he was being watched, and accordingly he couldn't finger a newspaper or a pocketbook or a magazine casually, though he amused himself by thinking that maybe if old Dickering was watching him through his window with binoculars, Blackford should ostentatiously pick up a newspaper and read it upside down.

Why did his heart begin to beat, and his mouth dry up? I am twenty-five years old, a week away from a magna cum laude degree at Yale University, I shot down planes in combat in a

18

world war, I have faced down deans and generals and brothel-keepers, and I am suddenly nervous at meeting a GS-14 in a New York apartment. . . .

He put down the newspaper, buttoned the bottom of his seer-sucker jacket, and strode purposefully to the door he had already, by a process of side-wise visual elimination, calculated as, necessarily, being No. 23. There were eight buttons to choose from in the dingy exterior. Dickering's was First Floor, Rear. He pushed the bell and, as he did so, looked at his watch and cursed himself. Only 10:05. The buzzer sounded, and he pushed open the door and walked through the dark corridor with the old linoleum on the floor toward a green door. Well below Blackford's eye level was a card, LAWRENCE DICKERING. He looked for a bell but there wasn't any, so he knocked, and Anthony Trust opened the door.

Blackford was at once relieved, intrigued, and enraged. He said nothing as he walked into a room with two armchairs and a sofa, a desk of sorts, and a fireplace that probably hadn't been used in years. The walls were papered, and two or three prints of Olde New York hung haphazardly, here and there. There was a coffee table, with the morning's New York *Times* and *Wall Street Journal,* and a large bookcase, with books but no book jackets, as though they had been accumulated over a number of years, none of them recent. The door leading presumably to a bedroom was closed. On the floor the carpet was brown, and old.

Blackford sat down on one of the armchairs.

Trust stayed standing, and began to pace up and down the room. A minute or two passed.

"This wasn't my idea," he said; and, after another pause, "But I suppose it's not such a *bad* idea. But *I* didn't volunteer."

Blackford remained silent.

"Blacky, this is going to take time, and only part of it is my fault. Look. In the Company—the CIA—there are lots of categories and distinctions. One of them is between the *deep-cover agent* and the agent who is—well—something else. The decision was made in your case—don't ask me why—to accept your application and to train you as a deep-cover agent. Now this means a lot of funny things happen to you, like the business last night on the goddamn train. *He* knows who you are for the simple reason that he was the principal leg man checking out your background.

He knows *everything* about you—well, he doesn't know the Greyburn bit; but he even poked around Cambridge and checked out the drunk charge at Bailey's wedding.

"Now"—Trust had obviously done this before, and Blackford wondered how many times—"get a load of this. *He* knows you're headed into the Company; *I* obviously know it; but apart from the two of us, there is *exactly one other human being who knows it*. A committee of men know you exist, in the sense that they know the qualifications of a certain applicant. But before they went over these qualifications, all identifying figures were removed or disguised. They decided to take on, as a covert agent, a young guy, freshly out of college, competent in French, highly skilled in engineering and theoretical physics, with a mother living in London with her well-connected and prosperous husband, a British businessman. Subject's father is a sort of commercial gypsy fly-boy genius in the airplane brokerage racket. Subject is well regarded by faculty and students, is healthy and smart, physically attractive, indeed is known to have been irresistible to several ladies, was an officer and an ace during the war, is said to be well adjusted, tenacious, and coolheaded, and—forgive me this, Black—fond of his country and of its liberal institutions.

"They know you as Geoffrey T. Truax. By the way, Black, you may as well commit that to memory, since that is now your 'name.' You'll be assigned under that name to some mission, nature undisclosed and, for all I know, unformulated. This much I *have* been told: that you will be sent to England. Deep-cover agents need above all things a convincing cover. A mother who lives in London is considered good natural cover. You haven't really visited with your mother much since the war. It's natural you should join her, and since your stepfather is both wealthy and an architect, it makes sense that he should vaguely welcome you to England for a year or so, maybe to see whether a young Yale-trained engineer could make out in London. Details to be worked out.

"First: At this end you'll receive, in the next day or two, an order to report for an army physical. When you check in, you'll be put through the usual routine. Your chest X ray, when developed, will show a tiny spot on the lung. You'll be reassured that with modest precautions, it won't keep you from living a full and vigorous life, but you will be instantly discharged from the reserves. This heartbreaking news you'll make known to your friends"— Anthony now mocked his friend's formal verbal formulations— "with an appropriate blend of joy and sorrow, a formula the Central Intelligence Agency is pleased to leave to your own devising. You will then approach the dean and tell him your doctor has recommended a year of relative leisure, and that you are therefore withdrawing your application for graduate school and going to England and the Continent for the next year. Say that you will advise the dean's office next spring what the doctor says about the prospects of your re-entering school.

"Now, here is a ticklish one. *You must spend two months during the summer in Washington.* There you'll get whatever training the deep-cover people get—which is scant, in contrast to what the in-house professionals get. None of the specialists who handle you will see you for more than five consecutive sessions, and you won't be in the same building—we call them 'safe houses'—more than five times. Everyone will know you only as Geoffrey or Mr. Truax. While in Washington, you'll be paid in cash. You are expected to pay the usual income tax and will list your salary— $4,400 per year, by the way—as 'miscellaneous receipts.' Now: We have been fussing over the question of what could plausibly take you to Washington, and though we have ideas in reserve, we'd like to come up with something better."

"Sally lives in Washington." Blackford spoke for the first time.

"Is she going to be there this summer?"

"Yes. She has a job with a congressman. She's doing a master's in Congressional Government. She chose the biggest bore in Washington, on the grounds that she wanted her book to be authentic."

"Well, what about it? Why not follow her to Washington for a couple of months? Even if you're not inclined to do so, would you be willing to give her the impression that that was why you wanted to go to Washington?"

Blackford appreciated the way Anthony moved into the subject: delicately. A liaison with Sally in Washington had not quite yet got itself framed as a CIA directive, but it had all the makings of one.

Yes, he thought. He could go to Washington. He wasn't ready

to marry Sally or even propose to her. And anyway, Sally would know he was too industrious by nature to go to Washington merely to be with her when the congressman wasn't. He would have to concert the advantages of a summer in Washington: Sally *plus* something else. . . .

"Is there a clinic or a specialist or somebody who could spend the summer nursing my poor lung?"

"Washington isn't a center of pretubercular research." Anthony spoke as though to himself. He looked up: "But the doctor at New Haven *could* give you the names of a half dozen doctors associated with a half dozen clinics around the country and recommend you spend a couple of months with any one of them. You are left with a reason for choosing Washington—"

"And I obviously have that reason with Sally there . . . though there should be something academic thrown in. . . ."

The tension was drawing out of the room, and soon Black's questions were asked without tension. Was he to tell his mother the same business about the lung? How could his stepfather actively co-operate without being brought into the conspiracy? To these questions Anthony had ready answers. His mother was to be told about the lung, but once across the Atlantic, the disability could safely be minimized, even ridiculed. The stepfather was a different problem. He was perfectly capable of informing Black that no research was necessary to establish that opportunities for young engineers in America were infinitely greater than in England, that in any case Black didn't have English working papers and would need to associate himself with an American company actually to do any work, and so on. His stepfather, an indulgent type, wouldn't much mind a leisurely year after college, but since Black had no other means of support, except for one of those episodic checks from his father on the infrequent occasions when he sold three DC-4s to the Paraguayans, it would be a little ungainly to have to ask the stepfather for a regular living allowance.

It had all been anticipated.

"A foundation here in New York will make you a grant to report on the effect of Point 4 on the English economy, with special attention to differences in historical British and American engineering techniques and theoretical inclinations. You'll make the application to the foundation right after you see the dean at Yale. Here are the forms. They are already completed, needing only your signature. You will see that the foundation expects an application from you, and you will have to come up with letters of recommendation"—Blackford groaned at yet another raid on his friends on the faculty, but, after all, they would have saved copies of the letters they had already sent to the graduate school.

"Now," said Anthony, "there's one more thing."

"What is it?"

"Greyburn."

"What does that have to do with this business?"

"I don't know. But I shouldn't have concealed it. I had to fill out a form telling *everything* I know about you. Greyburn was important."

"Why?"

"Because it was a primal experience. You were shaken by it and it belongs in your psychological profile. I don't know how much scar tissue is left, but I know there is some, and *I* honestly don't know whether it will get in the way of your operating successfully in England. You haven't been there since you left school, and I've heard you on the subject of some unpleasant characteristics of English institutional life. You still have a lot of passion. . . ."

"I've still got a lot of passion about Dr. Chase. And Simon. And what they got away with—still do get away with, for all I know. I'd like to think the war wiped out the whole bloody lot of them. Sometimes I wondered in France: God! Do you suppose I'm here to save *Dr. Chase?* . . ."

"That's the kind of thing I'm talking about. Tell you what I've decided. *I'm* charged with writing on the record any 'significant experiences' I know you've had. I won't. On two conditions: You ask me not to. And *you* tell me that you're asking me not to because the experience is behind you."

Blackford was pale, and, hands deep in his pockets, slouching on the armchair, he pinched the flesh of his thighs sharply and answered in a matter-of-fact tone.

"In answer to your first condition: Yes, I ask you not to. In answer to the second: You don't put something like that 'behind you.' I've met a lot of English people since leaving Greyburn, and haven't had any quarrel with them. Only once, when someone was preaching about the virtues of English public schools. Even then, I just left, without throwing up. To answer your question: It won't impair my work."

Anthony said lightly, abruptly changing his tone: "Okay. But I know you, Blacky"—he smiled. "One of these days you're going to say to yourself, *'We're even.'* I don't know what will make you say that. What will it take? I've got no business worrying about it since I'm satisfied you won't give English secrets to the Russians. And I don't think the English have any secrets from anybody else. As far as I'm concerned, you're at liberty to give the secret menus of Greyburn to the Soviet secret police."

"That would bring the Soviet revolution to a quick, constipated halt," Black smiled, getting up.

Three

IT WORKED, NO HITCHES. His friends turned out to be less concerned over his health than happy for him that he was now safe from a war that was getting bloodier every month. The final days at Yale were carefree, and consisted in part of the nostalgic task of dismantling the accretions of four years, and attempting, shyly, to repay some special debts.

Black felt a great, however unarticulated, affection for three of his professors. He sat and wrote them, in his meticulous hand, the reasons why each one had meant so much to him, and in what ways. He had been afraid he would stifle that impulse, but he wrote out the letters all in a single night and was relieved to have done so. He went for the hundredth time to David Dean Smith's to bargain-hunt for some of the 33 rpm records, and sent the three professors each a two-volume set of the Diabelli Variations, played by Leonard Shure, which he charged, giving his stepfather's address. He sold most of his books and instantly regretted it. They yielded $110, had cost him six times that, and he suspected that one day he would like to be able to reach for the *Antigone* and find the passages he had marked, because they pleased, or perplexed, him. He attended two functions at the fraternity, one of them stag, the second open to Sally, who was girlishly happy at Black's news that he would be spending the summer in Washington. For once she permitted herself to act, in public, as something less than a lofty graduate student crossing the tracks to condescend and minister to undergraduates. (Poor Sally, for all her academic seniority, she was only twenty-two. *She* hadn't had to take time out to go to France to save England.) He looked at her with the mint julep Jud, the Negro bartender at Zeta Psi, specialized in for the rites of spring, and wondered if anywhere in the world there was at this balmy moment a girl more lovely, with her loose brown hair, wearing white, and pearls, and a glossy red belt, her lips barely separated, her eyes gazing at the mint julep, but directed at him, her conversation routinely bright, with the little cynicisms she affected distractedly. It was then that he saw the message, as vividly as if it had been sewn on her blouse: *Blacky Oakes is deceiving me, Sally Partridge.*

She looked up at him squarely, and the banter stopped.

"What's going on?"

He stood there, tall and tanned, the straw in his hair blooming after the long winter, his white pants and blazer and fraternity tie making him look suddenly like a sixteen-year-old schoolboy, his thin, molded features without sign of age or strain, his eyes relentlessly intelligent, discerning, blue-frank, blue-cunning. He said simply:

"I bribed the doctor."

Her hand reached out and tightened on his.

"Blacky, what if you are caught?"

"I won't be," he said, "but I'm not going to give you any details."

"Then—you won't be coming to Washington after all?"

"Sure," he said. "But I won't be going in and out of clinics. I'll be sitting in on some engineering courses at the summer school at George Washington." In the two years he had known her, Blackford had never seen in Sally a scintilla of curiosity about anything scientific, and he felt safe invoking engineering to abort any impulse to specific curiosity.

"Blacky, I'm glad. It was just stupidity that you signed on for the reserve in the first place. You've done your tour of duty. You're not dodging anything. But oh God, if you get caught."

"Look, I told you it's not going to happen. At worst they'd discover that somebody else's chest X ray was confused with mine. That *has* happened before."

"Well, why did you pull out of graduate school?"

"I wanted to make the story sound right, and, to tell the truth, I wouldn't *mind* a year off. And I *have* neglected Mother."

"So you'll be neglecting me instead."

"Sally, next year you'll be working toward your big degree, and you care about that more than about anything else in the world right now, including (a) me, (b) a victory in Korea, or even (c) the goddamn United World Federalists. There is a lot of time. Meanwhile, it's not impossible that there's going to be a very general and very grisly war, in which case each of us is going to end up taking orders from somebody."

He finished his drink, and felt sick and smooth, and supposed that as time went on, he would feel less sick and more smooth. He thought, Well: at least this lie around, I took the brunt of it. There are bound to be others, where the victim will be someone else. He wondered whether, at any of the sessions he would have with the CIA instructors, they would discuss ethics. He hadn't studied ethics formally at Yale, and he was impatient with some of the niceties that preoccupied his Thomistic friends, particularly after two or three drinks. He tended to rely on instinct, and unlike Anthony, who was steeped in the literature of the Cold War, Blackford was content simply to know that there were the bad guys and the good guys, and that nit-picking about the good guys didn't make the bad guys less bad, that the world was going through an ideological ordeal concerning which he intended to inform himself, and that events had conspired to give him an anonymous role in the struggle. He began, suddenly, to feel less the conscript of events. Though the idea might not have occurred to him to enter CIA if he hadn't had the reserve hanging over him, now he wondered whether providence mightn't have had a hand in it all—he liked the word "providence" because he thought it a respectable, New Englandish way to avoid the word "God," which was altogether too personal and . . . intrusive, sort of. He didn't like it much that, in the classrooms, God was pretty defenseless against the wisecracks of the teachers. But, he thought philosophically, God is used to a lot worse than he gets at Yale, and anyway, isn't He overdue for a miracle if He really wants to engage our attention? Last November he had attempted to argue seriously with friends at Zeta that Yale's victory over Harvard was that long-awaited miracle, but nobody was in the mood for Black's frivolity.

Later that night, in Sally's car, they did it for the last time under the shadow of West Rock. She was silent, but prehensile.

He was distracted, but taken by lust, and he had to remind himself to be tender, and was glad when the moon was suddenly blotted out by the huge stone because she would be opening her eyes any second now, and she wouldn't be able to see, in his face, that he was thinking about subjects other than Sally, and the Last Copulation at West Rock.

He rented a one-bedroom furnished apartment. An agitated landlord explained that if the apartment's *regular* tenant were suddenly to return, some adjustment would have to be made respecting the furniture. But since Mr. Ellison hadn't shown up for seven months, and was thereby six months behind in the rent, the landlord decided he would simply appropriate the use of the furniture until *some* sort of settlement was made, and he asked Blackford whether he didn't think that was entirely reasonable since the landlord had made no effort until recently to rent the apartment, confident that Mr. Ellison would show up with an explanation and a lot of back rent. Blackford asked whether he had gone to the police, and the landlord said, Oh yes, *and* the Bureau of Missing Persons. What did Mr. Ellison do, Blackford asked, thinking to himself, God, I bet I know what racket *Ellison* was in. Mr. Ellison, said the landlord, was a winetaster, who took his duties very seriously. He pointed to a large closet.

"I've locked this because there are a great many wines in the closet and Mr. Ellison told me some of the wines he tastes are worth fifty dollars a bottle, so I don't want him coming back and telling me the tenants drank up a thousand dollars' worth of wine."

Blackford said he was surprised that there *were* winetasters in Washington, but the landlord wasn't surprised at all, or at least hadn't thought about it, and when the police searched the desk, there was nothing there to give them a clue as to whom Mr. Ellison worked for or who his clients were.

"On the whole," he said, "he was an ideal tenant, except for his disappearing. I've never had a disappearance before, and they are very expensive. I suppose you can use his record library"—it was extensive, Blackford noted, and eclectic—"but you'll be responsible for any damages. We have a detailed inventory of Mr. Ellison's possessions. There, that's a picture of Mr. Ellison. He doesn't look like a winetaster, does he? Although," he added pensively, "I'm not sure what winetasters look like."

Blackford turned to the framed picture of a man with slick hair and a mustache, Don Ameche slightly unfocused, a prim handkerchief in his jacket pocket, smiling lasciviously, as if he had just tasted a great burgundy. The two rooms were vastly overfurnished, crowded with bric-a-brac and old issues of *Life, Look, Time, Saturday Evening Post, Collier's*. Blackford wondered where the oenophiles' journals were and thought Ellison must be a real sport to pass himself off as a winetaster, working in the sunkissed vineyards of Washington, D.C.

He wondered when the landlord would stop talking and, thinking it might help, took off his coat and tie, complaining of the awful damp heat, which would in fact plague him during the next nine weeks.

"Is there such a thing as an air-conditioned safe house?" he asked "Tom"—the instructors gave only a single name, a Christian name.

"I've never been in one," was all he could get out of Tom, whose specialty was Visual Identification. At their first meeting in the house on O Street, Tom greeted him economically, signaling to follow him into the adjacent room, where two card tables were set together. Tom closed the door:

"Now, draw or list on that yellow pad everything you noticed in the living room we just walked through."

Black was always confident when in possession of a pencil and paper and under orders to sketch something. He had been born with the facility and it had developed into the craftsmanship that got him into trouble at Greyburn and an A in mechanical drawing at Yale; but other than the window they had passed and, he thought, a bookcase on the left and some sort of a couch, he now remembered nothing. Finally he let the pencil drop.

Tom was not censorious. He had seen it too often in his pupils.

"An agent needs to notice everything. Not only the unusual. If I had led you through a room with a nude girl lying on the couch, I'd want you to notice the color and shape of the couch."

"You mean, *not* the color and shape of the girl?" Blackford asked; but Tom wasn't the kind of instructor you make that kind of comment to, because all he said was, "Geoffrey, don't smart-ass me. My job isn't to tell you whom to screw. It's to notice whom you screw, and where."

Blackford learned that there are techniques for developing powers of observation, and after three long afternoons with Tom he was stuttering out details about the people he saw on the bus, and the advertising signs, and the beads of sweat that accumulated on the Washington *Post* merely from leaning over and reading it in that awful, hot summer. Blackford told Tom that at Yale he had signed up for a course in mnemonics taught, "would you believe it?" he asked Tom, who by the third day was indulging an occasional idiomatic familiarity, "by a freshman. The freshman had been a student of Bruno Fürst, who had written a book about developing your memory, and the freshman persuaded the chairman of the *Yale Daily News* to give him a big spread prior to a public demonstration."

Blackford and two hundred other curious students attended, and the freshman had two fellow students on the teaching platform with him—with a copy of the *Life* magazine that had been distributed that morning.

"The freshman pointed to a member of the audience and asked him to call out a number between 1 and 160.

"'129,' somebody said.

"'All right, Joe, what's on page 129 of the current issue of *Life?*' The trainee closed his eyes for a minute and said, 'A half-page run-over story on Margaret Truman's singing career and a half-page ad for Firestone tires.' The freshman triumphantly opened *Life* to page 129 and held it out for the audience to verify."

"A stunt," Tom said.

Blackford said he had sensed that, but that he had taken the course, thirteen two-hour seminars for which he paid the freshman instructor thirteen dollars.

"One of the sessions was devoted to how to remember somebody's name, and the idea," Blackford explained to Tom, "is to decide what *individual* feature in a particular person is most susceptible to caricature—

"For instance, Tom, I'd say hair, in your case. Your hair is very —neat—so I would try to find an association between *neat* and *Tom*. And the more absurd the connection, the more it fastens in the memory. For instance"—Black was suddenly wondering whether he would be able to bring this off—"*Tom* has only two consonants, *t* and *m*. In the Fürstian system, *t* is the letter that corresponds to the number 1 and *m* to the number 3, so that if I can establish a relationship between *neat* and *13*"—Blackford, beginning to perspire, was trying now to remember what Alan, the first instructor, had told him about never losing control of any situation—"I'd say to myself: It would *certainly* ruin the neatness of your hair if someone propped a great big wooden 13 on top of your head. Every time I saw you, I'd think of a 13 sitting on top of your hair. *Then* I would know that your name began with a *t* and ended with an *m*. I would then go quickly through the available possibilities, following the conventional vowel order—*a, e, i, o, u: Tam, Tem, Tim, Tom, Tum.* Two possibilities emerge, since we can reject the first, second, and fifth"—Tom was beginning to look at Blackford with a trace of concern, which he showed by running his hand through his hair, leaving it distinctly tousled, and damaging Black's whole mnemonic construction—"so it boils down to your being *Tim* or *Tom*, and here"—Blackford's relief was palpable—"here, at this stage, you have to rely a little bit on your plain memory, like, *Tom*, not Tim, is the man I knew with the neat hair and the wooden 13 perched on top of it."

"I see," Tom said. "Whatever happened to the young man who taught the course?"

"Oh yes, I forgot about that. Well, he taught the seminar during the spring, and that summer I ran into him on Park Avenue and we greeted each other, only he couldn't remember my name, and I couldn't remember his, though I couldn't imagine him except on a rocking chair, but I couldn't remember what a rocking chair was supposed to remind me of . . . I think it's a system you have to practice all the time—no summer vacations." Tom seized on the apparent consummation of the story to tell Blackford that the quality of observing things and people was something an agent *never let up on*, that it became a matter of habit. Other instructors, later in the month and in the next months, would keep prodding Truax on the point, to keep him alert.

Actually, Blackford's formal—as distinguished from his observational—memory was not only good, it was something of a phenomenon. As a child his father used to show him off by reading a verse, which Blacky would then repeat—word for word, syllable by syllable—with high seriousness, ignorant, at age three, of the meaning even of Hilaire Belloc's kindergarten verses. Blackford had been wondering whether it would be vain in him to apprise Tom of this particular facility, and now decided that perhaps this was the opportune moment to come out with it.

"When I signed on for the memory course," he explained, "it was to learn the trick stuff. The simple act of memorization— figures, dates, poetry, that kind of thing—I've always been able to handle pretty well."

"Good," said Tom, pulling out his note pad and scribbling something on it. Black wondered how many marines were required to protect the contents of Tom's notebooks. *Personal Observations of the Habits, Skills, and Idiosyncrasies of Deep-cover Agents I Have Known.* Was there enough there, under Truax, to triangulate in on Blackford Oakes?

He was given a dozen books to read, none of them technical. He supposed that if he was assigned to a dynamite-wielding mission, someone, somewhere, would pop up to acquaint him with the fashionable uses of dynamite, his introduction in that subject at Maxwell Field ("How to be useful if shot down and incorporated in the resistance movement") having been cursory and, in any event, six years ago. Nor was he shown any fancy rifles or secret weapons or miraculous chemicals. He wondered—and at one point came close to asking "Harry"—whether he was, really, still on probation. He realized, at this point, that if at this moment he defected, went to the Soviet Embassy, and told them everything he knew, the Soviet Union would know nothing it didn't know already except the addresses of three safe houses which in any case were abandoned as a matter of precaution every ninety days.

The books, far from being esoteric, were in some cases recent best sellers. There was one about a young Nazi soldier who in an excess of conscience decides he is shooting at the wrong people. He makes his allegiance known to U. S. Intelligence, who use him to relay to the western front information he gathers at great personal risk inside Germany. It was a gripping story, and Blackford found himself wondering for the first time—why hadn't it been a subject of conversation, or thought, when he was fighting in the war against Germany in France?—about the strange, corporately benumbed conscience of the German legions who fought bravely (most of them), dutifully (almost all of them), enthusiastically (an impressive majority) for an indefensible regime? These, surely, were sins of commission, yet the universality of the hypnosis, somehow, rendered it all passive. Here was a book about a Nazi soldier who, somehow, had tripped on a shard of conscience, which magically reordered his perspective. Blackford wondered: Was there now—was there in prospect—a Western counterpart? *He* had not been moved purely by conscience to join the CIA, though Trust surely had, even if he would not put it so. Would there be books in the future, and if so how would the author contrive the moral drama that would put Trust in the kind of light that shone now so brightly on this young German? He wondered, too, how many such there were within the Soviet Union. Another book described in detail the fate of hundreds of thousands of Russians who, in the course of the war, during the high tide of Nazi military success, had been captured by the Germans and made to perform services, military, paramilitary, and menial. By Allied agreement with Stalin himself, these were forcibly repatriated to Russia in the months after V-E Day, even though they implored the British and the Americans to permit them to emigrate.

"Nobody on our side believed," "Alan" explained, "that they were anything but paranoid in insisting that they were being taken back to Russia to be tortured and slaughtered."

But that, according to this account, was exactly what happened. It was "Rudolph" who was most passionate on the implications of that theme. There was just a trace of an accent there, and Blackford could not guess its provenance, and of course would not have presumed to inquire. He suspected Rudolph of having an academic background, because he was given to academic formulations. "Violence in pursuit of a national objective is a social characteristic, not a social anomaly"—that kind of thing. But Rudolph, discussing Koestler's *Darkness at Noon*, mostly in italics, told Blackford that it was necessary to recognize that Stalin operated without any *predictable* restraints.

"That's *very hard* for *us* to understand"—Rudolph spoke, unrelentingly, in weighted phrases—"because even *the most cold-blooded of us* know intellectually that *it is wrong,* for instance, to *kill people* wantonly, or torture them to no purpose. We know enough about Stalin to know that—on the contrary—he *takes pleasure* in killing and in causing pain. And he has a vehicle to justify what he does: *the revolution."*

Blackford asked why there weren't wholesale defections from the system, and Rudolph explained that the principal reason was fear—fear of defiance and fear of the futility of individual gestures in the age of totalitarian sophistication.

"But there's something else, and it was expressed by Bukharin when he was condemned to death by Stalin's court while absolutely innocent." Rudolph stood, tapped his cigarette ash—too late as usual—in the general direction of the wastebasket, and walked excitedly to a bookshelf, pulled out a book, and looked at the index. . . .

"Here," he said, "listen—these are Bukharin's words to the court. Now understand, Bukharin is *innocent,* but he makes a public confession of guilt. '*I shall now speak of myself* "— Rudolph's voice was grave with emotion—" '*of the reasons for my repentance. . . . For when you ask yourself: If you must die, what are you dying for?—an absolutely black vacuity suddenly rises before you with startling vividness. There was nothing to die for if one wanted to die unrepentant. This, in the end, disarmed me completely and led me to bend my knees before the Party and the country. At such moments, Citizen Judges, everything personal, all personal incrustation, all rancor, pride and a number of other things, fall away, disappear. . . . I am about to finish. I am perhaps speaking for the last time in my life.'* "

Rudolph looked up. His eyes were moist, and Blackford looked away.

"There," Rudolph said, "*that's* why. The revolution is still a matter of *faith,* and if you haven't that faith, you must stimulate it in yourself, otherwise you are living for nothing. Pascal posed much the same problem when he asked Christians to believe. Let's eat."

He opened a brown paper bag, Blackford opened his, and they ate silently for ten minutes, and Rudolph took Coca-Cola from a refrigerator. In ten minutes they were back at work.

34

Rudolph knew something about the history of the Soviet secret police, about the kind of training its agents got, the kind of assignments they carry out.

"We in the Company spend several hundred million dollars a year collecting information about the Soviet Union the equivalent of which, about the United States, the Kremlin can get by subscribing to a half-dozen technical journals. In the Soviet Union *everything* is secret. Every crumb of information we have, we have wrenched out—and even then, we cannot make projections. It isn't just Stalin. There is a loose dynamo in the Soviet will, and you cannot tell where it is going to take us: *Nothing is predictable.* Though some things are nearly so, among them that—just to give you an idea—a copy of all Ivy League 1951 yearbooks"—Rudolph had taken a flying leap at Truax's immediate past—"is in Soviet hands, and a record is being entered of names, faces, dates of birth."

"All of them?"

"Yes, all of them. They aren't short of man power. And they know that maybe thirty-five to fifty members of the graduating classes ended up with us, and they will work years to try to find out (a) who and (b) what are they up to."

Black yearned to see Anthony. He needed to *talk*. Four weeks had now gone by, and his life had fallen—hardened—into a pattern. Two or three evenings a week he spent with Sally, the others reading. He began to feel a restlessness that neither books nor exercise nor sex could satisfy, and he couldn't diagnose it, which worried him. He called Anthony on the phone not knowing exactly why. The obvious reason—that Anthony was still his closest friend—was blurred by an inchoate resentment that Black's dissatisfactions, his awful feeling of emptiness, restlessness, directionlessness, were something General Trust was somehow responsible for. Black ruled against an introspective examination of his motives, deciding, simply, to call his best friend. In doing so he found himself conforming not resentfully, but with a combination of good sportsmanship and institutional pride, to the specified procedures.

He made the call from a pay telephone in central Washington.

He dropped the requisite coins in the slot, and the number rang. A strange voice answered, a man's voice.

"I want to speak to Mr. Trust."

"Who is calling?"

He hesitated only slightly. "Mr. Truax."

Anthony's voice came on in a matter of seconds. There was in it the formal strain (somebody-in-the-room). But the undisguised pleasure that flooded his clipped words was what Black most longed for and needed: He had had intensive corporate solicitude for weeks now, and wanted, now, individual solicitude, and the opportunity he still felt he needed to confide, confide with someone with whom his relations were of long standing, uncomplicated by sex, moodiness, petulance, jealousy. He struggled to make his request appear—if not exactly casual—at least something less than imperative.

"Listen, I just called to ask—you coming this way soon?" He paused, but only for a moment, fearing that Anthony's schedule might yield a negative before he could know the underlying urgency of the invitation. "If not, I'll get up to New York to see you."

Anthony absorbed the whole of the message, as if through a single electrode. His hesitation was purely administrative. Though he did say, "Hang on a minute while I check my schedule," Black knew that he would be seeing him about as soon as the transportation system between New York and Washington could get him there.

It was less than a minute.

"I'll see you tomorrow, Geoffrey. But look, I can't make it till nine. We'll have a late dinner. It will have to be at your place. Buy a hamburger. Goddammit, buy a steak, you stingy bastard."

Blackford did more than that. Early in the morning, before his class on Contact with "Harry," he went to the delicatessen and bought steak and caviar, potatoes, and vodka, two wines, French rolls, some celery remoulade, and an ice-cream cake. When Anthony rang the bell, Blackford followed exemplary procedure. First he turned off the overhead light. Then he raised the curtain slightly, permitting him a view of the caller, two stories below. The curtain then went down, the light on, and the release button was depressed.

Anthony put his arms around Black, bussing him, in the French manner, on both cheeks. It was late, so Black started directly with the vodka and caviar, and they talked until two in the morning. Anthony waited until Black talked and talked about his experiences, his questions, his doubts, his anxiety—what was the nature of the anxiety? What was the restlessness he felt? When oh when would he have some idea of what specifically he would be doing? How was he doing as far as the Agency was concerned? Did Anthony receive any reports on him? How do you measure progress? How do you keep from going crazy with loneliness?

"Fortunately, I'm used to Sally never asking me anything about my work, because she decided some time after she learned long division that the limits of her scientific understanding had been reached. But at Yale I could talk to her about *personal* experiences, about the teachers, about other guys. Now I have to make all that up, and it's driving me nuts. I invented a character called Costello, who is allegedly taking a course in advanced structural physics with me, and I found myself night after night describing Costello and his general attitudes, and by God *now* she wants me to bring Costello to dinner next time, so *tomorrow* I'm going to have to kill the poor bastard off, or have him leave to see his sick mother in Canada. It's driving me crazy."

Anthony was soothing—and understanding, Blackford thought later. In a way, what he said was boiler plate. But what else could he say? He had seen it before, with other deep-cover agents. It won't always be this way, he said, because precisely the point of a deep-cover agent is that he is destined to lead a normal public life, as in due course Black would be doing. And *that* life you can talk about as freely as you care to, and to anyone you like. The duties of such an agent are very carefully calculated not to occupy so much of his time as to run the risk of blowing the cover.

"Some agents," Anthony said, "have regular, full-time jobs, and what they do for us either is done after hours, or else is in some way related to the job they are holding down. . . . In your case, your work is for the foundation, to be done more or less at your own pace. If it becomes necessary to have physical evidence of the work you have done, that can be arranged. And remember, there will be one man in London you will see on an entirely candid basis—your superior. You'll be talking to him as candidly as to me. More so, because he will know your assignment.

"And"—this took Black a little by surprise, even as Anthony's language did when it shucked off the aw-shucks integument he usually wrapped it up in—"you'll find something strange. Something not so lonely. There's a funny incorporealized solidarity out there. You don't know who they are, but you *do* know that you are all straining to achieve the same end, and a day comes when their invisible forms are as palpable as the members of your swimming team.

"But," he said, "that takes a while. It took me about a year, and I'm not a deep-cover agent. I'm not sure whether that means you'll have it sooner or later. But you will have it."

Black woke up feeling better, and rather keen to experience the practical test to which, he had been told, Harry would put him. Blackford was to draw up a plan for transmitting to Contact X an envelope containing five thousand dollars in cash. In other words, a fairly thick envelope. Contact X, a woman, was unknown to him; Black would have only a telephone number for her. The rendezvous must be for later than 5:30, giving X time to get away from her work, and before 6:30, when X was due at home. The conversation over the telephone should not last longer than thirty seconds. Truax's code name: Angel. X's reply, in response to Angel's identification, would be:

"Could you please wait until I get a pencil?"

If a different answer was given, Blackford should apologize for ringing the wrong number.

Blackford should now devise a plan of maximum simplicity, least likely to alert anyone who might be tailing him, or the person he was contacting. The plan required that he specify: an identification for X, an identification for himself, time, place, technique, and emergency signals. The minimum physical contact, the better. Blackford was told to take as long as he wanted.

He called Harry back into the room an hour later.

"How's this?" He handed Harry the text of the telephone message he would give Contact X. It read:

This is Angel.
(Assume contact gives proper reply.)
Tonight, at 5:36, approach the newsstand at the ground floor of the National Press Building. The first magazine on the bottom rack, all the way to the left, is usually *Yachting*. Behind it is usually another copy of *Yachting*. Whatever is behind the outside issue, the envelope will be clipped to the inside of it at 5:35. At 5:36, ask the newsstand vendor whether he carries *Yachting*. If he's busy talking to someone else, just say, "*Yachting?*" If by 5:38 no one has asked that question, within the earshot of someone six feet away, I'll remove the envelope. If when you ask for *Yachting*, you hear someone say: "It's last month's issue," walk away without purchasing the magazine. Any questions?

He looked up at Harry.
"I figure you don't need more identification than that, is that right?"
Harry pursed his lips. "What if the magazine behind *Yachting* is a man's muscle magazine. She going to be forced to buy it because the money is inside?"
Blackford was ready.
"If that's the case, I'll slide a decorous magazine behind the *Yachting*, or else I'll put *Yachting* behind the muscle magazine."
"All right," said Harry. "Now: Work it out as if you needed a receipt—how does she hand it to you?
"After that, work it out so that you need to find out first *where* the contact usually goes after the office, so that you don't have to derail her to an arbitrary drop, like the National Press Club.
"After that, work it out so that the contact has to work alongside a companion who can't know anything that's going on.
"After that, work it out so that the package you have to deliver is the size of a portable typewriter.
"After that, call me."
Black enjoyed the variables, and he indulged himself in a formulaic way of writing them out. By the end of the afternoon,

Harry was well pleased, and gave him the address to which he should report the next day.

When he got home, the telephone was ringing. It was Sally, in some excitement. Her roommate, during the year Sally spent studying in Paris as an exchange student from Vassar, had married the the Shah of Sinrah, or, more accurately, had been married by the Shah of Sinrah. Well, this morning the White House social secretary had tracked Sally down at Congressman Gordon's office to say that the Empress had requested that her old roommate be invited to the dinner being given for the Shah. And that the invitation extended to Miss Partridge's escort, but his name would have to be given right away to the Secret Service.

"I called every engineering professor at George Washington trying to track you down."

Black swallowed.

"You've got to admit it, Black, you haven't exactly hit George Washington like the Messiah, but never mind, the Messiah hasn't hit George Washington that way either. Anyway, I couldn't find you, so I gave your name just the same, and the Secret Service people cleared you in a couple of hours, and . . ."

"Sally! Hold it! Hold it a minute! You cleared me with the Secret Service? And *we're* going to *the White House* for *dinner?* When?"

"Tonight."

"Tonight! What am I supposed to wear, my lacrosse uniform?"

"I knew you wouldn't have your tux with you, so if you'll look in your closet, you'll find Jim's, he's exactly your size. It wasn't easy to get it from him. He wanted to pose as you and go as my escort, but I told him *No incest* at the White House."

"What time?" Black's heart was pumping, less with excitement than with acute pleasure—he had done a tourist's tour of the bottom part of the White House, his first, as recently as last Saturday; and he had never regretted giving Sally a key to his apartment.

"Eight. That gives you two hours. Get a cab and pick me up—no, you might have trouble getting one. The bar at the Hay-Adams—I'll get there at 7:30. You come there, and we'll saunter across Lafayette Park and have dinner with the Trumans and the Shahs. Black?"

"Yes."

"What shall I call her?"

"Call who?"

"The Empress. I mean, I used to practically lend her my toothbrush, and it was only four years ago. Do I have to curtsy?"

"Americans don't curtsy."

"Not even to the Queen of England?"

"Not even to the Queen of England."

"How would you know—all you know is how to build bridges."

"Sally, we are a *republican* country. Can you imagine Benjamin Franklin curtsying?"

"That's silly."

"Well, can you imagine his wife curtsying?"

"Yes."

"Look, we'll be in a receiving line. Do what the women ahead of you do. But don't call her Tootsie, or whatever you called her—"

"Michelle."

"Well, don't call her Michelle. If it's impossible to call her Your Highness, just don't call her anything. That always works."

"So do you. Stop talking. I'm going to start dressing."

They met at the Hay-Adams and Sally ordered a daiquiri, Black a tom collins. He bent his head over obediently—he had become used to it—as Sally recombed his hair, and was embarrassed when she whispered, within earshot of the bartender, "You look divine tonight."

He felt pretty divine, he thought to himself. He had taken to exercising in the morning and weekends, and was a trim 170 pounds, and his light suntan belied the troglodytic life spent plumbing the mysteries of the spooks. Sally was animated and sparkled like the window of a jewelry store, from whatever angle, her eyes, nose, ears, hands, throwing off rays of animation.

"Shall we have another?" It was 7:40.

"No," he said, paying the bill. "Let's saunter."

They had to walk slowly to avoid being early. Most of the guests were arriving in limousines, so there was no wait at the northwest gate when they showed their invitation to the guard. He checked it against a master list and waved them in. They walked leisurely on by the shadows cast by the descending sun on their right, around to the ground floor, and began to mingle with people for the most part twice and three times their age, looking at the brightly lit displays of china given to the predecessors of President Truman by affectionate, grateful, intimidated, and vanquished chiefs of state. Waiters with trays of drinks circulated. Sally refused, Black accepted champagne. Word passed around that the guests should now go up to the foyer, that the President and the Shah would be descending the staircase in a few moments. When they did, grandly, "Hail to the Chief" sounding out in majestical tempo by a division of the Marine Band, followed by the national anthem of Sinrah, the guests were stock-still. Truman, with Michelle, came down first, followed by the Emperor and Mrs. Truman. Truman was talking away, and smiling, and passed through the crowd purposefully to anchor the receiving line. He smiled robustly at faces he recognized. When he brushed by Black and Sally, they found themselves standing more or less at attention, which the President evidently noticed, because he paused, leaned over to Black, and whispered, "At ease." Black smiled, and the aides who overheard the President chuckled. The Empress, meanwhile, spotting her former roommate, broke away from the President to embrace her. The Shah's expression, behind, was inscrutable, though Black, viewing it coolly, decided Michelle had better bear the Shah a son very quickly. He guessed that royal spontaneity in Sinrah was not a specialty of the house.

The receiving line was an anticlimax. The Empress had only time to ask Sally for news of Priscilla Lane, their third roommate; and Truman merely said, "Good evening, son."

They sat at a table for eight. He was between the wife of the American ambassador to Egypt and the wife of the president of General Motors. Sally, opposite, had Mr. General Motors and the Ambassador.

Both ladies asked the usual questions and Black re-established, for the thousandth time, that one had only to say one was an engineer to catalyze that haze-in-the-eye behind which all attention wanders. But this time, buoyant from wine and excitement, he decided to press on, and re-engaged Mrs. Motors during the main course.

"I'm a Republican," he said, "but I think Truman will go down in history for Operation Down Under—that's what I've been working on since I graduated."

He tried to sound a little pompous and was a little frightened at the ease with which he succeeded.

"Operation Down Under?" She looked up, struggling to refocus. "What's that?"

Black looked around him, as if by instinct, and leaned closer.

"That, Mrs. Wilson, is secret information." He paused, having brought his fork to his mouth. Then he stopped, lowered the fork, and said:

"But I suppose it can't be a secret from you and your husband. Nothing is, I guess." He allowed a moment's pause, and was gratified that she had moved her head closer to his, to catch his words.

"Operation Down Under," said Blackford in a semi-whisper, "is the mechanism that sinks the whole of central Washington underground, under an atomic-proof carapace."

"When are they going to do that?" Mrs. Wilson looked startled.

"They *have* done it, Mrs. Wilson. The biggest project since the Manhattan Project. It was completed a month ago. I'm only in on the maintenance. All the President has to do is push *one* button and most of the city of Washington sinks down five hundred feet, and a concrete dome envelops us. In fact"—Black was carried away—"the button is over there right behind the President." Blackford, with Mrs. Wilson arching her neck in parallel, craning his neck, stood up slightly, then sank back.

"No. You can't see it from here. It's behind the curtain. Remember, that's *secret information.*"

The toasts were effusive, as Black expected, though the Shah seemed nervous—he had had limited experience with chief executives like Truman—but there were no discordant notes, and the President invited everyone to the East Room for a "little entertainment." As they got up, Blackford saw Mrs. Wilson dive for her husband and point toward the curtain behind the dais. Her husband listened, spoke a single word, looked in disgust over at Black, shook his head, and escorted his wife to safety. Black dove for Sally and they walked out, animatedly exchanging monologues about their experiences during dinner. In the Green Room the guests were given coffee and liqueurs. Black spotted the new president of Yale, Whitney Griswold. He approached him.

"Blackford Oakes, Yale 1951. How is our alma mater?"

Griswold, unattached at the moment, was genial, and asked what Black was doing.

"Well, among other things, I've just read Buckley's *God and Man at Yale*."

"You must have a lot of time on your hands," Griswold said, allowing his eyes to catch those of a crusty figure approaching him. They exchanged greetings. Griswold turned—

"What was your name?"

"Oakes."

"Mr. Oakes, this is Mr. Allen Dulles, deputy director of the Central Intelligence Agency."

Black shook hands, and then winked mysteriously and asked sotto voce: "How's tricks?"

Dulles stared at him silently, then turned to talk with Griswold. Black eased away toward Sally—his querencia, his love—to lick his wounds. She was chatting with an overly handsome marine captain, one of the White House escorts bobbing about, performing duties official, semiofficial, and quite unofficial. This one, for instance, was asking Sally what she was doing later that evening.

"What she is doing later is with me," Black interposed, pleased with his timing. The captain moved to withdraw, though not until after he had maneuvered Black's eyes down toward the chestful of war decorations.

"Sorry, sir," he said, leaving, in favor of caution—for all he knew, Black was the son of the chief of staff or Truman's nephew or Pendergast's natural son. Sally was generally pleased, and they went together to the East Room and listened to Eugene List play Chopin for about twenty minutes. Then President Truman rose, approached the microphone, thanked List, and invited the guests to stay on as long as they wanted to and dance, and everyone stood up, and he escorted the Empress out of the room, followed by the Shah. The room lighted up with talk and laughter, and Black thought it must have been so when Louis XIV went off to bed, though in those days there would be somebody missing, somebody like Sally, he mused, but tonight again she would be all his, and as they lay in Mr. Ellison's bed, listening to his soft music, they would tease each other and observe an oh-so-strict protocol.

44

Four

ONE WEEK TO GO. It was almost over. Black's final instructor, "Alistair," had obviously spent much time in England. He was a gray man, his mien, hair, face, suit, shirt. But he had an air of competence and experience which Black quickly deferred to, concluding that he was now in the company of someone high in the organization. He felt like a freshman taking introductory physics from Edward Teller. Alistair began by telling Black that he was expected, during the next two weeks, and indeed until otherwise notified, to read in great detail about the English Establishment. He was to go over, every day, a half-dozen English journals, the serious and the yellow press. He was to develop a knowledge of the principal members of the two major political parties, of the Houses of Lords and Commons, of the court, and of the diplomatic and business world.

"That is a tall assignment, and obviously you are not expected to arrive in England two weeks from tomorrow with the same knowledge of English affairs that a native would have. It is only the beginning of an extensive program of familiarization, the purpose of which will be explained to you when you get to London."

When Anthony Trust had first told Blackford that he would be going to London, his general submissiveness before the counterintelligence discipline prevented him from asking questions about the oddness of his destination, or even from wondering very much about it. Apparently that his mother lived there was the operative point. Perhaps if his mother lived in Pago Pago, he would be sent there, on the grounds that cover means all. But in due course he had permitted himself to wonder. London. There was a sense in which that was the equivalent of dispatching a young counterintelligence agent to Chicago. Surely London, crawling with British agents, was presumably more concerned about the activities of an exuberant revolutionary nation from which she was insulated only by France and the English Channel, not necessarily in that order of importance, and had altogether adequate intelligence facilities, in contrast with a republic insulated, besides, by three thousand miles of ocean? But, of course, London was a great metropolis, where even people who looked like Peter Lorre sank into the woodwork, and Blackford's job, presumably, would be to help the English locate the bad Peter Lorres. He thought for a while about it, but soon dismissed it, having by this time come around to the proposition that if the CIA was nuts, there was little he could do about it except discover it in due course and get the hell out. If it wasn't, it would do him no good to try to outguess motives which very intelligent Americans were making it their business to make it hard for very intelligent Soviet agents to guess at, let alone bright young Yalies, fresh from their bright college years.

Alistair told him that there was no point in his trying to answer questions until Black had gone through some of his homework. Most of those questions would be answered in his reading. But in each of the succeeding days, Alistair would brief Black on a technical aspect of his deep-cover life in London, and he would begin now, on the question of communication.

As a general rule, he began, all communications will be oral—to your superior, given under circumstances prescribed by him.

"If your superior fails to make a rendezvous, or if communication with him through routine channels should lapse, you are to write a letter to"—he gave Black a note paper on the stationery of the Hay-Adams Hotel on which was written: "Mr. Alan Wriston, United States Embassy, Grosvenor Square, London."

"In that letter you will say, 'Dear Mr. Wriston: I am informed you are the gentleman who can advise me what the duty is on taking English-made suits into America. I am traveling about Britain, but will telephone you in two or three days. Meanwhile this note, in the event it is necessary to undertake any research. Yours truly, G. Truax.'

"Two days after dispatching that letter, you are to sit by your

46

telephone between five P.M. and seven P.M. and a substitute contact will be made. The person who telephones you will say, 'This is George Allan from the Embassy.'

"Now, if he says anything other than that, listen to what he has to say, and play along, agreeing to any suggested rendezvous. Then pack a bag and follow the same procedures you would follow in the event you find you need to leave the country."

"What are those?"

"I'm coming to that."

He gave Blackford another piece of paper, on the stationery of the Pullman Company. Written on it was: "1. The London Library. 2. The Shakespeare Hotel, Chapel Street. 3. The Adelphi Hotel."

"The London Library is in St. James's Square—you will of course know the streets of London thoroughly, even before you arrive there. The Shakespeare Hotel in question is in Stratford-on-Avon. The Adelphi Hotel is in Liverpool.

"At the library, at the information desk, you will ask if there is a message for Geoffrey Truax. If there isn't, proceed to Stratford and ask the same question at the Shakespeare Hotel. If there is none, you are to stay twenty-four hours waiting for a message. After that, go to Liverpool, same procedure, only you stay at that hotel for two days."

"What if there aren't any rooms?"

"The hotels we're talking about always have rooms. If you hit Liverpool the day of the Grand National, find someplace to stay and keep coming in for messages. . . . Now, short of a world war, one of our people will have approached you by the time you have reached Liverpool and will give you instructions. If no one does, do your best to get out of the country. You will not be given a false passport unless London feels the situation requires you to have one. That decision will be made depending on how your mission goes. Remember, you are whoever you actually are, living a perfectly normal life in London, pursuing whatever it is you are pursuing."

Blackford took the note papers, read them over, and returned them to Alistair.

"Now a general word on the British situation. On the whole, the British don't like American intelligence operations conducted in their country. I say 'on the whole,' because since the Klaus Fuchs affair, they have grudgingly admitted that we have certain information they don't have; or that, in any case, if only on account of the proddings of McCarthy, we'll act on certain information they can't, or won't, act on. But they don't really want to know about it in any formal way. At the highest level, the P.M. is aware that we're a presence. But anything we turn up, they want handed to them through diplomatic, not intelligence, channels. This embargo on any official contact between British and American intelligence in England is so rigid that when we need stuff they have that we are sure they'd be willing to give us, we ask for it from Paris or directly from Washington. Never from London.

"Now," he said, "the situation in England is very grave. Fuchs stole atomic secrets and gave them to the Soviets. That was a considerable public scandal, and they tightened up security at the obvious levels—atomic research plants, that kind of thing. But the Soviets have people everywhere. I mean *everywhere*. I mean, places you would never dream of. Recruiting by the Commies during the late thirties was very successful. And, during the war, there was the grand alliance. Now, in the Cold War, there is a surviving band of pro-Soviet Englishmen who think the West is on the wrong side of history. We know something about the general sources of Soviet intelligence, a lot about the actual information they're getting away with, and very little about who the people actually are. Their cover is superb. We are operating now mostly by deduction: Somebody, in this office, is leaking information. Who? Is that somebody a clerk-typist? A branch head? A division head? An Agency head? A spy? Or is he merely careless? We aren't in a position to check whether the Brits have their own man trying to penetrate an operation, and we've even had a grotesque situation in which after fourteen months of diligent work, we fingered the guy we knew was guilty—only to discover he was a deep-cover British agent dogging the same trail. We blew his cover. That one required a long afternoon's chat between Acheson and the British ambassador.

"The Soviets obviously have to be more cautious operating in London than they do in most places. But the purges back home have been flogging them on to tremendous efforts—"

"Tremendous efforts to do what?"

Alistair looked at once disappointed and patient.

"The Communists always have a lot to do. Right now they want to put pressure on Attlee to put pressure on Truman not to use the bomb in Korea. They wanted MacArthur fired. They want to get in the way of any moves toward European solidarity. They want to heighten English suspicion of French and German intentions. They want knowledge, on a day-by-day basis, of the disposition of NATO forces, with special emphasis on the location of atomic warheads. They want to know what kind of progress the Brits are making on the development of a tactical and a strategic missile. And they want every piece of dirt they can accumulate on anyone, just as a matter of course.

"As I was saying, they have to watch their step in England, and they do. But when they get desperate, they act all the more ruthlessly. We have two men in the field missing this last year, no explanation, no record, no trace. The two had been on the trail of Klaus Fuchs. Both were deep-cover agents with satisfactory and plausible public identifications. We were able to put routine heat on Scotland Yard through the ambassador. The decision hasn't yet been made whether to tip off MI-6. That's one of the questions Dulles and Acheson will have to settle. The circumstances are pretty convincing. The two operatives were bearing down on Fuchs from different directions—they didn't even know about each other. One of them left his flat to go to work on a Monday, at an engineering firm used by the government to check out research done within the secret atom laboratory. He never reached his office. The other worked as an accountant in the firm that handled Fuchs's personal affairs. He got a phone call the following Tuesday and asked permission to take an extra half hour for lunch because he had to make an appointment a few miles away. Exit."

"Did you try the Adelphi Hotel in Liverpool?" Black asked. Almost instantly he regretted doing so. He realized that, for Alistair, and the others—even for Anthony—it wasn't a couple of characters out of E. Phillips Oppenheim who had disappeared, but two men who four months ago were alive, who might have sat where he was now sitting, listening to Alistair even as Blackford was now doing.

"No comment," said Alistair. "You will come to know, Mr. Truax, that although what frightens normal people may or may not be something frightful, in this case it is. Because the people we are struggling against take orders from a monster crazed by a frightful system. There are no bearable jokes about Vorkuta, any more than there could be jokes about Anne Frank. A single night, half frozen in a Soviet jail, knowing you probably will never see anybody again you care for, and that nobody knows where you are, or will *ever* know, is enough to change the texture of one's feelings about what this is all about."

Black knew suddenly that he was talking to someone who had had such an experience. He wished he could ask him about it, but knew he couldn't. Perhaps Anthony would satisfy his curiosity, if Anthony knew Alistair, or about him. Once more he strained at the silence with his colleagues and wished that he had been selected to sit behind a desk, behind a door lettered BLACKFORD OAKES, ESQUIRE, U. S. Representative, *Central Intelligence Agency.* Then it occurred to him that the engineer, and the accountant, must have heartily wished the same thing at that moment in London when, looking up or sideways or down, they suddenly realized that they had come, irreversibly, to the end of the road. He knew now, even from his limited and abstract experience, and his few weeks' training, that almost certainly they had been betrayed. In central London. The heart of civility in the civil world.

He left with his bundle of English papers, and he read solidly into the night, and, before turning off the light, he found himself reading even the Court Circular in the *Times.*

"This afternoon, Her Majesty Queen Caroline graciously received His Excellency Mr. Jonathan Hanks and accepted his credentials as ambassador to the Court of St. James's from the United States of America."

Five

He arrived on the last day in September, and as the Super Constellation circled the field, he was not surprised that the neat hedgerows and the green green, and the light mist and tidy cottages and factories were as fresh in his memory as the campus at New Haven. The ten years since his last arrival in England had been among the most tumultuous in world history, and he had participated in them, in a minor way, landing in France from North Africa, and fighting—brilliantly: His prowess as a pilot, who had soloed at age twelve, was legendary in his outfit—established in a few tangential air engagements until his transparent physical weakness got him ordered to the sick bay, and home. But these events hadn't changed the landscape, though he had never seen it from the air, because the first time was on the train from Southampton, in the chaotic weeks at the end of his fifteenth year.

When the letter from his mother arrived he was at Camp Blakey, in Maine. He opened it eagerly, in the presence of his tent mates, and read. His eyes blurred so that he couldn't see, not even his two silent companions, but when his vision returned, he streaked out—by the Old Schoolhouse, along the shore of the lake, past the dozen tidy canoes, into the forest, whose shadows slightly slowed him down, but never to a walk—the whole two miles to the main highway where, breathless, he stopped, sticking up his thumb with that supernal confidence of the young that he would not, by that Providence he had grown up with on such companionable terms, be kept waiting, which he wasn't. The farmer who picked him up took him as far as Bath. Then, in minutes, he was on a truck headed for Boston. The driver stopped for gas and

51

food and asked Black if he was going to eat anything, and Black said no, he wasn't hungry. He was very hungry, and he had no money in his pocket, only the letter, lodged permanently in his memory, word for word, after that one reading. The driver returned with two sandwiches, ate one slowly as he drove, and told the boy to toss the second one out at the next garbage can, because one had satisfied him after all. Black said that although he wasn't hungry, maybe he would eat it himself rather than waste it, and the driver said suit yourself. The driver asked Black no questions about himself, but volunteered copious details about his own humdrum life, confessing that he rather hoped the United States would get into the war, since he was still just young enough to join the army or preferably the navy in the event of a general draft, and would like to see something of the world besides the run from Portland to Boston before he got any older, and, frankly, he didn't think his wife would mind it all that much if he went away for a while. Black woke from his trance at this and sternly discoursed on the illogic and immorality of the United States getting involved in a European war, recapitulating with considerable skill, analytical and mimetic, the phrases and paragraphs he had so often heard his father so earnestly intone. The driver retreated, leaving the impression that his desire for war was at most a velleity and turned to other matters. Black listened, and commented as necessary, dozed off, wondering, detachedly, how he would get from Boston to New York—to his aunt's house—before dying of hunger.

He arrived in the late afternoon, the beneficiary of random highway philanthropies including a plate of french-fried potatoes from the Howard Johnson waitress who, when he had sat down after his driver dropped him to go north to Hartford, and asked, at the counter, for a glass of water, said he was cute, which, suddenly, he realized self-consciously, he probably was, wearing trim white shorts, and a T-shirt marked CAMP BLAKEY, and white socks and tennis shoes, a rope belt and a watch with an Indian bead band he had sewn himself. At 5′7″ and 120 pounds he was growing fast, but not in those mutant leaps and bounds that leave the mid-adolescent looking like a gazelle. His hair was a dark blond, with the same yellow-white strains that even now came out on the least touch of the sun. Though his lips were normally set, he was quick to smile, a charming and precocious smile, somehow wise and amused, and he smiled when the waitress, varying very little from the basic gambit of the truck driver, said there were excess potatoes, that a dumb cook had prepared too many. But after eating only a few, suddenly his stomach was narcotized by his mind's return to the letter, and he walked quickly to the men's room and wept silently in the toilet compartment, wedging his weight against the door because there was no lock. When he regained control, he left through the back way, and resumed hitchhiking, out of sight of the waitress, whose generous impulse he could not trust himself to acknowledge without betraying himself, or embarrassing her.

He flagged a taxi at 125th Street and Lexington—awful extravagance—but he did not feel strong enough to walk to 69th Street, and he knew of no other vehicle that would deliver him collect. He said nothing to the driver, and on arriving asked him to wait. Georgianna opened the door, black and dour as ever, but instantly docile when he said, "Georgy, lend me a dollar quickly."

He came back from the cab: "Is Aunt Alice here?"

No, but she would be back for dinner.

He went upstairs, not needing Georgianna's guidance, nor soliciting her permission, and took a bath in his cousin's room, lay down and slept until Alice Gonzalez prodded him awake. He reached to the chair and pulled the letter out from his shorts and gave it to her. She went to the end of the room to catch the light and read it.

"Did you know, Aunt Alice?"

"No," she said. "But I'm not surprised. At least, not by the first part."

The first part was his mother's information that she had secured a divorce from his father in England, where his father's work had taken them in May. "Darling, there's no reason to tell you *why*, and I don't want to say *anything* that would injure your father, or *you*, or your *relations* with your father. You'll just have to take *my* word for it that I *couldn't* go on."

The second part was her announcement that she had remarried.

"His name is Alec Sharkey. He is, in fact, Sir Alec Sharkey. His first wife died in a car crash a year ago, with their daughter. He is an architect, and a very kind man, and I pray that you will grow to love him. I know that you will like him—I promise you—and he knows already that he will like you."

There followed what he could only take to be instructions. He inferred that his mother was in charge of him. He knew, generally, that that was how it worked after divorces. Besides, he had had no communication from his father—which didn't surprise him because he was always bad about writing—and anyway, his father had set out in June for a trip to the Far East to look into the possibility of brokering some airplanes to the beleaguered Chinese, and the mail from the Orient was problematic.

Blackford's instructions were to take the S.S. *Wakefield*, sailing from New York on September 9. "Your stepfather has enrolled you in Greyburn College, his alma mater. It is very old, and very famous; you will get a fine education there before going to college, either here in England or in America." She gave the name of a lawyer in New York whom he was to write or telephone after Camp Blakey closed. I will write your Aunt Alice tomorrow and tell her what has happened and ask her if you can stay with her over the Labor Day weekend before sailing."

Black and Aunt Alice cried together. She was like Blackford's mother, sentimental, passionate, and generous. Clearly her sympathies were with her sister, but she wouldn't criticize Tom Oakes. Black knew that his Aunt Alice had been in love with his father before her younger sister, Carol, met him—after he had won the stunt pilots' prize at the same airport in Long Island from which his closest friend, Lindbergh, would set out a few years later on the great flight. The courtship had been ardent and overwhelming. Carol had gone to her older sister to tell her weepingly that Tom Oakes and she were engaged and would marry within the week. Alice's parents were at once relieved that Alice had got rid of Tom Oakes and distressed that Carol had fallen prey to someone who, however dashing and handsome, was manifestly irresponsible. But better Carol than Alice, they thought, since she was the stronger of the two. At one session they pooled their resources and tried throughout one wracking evening to dissuade her, predicting divorce "within a year." They were way off. Carol was glad that her husband's work took him around the world, away from New York and the reproaches of her parents, who however were both dead now and could not take satisfaction from the realization, however belated, of their prediction. Alice meanwhile landed on her feet, happy with her husband and his steady job at the bank, and with her son, a year younger than Blacky, off now at a dude ranch near the Rockies.

"Frankly," said Black at dinner, to his aunt and her phlegmatic, ever-silent husband, "the idea of going to school in England gives me the creeps. Don't you have to dress like an ambassador? And don't they beat you all over the place?" His aunt soothed him and told him he would have a great experience, which was correct.

His mother was waiting for him at Waterloo Station, and they hugged like lovers. The schedule provided for three days at home, and his stepfather had tactfully left London for the first of these to permit the reunion between mother and son without the restraint of an alien presence. Black realized quickly that his mother was not going to talk about his father, and indeed she never brought up his name again, though on the infrequent occasions when Blacky gave her news about him, she was affectionately attentive. Black stopped mentioning his father. During the war years, he saw him less than once a year. On those occasions, and while Blackford was at college, there was a strained man-to-manness, a lot of bluff advice, which grew progressively vinous as the evening wore along. Yet however desultorily, his father always kept in touch with him, and the more easily as his son grew older, and the two, though apart, did not grow apart.

Mother and son went by taxi to 50 Portland Place, a comfortable house in a fashionable area by Regent's Park, a block or so from Queen's Hall. A cook, a butler, and a maid were in attendance, but the butler had given notice—the War Office required him to take a war-related job. It was expected that the same would happen soon to the maid. The cook, old and devoted to Sir Alec, would stay.

Black was struck by the signs, paraphernalia, and scars of modern war. The streets were filled with martial posters, cluttered with soldiers and sailors. Half the air raid wardens were women. The next morning, he had been advised at Southampton, he would be required to be fitted for a gas mask. He passed several areas of recent devastation—from fire bombs, mostly; and he noticed how dim the lights were, how dark the central city as they drove through it.

He bathed and went down to dinner, and his mother, who looked younger than in the spring when he had last seen her—more beautiful than he ever remembered her—gazing adoringly on her beautiful son, said that they must be practical for a moment.

The next morning would be given over to outfitting him for Greyburn. He would need three pairs of gray flannel pants, two vests, two school blazers, a cap, sports shoes, gray woolen shirts, two school ties, socks and underwear, all of it available at Harrods.

"They have a quite extensive store of sorts at the school and you can buy there, or order, anything else you need. Your stepfather drove up there a week ago after he got your school records from Scarsdale. The headmaster went over them very carefully. You would be going into your sophomore year at Scarsdale. The equivalent at Greyburn is the fourth form. Dr. Chase thinks you'd be better off, and happier, entering the third form. Later, in a year or two, you might be able to skip a form. But right now, you haven't had as advanced work as the English boys of your age in Latin and French. And, of course, they've done a lot of English history and you've had none. Your stepfather decided we should take the headmaster's advice."

"Was there any choice?" asked Black, rueful at repeating an entire year.

"No, darling. There really wasn't. Greyburn made a huge exception in taking you. Everything is very tight with the war, and in any case Greyburn has a very long line of boys waiting to get in." Black wondered whether in Greyburn there was a very long line of boys waiting to get out; but he said nothing. The whole thought of the place—he had never been to boarding school—depressed him; he supposed he would get used to it, and his naturally high spirits, since his flight from Camp Blakey, were restored, though he was nervous at the prospect of meeting his stepfather.

This happened at lunch; and this time, his mother slipped away.

56

Sir Alec was, Black guessed, forty-five years old. What was most conspicuous at first was the formality of his dress. He could have walked directly into Westminster Abbey with that costume, Black thought, and married a princess at high noon. Even the carnation was there, and on coming into the hall, he had put aside an umbrella and a derby. He was middle-sized, and balding, with heavy glasses, a beefy face, and a trim red mustache. Black had studied, the night before in his stepfather's study, pictures of him as a boy: on the rugger team at Greyburn, crewing at Cambridge. He had then a profusion of what must have been red hair, and he always looked solemn, as though no other pose was suitable for a gentleman to strike before a photographer. There was a picture, in a black frame, of his wife, who looked austere and rather helpless as she held, self-consciously, the hand of their ten-year-old daughter, only a few months, he deduced from the date of the inscription, before the fatal accident.

"This is rather awkward, isn't it?" he heard his stepfather saying. "Sit down. I have given it a lot of thought, and it occurs to me we should handle some of the practical problems first, such as how you are to address me. I expect you do not want to call me 'Father,' and of course I shan't ask you to. There is, in England, a surviving tradition which permits calling one's stepfather 'Stepfather.' But it is shaky, even as the bourgeois tradition of calling one's cook 'Cook.' If I hadn't been knighted, we might have experimented with your calling me 'Mr. Sharkey.' But 'Sir Alec' is, I think you would agree, uncomfortable.

"Thus I have been driven by the process of elimination, which, incidentally, Blackford, is the secret behind most successful architecture, never mind the popular superstition that all those beautiful contrivances are born of poetic inspiration or theoretical sunbursts, to conclude that you will have to address me—brace yourself—as *Alec*."

He pronounced the syllables distastefully.

"I never thought before now that there were uses in being christened something more formal, like 'Algernon' or 'Auberon.' Now, *I* have the same objection to this that *you* may be thinking. In the first place, I dislike precipitate informality. In the second place, I dislike it *in particular* when it is otherwise fitting to emphasize a relationship, one of the parties to which is subordinate—

as you, necessarily, will be subordinate to me over the next few years. It is useful that terms of address should suggest such authority. And, finally, there *is* a hint of modernism in the arrangement, and *I resist modernism in all its forms,* with conviction, and indeed *implacability.* At the same time, if there are no alternatives, there are no alternatives. Under the circumstances, I am: Alec. Good afternoon, Blackford."

Black was breathless. Still, as Sir Alec sat down, he caught a trace of a smile in the studiedly dour countenance, and his whole frame—as when, tensing up again for another painful shaft of the dentist's drill, one is told that it is all over—relaxed. Black didn't feel he could let down his guard. Nor could he predict he would ever feel affection for his stepfather. But he felt, already, a certain . . . security in his presence. And no feeling at all that doing so implied any infidelity to his father.

Sir Alec rang a bell, and a tray of sandwiches and hot soup was brought in, with a glass of milk and a half bottle of claret. He spoke at a rapid rate about war developments and asked Blackford if he had any views of his own on the matter.

Black took a deep breath and said he did not believe the United States should intervene.

"Well," Sir Alec said, casting a cautious glance at Blackford, "Churchill has said to you Americans: 'Give us the tools and we will do the job.' That seems fair, doesn't it?"

"I guess so," said Black, electing not to recapitulate the ardent analyses of his father, that U.S. aid would necessarily lead to full U.S. participation in the war.

"Well," said Sir Alec after a pause, "we will have to see. Meanwhile it is not to be overruled that that madman will, in his triumphant exuberance, portage his army across the Channel, and it is by no means certain that if he tries it he won't succeed. But that kind of talk we reserve for *indoors. Outdoors* we use only defiant rhetoric. *Grrr!!*" Black looked up at his stepfather making a most hideous face. He laughed. So did Sir Alec: long laughter, waves of relief, submerging, slowly, and forever, a web of nerves exposed.

That afternoon they walked together, through the Tower of London, and Madame Tussaud's, and into Westminster Abbey, and past Buckingham Palace, taking tea—Black's first—at a Lyons, with cookies and fancy pastries of assorted kinds. Sir Alec asked for chocolates and the waitress said, "Sir, you know there aren't any chocolates these days." Black suspected that Sir Alec did know this, but that he had asked for them anyway, to show his American stepson how grave was the situation. Black understood, but thought that, really, he *should* be given credit for being almost sixteen. After all, he didn't think a shortage of chocolates was the surest sign of a collapsed order. Though he did wonder, idly, whether Aunt Alice could be got to send him some Milky Ways to Greyburn, as she had to Camp Blakey.

School! The day after tomorrow.

He looked up at his stepfather—he had not yet brought himself to refer to him as "Alec," was looking for the opportunity, and meanwhile he called him—nothing at all—

"How big is Greyburn?" he asked suddenly.

"Greyburn has six hundred and twenty-five boys and thirteen forms. The top four forms—the Upper School—have seventy-five boys in each form, approximately. The school was founded in the eighteenth century, under the special protection of the Duke of Caulfield, on whose estate it was built. The present Duke, who is all of twenty-three years old, is ex officio the chairman of the board of trustees. It has supplied as high a percentage of graduates to Oxford and Cambridge in the past century as any school in the kingdom. I finished in 1914, just in time to fight in a very long war, from which, for reasons I cannot understand, I emerged not only intact, but positively roaring with health, which made me hugely conspicuous alongside my emaciated and mutilated classmates who went up with me to Cambridge in 1919.

"Greyburn is a rigid school, insists on the highest standards, academic and other, and has means, mostly painful, of forcing the boys to meet these standards. I don't know the present chap, Dr. Chase, at all—met him for the first time when I went over there to discuss you. He was headmaster of a grammar school before going to Greyburn, and wrote a research study on medieval pedagogy, for which he received an advanced degree. Cold fish. But the trustees think highly of him, and now that the whole bloody country is regimented, the regimentation at Greyburn doesn't strike one as all *that* unusual. It will take you time to get used to it. But if you are like most of the others, you will find it an exhila-

59

rating experience. I did, though of course I had my unhappy moments. You get one weekend a term to come home, and we are permitted, after you have been there for ten weeks, to take you out three Saturday afternoons, provided you have not been 'confined'; and we may attend—again, after your initial ten weeks—any school game and have tea later on the grounds. You look fit for the junior teams, but first you'll have to do something to bring order to your rather chaotic academic background."

"Why 'chaotic'? Scarsdale High School has a very good reputation," Blackford said defensively.

"Nothing personal. All other educational systems appear chaotic alongside one's own. No doubt Scarsdale High School would find a matriculant from Greyburn dreadfully in need of adjustments. By the way, you will find an almost uniform ignorance, at Greyburn, of the causes, and ideals, of the American War of Independence."

That night all three had dinner, and Sir Alec announced, just before the soup was served, that they must hurry, because he had three tickets to a film being shown down Oxford Street, within walking distance. It was a thriller, in which Walter Pidgeon very nearly shot Hitler at Berchtesgaden, and the anguished disappointment felt by Black's fellow viewers at Walter Pidgeon's failure to squeeze the trigger when the hairline neatly and lethally bisected the Führer's head was emotionally overwhelming in the packed theater. To think of it! That one man, with one rifle, might have spared England the ordeal into which she was entered. After the movie ended, Black, seated by the aisle, rose and stepped automatically out. His mother grabbed him by the arm. The audience was risen and motionless, while the loudspeakers gave out the majestic chords of "God Save the King."

Six

As BLACKFORD CHEERED ON THE TEAM, he suddenly realized that what had been, up until only a week or so ago—at last Saturday's game—purely perfunctory cheers for the home team were now genuine. He really did want his school to win the game against Harrow, and he wondered why. He wondered, to begin with, how he had survived the first week, and the nights, when in his solitary cubicle, his pillow over his head so that he would not be heard by his neighbors through the flimsy plyboard partitions, he wept, longing for his mother, his friends at Scarsdale, and above all for the easygoing liberties that had been taken from him as abruptly as if he had been clapped into prison.

He could not *believe* the supervision. The detailed concern. When, on the first morning, while still brushing his teeth in his dressing gown, he saw his classmates, similarly dressed, leaving the communal lavatory with its forty washbasins, queuing by a master before whom they opened their mouths wide and exhibited both sides of their hands, Blackford thought he must there and then laugh, cry, or flee. He did none of these, but in showing his hands and opening his mouth, he inaugurated that cultivated air of discreet defiance which had made him now, after only eight weeks, something of a celebrity.

He found, for instance, the cloying repetition of the word "sir" obsequious to the point of debasement. "You know, Aunt Alice," he had written from the depths of despair on the fourth day, "around here you are supposed to say *sir* every other word, practically. I'll give you an example. You want the butter, and it's sitting in front of the master. You're supposed to say, *Sir? Please, sir.*

Would you pass the butter, sir? Well, as they say here, I'm bloody well not going to do that c-r-a-p."

He wondered, worriedly, whether, at this safe distance, he wasn't taking cowardly liberties—using an obscenity in a letter to his aunt. He reckoned correctly that in her absorbing concern for him she would not pause to reproach him on this count. She wrote: "My darling Blacky: You mustn't be defiant, dear. The English are after all a different people from us, and they have their own customs. Remember, dear, they didn't ask you to go to their school, you asked (through your stepfather) to go, and they let you in, so it's only fair to do it their way. Besides, you will be a lot happier."

But Blackford found himself happiest when skating breezily along the edges of defiance. ("Would you pass the butter? . . . sir?") After the first week his reliable spirits began, after measured decompressions, to revive. He was, in any case, desperately busy, from 6:45 A.M., when the bell in the cold-cold antiseptic dormitory clanged and the boys in dressing gowns rushed down to the lavatory, until 9 P.M., when a master at one end of the dormitory recited the psalm De Profundis, and the boys gave the responses in Latin, read out in the dim light of their cubicles, from a printed card permanently tacked to the inside of the door of the dresser which opened so that, lying on their beds, they could discern the ten-point print; whereupon all the lights went, implacably, out.

Blackford's first concern was his academic work. He had no trouble in English or in history—it was as easy to learn about the Plantagenet Kings as about the Founding Fathers; in fact, he found the Kings, on casual acquaintance, less confusing and (he did not divulge this) rather more exciting. In beginning French he found he could easily stay abreast of his class, and in mathematics he showed the flair that later would put him at the top percentile in his college aptitude tests. Geography was a bore—simply another subject—and his quick memory was wonderfully useful to him.

His trouble was with Latin. Although he had had a year of it at Scarsdale and was only in second-year Latin at Greyburn, here the boys were already reading Caesar, and Blackford found Caesar *utterly impenetrable.* The master, Mr. Simon, was a veteran of

62

generations of ineptitude in teaching Latin and reacted to student mystification with a blend of scorn and tyranny. A grizzled man in his late fifties, with sideburns and spectacles, Mr. Simon—one of the boys told Blackford—had many years ago proposed to a lady in Latin and, on finding her response ungrammatical, resolved upon celibacy. Latin was his wife, and mistress, and catamite. He wooed his muse with seductive little mannerisms he had over the years satisfied himself were endearing to young boys, and marvelous instruments of a successful pedagogy.

Blackford began on the wrong side of Mr. Simon by suggesting that, as an American, he should, by all rights, be permitted to continue to inflect Latin nouns according to the American sequence rather than the English sequence—on the grounds that to change now from nominative, genitive, dative, accusative, and ablative to the English sequence would terribly and prejudicially confuse him.

The other twenty boys in the class were awed into silence. Only the older boy in the back row, a fifth-former and prefect who, because he too was behind, was required to take third-form Latin with his juniors, dared to speak out.

"Sir, that's a pretty good point."

The boys all laughed, because he was the *other* American; though in fact he had begun Latin, last year, at Greyburn, and had been trained ab initio in the English sequence.

Mr. Simon replied: "You will have harder adjustments to make, Oakes, than slightly to rearrange the order of noun inflections. I *suggest* you resolve to learn it the right way, or, I suppose, I had better say"—and he smiled, lifting his hands to tug on the lapels of his academic robe, the characteristic posture when he thought himself about to say something withering or amusing—"the English way."

"Hear, hear!" the boys said, at once docile and chauvinistic.

"Do you also conjugate the *verbs* differently in America, Oakes? Another habit acquired from the Indians?"

The boys roared. Oakes flushed, doodling on his pad, conscious that everyone was looking at him, unlearned in the artifices of appearing indifferent. Mr. Simon then delivered what Blackford came to recognize as his favorite homily: the necessity of learning Latin nouns and their declensions, and Latin verbs and their con-

63

jugations, particularly the irregular verbs, by repeating them to oneself *in every circumstance.*

"Don't put the subject *out of your mind* when you leave the classroom. *Think* about a *difficult* verb when you are walking along the corridors between classes. When you are having your *tea.* When you are *running out to the playing field.* Remember: *Qui cogitat quod debet facere, solet conficere quod debet facere.*" Mr. Simon beamed as he attempted to dittify his maxim in English: "Those who think about their duty / Are those who end by doing their duty!"

At tea that afternoon—the sole, blissful repast at which the boys were unsupervised, and their banter unheard by a presiding master—Blackford remarked to the boy opposite, who was also in the class, that Simon was a pompous ass, and the boy replied in the public school drawl (one Blackford was determined would never be allowed to creep into his own speech) that how else could he have achieved such high standing at Greyburn? The veteran Greyburnian remarked: "Simon's been here practically since he left his blubbing mother's arms. He used to recite an original poem in Latin at Class Day exercises, until five years ago when he just plain overdid it—he recited thirty-two verses. When Dr. Chase came in, he changed the ceremony, moving Mr. Simon back to the 'Academic Reminiscences' hour scheduled the day before, which is voluntary. . . . He's always in a bad humor now, because he really thinks that, though he is tops in Latin, he really ought to be a *general!*"

The boys laughed. "He was a lieutenant in the last war. He'll tell you about it."

"He'll tell you about it for three hours, if you don't watch yourself," another boy chimed in, reaching over Blackford for the jam.

"*I'm* surprised," a third boy said, munching a piece of bread piled high with butter and marmalade, "he doesn't begin his classes with 'God Save the King.' He tunes in to the BBC five times a day to get the war news. The man he hates most in the world, after Hitler, is Charles Lindbergh."

Blackford said nothing. He was paralyzed with indignation. The great hero of world aviation! Charles Lindbergh, the scientist and patriot! Charles Lindbergh, the great advocate of American peace! Charles Lindbergh, his father's *earliest and best friend!*

Blackford had had experience in America, as the divisions over there hardened between the interventionists and the isolationists, with boys who, usually echoing their parents' views, disparaged Lindbergh, the leader of the America First movement. Blackford had a fist fight with a Lindbergh iconoclast at Scarsdale. But here, three thousand miles away from America, he found it a corporate affront that a sacrosanct master should feel free to belittle so great a man (who, when Blackford was ten years old, had taken him up in his own airplane for a joy ride that unforgettable afternoon when his family visited the Lindberghs in Rhode Island).

Dear Aunt Alice:
This is very important. Please, even if you forget to send me the Milky Ways, don't forget this. I want you to send me right away two buttons (the kind you stick into your lapels), one button that just says on it *America First*, another button that has Lindbergh's face on it, with his name under it. If you don't have these buttons around, please go, or send Billy, to the America First Headquarters, where they will give them to you for nothing. It is on 44th Street, Lexington Avenue. DON'T FORGET!!!

Much love,
Blacky

At the end of the second week at Greyburn, he attended the third, and final, compulsory lecture about school life given for the new boys, of whom there were thirty in the Upper School, twenty of them third-formers. The first two lectures had touched on school practices, holidays, vacations, sports, academic schedules, regulations involving health, writing home. This one concerned discipline.

The speaker was a tall, spare, youngish man whose title was School Secretary and Assistant to the Headmaster. He taught one class in ancient history and was otherwise occupied helping the headmaster with his administrative chores, interviewing prospective students, collating the grades that went out to the parents, and occasionally representing the headmaster at official functions.

His face was pallid, and without expression, except for what seemed like a running, permanent, ineradicable leer (his name, as if to rub it in, was Mr. *Leary!*). His accent was the most exaggeratedly British Blackford had ever heard. It was a strain even to understand him.

What Mr. Leary said was that the standards of Greyburn had always been high, but that in time of war they would be set higher than ever before, that this was a time of great national tribulation, that the sons of England's most privileged families in particular should recognize their special obligation to grow quickly, to do their work well, and to obey their superiors.

"Now," he continued, "as some of you no doubt have heard, Dr. Chase, on becoming headmaster, withdrew from the school's prefects the privilege, or rather the *duty*—a much better way to put it —of administering the rod. It was widely suggested among some Old Boys that Dr. Chase was 'modernizing' the school and permitting its standards to deteriorate. *That*"—Mr. Leary . . . leered —"*any* boy who has been at Greyburn during the past five years would now know better than to believe. Although the use of the rod is now reserved to housemasters and to the headmaster, its use is not for that reason any more . . . disdained. There is no reason for anybody sitting in this room," said Mr. Leary, "to experience the birch before graduating from Greyburn. But," he warned, with a tight smile, "the statistics are heavily against such a probability—that boys *will be* boys is *more* than a *mere* truism— but after all, the *purpose* of punishment is to *advance* a boy's understanding of his obligations, and therefore the use of the rod is, really, *designed* to bring boys to the stage where they *do not need the rod* to behave like civilized human beings."

Friday, he said, is the day in which the headmaster interviews miscreants and administers punishment, after weighing reports on the behavior of individual boys. At tea time, any boy who is to report to the headmaster's office will find a blue slip on his plate with his name on it.

"As for the housemasters, they attend to their own corrections in their own way at their own time."

Were there questions?

There were none. The room was as silent as any Blackford had ever been in. He could hear only his heart beating, and he noticed that even after Mr. Leary had left the platform, the boys stayed briefly in their chairs, before getting up and, silently, filing out.

Another month went by, and now instead of cheering the team, Blackford was on it—the junior team to be sure—being cheered. He had quickly adjusted to rugger, and his fleet-footedness and natural sense of tactical guile were of great advantage—to be preferred, he reluctantly concluded, to the hulking Maginot Line of football at Scarsdale, where the huge shoulder and hip pads always made him feel a little creaky, and the quarterbacks thought in terms of feet and even inches gained, as against tens of yards. He made dazzling runs on three successive Saturdays, and there was even talk that he might be put on the senior team, though he was a little light for the senior scrum, and it was said that Mr. Long thought it advisable to wait until the next season. Meanwhile, Oakes would be tried out in cricket.

He was popular with the boys quite apart from his athletic prowess. They liked his natural manners, his frankness of expression, his ingenuous American informality, especially in tight situations involving the masters and the prefects. Mr. Manning, his housemaster, observed him with something like fascination and desisted from pulling him up short, which he had several concrete provocations for doing, most concretely after *twice* discovering Oakes calmly reading in bed with a flashlight—strictly forbidden in the rules. He excused his indulgence on the grounds that Blackford was after all American, and needed time to make the sharp adjustment to English ways. At a faculty tea, Mr. Manning defended his permissiveness toward Oakes in a casual comment that suddenly engrossed the entire company in a general discussion about the extraordinarily self-assured young American who was lightheartedly making his way through Greyburn with an indefinable cultural insouciance, the most palpable feature of which was a total absence of that docility which was universally accepted as something on the order of a genetic attribute in Greyburn Boys.

"I tell him to fetch the atlas," the geography teacher, lowering his teacup, remarked, "and he pauses—for *just a moment*—as if he is *considering* whether he will *grant* my request! And then, just one second short of refractoriness, he will say, with an incandescent smile, 'Sure!' Somehow *I can't make myself* say to him: 'Say, "Yes, *sir!*"' It would leave me feeling not only the martinet, but as if I had earned his absolutely predictable condescension . . . the strangest, most independent boy I have ever known, and frankly, one of the most attractive."

Mr. Long, the athletic coach, saw an opening and moved in heavily—as an outspoken defender of Oakes. "I have never found him insolent, and he is every bit the team player. With his legs and lungs he could hang on to the ball and play only for the gallery. He works with the team, though, and they like and admire him even though he is . . . different."

Dr. Chase, in an infrequent appearance at the weekly faculty tea, said nothing.

Nor did Mr. Simon, for fear he would betray his very strong feelings about Oakes.

Mr. Long—under fire from Oakes's history teacher—admitted that Oakes's outspoken advocacy of the cause of American isolation *was* galling.

"You would think," the history teacher said, "he would keep his views to himself for so long as he is a student at a British school."

At this Mr. Simon could not keep silent. "You would think he would take the trouble to learn something about Hitler's global ambitions before urging the position that only the British should shed blood in defense of the English-speaking world."

"Actually," Mr. Long persisted, "I overheard him yesterday arguing with two of the boys at lunch, and his arguments are remarkably well marshaled. He made it a point of saying that *he* doesn't bring up the subject except when one of the English boys does, and that far from being presumptuous in speaking out on the subject, he is presumptively—that wasn't the word he used—better entitled to express himself on what America should do than Englishmen."

Dr. Chase spoke up, lifting an eyebrow customarily set in concrete. "He said that?"

"Yes, Head; exactly that."

Dr. Chase was silent; then he rose, and without looking to right or left, intoned quietly, "Come along, Leary," and they filed out of the faculty lounge, the headmaster and the assistant to the headmaster.

"Good afternoon, gentlemen," he said on reaching the door, again without looking aside.

"Good afternoon, Head," was the chorused response.

By early December, it was somehow palpable that the crisis of Blackford Oakes must come. It had to happen was the consensus, and even the strongest partisans of Blackford sensed inevitability —the institutional integrity of Greyburn required the formal subjugation of this coltish alien. Last week he had shown up at Mr. Simon's class, a serene expression on his handsome boyish features, flaunting, on his lapels, an *America First* button and a *Lindbergh* button. Mr. Simon had looked down on him—Blackford sat, as a new boy, in the front row—very nearly speechless (indeed he had to clear his throat the better part of a full minute before proceeding), and then delivered, defensively and to gain the time necessary to settle his emotions, his standard lecture on the need to Think Latin outside the classroom. Blackford pocketed the buttons on leaving Mr. Simon's classroom; but every day, at ten in the morning, which was the Latin III hour, he would reach into his pocket, fasten the two buttons on his lapels, and stride jauntily into the room, sometimes whistling a tune. At this he was not competent, since he could not carry a melody, but those who listened hard could discern an effort at "Yankee Doodle Dandy."

The end came early in December. The French teacher announced that he would have to leave his class at a quarter before the hour because he had to catch the eleven-fifteen train to London. So, finding ten minutes of leisure, the six boys from the French class who would also meet together for Latin III at ten strolled down the hallway, passing a half-dozen classrooms in session, reaching Mr. Simon's ten minutes early. It was empty. Blackford, giving way to a pent-up fancy, found himself at the blackboard, chalk in hand, sketching furiously. From the swift and authoritative strokes there emerged a most recognizable caricature of Mr. Simon, bushy sideburns and all, academic cape flowing in the wind. His legs, however, were awkwardly separated, his member exposed, the stream issuing from it arcing splashily to the ground. A dotted line from the lips of the master led to a balloon, within which Blackford, imitating the holographic style of his teacher, who a few days earlier had explained the English evolution ("micturate") of Caesar's word to describe his soldiers' careless habits when emptying their bladder, indited the words: "Mingo, Mingere, Minxi, Mictum." Triumphantly, Blackford autographed the sketch: "B. Oakes, discipulus."

The boys howled with laughter and glee, overcome with pleasure at the artistic feat of retaliation. One of them in due course said, "Oakes, you had better rub it off. It's five minutes to ten."

But Mr. Simon was always *exactly* on time, and Blackford wanted to share his creation with more of his classmates, who already were dribbling in and, alerted to the cause of the excitement, looked instantly at the cynosure on the blackboard and exploded in squeals of delight and ribaldry.

It was those yells, issuing from his own classroom, that prompted Mr. Simon to snuff out his cigarette, rather than finish it outdoors, so as to time his entry, as was his habit, to ten o'clock exactly, and stride into the Caulfield Center building. As senior master, he had title to the first classroom on the right. Thus he entered the room two and one-half minutes before the hour. There was sudden, stunned silence. He followed the boys' eyes to the blackboard. He lifted his head slightly to study the sketch through the appropriate lenses of his bifocals. He then shut the classroom door and walked deliberately down the passage to the teacher's platform, up the single step, sat down at his desk, hinged open the cover, and drew out stationery and, from his vest pocket, a fountain pen.

"Jennings," he said, without even looking in the direction of the boy who that week was in charge of wiping the blackboard before, during, and after Latin III, "wipe the board."

Quickly, nervously, Jennings, plump and bespectacled, slid in the continuing silence to the board and with a few vigorous strokes, beginning furtively with one that erased Blackford's signature, eliminated the lapidary caricature of the Latin master, shown constructively engaged in following his own advice of Thinking Latin on every occasion.

You could hear in the room only the stroking of Mr. Simon's pen on his note pad.

"Dr. Chase, FOR IMMEDIATE ATTENTION," he wrote.

Sir:

B. Oakes, who is in my division Latin III, has committed an offense, gross, insolent, and obscene—a drawing on the blackboard seen by all the other students—more disgusting than anything I have seen in my thirty-three years' experience as a teacher. I request—nay, I require—that he receive the most vigorous punishment, or else that he be expelled from Greyburn. No alternative treatment of him would make it possible for me to continue to discharge my responsibilities.

Yours truly,
A. Simon.

He folded the note into an envelope, scratched out "Dr. Chase, For Immediate Attention," and called out, "Prefect."

"Yes, sir." The other American stood at the rear of the room.

"You will take this message to the headmaster at his study and conduct Oakes there—immediately."

Anthony Trust waited at the door as Blackford, turned faintly white, rose, walked across the classroom, and came back along the length of it to where the prefect stood waiting. Trust closed the classroom door quietly behind them and led the way to the front door.

The headmaster's office was diagonally across the huge campus, a ten-minute walk.

"What will he do?" Oakes found himself asking, as he walked alongside Trust. The morning's frost lingered on the pathway in the cold winter gray of Berkshire.

"What will he do? He'll beat you."

"When?"

"Probably this afternoon, after tea. I doubt he'll put it off a whole week till the usual time on Friday, if I can guess what's sizzling inside this letter. Maybe he'll even do it right now."

"Has it ever happened to you?"

"Sure. Twice, last year—once in the fall, once in the winter."

"Is it pretty . . . bad?"

"It's bad. It is indescribably bad. But really, Oakes, you *were*, as the guys here say, an awful *ass*."

They passed by his dormitory, and Oakes's housemaster, walking in the opposite direction, gave him a cheerful greeting, which Oakes returned, with effort.

"How do they do it?"

"How?"

Trust groaned at the ignorance of his compatriot. "Well, you get a lecture first. Then Leary-deary will pull over the library step—what you use to reach for a book on a high shelf—and drag it over until the back is up against the arm of Dr. Chase's big black leather sofa. Then you kneel on the block—that's what they call it—over the arm of the chair. But before, they make you take off your coat and loosen your suspenders—they call them braces here, in case you don't yet know that. Then Leary slides up your shirt and pulls down your shorts."

"*Pulls down my shorts!*" Oakes stopped in mid campus, his mouth open, eyes flashing. "You're *kidding!*"

"I am *not 'kidding.'* They've been doing it that way for three hundred years, and the Old Boys wouldn't want any detail to change, no siree. After all, they went through it, and look how *marvelous* they are—that's the argument."

Oakes was silent again as they resumed their walk toward Execution Hall.

"How many strokes will I get?" he suddenly asked.

"It's usually six maximum. You'll get the maximum, all right."

"What does a birch rod look like?"

"Like a lot of long twigs, maybe a dozen, tied together at the bottom by string. They're made up by Johnson." Oakes liked Johnson, Greyburn's kindly man of all trades who only last week had fixed Blackford's bicycle chain. "After two weeks, Leary will tell you with great pride, *all* Dr. Chase's rods are automatically replaced. He doesn't like them to get stale. Less sting. Only the best of *everything* at Greyburn."

"Will I . . . cry?"

"If you're normal."

"Is it only Leary and Dr. Chase in the room?"

"No. There's a prefect. I hope to *God* he does it after tea, or next week, because then some other prefect will be there. If he does it now, it will be me, sure as shooting. How do you like that! Come all the way from Toledo, Ohio, to Berks., England, to hold down a kid from New York being spanked on his ass—that's great!"

They arrived at the stone building, the Elizabeth Caulfield Memorial Building, the first floor of which was occupied by the record and bill keepers, the second reserved for the headmaster. Trust led the way, going up the steep stone staircase. He knocked on the door of the headmaster's antechamber. Mr. Leary's voice sounded through the thick oak door.

"Come in."

Mr. Leary sat at his desk, opposite a sofa. At the far end of the long room eight or ten chairs were spread about and a few old magazines on a small table. On the walls, a half-dozen etchings and photographs of Greyburn, four of them, dating back to the eighteenth century, faded into a sepia brown.

"What is it?" asked Leary, looking up at the two boys.

"I have been instructed by Mr. Simon to bring Dr. Chase this, sir," Trust said, handing the letter to him.

Leary seized it. Though it was addressed directly to Chase, he broke the seal without a moment's hesitation, passing his eyes, unhurriedly, over the enclosure.

He looked up.

"Sit down, both of you." And to Oakes, softly, with a hint of the hangman's humor: ". . . while you can."

He opened the door on the left end of the room by his desk, closed it, and strode down the length of the dark library, past the single window, opening, without knocking, a door at the left, at the far corner.

Dr. Chase was on the telephone.

The inner sanctum of Greyburn College was not large. When Dr. Chase had more than two visitors, he would elect to sit with them in the roomy library next door. Here it was just the two chairs opposite his authoritative desk, a few shelves of books, one or two pictures, a door to a private lavatory, and, through a bay window, a fine view of the college quadrangle. But the light, in the winter, was weak, so that the lamp on Dr. Chase's desk was lit, X-raying his long thin hand, outstretched, now, to receive the envelope his automated servant Leary had wordlessly extended to him.

Whoever was on the line was doing most of the talking. By the time Dr. Chase had got around to saying, "Very well, then, we'll meet in London rather than here, Your Grace," he had read the missive Mr. Simon had handed him. He hung up the telephone and eased his chair forward into the light's territory, no longer a penumbral figure with a disembodied hand reaching like a tentacle from under the rock into the lit spaces of the world to transact necessary business. His rhythm through it all was unbroken, from the shadow of his telephone to the operating-table brilliance of the appointments calendar on his desk.

"Well, I suppose we shall have to have him come in after tea. No, dash it, I see I shan't be here—a council meeting in the town . . . tomorrow seems too far away. Sunday is bad for this kind of thing. And anyway, it's no way to placate old Simon. He is very riled, and"—Dr. Chase exposed for the first time his extra-perfunctory interest in Blackford Oakes—"I wouldn't say I'd blame him, dealing with that cheeky American brat."

"May I make a suggestion, sir?" Leary was valuable not only for making helpful suggestions but for making suggestions of particular, though not obvious, appeal to Dr. Chase. "Why not do it now? Your appointment with Dr. Keith isn't until eleven, and it's only ten-twenty. You wouldn't have to leave here for fifteen or twenty minutes in any case."

Dr. Chase reflected, primarily for the sake of appearing deliberate. He made decisions quickly.

"Very well. But is there a prefect about?"

"Mr. Simon thinks of everything," Mr. Leary smiled. "He sent Anthony Trust along as an escort."

"Very well." Dr. Chase was now the man of action. "Never mind bringing the boy in here first. We'll omit that. Put him straight down. I'll talk to him when he's ready."

Mr. Leary walked back to his office, saying nothing to the boys as he opened the door of the antechamber and posted, on the permanent hook outside, the frayed cardboard notice, "PLEASE DO NOT DISTURB," normally reserved for late Friday afternoons and for faculty meetings. Then he turned to the boys, who had risen respectfully on his entrance. "Follow me."

74

They went into the library. Sitting in a chair and leafing through a black-bound register, Leary addressed Anthony without looking up at him, standing across the way, self-consciously, in the gray light, Oakes at his side. "Trust, it hasn't been all that long since you were here on . . . official business. You do remember what is expected of a prefect?" Trust said nothing, from which Leary assumed he had the answer he wanted.

To Oakes:

"Take off your coat, put it on the chair over there"—he pointed to an upright chair all but hidden behind the window light—"and loosen your braces. It's quite *simple*, Oakes, merely unbutton the buttons forward and back; or, if you prefer, take off your vest and slide the braces off your shoulders."

Leary went off to the corner of the room and lifted the two-tiered block from under the bookcases, depositing it up against the sofa. It reposed now directly under the window, the shaft of light sharply but severely illuminating the block, isolating it altogether from the shadowed arm of the sofa to which it was now conjoined.

Oakes stood, coatless, not knowing, exactly, what to do. His trousers did not need the braces to keep them up, so his arms hung limp by his sides.

"Come here," Leary motioned.

Oakes approached him.

"Unbutton your fly buttons." He waited.

"Now, kneel on the *lower* step, and bring your arms over the arm of the sofa."

Blackford did so. He felt, then, the cold hands of Mr. Leary taking up his shirttail and tucking it, tidily—was there an unnecessary motion there?—under his vest. And then, with a snapping motion, Leary yanked down the shorts, leaving Oakes with naked posteriors, cold, and—he thought in his fright and amazement—trembling, as they jutted up at a forty-five-degree angle, as exquisitely postured as any guillotine block to oblige the executioner.

"Ready, Head," Mr. Leary sang out without actually approaching the headmaster's door.

Dr. Chase did not materialize instantly. There was a long minute's wait before Blackford could hear the steps approaching. He looked up as best he could at the tall and silent face of this man who ruled thus conclusively over the bodies and minds of 625 boys. Dr. Chase moved to a long cupboard directly opposite from that part of the sofa over which Black's head was suspended, took a key chain from his pocket, located the right key, and opened the cupboard. At that moment, back in the study, the telephone rang. Leaving the door open, Dr. Chase walked resolutely, unhurriedly, back into his study, and though the sounds of the brief conversation reached the library, the words did not. Meanwhile Black, bent over, stared at the contents of the open closet. Two or three bundles of birch rods, several bamboo canes, and what appeared to be a collection of slippers, sitting at the bottom. Dr. Chase returned, selected, after some deliberation, a particular birch rod, withdrew it, laid it on a table by the far end of the sofa, sat down opposite Oakes, and took the black leather register handed to him by Mr. Leary, opened at the right page. Dr. Chase spoke for the first time.

"Oakes. O-a-k-e-s. I have a good many complaints here about you, Oakes, though I have not previously acted on any of them. My mistake, I can see now. Tell me, sir, have you ever been beaten?"

Blackford was hot now not only with fear but with rage. But he knew that nothing—no threat, no punishment—would deprive him of the imperative satisfaction of answering curtly. "No," he said.

Dr. Chase seemed to grow whiter, but then the same chalk-white shaft of light that shone on Oakes's rear end now flooded Dr. Chase's face as he bent over his register, scribbling on the page reserved for *O-a-k-e-s, B.*, a record of the forthcoming ministration.

"Perhaps, sir," Dr. Chase said icily, "that accounts for your bad manners?"

Oakes said nothing.

"We have a great deal to accomplish, here in Britain, during the next period. But we are not unwilling to take time for a little foreign aid. Perhaps America is not prepared to help Britain. But here at Greyburn, Britain is prepared to help America"—he stood up, handed the book to Mr. Leary, and walked over toward the rod—"even if our aid is administered to only one American at a time."

The moment had come, and suddenly Oakes found Trust's

76

hands grabbing him at the armpits, forcing his head down. Now, his face on the leather cushion, he could see the bottom half of Dr. Chase, walking over toward the executioner's position.

"You will receive nine strokes."

Black could hear Anthony gasp.

Again there was a pause, and the whistling sound of the rod as Dr. Chase limbered his arm. After that, a moment such as, Oakes thought—in the furious state of his mind, recalling the war stories he had read so avidly that summer—the soldiers experience just before beginning their charge: the whole body and mind frozen in anticipation. What happened then he could not have anticipated. The rod, the instrument of all Dr. Chase's strength, wrath, and resentment, descended, and the pain was indescribable, outrageous, unforgettable. Oakes shouted as if he had been hosed down by a flame thrower. His legs shot out from the block. *"Hold him tight,"* Dr. Chase hissed at Trust, who applied his whole body's strength to holding Blackford down. The rod descended again, and Oakes's lower body writhed in spastic reaction, but could not avoid the descending birch, which came down, again; and again; and again. There was a slight, endless interval between the strokes—five, ten seconds—during which Dr. Chase, grim satisfaction written on his face, studied Oakes's movements like a hunter the movements of a bird dog, the better to anticipate, and connect the rod to, the buttocks with maximum effect. Oakes's screams were continuous, uncontrollable, an amalgam of pain, fear, mortification. But when the ninth stroke was given he suddenly fell silent, as Trust's grip relaxed. The room was noiseless. Dr. Chase, breathing heavily and drawing back his rod, red with Blackford's blood, said raspily:

"Courtesy of Great Britain, sir."

He handed the rod to Leary, disdaining to return it himself to the closet, walked rhythmically to his office, and closed the door. Oakes did not change his position for a minute or two during which he was convulsed with a silent sobbing. Leary busied himself for a moment with unimportant details, shutting the closet door, replacing the register in the drawer; and then, finally, left to go to his own office, leaving the library to Trust and Oakes.

"You'd better try to come along now, Oakes." Trust discreetly pulled up the shorts, and gently prodded him by the shoulder, first to lean back, and, finally, to stand up.

"Now, try raising your pants. Easy."

Blackford's blond face was ashen, but his eyes had dried. He struggled to lift up his pants. Without bothering to fasten his suspenders, he reached for his coat, and Trust helped him put it on. He groped his way to Mr. Leary's back door, opened it, and passed through the antechamber without comment to the assistant to the headmaster, walking, as best he could, down the staircase. As he passed through the front door, held open for him by Trust, he detected the gaze of the two ladies in the administrative office, who no doubt had stopped their work to pity or—who knows?—perhaps to celebrate the youthful screams, which must have penetrated the ceiling like a burglar alarm. He felt like flinging open the side door and shouting out, "Would you like a repeat performance tomorrow, ladies? Same time? Same place?" But his imaginary resilience proved very nearly nauseating, and he felt he had to stop to swallow, or be sick. Trust stayed with him, saying nothing as Oakes, head down, waddled, which was all he could manage to do, in the direction of his dormitory. He didn't know exactly why he was headed there, but at that point Trust's voice, rather shakily, but in unequivocal accents of pity and shared outrage that gave a moment's life to Oakes's spirit, said, "We'll go to the lavatory. Cold water will help a lot, and right away."

Trust brought up two empty wooden cases from the store closet opposite the empty lavatory, on which Oakes's feet could perch. Then he poured cold water into the large washbasin, and once again Oakes pulled down his clothes, and sat. The relief was immediate, overwhelming, blissful. He perched there while Trust kept running in cold water. They said nothing, as Blackford's mind settled. It did so quickly. In ten minutes, he said, "Can I call you Anthony?"

"Sure."

"Well, I have to leave Greyburn."

"Don't. Chase has got it out of his system. Now Greyburn is *secure*." Suddenly Trust was less positive. "I don't think they'll keep after you."

Blackford went on without comment. "Anthony, I want you to do one thing for me, which I can't do for myself."

"What is it?"

"I want you to use the telephone in the prefects' lounge to order a taxi to meet me outside Caulfield Hall at one o'clock. I can't approach the housemaster and ask permission to use the telephone at this point."

Anthony's orthodoxy collapsed. Suddenly, willingly—enthusiastically—he was the co-conspirator, sharing the wrath Blackford felt at the sadistic and xenophobic episode in which, the guilt began to assault him, he had somehow served as co-executioner. He wondered, should he have *refused*? Told Dr. Chase that *no*, he, Anthony Trust, *declined* to pinion down a fellow American to accommodate one Briton's vindictiveness? But, he reflected— Anthony was always judicious—the anti-American animus was not really all that transparent until just before the punishment began, and on through the ferocity of it and the hideously redundant final blows. . . . There *was* that premonitory crack, at the beginning, about foreign aid. . . . For a wild moment Anthony thought of taking off with Blackford; but reality quickly overtook him, as he tabulated the arguments, and reckoned that from such a flight he had everything to lose and nothing to gain, except a moment's satisfaction.

What Blackford had to gain, or lose, Trust could not know. But Anthony, unlike Blackford, was an unqualified success at Greyburn. He was elected prefect as a fifth-former and as an American. A slight, dark boy, with unspoken thoughts always obviously on his mind, he was, in a taciturn way, an enthusiast, whose paradoxical detachment, however, was always an unshakable presence. He made his mark early by singling out the house bully and challenging him, notwithstanding the disparity in size and experience. Anthony was trounced, and a week later he challenged the bully again, and again was trounced, and a third time, to meet the same fate. But soon the young oppressor appeared to lose his appetite for bullying, and Anthony, only a few months later, was named prefect by the boys in an overwhelming vote and found himself exercising formal authority over the bully, which he did not abuse. He occupied himself by quietly excelling in everything —his academic work, athletics, the maintenance of his privacy. He

79

was a comfortable and respected member of the Greyburn community. He would remain in it.

Meanwhile his enthusiasm for Blackford's resolution had become a commitment, at whatever risk to his own standing.

"Okay. I'll call Leicester Drivers. But why one o'clock? It's only eleven-fifteen. If you want to slip away earlier, I'll help you pack."

"I don't *want* to slip away. I can pack in fifteen minutes. Then I'll go to lunch."

"You must be nuts! Go to the refectory and advertise the fact that you're running away from school because you were beaten?"

"I am not running away from school. I am leaving school."

"Great God." Anthony wondered: Would the school forcibly stop him? He could think of no real precedent. Last year one of the boys in the Lower School ran away, but he sneaked off at night, taking the bus from Greyburn Town. He was back in two days, driven to the school by his irate father, was soundly beaten, and—Anthony vaguely remembered being told—was doing very nicely this term. Anthony could not conceive of a protracted, let alone ceremonial, departure from Greyburn when the departure was *itself utterly illicit.* He was certain only of this: He could either co-operate with Blackford or desert him; nothing in between. Anthony had not been invited by this strangely independent fellow-American to help formulate his plans, merely to help execute them. The boy sitting half naked in the washbasin gave off a nearly regal sense of rectitude and authority. Anthony had only to see how it would all proceed. He was not there to interpose.

"We'd better get moving. I'll help you up. It's going to hurt again in a matter of minutes, after the cold wears off. After I call the taxi, I'll bring you some stuff I have left over from last year, which you can apply. It's for burns, and it dulls the pain."

Blackford stood up, shakily, stepped off the wooden cases, and drew up his trousers. The pain resumed, intensely, and his eyes were once more hot with pain.

He tried walking naturally. It was very difficult, but by the time he reached the staircase, he was managing a kind of deliberate and synthetically symmetrical gait.

"I'll make the call, then I'll come to your dorm—what number are you?—and help you. Five minutes." Anthony streaked out, and

Blackford, his hand on the railing, moved himself, the left foot up, the right following, the left foot up again, the right following. He reached the landing and walked toward his little cubicle, along the neat row with the white hanging curtains drawn, the beds, the window sills on which personal belongings were permitted, pictures of parents and sisters, school photographs. He came to his own, halfway down the corridor, closed the curtain behind him, and, leaning against the dresser, wept convulsively. He must stop, he thought. Quickly. He leaned over, painfully, to open the drawers of the dresser, to take out his clothes. His suitcases were stored in the locker room, inaccessible. He would leave them there and pile his clothes into two laundry bags. He had already begun to do this when Anthony slipped through the curtains and whispered, "The taxi is all set." He helped Blackford stuff his clothes into the bags. Suddenly he stopped.

"Blackford, you'd better change your pants."

Blackford moved his hand behind him, felt nothing, and asked, "Why?"

"Because. Take them off."

Blackford did, and saw the spots. He removed his shorts, gazing with awe at the streaky bloodstains. He accepted from Anthony the proffered tube. With great care he applied the unguent first on one buttock, then on the other. He took fresh drawers and stepped into them. Then another pair of pants, and suddenly, the balm taking hold, he felt better, and his appetite increased for a last lunch at Greyburn College.

By the time he reached the refectory, promptly at 12:15, the word had obviously traveled to all corners of the school—it is so in schools—that the problem of Blackford Oakes had been disposed of, and all eyes were on him as he filed silently (the boys were not permitted to talk until the presiding master had said grace) to his customary place at the table. After grace, everyone sat down, except Blackford, who in any case could not have done so. Freshly birched boys routinely ate off the mantelpiece for a day or so, and it was expected he would go there, where a plate would be brought to him, and where he could chat with several survivors of Bleak Friday, the afternoon before. Instead he turned to the boy on his left, stretched out his hand, and said, "Good-by, Dodson. I'm leaving Greyburn. It has been very good to know you."

Dodson, who found all things amusing, was tempted to laugh, but decided, his soup spoon barely out of his mouth, against doing so; instead he dropped the spoon and stuck out his hand. There was a terrible gravity in the good-by he had just received from Oakes, who now was saying good-by to Oldfield, continuing his tour around the table. The master, a young physicist called Mr. Brown, watched with fascination and suddenly found that it was his turn.

"So long, Mr. Brown. It has been very nice to know you."

The table was now quiet, and as Blackford walked off stiffly to say good-by, selectively, to special friends here and there at other tables, the entire refectory gradually fell silent. Blackford appeared not to notice, and the whispering then began, in accents of awe, disbelief, and dismay. But no one did what Anthony most feared someone might do. Perhaps because everyone knew Blackford enough to know that to call him a coward would be implausible. And there was something in the precocious solemnity of the courtly tour around the large refectory that gainsaid schoolboy jeering. He did it all—from the lowly Dodson to the final occupant of the main table, the formidable head prefect, the Scottish aristocrat who, at age seventeen, was already a world-renowned equestrian—in six or seven minutes, his voice audible only to the person he was addressing. When passing by the presiding master—this week it was an utterly dumbstruck Spaniard, who taught his own language and Italian—he merely bowed slightly, stopping to shake hands with a genial prefect on his right. Then, without looking back, he opened the door of the refectory, and closed it on to an explosion, the animated bustle of three hundred boys wondering whether they could believe their eyes.

Anthony rose from the main table, whispered to Mr. Castroviejo that he was suffering from a stomach ache, left the refectory sedately, and then rushed down the hall, catching up with Blackford at the door. Together they crossed the quadrangle and climbed the stairs to Blackford's room, where Anthony insisted on picking up the two bulky laundry bags.

"I'll write to you, Anthony."

"But Blackford, your old man is bound to send you back. Oh God, what will they do to you then?"

"I won't be coming back," said Blackford, as they walked down to find a Leicester taxi waiting. There was no one else in sight. Blackford opened the door, put one of the laundry bags on the back seat, smoothed it out, gave the other bag to the driver, eased himself in, and, gently, lowered his weight on his cushion.

"We are driving to London," he told the driver, and returned Anthony's wave as the car pulled out.

Mr. Castroviejo, revived, rushed across to the headmaster's home to give him the news. Dr. Chase, caught at lunch with his wife and twenty-five-year-old daughter, clenched his fists on the seat of his chair, his mind racing. He *could* stop Oakes. But that would require physical force. And what then would he do? There were no *prison cells* at Greyburn. He could hardly, in Oakes's present condition, beat him again. He resolved that at best, by attempting to detain Oakes, he would risk indignity. Oakes would be back. If it required a few days, or a week, so much the better— he would be ready for another dose of the birch, he thought smugly.

But Dr. Chase experienced a real alarm. What if, on reaching London, Oakes should exhibit his backside to his parents? The nightmare took wings, and Dr. Chase had visions of Blackford Oakes reporting to Ambassador Kennedy or the American Embassy, and calling in the press to photograph his lacerated posteriors. What would the press in America do with that—the story of the American boy who spoke his mind in an English school!

Chase snapped out his orders to Castroviejo. He was to go fetch Mr. Simon *instantly*. He would get an affidavit, Dr. Chase thought, and maybe signed statements from several of the boys in the class, testifying to Oakes's unparalleled insolence. He *did* wish now that he had beaten him a little less viciously, a little less . . . thoroughly. Too many people are too easily shocked by the stern discipline of fine public schools, he thought. But the trustees would *not like* the publicity. And what if, in America, it did become a cause célèbre? How he wished he had never consented to admit young Oakes. Trust! Trust!—he remembered. He had been witness to Dr. Chase's acid remarks about America.

"Geraldine," he barked to his daughter, "go right now to the refectory and get a prefect—any prefect—to find Anthony Trust. T-R-U-S-T. Have Trust come here *instantly*."

He wondered whether he could strike pre-emptively by telephoning Sir Alec. It would be an hour and a half before Oakes
reached London if he took the taxi all the way in. If he was
headed for the station, it would take him—he looked at his watch
—two and a half hours. Yes, that was it.

"Camilla," he said to his wife. "Get me the registrar on the telephone." She would have the home telephone of Sir Alec Sharkey.

He was not surprised, when he rang the bell, that his mother
should open the door. It was obvious that Dr. Chase would report
his absence and take the opportunity to vindicate Greyburn. He
had steeled himself for this encounter, not knowing certainly
whether her sympathy for him would be muted by dismay at his
mutiny. Whatever she had planned to do, she in fact broke into
tears as she hugged her boy, who had grown taller than she in the
two months he had been away. He returned her embrace, but was
dry-eyed.

"I'll be all right, Mother."

When she saw how he had to walk, ascending the staircase, she
broke down again.

"Don't," he said, climbing slowly to the living room to face Sir
Alec.

In the hour and a half's drive he had gone over it and over it,
and he found himself strangely calm. He knew only that he *had* to
communicate to his stepfather, early in their conversation, that he
would go to a reformatory school before he would go again to
Greyburn: that Greyburn was *out*. What to do then would be a
matter of probably prolonged negotiation. He was ready to begin
it.

Sir Alec was not. He looked awfully black and severe in his
morning coat. But, rising, he extended his hand to Blackford and
said, "We will go over the whole thing tomorrow. There is no
point in doing it today. You are upset, I am upset, and your
mother is upset. We shall have some tea, and talk about other
matters."

Blackford feared that any extravagant gesture of caution, as he
lowered himself into the sofa, might be interpreted as an appeal
for pity. On the other hand, he guessed that his stepfather was

practiced enough in the ways of Greyburn to distinguish between a routine, as distinguished from an abusive, punishment, by the precautions the victim had thereafter to take before sitting down. Blackford decided to do as he would if they were not in the room; so he sat down slowly, carefully. Even so, on the soft cushion, it was painful, as it had been in the taxi, and he yearned to go to his room and try to nap sleeping on his front.

"Tomorrow," his mother said, attempting cheer, "is your birthday, Blackford. I went out an hour ago and bought you one or two things, nothing in particular. We had sent a package to . . . Greyburn."

"Thank you, Mother."

There was silence as they stirred their tea. Sir Alec cleared his throat.

"The war news is uniformly bad. Unless we get a great deal of instant help from America, we are very probably lost. If the Russians don't check the winter offensive of Hitler, he'll have all of Europe. But the situation in America is coming to a head. Roosevelt has in effect given an ultimatum to Japan, and there is no reason to suppose that Japan will stand for it. . . ."

Blackford had tuned out. He was suddenly nearly sickened by fatigue, by the strain of the past four hours.

"Would you mind"—he paused—"Alec . . . if I went to my room?"

"Of course not. Carol, help the boy upstairs."

Mother and son walked up the second flight. His room was ready for him. His mother did not linger, kissing him lightly on the cheek and giving him two capsules and a glass of water. He disrobed, and lay down on his stomach, and awoke at eight the next morning.

At 9:45 they drove off to church. "Look, Alec," Blackford fought through his embarrassment, "I won't be able to sit in the pews. So when I stand in the back, please no fuss."

The church was very nearly full, and the minister prayed for national strength at this time of adversity. There were soldiers and sailors there, mostly accompanied by wives or mothers, and some very old people, fatalistic in the set of their faces, and in

85

their routinized responses, and in the singing of the hymns. Blackford missed—for a moment, until he decisively suppressed the nostalgia—the Greyburn College choir, half of it made up of boys from the Lower School with their bel canto soprano voices, half from the throaty Upper School, under the spirited direction of Mr. Clayton, the gifted pianist, organist, and cellist, for whom the boys in the choir would do anything, so transparent was his pleasure when they did it right. He looked at his watch. The services at Greyburn would be over by now—they began at nine—and the boys would be free to do as they pleased for the balance of the morning, the balance of the blissful morning, that went so fast.

His mother had decided they should all go out for lunch. The awful hour was approaching when husband and son would discuss the future. Meanwhile there was a birthday to celebrate. The lunch was strained, but the food was good, and Blackford ate ravenously. In the taxi on the way home there was no conversation at all, and, once inside the door, his mother said she would be going up to her room; and so left the study, and the living room, for the privacy of "the two men"—"that's what I must think of you as, Blacky, now that you are sixteen."

They sat down.

"All right, tell me about it. You should know that Dr. Chase had me on the telephone for twenty minutes. So I know his side of the story."

Blackford related, without embellishment, in something of a monotone, the events that led to his session with Dr. Chase. He did not omit any detail of his drawing on the blackboard. But he repeated, exactly—the words were engraved in his memory—what Dr. Chase had said, before and after the punishment.

"He said, 'Courtesy of Great Britain, sir'?"

"Yes."

Sir Alec had risen and was pacing back and forth.

"Blackford, stand up. Turn around, and drop your pants."

Blackford did as he was told.

"Take them up again."

Blackford did so, buttoned them, and turned around. His stepfather had left the room.

He saw him again at dinner.

"Blackford, we'll resume the discussion tomorrow. There's

time, and your mother wants a proper celebration." In due course a cake with sixteen candles was brought in, and four gift-wrapped packages, a book of etchings, four ties, and a large box of chocolates sent over by Aunt Alice. The telephone rang, and Sir Alec answered it in the next room. They could hear him shouting and slamming the receiver down.

He ran into the dining room. "The Japanese," he said, "have attacked the United States Navy at Hawaii!"

They spent the rest of that night listening to the radio.

The next afternoon, the American ambassador was quoted in the newspapers as making an appeal to all American residents in England whose work was not related to the war effort to return home. Two passenger ships, under convoy, would leave on successive days, Wednesday and Thursday; and again, a fortnight later. Embassy officials were standing by, at the indicated numbers, to take reservations. Priority would be given to school children and the elderly. But men and women of any age would eventually be accommodated. The ships would ferry Americans until the last request for transportation was met. After that, there would be only irregular opportunities to leave the British Isles.

Late in the afternoon Sir Alec advised Blackford that he would be on the S.S. *Mount Vernon*, leaving that Wednesday from Southampton. Sir Alec had two envelopes in his hand. He gave one to Blackford and told him to read it. It was a letter to Aunt Alice, endorsing a bank draft of five hundred pounds. He handed him the second envelope—a copy of a dispatch he had written the afternoon before to Dr. Chase. Blackford read it, lowered it, then rushed impulsively to his stepfather, hugging him tightly—his judge, vindicator, and protector. He wept one final time, with relief and gratitude, and prepared to leave his parents, whom he vaguely suspected he would not see again until the war was over; perhaps never again. On Wednesday, feeling strong now, and self-assured, he waved from the crowded, noisy, boisterous railroad car at Waterloo Station crammed with very young and very old Americans, until they were all gone. Sir Alec's bowler was the last object to slip from sight. He sat down with considerable aplomb, pulled out a chocolate from the recesses of his leather hand-case, popped it in his mouth, and sat comfortably, though still a little edgily, studying the sketches of Michelangelo.

Seven

HE HAD CABLED HIS MOTHER not to attempt to meet his flight, the schedules being as wayward as he knew them to be, so he arrived at Portland Place by taxi and sat briefly staring up at the neat Georgian entrance, so similar to the abutting entrances on that spacious street, recalling the last time he had approached it alone, by taxi, a frightened, wounded schoolboy, ten years ago. He took the large suitcase from the stooped-over septuagenarian who was trying, with difficulty, to cope with it, paid him the fee, rang the doorbell, and embraced his mother, whom he hadn't seen for a year, since she last visited New York. Sir Alec he had not seen since he left England as a schoolboy. He came down the stairs looking a great deal older, but robust, dressed in formal garb as always—a smoking jacket this time and velvet slippers. It was very late, the airplane ride had taken eleven hours, so they sat with cheese and port, and caught up. Black gave his mother perfume—she delighted in novel brands, and Sally had introduced him to Sortilège. And for his stepfather, a first edition of Johnson's dictionary, which Black remembered he wanted and which had soaked up all the money realized by the sale of Black's textbooks. And for both of them, from his suitcase, a ten-pound Virginia ham, a rare event in meatless England, 1951. He told them he would be busy throughout the following day but proposed to take them both to dinner at the 400—they wondered how he came to know about the 400—in the evening, "Because I have lots of foundation expense money I'm dying to burn up. . . . One of these days, Alec, I'm going to pay you back all the money you sent me while I was at Yale."

"If you do, you'll get me arrested," Sir Alec said, affecting, with some success, a Colonel Blimp chortle. The allusion was to the intricate arrangements necessary for getting money out of Great Britain to America during the "austerity" instituted by the Labour Government to husband precious dollars after the war. Sir Alec gave pounds to American friends who traveled regularly in England, which they consumed there; and, in America, they reimbursed Sir Alec through a lawyer, who paid Blackford's bills in due course. The struggle was to keep the two figures in rough equilibrium. Anyone caught doing that kind of rinky-dink was severely handled—or so, in any case, Her Majesty's Government was always threatening. Black kissed his mother good night, clapped Alec on the back, and walked upstairs where the butler, returned to service after the war, had unpacked his things. On his bed was a note from his mother: "Darling, I've dreamed of your coming back and living in London. I am too happy to tell you how I feel." His eyes swelled with tears, and he looked down at the bed in which he had fitted so comfortably returning from Greyburn. It was a snug fit now, but he slept soundly, and serenely, and wondered what Singer Callaway would be like, that being the name of the single man in Great Britain aware, at this moment, that "Geoffrey Truax" was now in London.

Tomorrow at ten they would meet at a safe house, 74 Park Street, and he hoped he would learn what he would be doing on the London scene, with which he felt now a fingertip's familiarity. Callaway would be pleased, he thought to himself as sleepiness began to overcome him. Not quite like Macaulay, who could name all the Archbishops of Canterbury (how many had there been, he wondered, in 1815, when Macaulay was a schoolboy?). Let's see, mmm, the incumbent is the 98th, subtract, hell, maybe one every fifteen years, that's about how long they serve. 1951 minus 1815, mmm, that's, mmm, 136, divided by 15, mmm, well, less than 10, because 150 divided by 15 *is* 10, and 136 from 150 is very nearly 15, call it 15, so that comes to 14, subtracted from 99, makes 85. Just think of it, Oakes, he said to himself, if you had gone on and finished at Greyburn, you wouldn't be counting Archbishops of Canterbury at night before you went to sleep, you'd have all the answers memorized. . . .

He rejoiced the next morning, not only in the unexpected brilliance of the sun—he thought for a moment of Casablanca as he stepped out into the sandy white—but in the self-confidence with which he stepped out, his stepfather's *Daily Telegraph* rolled up in one hand, heading in the proper direction. I'll walk down to Oxford Circus, he said to himself, then right on Oxford Street until I hit Park Street on the left. There was a bustle on the streets, and he remembered the cynical economist at Yale who commented that nothing so invigorates a city as to all but destroy it every generation or two. He was amused by the formality of the businessmen, some of them driving about in great dignity with bowler hats on tiny motor scooters they called Corgis. Twice he bumped into people, or was bumped into, and in both cases, one an older man, the other a young girl, the disengagement was accompanied by a "Sorry, sir." The buses seemed old, and a little toy-store quaint, but there was animation everywhere, even around the war's potholes, several of which he passed by, most of them already in the process of reconstruction. The air was brisk and light, and he could not remember a day from his school days quite like it, and wondered whether the weather was a function of his mood or the other way around.

He knocked at #74, and a slim man, in his late forties, opened the door, at exactly 10:03 by Blackford's watch.

"Come in, Oakes," he said, rather more genially than was the custom in Washington. Blackford walked in and sat down in the living room immediately to the right of the entrance.

Callaway poured coffee.

"It's hard to know where to begin. By the way, in England, anyone wearing the kind of costume you have on is very conspicuous. A blazer and gray trousers won't do. They wear suits here, on all occasions. Anyhow, I'm an assistant cultural affairs officer at the embassy, two and a half blocks from here. The cultural affairs officer and the ambassador know what my job is, no one else. I spend about four hours a day on cultural affairs of one kind or another, and no one knows when I'm away from the embassy what I'm off doing—presumably listening to poets or watching ballet groups that want to visit America. I have a superior in England from whom I am currently detached, reporting instead to a single man with a single mission whose presence, indeed whose existence, is not known to anyone else in London."

Callaway's voice was midwestern, though not twangy like Senator Taft's. He spoke with energy, contained only by a seeming fear of running away with himself: Every few minutes Blackford had the sense that Callaway was reaching up and putting on the metronome to rein in his speed. He spoke with spontaneity, but in large figured patterns, like a skier slaloming carelessly down a mountain, tracing loosely perfect curves.

"The heat is on. Stalin knows we're developing the hydrogen bomb, and that he can't speak back to us persuasively unless *he's* got one too. The Brits have had teams of people going over, and over, and over again, everything Klaus Fuchs probably took with him. They don't know what he was doing during the long hours he spent in the library and away from the office. Alan Nunn May has been in prison six years, and I've waged a campaign to get him sprung."

Black raised his eyebrows.

"He's not doing anything in prison except serving time. Outside, he might resume his activity, and we can keep an eye on him. The restrictions voted by Congress are useful. It gives us the handle for asking questions relating to security, and we have already established the practice of asking to see the personnel records of anyone involved in nuclear stuff. That situation has improved a lot in the past few months. Two foreign service officers have been missing for six months, and we haven't yet given out a general alarm, but we've got to think they're in Russia —or dead. But if they're dead, it's not our doing. They weren't working for us, and we have now dug into their college records: one Commie, one fag, Guy Burgess and Donald MacLean; Burgess was in Washington for a while with the British Embassy and did a lot of contact work with our people. Oh my God, is there no end to it?"

"End to what?" Blackford asked.

"End to *not* knowing whom you can trust and whom you can't trust."

"I would suppose not," said Blackford, "since there will be defections in both directions always."

"A lot of the guys we've come across, and are looking for, became Communists before the war, for reasons you are familiar with—social idealism, and, now and then, political exigency. Some of them, but not many, came in through the study of Marx. The war fused a lot of disparate impulses together: There was only the one cause—beating Hitler—and the consensus was entirely negative. After the war came the great diaspora, but many of our people clung to the Soviet star. I can't help but think they will diminish in number. There is too much information flowing out of the Iron Curtain that can't be assimilated by British stomachs, which tend to be healthy—the Communist party has about thirty thousand members. Stalin has right now maybe ten million people in concentration camps. That has got to affect, sooner or later, the success of Soviet recruiting in England—and in America. They don't have a Joe McCarthy here, but it's getting pretty unpopular to be a Communist or an apologist. They didn't used to care; now they do: so that social pressures within the universities, and in the professions, are blowing away a lot of the loose-hanging supporters the Commies used to have. The other day, Professor *Meachey* signed a protest against the Czechoslovakian purge, which is the first Communist purge in history Professor Meachey has reacted against. Of course, he's only seventy."

Blackford knew all about Meachey. He had led the Oxford Committee to protest the imputation of guilt to Stalin during the show trials in the late thirties. He had defended the Stalin-Hitler Pact with fiery eloquence, and he had warned as recently as four months ago against the "McCarthyization of Great Britain." Would the Red Dean of Canterbury be next? Blackford wondered.

They drove out in Callaway's car, west, toward Windsor, and lunched at Maidenhead. Callaway spoke steadily. Attlee, he said, was going to Washington, among other things to persuade Harry Truman on no account to use the atom bomb in Korea. The British election was coming soon, and the chances were very good that Churchill would come to office again. The peace party in England, demonstrating against the atomic arsenals maintained by NATO, was dominated by the Communists and financed by them. The British labor unions were pretty solid and were turning against Horner of the coal workers, who had said two years ago that his union would strike and refuse to supply coal for any war against the Soviet Union. The Marshall Plan was working well and, in West Germany, accomplishing some kind of a goddamned miracle.

Blackford enjoyed the quaintness of the five-hundred-year-old inn, and the trim garden where they sat, to celebrate the sun, eating dried-out fish and cold potatoes.

It was then that Callaway said, "You're going to have to step out into London society. That takes money, a lot more money than we are paying you. I've gone over it in some detail with the boss. We figure you will have to spend four or five hundred pounds per month to live the kind of life we want you to live. That means you get a large apartment, in a right part of London, maybe somewhere near Mayfair, and you start mixing with the social set—you know who they are.

"Now, there are two cover problems. The English present no problem; they're used to rich Americans, and one more won't surprise them. The problems are your parents; and your friends from Yale, and so on, coming over and visiting with you.

"As far as your parents are concerned, I think you can bring it off by saying that your flat belongs to the foundation. It is part of your job to entertain British engineers and scientists, to persuade them to co-operate with you on your project. Will that satisfy your mother and stepfather?"

Blackford thought.

"Mother wouldn't give it a moment's notice," he said. "But my stepfather is capable of wondering about the extravagance even of American foundations. On the other hand . . . he wonders about the extravagance of everything American. So unless you're going to have me buying race horses, I think I can persuade him that everything I do is accounted for by the foundation using blocked and otherwise illiquid assets in England. He'd understand—even sympathize with that."

"What about your friends, coming in and visiting?"

"That's tougher. On the other hand, they can be led to believe it's my stepfather. They know he's well off, but not how well off, and know he had difficulty getting money to me in New Haven. But he wouldn't have that problem here. . . . I suppose it would help not to have my stepfather and my friends at the same party."

"I shouldn't think that would be too tough."

"No," Blackford agreed, smiling at the thought of presenting his stepfather, who dressed like Jeeves, to some of his friends.

Callaway thought—they were back at Park Street now—and said, "Okay . . . the money itself will come in from the foundation. At the end of every month, write out a very general voucher, and bulk the expenses under the heading: 'Entertainment in re Project.'

"Now," Callaway said, "I'm going to leave you alone for three months."

"Three months!"

"Three months. You can get in touch with me anytime you want. But we know that organic relations are best developed by an agent operating naturally. Get your own apartment—"

"Flat."

"Yeah, flat. Get it furnished, drift around as you find yourself drifting naturally. All you need to do is remember the objective: We want *you,* a wealthy young American engineer, a former air ace, handsome and intelligent, popular, a uniform success, except for an ugly and ambiguous episode at Greyburn College years ago"—Blackford flushed, but did not interrupt—"inside the English social set, maybe even a guest on some occasion or other at one of the affairs the royals attend, an extra man at one of those parties. Something of a social fixture. If you can't manage that, we have alternatives. We can try, using our own resources, to get you into the milieu we want; we can assign you to another covert operation; we can pull you out of deep cover and give you a desk job in Washington; or we can fire you."

"There's one more. But I'm glad you didn't add: 'Or dispose of you,'" Blackford said, rising.

Callaway smiled, with great warmth. And Blackford experienced the current of faith that lit up that smile. Now Blackford knew Singer had that faith in him—knew it with a scientist's detachment. It was well founded. Blackford was not in the least dismayed by the assignment. He had the wherewithal, the background, the manner, the looks, his father's gypsy glamour and audacity, his mother's quiet and gentle tenacity; and now he had money to buy the paraphernalia without which you do not, in London as a foreigner, get very far past the doorman. Why should he not end up among the dozens of young men who make it to the best parties? Of course, it would help if the CIA had made him a young duke, but failing that, better an untitled American than an untitled Englishman: They can't hold these misfortunes against an American. He dreaded only the prospect of running into the Old Boy network of Greyburn College, the thought that tongues would wag. He wondered how his experience had survived in Greyburn mythology. . . . Anthony Trust could not tell him; after settling for the security and certainty of Greyburn, he had been ordered to America by his mother twenty-four hours after Blackford left, minutes after Pearl Harbor. The chances were overwhelming that he would meet one of his former classmates, and that The Story would circulate. Nothing to be done about it. Beyond a little embarrassment, there was nothing in prospect that would impair his mission, whatever the mission proved to be.

"I take it you're not ready to tell me what it is I'm supposed to look for once I'm a social lion? Just a routine check under the potted plants?"

Callaway stood up. "All in good time."

He opened a drawer and pulled out an envelope with a thousand pounds in it. "Sign here," he said, giving Blackford a foundation report form, "and send it in yourself to your contact at the foundation. Don't let me hear from you unless you really need me. Good-by." He had led Blackford to the door. "And good luck."

Eight

Q ueen Caroline was awake, but did not ring for her tea, toast, marmalade, and one sausage. ("I said *one* sausage, Emily, one-one-one-one sausage," she had exploded almost two years ago. "Do I have to pass a royal decree to make that clear? I *know* my larder is full enough to provide me with six sausages, and I *know* I am a constitutional monarch with very limited powers, but I should have enough authority—or maybe I should consult the Prime Minister on the question?—to get *one* sausage when *one* sausage is all the sausage I want!" "Yes, ma'am," Emily had said, and rushed down to the chamberlain to ask him please personally to instruct the kitchen.)

She was not exactly tired, but she was a little bored and saw no point in unnecessarily accelerating her schedule and thereby increasing the length of her day. Being Queen was a marvelous job, really, with no end of compensations, but she had to admit that whereas she was awfully skeptical when her cousin, during her brief reign, complained on one occasion at Sandringham about the burdens of office, she knew now that her predecessor had been entirely correct. Not that she had given it much thought. No doubt if she had had to submit to one of those tests they give to common criminals (*"You say you were at Brighton when Nellie was murdered?"*), in the course of which she was asked: *"Did you ever dream about being Queen?"* she would have to confess that yes, she did, but it was psychically meaningless—after all, Emily and every other serving woman probably dreamed from time to time about being Queen. Caroline's dreams had been purely in the nature of fantasy. That an exquisitely tended airplane would crash, killing a pregnant Queen and her younger and only sister, was statistically outrageous. The House of Commons had since passed a law forbidding the sovereign, and the next in line for the throne, from traveling together in the same plane. She mused, all the time that debate was going on, on the inexplicit premise of the bill, namely that nature should not be permitted to strike again in such a way as to saddle the kingdom with another Queen Caroline. But that was perhaps too personal a way of looking at it, really. The protest was more in the nature of a routine precaution against multiple tragedy than a bill of attainder animadverting on the performance of the incumbent monarch.

As a matter of fact, it had turned out quite the contrary—Caroline took fugitive satisfaction out of it. Her manifest concern for every English problem struck neither her ministers as officious nor her public as imperious or even unfeminine. She was on the one hand unequivocally pro-British—the least penitent monarch who ever lived, by no means given to ostentation for its own sake, but utterly prepared to use the huge resources of the crown for public effect. So that when she was putting on a state dinner she was a great theatrical success. But she was a great success also when she visited bits of her kingdom laid waste by tragedy—fires, pestilence, storms, whatever. She would talk quite freely within the range of the microphones and television cameras to the victims, make practical suggestions, show a familiarity with the mechanical availability of state services. And—altogether unusual—she would sometimes express a pulverizing royal impatience over the failures of the state bureaucracy. She was in that sense an ombudsperson: always on the side of her subjects, opposed—theoretically—to herself, the embodiment of the state. But she would be seen, sometimes in these extraordinarily frank glimpses of her on television, thinking out loud; inquisitive about things; naturally curious. Her reactions were never packaged, and not entirely predictable, except for that predilection to side with the victim and against the man who specialized in rushing forward with forms to fill. In a year, she had become an omnipresence—eccentric, autocratic, desirable, feared, and quite frankly beloved.

To be sure, thought Caroline, reaching down with her toes to touch the gilt footboard, which she liked to do to remind herself how very tall she was, in contrast to her predecessor—she was by no means a perfect Queen. For one thing, she was perfectly capable of making it perfectly clear that she was bored to death. She did not shirk those duties she had to perform in virtue of her office; but she did not see it anywhere specified that she should *pretend* to enjoy them. Some she enjoyed hugely: receiving the weekly report from the Prime Minister in particular. She was deeply and meticulously informed about politics, in which she had been interested even as a girl, her father's favorite, with whom he would discuss political matters as animatedly as if he were talking to a party leader. The Prime Minister, accustomed to thirty-minute ritual sessions with her predecessor, found himself, before the flowers had bloomed on her predecessor's grave, required to allocate as much as two hours to answering Queen Caroline's searching questions.

She had begun by meticulously observing the rule that she was merely an auditor. But, really, that was unrealistic, she soon discovered. If she were entirely passive in receiving the news of her first minister, why could he not send his reports over on magnetic tape—or rather, Caroline smiled, on Royal Magnetic Tape? *"Excuse me, ma'am, the Lord Chamberlain is here with the Royal Tape from the Prime Minister." The Lord Chamberlain, in his silk knickers, advanced reverentially toward her, his hands extended under a velvet cushion on top of which was one sixty-minute tape.*

She was smart enough to advance herself slowly, and before long the Prime Minister really had no alternative than to talk to her as he might talk to the Home Secretary. He had explicit authority over the Home Secretary, and she had explicit authority over the Prime Minister—she could discharge him if she wanted to. But that would result, as she learned from her tutor twenty years ago when as a precocious child of eleven she had asked about it, in a "constitutional crisis."

"What is a constitutional crisis?" she asked.

"That"—her father, sitting nearby smoking his pipe and reading the afternoon paper, interposed—"is, for instance, when the King fires his Prime Minister, the Parliament calls a general election, the same party is returned to power, and elects the same man as Prime Minister. The monarch would have to resign."

"Why?" Caroline had asked.

"Why? Because, dear, Parliament is really sovereign."

"Then why do they call the King the sovereign?"

"It is a protracted metaphor," her father had said; and she did not quite know what that meant, not for a few years. The phrase had stuck in her memory, and she had decided, on finding herself suddenly the sovereign of Great Britain and its diminishing empire, that if other people were going to play along with the metaphor, she might as well see what was in it for her. The Prime Minister, who had inexplicit authority over the Queen, could not really exercise it without weakening, perhaps even destroying, the metaphor. And this no Prime Minister was likely to want to do. Under the circumstances, she began to exercise not her theoretical powers to command compliance, but her indisputable powers to command attention—anywhere; for just about as long as she chose. Moreover, she insisted on talking about the things that interested her. At the third session with the Prime Minister, who had been rattling on for at least ten minutes about what the Houses of Parliament were intending to appropriate to preserve the parks' deteriorating rose gardens, she interrupted him:

"How many atom bombs do we have?"

"How many what, ma'am?"

"Atom bombs."

The Prime Minister—an old Etonian, who had cultivated the public school stutter to political advantage—half opened, shut, half opened his mouth again, and said, "I d-d-don't know exactly, ma'am."

"I don't need to know *exactly*, Prime Minister. Is it more like *ten*, like *one hundred*, or like *one thousand?*"

"Do you mean, m-m-ma'am, those held in Great Britain by the United States, pursuant to the codicils of the NATO Treaty? Or d-d-do you mean those bombs over which we have total authority?"

"The latter."

The Prime Minister let out a half sigh—he would not have given out this information to his own Home Secretary.

"Twenty-six, ma'am."

"How many do the Americans have?"

"I don't have the e-e-exact figures. Approximately ten times as many."

"How many do the Russians have?"

"We assume they have only a dozen. But they are manufacturing them very rapidly."

"How do you know?"

"American intelligence, ma'am. They have contacts." He was vastly relieved to be able to add, "We don't know, of course, who those contacts are, or how reliable they are."

"I see. Well, get on with the rose gardens."

The Prime Minister did, but it had become a listless performance.

She yawned and pressed the button. Instantly the large white-gilt doors opened, and Emily entered with five newspapers, walked to the Queen's left and drew the curtains letting in light from the garden, walked to the bedside and bobbed a quick curtsy as she handed the papers to the Queen.

"Good morning, ma'am."

"Good morning, Emily."

She flicked on her bedside light and began reading. "Emily," she called out, just as Emily had reached the door.

"Yes, ma'am?"

"Please tell Lady Mabel to attend me."

"Yes, ma'am."

Lady Mabel Lunford knocked and entered.

"Mabs, please take this cablegram."

Lady Mabel, who had been a secretary before marrying her husband, had eagerly revealed her knowledge of shorthand to the Queen on being retained by the court after her husband's death. The Queen was delighted to learn this about her family's old friend, having resisted the dictation of intimate communications through her official personal secretaries. It was always Lady Mabel she asked for when she wanted to communicate with her husband, which was infrequently, during his absences, which were frequent.

She munched on her toast and toyed with the sausage, looking up at the ceiling. *"To the Duke,* wherever he is in the Gold Coast, wherever the Gold Coast is. *Dear Richard: I plan to give a party on January*—what is the second Monday in January?"

Lady Mabel paused only briefly. "That would be the fourteenth, ma'am."

—on the fourteenth of January in honor of Margaret Truman comma whose father comma you will recall comma will be entering his final year of office with visible reluctance period I need to know now whether you will be in London on that day comma as if so comma I shall plan one kind of party dash stuffy end dash semicolon if not comma I shall plan another kind of party dash more amusing period Please advise by return cable period And if you can possibly bring yourself to refrain from doing so comma dear Richard comma I should deem it a personal favor if you can complete your tour of Africa without publicly apologizing for Great Britain's history of imperialism period Affectionately Caroline.

The Queen stuck the sausage into her mouth and munched it happily, ringing for Emily who, waiting in the next room, came in instantly.

"Bring me another sausage, Emily."

"Yes, ma'am."

"And Mabs, kindly instruct the Lord Chamberlain to instruct the Foreign Minister to instruct the ambassador in Washington to convey to Miss Truman an invitation by Her Majesty to be the guest of honor at a dinner dance at Buckingham Palace on January 14. You will note, Mabs, how readily I have mastered royal procedure?" Lady Mabel said nothing, but smiled respectfully. But Caroline felt the affection behind the official smile. "Thank you, Mabs."

"Yes, ma'am."

She bobbed, turned, and went out the door, and the Queen settled down to reading her five newspapers, to which she would give a full hour.

Nine

BORIS ANDREYVICH BOLGIN peered through the little round port-hole on the tatterdemalion IL 12 as the pilot circled the airport. He sometimes felt, approaching Moscow, that it might all end better for him if the pilot would miscalculate while landing in one of those frequent snowfalls, plunging the airplane straight into the ground. He recalled that, as a matter of fact, Comrade Stalin had not eschewed this as an expeditious means of execution. His old superior, Constantine Oumansky, was ambassador to Mexico and in active charge of the entire NKVD operation in Latin America when Comrade Stalin sent for him in 1945. The plane took off, reached fifteen thousand feet, and exploded. For a few months, toward the end of the war, when Stalin was cultivating the image of the fatherly protector of the Russian homeland and the memory of the great bloodshed of the 1930s dimmed, it was possible to talk about Stalin, discreetly to be sure. But his colleagues had talked candidly about the execution of Oumansky and the novel way in which it had been effected.

"Mexico is becoming a laboratory for Comrade Stalin's executions," his counterpart in Norway had commented, not without a trace of admiration. "Trotsky they bungled the first time, but, Boris Andreyvich, you don't bungle when you put an explosive in an airplane and set it to go off at fifteen thousand feet. Of course, there are a few innocent victims, but isn't that true in any situation?"

Boris Andreyvich had learned merely to nod his head, rather than contribute verbally to any discussion that might find him suddenly co-opted by the speaker to a point of view.

102

Boris Andreyvich Bolgin was not born laconic or passive. As a young exuberant revolutionist in the twenties he had experienced great joy rising up through the party ranks, obeying orders with will and verve, and practicing his catechism in extended ideological conversations over a bottle of vodka with his colleagues and even his superiors. In 1933 the superior in question calculated that at the rate Boris was rising, it would be approximately one year before he would be displacing—the superior in question. Accordingly, on March 30, he was brought in to the headquarters of the OGPU (as the NKVD was then called), and there he was confronted with a sworn statement. He had been overheard to say that however justified Comrade Stalin's control of the party, someday it would necessarily yield, according to Marxist dogma, to the stateless society.

He had never said it, the sworn statement was a fabrication, the trial was swift, and the prison sentence was ten years, seven of which he served at a forced-labor camp in Siberia until the requirements of the war effort took precedence and he was assigned to the army, then to army intelligence (he was fluent in German and English), then to the NKVD, though he continued to serve, ostensibly, as military attaché to the Soviet ambassador. Seven years in Siberia permanently dampened Boris Andreyvich's spirits, and the frostbite permanently altered his physical appearance, so much so that his wife, on seeing him when he first arrived at their tiny flat in Kiev after seven years, screamed; in due course suffered a nervous breakdown; and finally went off with their fourteen-year-old daughter to live with her mother. During the war, she quietly divorced him. Boris lost his final link to his spirited youth and settled down to the job for which there was no practical alternative, as agent of the will of Joseph Stalin, about whom he asked no questions, and permitted himself to think no heretical thoughts, except, in respect of himself, that he hoped he would not live too long, that when he died it would not be in a torture chamber of the NKVD, and that no day would go by in which, at night, he would be deprived of the solace of his own little apartment, his large glass of vodka, and the huge library of the Russian masters of the nineteenth century, which he would not complete, at the studious rate he read them, in the ten years or so he had left to read.

He shook himself awake from the trance when the airplane touched the ground and wondered whether this would prove to be his last landing. He had been recalled frequently for consultations in the preceding three years, but never quite so abruptly as this time around, and he knew—everyone in the embassy knew—that the center of their earth was heaving and fuming and causing great eructations of human misery in its writhing frustration over the failure of Soviet scientists to develop the hydrogen bomb at the same rate as, he knew, the Americans were proceeding with it. Stalin knew, because Boris had passed along the information, that Clement Attlee had secretly promised Harry Truman to endorse the American use of the bomb in the event a cease-fire in Korea was achieved, and then violated. And he knew, again through Boris, exactly how many atom bombs the British had, even though the majority of the members of the House of Commons were ignorant of the fact that the English had built a single bomb. In fact, Boris mused, his knowledge of British secrets was vastly more extensive than that of any one member of the House of Commons, except perhaps the Prime Minister. He knew, moreover, that the brilliant success he had achieved during the past two years would not satisfy his superiors, who were satisfied only with the satisfaction of their superior, which would not come in Boris's time on earth.

There was a car waiting for him. A driver, no escort. Bad sign. He stepped into the car—the only car that had met that flight—and the driver sped off down the lonely, empty highway, the snowy innards of the vast, awful city, where ten thousand bureaucrats dictated the movements of 350 million people, seeking only to please the one figure whose displeasure loosed the Arctic gales of Siberia, and whose wrath dispatched bullets to the brain.

It did not matter that it was now nine at night or that he had been traveling all day. He was taken directly to the Lubyanka Building and noted with relief that the driver had swung into the official entrance, rather than to that irreversible entrance, at the east end, where the prisoners were taken on what was so often their last ride.

A plump and cheerless woman with dirty blond hair and fingers that looked as if she had been changing typewriter ribbons all day long gave him a prepared pass, with a small identity photo, and told him to proceed to Comrade Ilyich's office—he knew where it was.

The initial greeting was perfunctory, but then it usually was; so far, Boris had detected nothing unusual.

"A cup of tea, Boris Andreyvich?"

"Thank you, yes."

Pyotr Ivanovich Ilyich depressed a button on the elaborate console in front of him and gave the orders.

"You are tired, comrade?"

"Well, it is a long trip, but it is refreshing to be back in the Soviet Union," Boris lied.

"Yes," said Ilyich perfunctorily; "yes." He had grown much older, Boris noticed, and surely he had not seen the sun in months? Years? His dark eyes were ringed with fatigue and tension. Once upon a time Pyotr Ivanovich would have dared to say, under the circumstances—to such a friend and colleague of long standing—that these days it was safer to be away from Russia than in it. *No more.* To *no one* would Pyotr Ivanovich say such a thing, save possibly his wife in moments of great intimacy. Never in front of the children or the maid or the butler—he wondered which of his subordinates the butler worked for, and who replaced the batteries in the microphones buried in his apartment.

Once, on the pretext that he feared the possibility of foreign intercepts, he had ordered his own top microphone-detection crew to sweep the place. They found three microphones, one in the bedroom, one in the lounge, one in the dining room. Fine. Only then did he realize the dreadful dilemma he was in. If he reached the official conclusion that the microphones were the work of foreign spies, he was guilty of not having exercised the necessary precautions to prevent foreign spies from planting microphones in the home of the director of the NKVD. But the alternative was officially to concede that he had less than the full confidence of Comrade Stalin, whose agents were listening to Ilyich's conversations. In a flash of inspiration, he solved the problem. He lined up the three members of the crew and, ceremoniously, praised them mightily, telling them that he had had an expert place the microphones in order to test the skills of the sweepers. They had passed their test with flying colors, and he would put in their names for a decoration. After they left, he carefully replaced each of the microphones exactly where it had been. And, sitting in the little drawing room that had served as the children's nursery, he explained to his wife why, in the future, they must retreat here for any intimate discussions, and routinely after dinner, when, he knew, the postprandial relaxation loosens the tongue. Experience in such survival tactics had equipped him for moments such as this—handling Bolgin. . . .

"Boris Andreyvich, we have got to get more information out of London concerning developments in the United States—don't interrupt me quite yet, let me speak. I am aware that security precautions have been taken in Great Britain as a result of the valor of Fuchs, Burgess, and MacLean. But in the United States, matters are far worse. The proddings of McCarthy have resulted in immobilizing many of our operatives. They have not been detected, but they are greatly neutralized. New security precautions taken in the laboratories where the work is going ahead on the hydrogen bomb has resulted in a nearly impenetrable situation. It has been a full year since we succeeded in getting any reliable technical data from the inside. In that year, however, great strides have been made in the development of the great weapon which Comrade Stalin so rightly tells us we cannot permit the United States to have without our having it also. It is *the key.* Alongside it our atom bombs are mere . . . what, *blockbusters,* as they say in America. The potency of the hydrogen weapon staggers the imagination. What would you say, Boris Andreyvich, if I were to tell you that our scientists estimate, on the basis of all the information we have been able to collect, that a single such bomb could destroy the whole of Moscow!"

He was breathing heavily.

"Now, the whole of Moscow means, among other things, *destroying Comrade Stalin.* Comrade Stalin, the heart and soul of the international Communist movement, and Moscow, the heart and soul of the Russian and socialist fatherland—all with a single bomb. There is only one certain way to contain its use, and that is to have one of our own. Comrade Stalin told us two evenings ago that there is no substitute for this achievement, no other priorities, save this one, no other sources of concern, save this one. That's when I sent for you.

"Now," he said, "you. Where do you figure? You have in the

past year fed us a most remarkable fund of important information. I don't mind telling you, Boris Andreyvich, that I consider your operation the most successful of any we have. I have said that to Comrade Stalin, mentioning you *by name.*" Boris Andreyvich shuddered. "He wisely concludes, with his usual magnificent grasp, that England has really become the center of our American intelligence effort. There is a close collaboration between British and American scientists, and a regular flow of information was promised by Truman to Attlee at their most recent conference. Some of that information has already come in to us. *But we must have* more. We must have some direct answers to certain technical questions, and some not so technical."

"Such as?"

"We need to know, for instance, when exactly it is projected that the United States will detonate a test bomb. And when it will go into production after that. And what are the characteristics of that bomb. How heavy will it be? What is the proposed vehicle for delivery? Are there American missiles yet designed which would carry its weight?

"Now, your contact, this 'Robinson.' I must know more about him. I trust greatly in your judgment, but it is only by a careful study of him and his entire range of contacts that we can conclude here whether he is passing along all the information he might have access to. I need therefore to know everything about him—everything. Begin."

"I know nothing about him, Pyotr Ivanovich."

The director of the NKVD rose behind his huge desk and shouted, "You know nothing about Robinson! What are you talking about! It is from Robinson that we have been getting information for over a year!"

"I know that, Pyotr Ivanovich. But Robinson is a very peculiar man. I have never laid eyes on him."

Pyotr Ivanovich was a volatile man who felt that genuine emotion cannot be communicated except by totalist vocal measures. So he cried out at the top of his voice. *"You have never laid eyes on him! Are you mad?"*

Boris replied calmly. "One question at a time. Three times I asked him to disclose his identity. The third time he told me if I made the request again he would disappear, never again to surface."

"How does he communicate with you?"

"In a confessional."

"In a what?"

"A Roman Catholic confessional."

"Where?"

"I shall answer that question if you insist, Pyotr Ivanovich. But I must have your request in writing, and I will insist that you overrule my written reservations. These reservations are based on my estimate of Robinson's turn of mind. If I give you the information, someone on your staff might decide, on his own initiative, to have Robinson followed so as to discover his identity. If that should happen, it is my prediction that Robinson will cease to be useful to us in any way. Remember, we could not blackmail him even if we discovered who he is: because there is not a shred of evidence that he is the source of the information we have collected. To attempt to get between me and Robinson is to jeopardize the most important source of information we have in the Western world."

Pyotr Ivanovich tapped his fingers on the desk, his eyebrows lowered in deep thought.

He would on no account overrule Boris Andreyvich in writing.

And he doubted that, when he conferred with him, Stalin would instruct him to do so. Boris Andreyvich's posture was bureaucratically perfect: He *would* obey *any* order, but that order had to be carefully and deliberately given.

"How does Robinson reach you?"

"By telephone, a pay telephone."

"Your telephone is surely intercepted by the British?"

"Not *surely*, comrade. *Probably*. Still, we proceed on the assumption that it is. The British are extraordinarily carefree about security, and they still feel it is somehow ungentlemanly to intercept private conversations. They are perfectly capable of commissioning an assassination, but half measures are frowned upon. In any event, at the first meeting—or rather, conversation—Robinson and I worked out a code, which is simple, but I think very effective."

"What is the code?"

"I must give the same answer as before, Pyotr Ivanovich."

"What happens then—you proceed to a prestipulated confessional?"

"That is correct. He is always there before me. The confessionals are vacant at the hour he sets, and the church is quite dark. Sometimes we spend as much as a half hour in conversation. He is, oddly, rather loquacious, and enjoys our intercourse. To be sure, during these sessions he is sitting, and I am kneeling, and no doubt that contributes to his sense of leisure and to my occasional impatience. Like all agents, he has no one else to talk to. When it is over, the understanding is very rigid. He leaves, I stay a full three minutes."

"Has he ever given you false information?"

"Yes, once. But he called me the very next day and set up another appointment. He then corrected the misinformation. He had himself been misinformed. But I should ask you, Pyotr Ivanovich—you who have far greater resources than I do to check the information I pass along. Have you ever found it to be false?"

"No," Pyotr mused. "No. Much of it we cannot know to be true or false, since there is neither corroborating evidence nor discrediting evidence. But so much of it has proved to be correct we are required to believe it is all correct, or in any case that it is correct insofar as he knows."

Pyotr felt stymied. He must report some progress at his next meeting with Stalin. (The thought of any such meetings caused the flesh to crawl with apprehension, and he was happiest when, as sometimes happened, a month would go without his being summoned. But this last week he had been summoned three times, and this recall of Bolgin had been at the specific instructions of Stalin.)

"Very well then. We are required to play it your way."

"His way."

"Yes. Your instructions, therefore, are to tell Robinson exactly what it is we want, and see if he can exert himself to get the proper answers. I will arrange for you to see Comrade Sakharov in the morning. He will familiarize you with the technical information we need, to give you an idea of the lacunae in our own work. You will acquaint Robinson with this information and urge him to use his own devices to come up with it. And you will ask him what is the American timetable." Ilyich scratched his nose. "Tell me, has Robinson ever asked any favors of you?"

"No."

"You recognize that you are authorized to grant him anything he wishes—*any*thing? Compensation; asylum—later."

"I have a feeling, Pyotr Ivanovich, that if I were to suggest compensation of any sort, Robinson would leave and I would not hear from him again. He is a very sensitive man."

"Comrade Stalin does not believe in Sensitive Men."

"I am aware of that, Pyotr Ivanovich." The moment he said it, Boris was sorry. It violated his rule: no inflections, ever, of any kind, that might be misunderstood. Quickly he added: "Comrade Stalin is a great leader of men, and individual sensitivity is often a way station to selfish and unproductive behavior. But there is no way we can change the character of Robinson. He is very self-assured and obviously disdains a lot of the things we find useful to reward our people. He is a very, very close student of Marxism, and likes every now and then to talk with me about the fine points. I remember once," Boris mused, "when he brought up a work of Comrade Lenin I hadn't consulted in thirty years. I went straight to the embassy and reread it right through and brought it up at our next meeting. Robinson told me that Lenin's predictions were often influenced by political crises, and that is why this tract isn't stressed so much nowadays. He gave me a learned lecture on the subject, and then suddenly he told me that although he knows nothing very much about me, he knows that I could never understand British society. 'You may prove to be very good at wrecking it, Boris,' he said, 'but you will never really understand it. I don't, though there is much to it that is entirely lovable.'" Boris began to feel, coming in across the desk, a certain fatigue—which awakened his own. He closed off the discussion. "He is," Boris said, "altogether unique—though, of course, I do not know many Englishmen on such a basis!"

The driver took him through the thickening snowstorm to the hotel. He went up to the hard currency store, open for diplomats and late patrons of the ballet and opera, and with a pound note bought a half bottle of vodka, two rolls, a small jar of caviar, a half pound of smoked salmon, and went down to his room, opened the novel by Gogol he had begun the day before, and ate, and drank, and gave thanks for the guardian angel who had whispered to him, months ago, that when asked, as surely he would be one day, to divulge the identity of Robinson, he must say that he did not know. As long as Robinson performed, Boris was safe. He took another long swallow, and looking up at the mirror he whispered, in idiomatic but heavily accented English, his eyes bright, a prerevolutionary smile on his face like Chichikov's trading off dead souls, "Here's looking at you, Robinson my boy."

Ten

BLACKFORD NEEDED to ask no one's permission before cabling Anthony, "OF COURSE I'LL MEET YOU. WILL ALSO BOOK AT FRANCE ET CHOISEUL AND WILL ARRIVE BEFORE NOON FRIDAY. REGARDS, BLACKFORD."

He was excited, having experienced Paris only glancingly on his way back to the States, and in a physical condition that excluded any experimentation with the city's celebrated delights. Almost two months had passed since last seeing Anthony, and he reasoned that although he would not be free to divulge the name of his contact in London, surely he could at least bring Anthony up to date on the general, and highly unusual, nature of his commission. And—who knows?—perhaps now that he was active in the field, Anthony could tell him a little more intimately something about the situation as viewed from Washington; perhaps even something more about the nature of Anthony's own work.

He told his maid where in Paris he could be reached if anybody needed to be in touch with him, and that in any event he would be back on Sunday night. He gave the same message over the telephone to his mother and asked if there was anything in particular he might bring her from Paris, and she said yes, a couple of ounces of any good perfume; and, packing a light suitcase and James Burnham's latest book, which he had been assigned in Washington, he took a cab to the airport and boarded an Air France Convair for the two-and-a-half-hour flight.

He was detained by the immigration authorities.

A moment of irrational panic touched him as the official studied his passport. What could they have seen in it to catch their attention? Was it, somehow, especially stained, for the benefit of Interpol? He quickly rejected these reservations, so obviously in conflict with his training. Yet the man was looking suspiciously at the passport number on his immigration form. His old army passport having lapsed, he had sent in an application for a new one, together with the nine dollars and the three pictures, directly to Ruth Shipley, head of the passport agency of the State Department, and his godmother, reasoning that it would give her a kick personally to expedite its issuance. Miss Shipley did more than he asked her to do. She sent him his passport with the note: "A belated birthday present. With love, Aunt Ruth." At first he examined the passport, but could not see what there was about it that was either festive or free—the nine dollars had not been returned. True, it had arrived quickly. Then he noticed the number: H 1234567.

He had thought that a truly elegant gift, like license plate #1, and looked forward eagerly to occasions that would require him to use it. Unfortunately, the French at Paris, even as the British had done at the London airport, sniffed not VIP—at his age—but impertinence when they noted his immigration form with H1234567 scrawled in the blank marked: *Passport No.* The tall unamused French official stretched out his hand: *"Vôtre passeport."* Blackford produced it, and, carefully, the inspector examined the number, visibly disappointed that he would not have the opportunity to reprimand, or even detain, the dashing young American on the charge of bureaucratic provocation. So, Blackford saw the mistake and wondered whether this passport number wasn't something like a dye marker, which would illuminate his trail in the event he needed, using his own papers, to hopscotch discreetly around Europe. But he pocketed it, smiled at the agent, and said a respectably accented *"Merci, monsieur."*

It was noon when he reached the hotel, built, he saw on reading the legend in the little cobblestoned courtyard into which the taxi took him, on grounds that once belonged to the Marquis de Lafayette. He was agreeably surprised to notice that he would be paying eight dollars a day, including breakfast, for a room positively awesome in its only slightly tatterdemalion Empire splendor. The bath was huge, and there were doors that opened out into the garden; and yet he was only two blocks from the Place de la Concorde. He stood, inhaling the sunny winter wind and smelling from the dining room below the conventional, inescapable, incomparable French bread, and then thought to call Anthony, rather than await his call; and he was in, and greeted Black's call for the first time, with unreserved joy.

"Don't ask me what we're going to do," he said when they met in the lobby ten minutes later. "Just follow me." Anthony had rented a car, and they drove through residential Paris, through the Porte de la Chapelle toward the country. Anthony, chatting away, did not disclose their destination until they reached the outskirts of Chantilly. "There's a little restaurant here, practically unnoticed in *Michelin,* but one of the best—I stumbled on it a while ago, accidentally. But first let's take a quick look at the château."

It was there sitting content, architecturally self-confident, in the lake, yellow-white and stately, with a Mediterranean grace lacking in its more somber counterparts in England.

"There's no time to go through the rooms now—just wanted you to have a look at it."

Presently he retreated a mile or so into the town and parked directly outside a small, inconspicuous set of doors with the traditional menu taped inside the window, facing out for discriminating French inspection. The Café Tipperary abutted, on the right, a shoe store, on the left, a pharmacy.

"Just wait!" said Anthony, bringing his right leg voluptuously over the chair and floating down opposite Black, separated by the usual red and white checkered tablecloth. He ordered, in authoritative if imperfect French, for both of them, having first achieved instant delivery of a bottle of dry white wine from the Loire Valley. The first course was an omelet of sour cream and tomatoes and elixir, unlike anything Black had ever tasted, and better. Then there came a steak and french-fried potatoes. But how to describe the steak? Black looked up wonderingly at Anthony. How had they managed to transmute plain steak into . . . this? And the *pommes frites* (served with a salad of endives). Then, for dessert, a peach tart covered with crème Chantilly, which he had never tasted before and which he would specify on execution eve. Black paid this tribute first in English to Anthony; then, his enthusiasm carrying him away, in French to the waitress, who was also the maître d'hôtel and the wife of the cook. Black's hold on the language being a little uncertain, this caused not a little confusion, and it was required finally that he and Anthony pool their resources, to persuade the waitress, after explaining the little indulgences granted to condemned men in America on execution eve, that the intention had been to compliment the crème Chantilly, not to suggest that it was fit only for convicted murderers.

"Sorry, Black, it won't do. I don't mean it isn't *likely* that you will be convicted or killed or executed in the line of duty, but I mean, crème Chantilly doesn't travel. You can't get it to the States fast enough and anyway there's something about the grass here— doesn't produce the right kind of milk. So you will have to arrange to commit your capital crime in France. As to the crime, I leave it to your imagination. And for the punishment, no problem: The guillotine is still slicing away. Speaking of guillotining, what have they got you doing? Now wait. Before you tell me, you know what you *can* tell me and what you *can't* tell me. Just in case you stray over the line—which try not to do—I won't repeat anything you say."

Black looked at him.

"Okay," Trust said, "just to set your mind at ease: I am *not* here as an agent provocateur to test your discretion. Shoot."

Blackford, afloat with confidence, security, warmth, told him everything, leaving out only the name of his contact, Singer Callaway.

Anthony ordered coffee and brandy and after a pause said, "Well, I'll be goddamned. I've run into some crazy ones. And to think, they are actually paying you *money*—the taxpayers' money, as Senator Taft puts it. Well, all right, tell me: Are you making out?"

Anthony smiled with a boyish self-pleasure he hadn't intended to contain.

He pulled a stiff card out of his jacket pocket.

"My boss hasn't seen this yet."

Anthony took the card in his hand. On top was the royal seal in gold. And underneath, in stately italics:

The Master of the Household
is commanded by Her Majesty to invite
Mr. Blackford Oakes
to a supper dance at Buckingham Palace
to be given by the Queen
to honor Miss Margaret Truman
on Monday, January 14, 1952   10 p.m.
A reply is requested to   *White Tie*
The Master of the Household   *Decorations*

Anthony grinned. "Not bad! How did you manage it?"

"By being charming. That is, by being natural," Black said, with heavy solemnity.

Anthony did not ask the details. So Black proffered them.

"It was easier than I thought. I was only supposed to get myself into high society, try to circulate, have the proper introductions—you know, all that stuff. It just took one. And that's got me to Buckingham Palace. What was required was that I—ingratiate myself—with the U.S. Ambassador's daughter, who is very easy to ingratiate oneself with. I am, in fact, her escort at this party."

"That must mean you are Number One with Helen Hanks."

"As a matter of fact," said Blackford roguishly, "I am. She is not, however"—he found himself saying this in an effort, intellectually unformulated, to suggest the survival of pre-CIA loyalties—"number one with me. Sally still is. All in the line of duty."

Anthony got up, paid the bill, and walked, his arm around Black's, the two of them sparked by the lunch, and the professional intimacies, and the reconnected circuit, through which the friendship flowed as fast as ever, and their pleasure in each other's company. Anthony, talking about nothing much at all, save bits and pieces of Chantilly history he recalled from a study of World War I, which, incredibly, was run from Chantilly during those disastrous months when, Anthony suggested, the generals must surely have made their battle plans after lunch at the Café Tipperary. They drove around rather aimlessly in the car, poking here and there, snuggling up to the perfect little Château St.-Fermin, owned now by Duff Cooper, before that the summer residence of the American ambassador William Bullitt, before that—Anthony decided to enjoy himself—"the little château where Marie Antoinette slept with Robespierre trying to dissuade him from carrying out the French Revolution."

"Oh," said Blacky, "so it was *here* that famous tryst took place?" Except that he was too stuffed with the crème Chantilly, he'd have taken out his notebook, further to extend the historical jape, but Anthony, sticking the gear into reverse (the château was strictly private property), uttered an amiable obscenity, and they lazed their way back to Paris. "It'll be hours before we're hungry again, Black my boy, so I'm going to take you to a little place in Montmartre, known only to the CIA, MI-6, Bao Dai, the Duke of Windsor, and Zsa Zsa Gabor. Promise you won't tell any of your friends?"

"Not even the Queen of England?" Blackford asked solemnly.

They had been there over an hour, drinking champagne, watching what Black assumed must be the world's most unlicensed floor show, when Anthony, having disappeared a full quarter hour, came back to the table.

It was the Entrepreneurial Anthony Trust (there was no mistaking him).

"Black, my friend," he said, making an effort just faintly discernible to steady his voice, "I have . . . after quite extraordinary efforts . . . taken some liberties in vouching for your reputation . . . and made arrangements for us to visit, not more than two blocks from here, two extra-lovely young ladies, so special they are not permitted to appear even in this select company."

Black could not, at that moment, have resisted an invitation to make a comfortable living as a double agent, provided he were fed at the Café Tipperary and entertained at—but the name, he brought his finger to his lips, would never pass them.

"Count me in," he said to Anthony.

"Not until after it's over and I talk with Doucette," Anthony leered.

"You are vulgar, Anthony. And good manners require me not to ask you how you know where to go."

Anthony replied gravely, as in an intelligence briefing, that during the past half hour, "during which, Black, you have done nothing more to further the movement of the universe than ogle, moreover, at the obvious places—did no one ever tell you that the mind is an erogenous zone?" Blackford was in good form for that kind of thing and could have spent a pleasant evening in badinage, but Anthony had gone too far, and Black felt that he was on the escalator, and to pull the emergency stop would somehow throw things off kilter for hours—maybe weeks and years, he thought solemnly, lifting his glass of champagne. "Let's go, Trust. Now."

They walked out, an elderly guide leading the way.

"What time is it, or does it matter?" Black asked, looking at his watch, which, he thought, said only 7 P.M.

"L'heure bleu, they call it in Paris. And, in Paris, no hour is inappropriate for, as you say, engineering studies. Mine is Michelle. She has the most splendid front and the most splendid rear I have ever seen."

"Don't talk to me about Michelle, talk to me about Doucette."

"Blackford my boy, haven't I always looked after you? Doucette is preferable even over Michelle. I elected Michelle only because when I popped in and took a look, Michelle was so obviously, so irresistibly attracted to me—there, on the spot—I could not bear to tell her she would be spending the golden hours of the afternoon other than in the arms of the best America has to offer, certified by the Marshall Plan."

"Shit."

"Please elevate your vocabulary, Blackford. We are going into a very respectable establishment, where the girls are easily shocked. To say nothing of Mme. Pensaud."

Anthony parked, and began walking, past any number of vacant parking sites, what would turn out to be three full blocks.

"By the way, the charge is F.12,500, about twenty-five bucks. Slip it in her purse. Or maybe your . . . nurse . . . already taught you the right way to do these things? And listen, we'll have to sit downstairs in the lounge with the two girls and madame and order more champagne, which will cost us another F.8,000 apiece, but that's expected—that's where Mme. Pensaud makes out."

Anthony rang the button. An old, squat woman wearing a spotless uniform opened the door.

"Nous avons un rendez-vous avec Mme. Pensaud," Anthony said; and they were thereupon led into a lounge, with three sofas of heavy red velvet, walls of heavy yellow damask wallpaper, and heavy red curtains, drawn. On every wall was a huge color lithograph of a member of the British royal family, and, over the desk, a group photo, published by *Paris-Match*, suitable for framing, and, here at Mme. Pensaud's, suitably framed. The coffee table had only that afternoon's *France-Soir* on it. Before they had sat down, Mme. Pensaud came in, lorgnette hanging over her bosom, dressed in black lace with pearl necklace and earrings, and a large diamond ring on her fourth finger. Her hair was elaborately coiffed, lifting up above her head, with ringlets down front, reaching ambitiously over her parched forehead. She wore light lipstick and was dabbed—impregnated?—with an aroma that excited Blackford, who made a note to try to remember to ask what it was exactly, if things went in that direction, so that he could buy some for his mother. Mme. Pensaud shook hands jovially with Anthony and greeted Blackford.

"Oo-la-la, you haarr beeyutifool!" she exclaimed, raising her hand slightly more formally, only to recall, and deftly divert her motion, that American men are not trained to kiss the hands of married women. She sat down and talked in halting English, until Anthony suggested that they might speak in a French, however clumsy, with her guests—*vos invités*. Blackford thought that most diplomatic.

"Yass, that ees bettehr," Mme. Pensaud said, switching now into French, "because anyway, Doucette and Michelle don't speak much English."

She began then to talk again and at length. Clearly, she loved the sound of words, especially her own. Anthony interrupted only to suggest they have a little champagne together, upon which Mme. Pensaud registered surprise and pleasure and rang the bell at her side, producing the maid and the champagne within a matter of seconds. She spoke of French politics, the dreadful mess into which the Fourth Republic had been dragged, and the infinitely preferable arrangements in England under Queen Caroline. Blackford, impatient for the more substantial course, groaned inwardly when Anthony affected to be primarily interested—more than in anything happening anywhere in the world—in the minutiae of French politics. They had drunk almost a full bottle before Anthony said: "But Madame, you cannot expect me to dispense all this political wisdom before such a small audience? Shouldn't we seek to educate Doucette and Michelle?"

"But of course," Mme. Pensaud rose, and left the room.

Blackford said in a whisper: "Listen, Trust, you discuss French politics one more minute and I'm going to smash this champagne bottle over your fucking head. Goddamn, Anthony, we've been here twenty minutes, and my . . . metabolism won't take it."

"Patience, Oakes. You must learn civilized ways of doing things. Otherwise you will stand out as a rube in Buckingham Palace, and blow your cover."

"Blow your own—cover, Talleyrand. No wonder the French population is declining if this is the rate at which they go at things."

Suddenly the girls were there. They smiled and shook hands, and sat down sedately, and Anthony suggested another bottle of champagne, which came in with two glasses.

"Well, Blackford," Anthony spoke in English, "say something."

Blackford raised his glass to propose a toast to the two voluptuous ladies, and froze. All he could think to say was: "*Allons enfants de la patrie!*"

The girls and Mme. Pensaud roared with laughter, and from that moment on it seemed that everyone spoke simultaneously, and a third bottle of champagne was half empty before Anthony said, clinking his glass with his ball-point pen, "Ladies, let us take these festivities upstairs. You are too beautiful to resist."

The girls, excellently trained, instantly rose, and Madame, ringing for the maid, told her to take up the half-empty bottle. The four of them filed up the staircase. Upstairs, doors were open, one on the right, the other on the left, to bedrooms with jumbo-sized beds and dim table lights. Blackford darted into the room on the left and began to undress.

"I see you managed to get what's left of the champagne," he shouted across the hall to Anthony. "*No, no no no no no,*" Doucette was giggling, pulling at Blackford, and, attempting English for the first time, saying: "We all go together!" Blackford and Anthony looked at each other in astonishment.

"Now wait a minute," Anthony began to say, but Michelle had already pushed him into the room on the right, and Doucette, taking advantage of his paralysis, his pants having dropped to his knees, was dragging Blackford in, pausing only once for a quick sally with her right hand down the front of his shorts. "Wheeeeee!" she said.

As they struggled, Anthony, his savoir-faire finally ebbing, muttered, "How in the hell are we going to handle *this* situation?"

Blackford, still resisting, but less forcefully, said fatalistically, "God knows. Maybe this way there'll be some sort of symbiosis."

At that moment, Mme. Pensaud reappeared, carrying a silver tray with a fresh bottle of champagne. She was utterly unperturbed by the commotion, and the girls continued to push the men playfully toward the one bed. She put down the tray, looked up and said, "Symbiosis? *Qu'est-ce que c'est, ça?*"

"After you, Webster," Anthony motioned to Blackford.

"Well, well," he said, with difficulty, because Doucette was now vigorously stimulating him, "that's when—ah!—two things together get—oh!—along better than one."

Mme. Pensaud knitted her brow in thought. "I do not know that word. That is not a French word."

"Well," said Blackford breathlessly, "I guess there's nothing we can do about *that.* . . ." He noted that Anthony had now completely surrendered, and stretched himself out on one side of the bed while Michelle quickly undressed him, then herself, and descended on him making cluck-cluck noises with her lips on the way, and exposing that splendid bottom which Anthony had if anything underrated. Blackford sighed, and went over to the other side, glad to note that he was several feet separated from Anthony from that great expanse—and found himself looking across at a huge and solemn portrait of the young and stately and, indeed, ravishing Queen Caroline of Great Britain. In a moment Doucette was accompanying Michelle, and uttering squeals of delight at Blackford's proportions, insisting on interrupting Michelle in order to display them. "Do you mind if I don't join the inspection, old chap?" Anthony commented, lying on his back, his eyes closed.

"Yes," Blackford groaned. "I mind greatly. Very poor sportsmanship."

At just that moment Mme. Pensaud opened the door without knocking, lorgnette in front of her eyes, a large Larousse in her hand, which she brought under the reading light next to Anthony who was horrified by the interruption. "I have found eet! I have found eet! Here in Larousse!" she exclaimed happily in English, and proceeded to read out, "*Symbiose: coopération mutuelle entre personnes et groupes dans une société spécialement quand il s'agit d'une interdépendance écologique . . .*" She looked up triumphantly, bestowed a motherly glance on the writhing bodies of her guests, and walked out, her head still bent slightly over the dictionary, repeating, thoughtfully, "*coopération mutuelle entre personnes et groupes dans une société spécialement quand il s'agit d'une . . .*" Her voice could no longer be heard, the door having closed quietly behind her.

The boys went to the hotel, napped, and met for a midnight snack at Le Bon Laboureur, on the Left Bank. Their appetites so recently sated, they ordered soup, a salad, cheese, and the house wine.

"Anthony, tell me what you are up to."

"No," he said. "Except this. We're worried as hell over what Stalin is up to. He has turned more secretive than ever. A purge, maybe of classic proportions, is under way. The tumbrils are full and, as usual, full of his own past intimates. At the last state funeral—Litvinov's—our people found as many holes in the array of mourners perched on top of Lenin's Tomb as there were mourners. There are terrific strains on Stalin. In the first place, it has become pretty clear that Mao Tse-tung is making his own decisions in the Korean War. We have reason to believe that some of those decisions have gone directly against the advice of Stalin. Stalin doesn't know how to handle Communist parties that don't do what he tells them to do—Yugoslavia is the perpetual stone in his stomach, and we gather he goes into periodic rages about it. He is so much convinced of his own infallibility that he quickly assumes that when something goes wrong, somebody has been unfaithful to him, and since it is not always possible to establish just which one man is responsible, he eliminates a whole category of men, just as he has begun eliminating—I'm sure he'll keep after them until every last one of them is gone—the top Communist leaders in Czechoslovakia. He feels the most intensive need for physical protection. His own personal security is the tightest ever, and virtually nobody knows, at any particular time, where he actually is. There are doubles, and a couple of people have actually raised the question of whether the man who was at Litvinov's funeral was actually Stalin. Meanwhile the apparatus, world-wide, is roused to a pitch of activity and suspicion. That part has in it things that work for us: We have had two or three very good defections in the past few weeks. We expect more. At the moment, we're getting the word around that if they defect, we'll see that they're looked after. At one meeting in Washington we even considered setting up a branch of the International Rescue Committee to man a huge truck, with lettering in English and Russian, to wander around the U.N. and the Soviet mission, promising instant safety to anyone who wants political asylum. Acheson vetoed it, even though the IRC, which runs its own show, was willing, provided they could also offer the same protections to refugees from Spain and Argentina—the usual thing. One defector has alerted us to Stalin's obsession over the bomb we're building. It's going to be a lulu, and the word is that we have got the toughest part of it licked—Truman, as you may know, is the personal sponsor of the project and has given its development top priority. The defector told us that Stalin won't rest until he has copies of our schematics. We've made security really hard-boiled." Suddenly he looked grave.

"What is it?"

"McCarthy. I had lunch, just before coming over, with a State Department guy at a restaurant in Washington. McCarthy's going after the fags, as you know, and the department dropped about fifty people already this year. This guy said, 'McCarthy's got us so goddamn self-conscious, every time we buy a banana at the State Department cafeteria, we eat it like corn on the cob!'"

Blackford wondered whether that was a story Helen Hanks might enjoy. Her father would not. The mere mention of McCarthy's name excluded jokes in the presence of the ambassador. Black felt himself curiously affected by the invisible network being managed at one end by Joseph Stalin, the principal agent—now that Hitler was gone—of human misery; and, at the other, by Washington, D.C., a network of its own, protective of human freedoms in design, but, also, necessarily engaged in the same kind of business: lying, stealing, intimidating, blackmailing, intercepting. He smiled again as he recalled an aphorism written on the blackboard by Mr. Simon: *Quod licet Jovi, non licet bovi.* He did not fully understand it then, but did now, and though he realized it could be used in defense of indefensible propositions, nevertheless, correctly applied, it was unchallengeable: That which it is permitted for Jove to do is not necessarily permitted for a cow to do. We might in secure conscience lie and steal in order to secure the escape of human beings from misery or death; Stalin had no right to lie and steal in order to bring misery and death to others. Yet, viewed without paradigmatic moral coordinates, simpletons would say, simply: *Both sides lied and cheated*—a plague on both their houses.

"I feel the tension, somehow, Anthony, and I know that I'm part of it. But it is awfully hard to remind yourself, when you are out in a London night club, having carefully selected your company so that it reaches closer and closer to the hem of the court, that you are doing your best for your country." His eyes were lowered, and Anthony had come to know that on such infrequent occasions, Blackford did not welcome wisecracks. He looked, by candlelight, like an innocent schoolboy still, of penetrating intelligence and seductive good looks, who was, somehow, lost; he looked as if he would have stayed there indefinitely, unless somebody thought to call for the check and leave. Anthony told him that though it was a banality that people serve their country in very different ways, no doubt his superiors knew what they were doing, and that, after all, it was only seven months ago that he was an undergraduate in New Haven, "drawing bridges, or whatever you people do"—how could he expect to have got his bearings? They left, and elected to walk across the bridge, up the Rue de Rivoli, and across to St.-Honoré. At the hotel they sat and had a brandy, and Anthony said he would not be free the next day and, whipping out a notebook, wrote down a few notes.

"Here," he said, clipping off the page. "Do what you want tomorrow before your plane. These are my suggestions, given the time you have. Get a driver in the morning and have him take you to Chartres, about forty miles, and—let me see how I can put this simply—it is the most beautiful man-made creation in the world. Then, on the way back, stop at Versailles. It's being rebuilt by Rockefeller money, and you can't see many of the apartments, but you can see the most splendid palace in Europe this side of the Winter Palace in St. Petersburg, I mean Leningrad. Then take a look at Napoleon's tomb, and think what that little man did to Europe; and yet even he was a flop, alongside Alexander. Caesar wept, on viewing the bust of Alexander and meditating what it was that Alexander had accomplished by the time he was half Caesar's age. Maybe Alexander wept, too, foreseeing how quickly the wops would take advantage of his great geopolitical consolidations. Then on the way back to the hotel, stop in at the Jeu de Paume, the old tennis court of the last emperor, where one hundred French Impressionist paintings are exhibited. It is a jewel house, dizzying, but it's maybe one one-thousandth of the Louvre. Then tell your driver you'll give him an extra thousand francs if he catches your flight, because you'll be late. And here, in case you find yourself unsated, and with time to spare"—he retrieved the note paper and wrote down some figures—"is Mme. Pensaud's telephone number. You might want to try it without symbiosis."

"Thanks," said Blackford standing up and clasping Anthony warmly by the hand.

"Be good, Blacky. And—oh yes: If by any chance you ever get to meet the Queen, Blackford, don't forget to call her ma'am." Black smiled at him and wondered whether he should bother to tell Anthony that it had not been all play and no work. By now, he knew as much about British protocol and British manners and British pecking order as the Lord Chamberlain.

Who, as it happened, was the first person presented to him at Buckingham Palace. The men preceded their ladies down the receiving line. The Lord Chamberlain had had a long day, having previously assisted in preparing the Duke's trip, representing his wife the Queen, on a sudden trip to Oslo, to attend the funeral of Queen Benedicta.

"Has it ever occurred to you, Richard," the Queen had said the preceding Friday when the news was brought of her second cousin's death and word requested whether Her Majesty would attend the funeral on Tuesday morning or would dispatch someone else, "that the favorite occupation of royalty in Scandinavia is dying? I am seriously considering buying a little castle in the area, as a convenient base of operations for attending state funerals. And the papers are *always* talking about the high life expectancy of Scandinavians. Not if they go into the royalty business. Or—do you suppose?—perhaps Benedicta committed suicide? If I were married to Kaspar, *I* wouldn't have lasted sixty years. Well anyway, Richard, I am *not going* this time. I cannot go to a ten o'clock funeral in Oslo and begin a state party for Margaret Truman at ten o'clock the evening before, not even if the air force—pardon me, my air force—jets me there in one of its two million guinea fighter planes. You go, and take Lord Stanley—he'll keep you out of trouble. And remember, Richard, churches and funeral receptions aren't ideal places to bemoan the slow rate of decolonization. Tell King Kaspar that Queen Caroline sends her deepest regrets, and cannot imagine that Benedicta is at this moment anything less than wild with liberty." Richard, who always looked slightly pained when with Caroline, managed to look slightly more pained—they were driving to Westminster Abbey for the baptism of a niece—and stared, unsmiling, out the left window at the motorcyclists who wedged the way of the royal limousine. Caroline noticed he had a fresh decoration.

"What's that one?" she pointed.

"The Order of the Full Moon, the highest award of the Paramount Chiefs of the Gold Coast."

"What is their lowest award, the Order of the New Moon?"

"Really, Caroline, you are a dreadful snob."

"I am nothing of the sort, really. But if it pleases you to think so, Richard, then I'll just say, very well, I am." Caroline was uttering these words through a fixed smile as she greeted her subjects with the royal hand-wave, which she had practiced in her bathroom the day after the Prime Minister came to Scotland to announce her accession to the throne (after giving the prescribed oath that she was not a hidden member of the Roman Catholic Church). "Try it as if you were slowly unwinding a large bottle top," her aunt had said. The wave worked.

The Duke of Norfolk, whose aide was discreetly behind him whispering the name of the next in line, intoned the next presentation:

"Your Majesty, I present Mr. Blackford Oakes." Directly in front of him, the American ambassador's wife was being embraced by Margaret Truman, thereby holding up the procession and requiring, between Blackford and the Queen, an extension of their minimal exchange. ("Good evening, Mr. Oakes." "Good evening, ma'am.")

". . . Are you living in London?" the Queen inquired.

"Yes, ma'am. In fact right now I'm living it up in London."

The Queen smiled and suddenly her eyes deglazed and she actually looked at the person she was addressing. She found herself most agreeably surprised by a young man of poise, with quite extraordinarily attractive features, blue eyes, dark blond hair, and an ever-so-slightly mischievous expression. She guessed his age, incorrectly, at twenty-three, and wondered whether he would guess her age at less than her thirty-one years. What she didn't know was that he knew exactly how old she was, where she was born, who her godparents were, where she had schooled, what were her talents, hobbies, passions—and he knew that she was impetuous and could be witheringly sarcastic. Yet he hadn't known for all that he had seen ten thousand pictures of her that she was a generator of power and sex. He sensed that she could, without serious emotional turmoil, order him shot, if she had the power, which she did not, or order him to her bed, which she had the power to do but would not.

"Whom are you escorting, Mr. Oakes?"

"Miss Helen Hanks, ma'am."

The Queen turned her heavily bejeweled head to the next person in line, who had been engaged in make-talk with the Duke of Norfolk.

"Helen," she said amiably. Helen Hanks curtsied. "Perhaps you and Mr. Oakes can join us at our table at dinnertime? We shall sit down exactly at midnight." Her finger had lifted, unnoticed to either Blackford or Helen Hanks, but it might as well have been a rocket for the Lord Chamberlain, who appeared from nowhere and to whom she whispered in a voice audible to the two guests in front of her. "Change my table. Remove . . . the Turkish ambassador and his wife and place them somewhere exalted. Put Miss Hanks and Mr. Oakes in their place." The line had begun to move, and the Queen smiled, evenly, at Blackford, and at Helen, and then greeted Viscount Kirk, who bowed, took her extended hand, and managed discreetly to tickle her palm.

"How are you tonight, Perry?"

"I'm fine, ma'am, and if I may, you look dazzling."

"You don't look mistreated yourself, Perry. When shall we ride together again?"

"I am, in this as in all other matters, at Your Majesty's service," said Kirk, with that exaggerated deference used only by flunkies and very old friends.

"Not tomorrow," said Caroline. "Wouldn't do for me to gambol about the woods on my horse while they are lowering Queen Benedicta into the sod. And Wednesday I must see the Duke off. I shall set out for Windsor from the airport. Join me there for a late family supper, eight o'clock."

"With great pleasure, ma'am."

Blackford found himself exchanging greetings with nearly one half of the two hundred guests at the party. He knew everyone by name, and Helen had long since become accustomed to Blackford's desire to meet everyone, which she attributed to natural gregariousness, a galloping Anglophilia, and an unconcealed desire to advance his engineering projects—the details of which Helen had never completely understood. He seemed to want to be in touch with influential Englishmen with contacts in the academies, in the business world, and in the great postwar construction enterprises. The orchestra played 1930s jazz. There was a vocalist, and the white-tied men, half of them in their twenties, half of them portly ministers and ambassadors, danced with their starched ladies, and retreated, from time to time, to their tables where their champagne glasses and smiles were refilled. Helen was a moderately attractive girl, and her father greatly influential, so that Blackford was left without a partner much of the time, and after dancing spiritedly with (a) the flighty daughter of a duke, (b) Margaret Truman, and (c) Helen's mother, he set out for his table to drink a glass of champagne. The Queen, who until then had sat up at balcony level, a miniature proscenium of sorts on which was the throne from which on other occasions she rose officially to greet ambassadors and gartered commoners, descended toward the ballroom stepping down two large, circular steps, led by the Duke of Gloucester, toward the same table. Blackford was seated, looking out at the dance floor, and did not notice the Queen's arrival behind him, at the head of the table. He was startled, on turning to fill his glass, to look up and find that the Queen, the Duke of Gloucester, and he, were quite alone at a table that seated eight. He wondered whether he should leave, but this would have appeared unnatural—he had just filled his glass with champagne—and by instinct, Blackford could not be awkward. So, without showing surprise, he looked up.

"Champagne, ma'am?"

"Yes," she said, "thank you," and turning to her companion, "and you, Uncle Harry?"

"Yes, dear," the Duke of Gloucester said absent-mindedly, stretching his glass toward Black. "Caroline, you will excuse me a moment? I shall be right back, but Madeleine is waving to me, and I fear I know what she has on her mind, and what's worse, she's right—I must dance with her sister—this is her first time out since Alan's death."

"Go right ahead, Uncle Harry. I shall talk with Mr. Oakes." The Duke of Gloucester, bowing almost imperceptibly, rose and left, and the Queen motioned Blackford to bring his glass and sit next to her.

"What are you doing, exactly, in London?"

"I guess the best way to put it, ma'am, is that American engineers have something of an inferiority complex. We build the biggest everything in the world . . ."

"You do not. The *Queen Elizabeth* is still the biggest passenger liner afloat."

"Well, yes, though our *United States* will be faster, and, though only a hundred feet shorter, much, much lighter."

"It is a new ship. What makes you think when we launch a new one it won't be even lighter, with respect to speed and size?"

"I don't know. But I hope to know all this by the time I return to America."

"What were you saying about an inferiority complex? If so, it would be very good news. Most of the Americans I know could use large transfusions of inferiority complex and still be pretty unbearable."

"Are you referring, ma'am, to all the Americans you met when they came over to give you the tools so that you could do the job? Perhaps they were just homesick."

Queen Caroline paused for the slightest moment; and then smiled. She wished her Prime Minister were a bit more that way—she would enjoy herself more. She wondered if she could ever say anything that would provoke him into speaking to her with the same ease as the young American. She had never traveled to America, but had read a great deal about it, had known many Americans, and read their journals. In some Americans, she reflected, the republican experience was truly profound. They accepted the paraphernalia and rituals of the monarchy with wholly good nature, but they would exhibit the same good nature in the court of the Paramount Chiefs who gave Richard that preposterous medal. It wasn't condescension—there hadn't been a trace of that in Blackford's manner. It was, really, an assured sense of metaphysical equality. She liked it very much. She wondered whether she was too spoiled to like such a style if she ever felt that she could not, with a wave of her hand, cause it to go away, or, through the use of her station, deliver an overwhelming rebuke—the force of which, however, would express not her linguistic resourcefulness, but her temporal rank. She thought it would be amusing to test herself with this young man, to whom she was greatly attracted. She found it increasingly easy to achieve informality—to the dismay of the more formal members of her household, in particular her impossibly punctilious husband who desired ochlocracy abroad but, at home, to be paid homage by the baboons at the zoo. Or, as he would insist on putting it, the Royal Zoo. After the funeral, he would be back for only one day, and then at noon on Wednesday he would depart for a blessedly long and detailed tour of Australia. She would not antagonize him during his last day here.

"Mr. Oakes, are you aware of the archives at Windsor Castle, which collect eight hundred years of engineers' drawings, specifications, and insights into the problems of constructing not only Windsor Castle but also some of the great cathedrals in England?"

"Yes, ma'am. I'm aware of that library—but not familiar with it."

"Would you care to examine it?"

"I would be very, very, very glad to examine it."

"You may do so. Call my lady in waiting Lady Lunford at the palace tomorrow, and she will make the arrangements."

"Does the palace have a listed number?"

The Queen laughed. "Over here, Mr. Oakes, we say: 'Is the palace's number ex-directory?'"

Blackford knew that, but knew also that idiomatic American solecisms carried one further, in certain circumstances, than total acclimatization. He smiled. "I'm glad you're in the book."

The Duke of Gloucester returned. Blackford stood. The Duke asked his niece if she would care to dance. She didn't really want to, but of course she did, and as they rose and approached the floor, the other dancers drew back, without themselves missing a beat—it is so prescribed by convention—leaving their sovereign a wide semicircular berth. She and the Duke went round and round, but did not move six feet from where they first touched the ballroom floor, so that they remained like the tip of the handle of an outspread, ornate fan, and from the table where he stayed sitting, Blackford was struck by the ornamental splendor of the scene, with the huge chandeliers, the gilt-red balcony, the steps behind him ascending to the regal eyrie whence Queen Caroline had descended, the muted whispering and laughing of the dancers and the popping of the champagne bottles, mini-drums written into a secret, melodic score firmly directed by the conductor.

"I guess," Blackford thought to himself, "the time has come to call Singer Callaway."

The contact was routinely established, and Blackford found himself back at Park Street on the afternoon of January 15.

"I knew you were making progress," Callaway said. "Your name has been in the social pages, and I've seen your photograph two or three times. I liked in particular the picture of you and the ambassador's daughter at the Aldershot Tattoo, though I must confess I felt a certain pang when the ambassador asked me at a staff luncheon the other day, 'Who is this Blackford Oakes, Callaway?'

"'Don't rightly know, Mr. Ambassador. Seems a pleasant-looking fellow.' I think you should know that he turned to his secretary and told him to remind him to make some inquiries. Anyway, since I gather you are pretty well launched, it might be a good idea to disengage a little from Helen."

"What for?"

"There are two disadvantages to being with her too much. First, everyone will begin to think of you as her property. Second is that old Hanks, if he thinks you are serious, will bring together a picture of you—in microscopic detail."

"So what?" said Blackford. "The Company did, and wasn't deterred."

"The only slightly frail reed in your tightly thatched cover, Blackford old shoe, is the American foundation's munificence. Hanks is not beyond calling in a top scientist and asking him to assess your mission. We would not welcome that. In fact before we permitted it, we'd have to consider bringing Hanks into the operation. The best thing is to ease away from Helen. She's scheduled to spend six weeks in Arizona with her father beginning in February, so that will help. . . . Now tell me."

"I was in Buckingham Palace last night. The Queen invited me to sit at her table. She subsequently invited me to inspect the engineering archives at Windsor Castle. I was told to call her personal secretary, Lady Lunford, to make an appointment, and it was not clear, when the invitation was tendered, whether the Queen would be around when I went over the papers. It became very clear this morning. Lady Lunford—she's the Queen's personal secretary—a little prim-sounding, but you get the feeling whatever Her Majesty wants, Lunford baby wants at least as badly—told me the Queen would herself introduce me to the keeper, that it would require at least three days for me to inspect the documents, that the Queen had reserved a suite of rooms for me at the castle and would look forward to welcoming me for dinner on Wednesday night."

Callaway whistled. "My God, Oakes, your instructions were to penetrate society, maybe the court. Not the Queen."

"What did you want me to do? Run off with Lady Lunford?"

"No, but I want you to leave here now, because there is nothing I can do at this point without consulting my superior. And Black, you know I mean, really . . . congratulations. Say, what's she like?"

"The kind who stays with you after you've gone. Everything about her. And of course the thing is to ask yourself: Is it the Queen business that makes her eyes that way, the voice intriguing, the skin luminous—her hair looks as if one shake of her head would make it all come down, it's that light. At nineteen she was a tomboy, riding horses all the time. You wouldn't know that now, though she rides all the time. You'd guess she was queenly when they changed her diapers. She is *something*."

"Be at your flat tomorrow at noon," Callaway said. "If you don't hear from me, then come here at two. You will be introduced then to the exact nature of your assignment."

After Blackford left, Callaway made a telephone call.

"Yes, I can be there in fifteen minutes—hell, I can walk there in fifteen minutes," which he did, rounding the park going west at Knightsbridge past Basil Street and the little hotel he had first stayed at in London, and on to number 28 Walton Street. The door opened as he approached it, and he walked down the staircase to the study of the man whose principal responsibility during the war had been to co-ordinate the deceptions that led Adolf Hitler to anticipate that Eisenhower's crossing would be to Calais, rather than a landing in Normandy.

His code name then had been "Rufus," and before Eisenhower gave the final command, he demanded that Rufus, whom he had never laid eyes on and whose whereabouts were never exactly known, should be put on the phone. This was done in about fifteen minutes, which was longer than General Eisenhower liked to wait, particularly in the hours before D-Day. "Rufus, goddammit," Eisenhower had said, in the presence of his five most immediate associates, "it's in your hands more than anybody else. If your deception has worked, we go. If you smell a rat, we'll call the whole goddamn thing off and save a hundred thousand lives." The disembodied voice at the other end of the telephone paused, then said, "Get going, General. The coast is clear, and I'm giving you information less than five minutes old."

"All right, Rufus. And when this is all over I want to meet you. And when I do, it'll be either to give you my dog tags or to plant a bayonet through your gut."

After the war, Rufus had retired to France, but when in January of 1952 he was visited late one afternoon at his farm near Haudon by Allen Dulles, Rufus greeted him cordially and, somehow, was unsurprised. When he offered Dulles tea or a drink, Dulles said no, he wanted him to come along and visit a neighbor. Rufus's wife would not have been surprised if Dulles had told him to go circle a galaxy in an unidentified flying object, and so she said nothing, stepping silently into the hall closet to bring her absent-minded husband his raincoat. In the car, Dulles whispered to his driver and lifted the separating glass.

"General Eisenhower wants to see you, and he's waiting for us at Villa St.-Pierre."

There being no man, ever, who looked like Allen Dulles and wasn't Allen Dulles, the guard, after squinting through the window, did not demand identifying papers, but ushered the car straight through to the residential compound of the Supreme Commander, North Atlantic Treaty Organization, in the old modernized villa. It was after six. Eisenhower was in his study, the fire crackling. He told the butler to bring them whiskey, pushed a key on his telephone, and told his secretary he was not to be disturbed.

Then he rose, and clasped his arms around Rufus. "That's the way I feel about you, Rufus—and I've only laid eyes on you once before."

"I was awfully relieved, General, that that other time you had your dog tags in your hand, not a bayonet."

"Do you still have them?" Eisenhower's expressive face looked up inquisitively.

Rufus unbuttoned, lowered his T-shirt, and pulled them out. Eisenhower reached for his pocket, put on his spectacles, and examined them. "EISENHOWER, DWIGHT DAVID 0-3822." He smiled. "I was issued those in 1915. I never thought I'd give 'em away. I don't know anybody—anybody—who did more than you did, Rufus, to save lives and help win the goddamn war. I had a funny feeling about you—couldn't explain it. Tried to once with General Marshall, and he thought maybe you had me spooked." Ike laughed. "I told Mamie. She understood. But that's the trouble with Mamie. She understands everything. But you've got to admit, Rufus, I could get through to Churchill or the President easier than to you, and I sometimes thought, goddammit, Rufus, that you didn't talk to me because you didn't *want* to talk to me. The Supreme Goddamn Commander!"

Rufus smiled. "I'd make a bad Prime Minister."

Rufus was clearly pleased that the years hadn't obliterated in Eisenhower's memory the awful responsibility Rufus had taken; and he hoped he would be dead before it ever became known all that he had done to accomplish his mission.

They sat down.

"Rufus, we are in the goddamnedest diplomatic mess I have ever known. Or ever heard of—does that go for you too, Allen?"

"Yes, Ike—*never* . . ."

"Look, let's not fart around. We *can't prove* it, but we *know* that some of our top secrets, our big-time stuff, are getting to the Soviet Union on a regular basis by someone at the top—the Home Minister, the Defense Minister, the goddamn Prime Minister, for all we know, and conceivably it's somebody around the Queen."

Rufus, though American, had lived in England, and all four of his grandparents were British. He stood up.

"Now wait a minute, Rufus; sit down. We're *not* saying that the P.M. or Queen Caroline is a Soviet sympathizer. We don't think so. On the other hand, we can't as a *theoretical* matter—I'm talking *your* language now, boy—exclude any possibility. That is, everything about this case is so bizarre you have to begin by forcing yourself to consider every conceivable goddamn possibility.

"Here's what we *do* know. Over the past couple of years, information that our people have given to the Prime Minister has regularly ended up in Soviet hands."

Rufus sat down.

"Not just *one* piece of information, or *two*, or a half dozen; but maybe thirty, forty items of information. What the hell am I calling it information for? Our *most vital secrets.*

"At first we all assumed the stuff had passed through Fuchs, and then Burgess and MacLean. Then we got comprehensive reports from British security on what those three bastards knew, and they knew a hell of a lot. But what we're talking about *now*, they *didn't* know, it turns out. In fact, a lot of the stuff we're talking about now *hadn't even been developed* when they took off.

"I'll give you an example." Eisenhower rose, and poked the fire.

"Two weeks ago, Urey and Teller came here, on Truman's orders. They give me up-to-date information on the H-bomb, so that we can make preparations in NATO in accordance. They came directly from California, no stopping even in Washington. Just before leaving, they told me they had collated reports from various labs and interviewed a few technicians, and *on the airplane* the two of them made projections—that the bomb would be ready to test by the first of November. They gave that information to *me*. No one else was in the room, not even Beedle Smith, Dulles's boss. I didn't send the information to the White House, because they were both due to stop off there in a week, on the way back from the atoms control business in Geneva. They are the tightest-lipped guys in America, but even so, the Bureau keeps a routine eye on them, partly to watch them, partly to protect them. There has never been a single leak traceable to either of them.

"The day after they left here, the Prime Minister was in Paris on an official visit, and the next afternoon he visited with me here. He asked me when the bomb would be ready, and I told him. You know, Rufus—or do you—the President, in consultation with the Atomic Energy Commission and the Senate people, ordered a complete pooling of scientific information between us and the Brits, provided they adopt our style security. I then asked the Prime Minister with whom would he share the information I had just given him. He told me he gives it out strictly on a need-to-know basis. So I said: *Who* needs to know?

"'Something like this, General,' he said, *'nobody* needs to know. Because the bomb will be something for NATO to deploy, not the British. We're poking along on our own in the direction of the hydrogen bomb, but we're several years behind you.'

"*One week later,* we pick up a defector in Prague. He's a young well-placed scientist at the Lossa laboratories where they're working on heavy-water something or other. *He* told *us* that the day before he cut out into West Germany, he and the six top scientists in his lab were taken into the director's room and told they would have to work overtime because word had just come in from the Kremlin that the United States would be ready to detonate on November first! I am not exaggerating when I tell you that a junior scientist working on a Communist bomb had that information before the President of the United States!

"I flew right away to No. 10. Theoretically to protest the budget cut announced in the House of Commons for NATO—dumb bloody thing to do, Rufus—I didn't want the P.M. to know we had figured he must have been the leak, so I said that Teller and Urey, returning from Geneva, had revised their calculations, and figured now it might not be until February 1, 1953, before we could safely detonate. Then I asked him—just like that—whether the November date had been given out to anyone.

"He replied: 'Only to the Queen.'

" 'The *Queen?*' Obviously I looked surprised.

" 'Oh yes, General. Queen Caroline does not like to talk to me, at the weekly audience, about royal charities, horse shows, or honors lists. She treats me the way your man does, on your program, what is it on Sundays?'

" '*Meet the Press?*'

" 'Exactly. Her Majesty treats me like Mr. Spivak, with the significant difference' "—Ike attempted to convey the P.M.'s chuckle, without great success—" 'that I can politely decline to answer Mr. Spivak's questions. But I am, after all, Her Majesty's Chief of Government and *her* subject, and as long as she has a running curiosity about top secret matters, I have a running duty to satisfy it. About our intelligence service and its activities, about our emergency war plans, about our hidden commitments with President Truman in Korea. And she never forgets anything I tell her. One time, forgetting to correct a piece of information I gave her which proved inaccurate, she reprimanded me sharply when a different figure was published in *Jane's Fighting Ships.* I must say, General, there is something to be said for the American way!'

"We then took *every leak* we have been aware of over the last two years that we hadn't traced to a particular person. A small staff was picked to classify these. We were able to establish, in a great majority of the cases, that the leaked information had at one point been given to the Prime Minister.

"We spent six months doing everything we could to study the habits of the P.M. For this, obviously, we couldn't very well crank up MI-6. Can you see a British intelligence official approaching the FBI to check on the security habits of the President of the United States? We obviously couldn't get *too* close to him. But we did a study that *seems* to make it clear that he *isn't* the kind of man that gives away state secrets accidentally, and we're obviously prepared to rule out his giving them away intentionally. In fact, he made commitments to Truman in Washington in September, stuff we wanted from him—which no one in the House of Commons is *yet* aware of—and yet we *know* the Russians know about them! Obviously these could have come from our side—from Truman or someone on Truman's staff. But there's only one common denominator in the bulk of the leaks we are talking about. These were secrets *given* to the Prime Minister. And, we got to believe, handed on by the Prime Minister to the Queen of England, and where, goddammit, Allen, do we go from here?"

Dulles answered: "We go to where your instincts have taken you, Ike. To Rufus. And I think we ought to go to Rufus with something like the mandate we gave him eight years ago. Stop what's happening, and don't let us know how you did it." He looked up at the ceiling. "Needless to say, Rufus, where nothing was excluded in 1943, 1944, one thing is absolutely excluded now. Under *no* circumstances is damage to come to the P.M. or anyone at the top, and under *no* circumstances is it *ever* to be known by anyone, except us, who the leak is. Will you take it on?"

Would they, Rufus felt like asking, take on his wife? But he had always half-expected that the rural life in France could not last forever; and, really, at fifty-eight he didn't feel exhausted any longer. Besides, it didn't look as if this mission would require him to shed blood.

But Rufus thought slowly, and it mattered not at all to him that others should wait while he thought, and those who knew him resented it least, confident that he was thinking about something they should probably themselves have thought of, but hadn't.

"Two things," he said after a silence of several minutes. "Do I understand that you wish me to clear the matter up but that you do *not* wish me to inform you in what way I have cleared the matter up?"

Eisenhower looked at Dulles. "That is my feeling. But Mr. Dulles here has the responsibility for answering that question."

Dulles replied thoughtfully. "I do not have the authority either myself to initiate any extra-legal operation or to authorize a subordinate to authorize one. I take my orders from the director and from the President of the United States, who acts on the recommendations of the policy committee of the National Security Council, which is guided by a piece of congressional legislation. I have never broken the rule. But then I have never faced a situation like this one." He turned to Eisenhower. "Ike, I need guidance. I know the sense in which the responsibility is mine, and I don't propose to shirk it. But it would mean a lot to me to know what you would do in my place."

"If I were in your place, Allen, I would hire Rufus away from his goddamn rose garden as a consultant, on the written understanding that Rufus was free—no hard feelings—to quit whenever he felt the load was too, ah, heavy. I would specify that all reports from him be given you orally on your frequent trips to London, or on his to Washington, or through no-hands cryptography, but that these reports should be made only when he is ready to make them. I would then proceed on the understanding that when Rufus hands you his resignation, you will know only this—that our problem has been taken care of."

"And what," Rufus interrupted, "do you propose to do about state secrets shared with the British, until old Rufus performs?"

"You will have to work out a plan for that, too, Rufus."

"All right. But I'll need a log of everything important that flows into the P.M.—from CIA, from the NSC, from the President, from the Joint Chiefs, from NATO, and from visiting scientists. That's not going to be easy. It isn't going to be easy."

Nothing had been easy for him in years, he thought, as he shook hands, and headed out to the car that would drive through the late spring countryside to his home, to his wife who hated England so, for the purpose of telling her that they were moving back to England for a few months, how many he could not guess. The next thing to do was get hold of Singer Callaway.

At dinner the night before there had been, in addition to Peregrine Kirk, Queen Caroline's mother; Henry, the nine-year-old Prince of Wales; and his second cousin who was tutoring him for a few months before going off to Stanford University in California to pursue graduate studies. Caroline had said a family dinner, and it was just that. The day had been crowded, what with the festivities that attended the departure of the Duke, and a number of

139

greetings and allocutions the Queen needed to execute for the Duke to distribute on his rounds through Australia and New Zealand. So that not very long after a dreadful dinner—she wished the Normans had colonized British cooking—and after listening to her son's proper tutor, James Gould, play a little Mozart on the piano, which had, at least, the undisguised effect of making the Prince of Wales sleepy, Caroline rose, a signal to everyone else to rise.

"Good night, dear Perry. We shall have a real visit tomorrow. Ring for your breakfast when you want it, and let's meet at the stables at eleven."

James Peregrine, Viscount Kirk, eldest son of the Earl of Holly, had found Cambridge boring, on the whole, after two years in the Royal Air Force shooting down, at a most extraordinary rate, Kraut fighters. He had come late to the war; he was only twenty-one when it was over, so they declined to demob him after V-E Day, sending him instead on an assignment unrelated to airplanes —helping to maintain order in Palestine. Though they had been brief, he was well hardened by his earlier experiences. Shot down over the lowlands, he spent one week in the bitter snows in command, by virtue of his rank, of a rag-tag band of foot soldiers whose own leader had been lost. For better than three days they were without food, with only water made by allowing the snow to melt in their frozen hands. Kirk resolved on that occasion that he would not complain, ever. His subordinates, eighteen in number, and resentful at having to take orders from an air force officer, complained with good and ill humor about everything, about the weather, the food, the hygienic facilities, the paucity of air cover, the stubbornness of Montgomery, the tenacity of the Germans. After the first two days, he did not hear even indirectly any complaints about his own leadership. He was approachable, permitting anyone to ventilate a complaint at almost any length. When he felt it was going too far for the morale of the unit, he would stop it short with such a comment as: "Wars certainly have their unpleasant side, Tomkins. Quite right." And he would reach for a straw of optimism. "But it can't be long now. Monty has got to protect his right flank, and when he does that, the area will be evacuated, and we'll be back with the main unit." There was the one occasion—it came on the second day—when these tactics had not worked on a soldier who from heaven knows what interstice in his equipment had come up with a reserve of whiskey, listened with expressive facial skepticism to Kirk, and then interrupted him. "I don't think you bloody well know one bloody thing about fighting. This aynt no cricket field, boy." Kirk had calmly walked over to him and delivered three crippling strokes, one to the stomach, the second to the nose, the third again to the collapsing stomach. Kirk motioned to a sergeant to remove the corpse, and resumed, as if there had been no interruption, his estimate of the surrounding military situation. He eased, without its catching the attention of the soldiers at first, into the metaphorical language of the cricket game and was soon referring to "teams" and "wickets" and "batsmen," as the men listened first with furtive amusement, finally with undisguised admiration.

He had gone straight into the air force from Greyburn and knew how, without saying anything very much, to stimulate a sense of community. Instinctively he guessed that the key to it was: never complain, always sympathize with those who do. At nineteen he was tall and strong, though light. His eyes were a dark green, in colorful contrast to his dark red hair which, characteristically, hung loosely over his forehead, leaving a wake of pale freckles that reached to his angular nose. His father squatted over his huge estate in Aberdeen and complained in all his communications to his son that if the war did not end soon, the pheasants would disappear from Scotland for want of feeding. Young Holly did not pool his father's complaint with those of his men.

Later, in Palestine, he was involved in the counterinsurgency movement. He found one morning a message under his door in the King David Hotel. His master sergeant Akers needed to confer with him instantly and could be found at the empty farmhouse two miles out of the city, on the Mebev Road, at which Kirk frequently met with two or three other counterinsurgency officers to co-ordinate their moves. He dressed quickly, called Roberts, the corporal who, like Akers, had served with him in the air force, and together they drove out in a jeep. He found his sergeant, hanging limply by the neck from a limb of an oak tree by the farmhouse. He ordered Roberts to bring down the corpse and went inside to telephone headquarters. There he heard the explosion, rushed out, and found only bits and pieces of Roberts. The sergeant's body had been booby-trapped. He walked back into the farmhouse and sat still for the hour it took a detachment of specialists to arrive, with their special tools for trying to track down the terrorists.

He wondered whether he would ever again feel so close a kinship as he had felt for the two men he had just now got killed. With morbid shame he recalled importuning them to request a transfer, after V-E Day, so that they could serve out the balance of their terms with him. "It should be very interesting work," he told them, and they both agreed. What could be responsible for the deaths, suffering, and mutilations he had seen in the last two years, he asked himself, and concluded there, in the stillness of the old farm, that there must be an explanation; that human nature must not be left free to do what he had seen it do.

At Cambridge he considered two options. The first was to get it done and over with by taking a heavy academic load. The second was to treat Cambridge as an extracurricular activity, even though it might then take him as long as five years to complete the required courses. He decided on the second, in part because he was not sure what he would be racing toward if he accelerated his education. And in part because it would give him more time with his horses.

He had begun hunting at the age of seven, closely supervised by his father. At thirteen he was riding competitively, high jumping in Dublin at the horse show and competing in the hunter trials. At fifteen he achieved, with his 14:1 pony, the highest jump ever recorded—eight feet one inch. In the summer before the war, he rode wildly hour after hour with his second cousin Caroline through the forest of his and her abutting estates—twelve thousand acres combined—and, toward the end of the golden summer before his final year at Greyburn, he confessed to her at the end of a long day together that he had nothing further to teach her in horsemanship. Though three years older, she no longer condescended to him. Her pleasure was total, and she smiled a heavenly smile that stuck in his memory until the experiences of war made him shrink from all childish, romantic memories.

The horses were no longer a source of pleasure. They were an obsession. He was a member of the British Olympic Team in 1948, and he drove himself, and his horses, in a furious effort to win a gold medal. On the last day, Perry was determined to bring his horse over the high pole the American had nicked, and all but derricked his depleted mount over it. The horse's heels, twisted sideways to avoid hitting the pole, struck instead the pylon that held it, breaking his leg and Perry's back.

It should have been cold, but wasn't, and though they might have eaten at the little lodge at the far end of the great forest, the day was sunny and they flew through the three-mile wooded lane leading to the Great Park. Perry was entirely well again, though he found himself indulging a certain instinct for prudence he had not known a few years back when competing for gold medals. Caroline had not gained an ounce of weight since she was nineteen, and when he had said to her then, in a flush of admiration at an equestrian feat she had performed, that he had nothing left to teach her, he was very nearly correct. A silk scarf around her head, wearing a well-tailored black jacket, capped with the pink of the hunt she had joined as a girl, her tailored breeches and boots soft and limber, she led the way, and they galloped, without stopping, a full thirty minutes. When she reined in, Perry approached her to listen to her breathing. It was as regular as if she had been sitting in bed.

"Come along, I have a surprise."

They darted into the lodge, and she came out bearing a basket and blankets that had been laid there for them. The sun was directly overhead, and through the young horse-chestnut trees she would see out onto the lake and the grass beyond. Their privacy was total, and she gave him the Alsatian wine to open, and quickly drank one and then a second glass, before she began opening and eating the finger sandwiches, and the eggs, and the cold pheasant, and cakes and coffee, by which time they were well through a bottle of claret, just cool enough, and she drew the blanket around her and snuggled close to Perry.

What she liked best about him was that he always talked with her, and almost never about the kind of thing queens get talked to most about. In great exasperation one time she had asked Mabs to help her calculate how many conversations on an average working day she, the Queen, had had respecting the weather.

"Such a nice day, ma'am!"

"Yes, it is a very nice day, isn't it, Lady Leonard? Quite unseasonable, for this time of the year."

"Yes, indeed, ma'am, but I remember once when we had such weather—I was a child, spending the winter in Shropshire—for two whole weeks, and it quite ruined the natural rhythm of the farmers. Let me see now, would that have been 1907 or 1908?"

"I wouldn't know, Lady Leonard, but surely it was 1907 because 1908 was the year of the great blizzard in Shropshire."

Lady Leonard would retire, trying to refresh her recollection about the great blizzard of 1908, which hadn't occurred.

"Is there no other neutral subject, Mabs?" she asked, when Lady Lunford, her pencil quiet at last, computed that Her Majesty discussed the weather approximately ninety-four times per day on a typical day.

"I'm afraid not, ma'am, though flowers are fairly reliable. Most people know *something* about flowers, even the men." The Queen said she would find a discussion of the weather a great relief over the discussion of flowers.

"What would I say? Are your petunias big and strong this season, Lady Shaftesbury? . . . Or: If you really want a great big petunia, Lady Shaftesbury, you can borrow one of mine. I must have the biggest stud in the vegetable kingdom, and he'll bugger anything you have in sight." Lady Lunford laughed.

"Oh, do stop it, ma'am!"

Perry asked her whether she had had a chance to talk to the Duke about his findings in Africa. "We spoke for a while," Caroline said. "Richard is, as you know, terribly anxious to oblige everything except British tradition."

"But you know, he's probably right. It's only a matter of time, and the whole lot of them will want to be free. What then matters is the nature of the Commonwealth."

"I have ideas about that," Caroline said. This sounded portentous, so she added, "Everybody does. . . . The problem is so much the problem of pride. When you think that the Stone of Scone was taken from Westminster Abbey in protest against an amalgamation several hundred years old, you can get a feeling for what the separatists want in Africa."

"And—I expect—what they'll probably get."

"Perry, do you know Westerley Aston well?"

"No, though Father does. Says he's an awful ass, but that could mean simply that he missed more than the permissible number of birds last time they shot together. Why, is he botching the Colonial office?"

"Not so much botching it," said Caroline, "as giving everywhere the impression—to which His Royal Highness, my husband, contributes—that we are the one surviving colonialist power. Occasionally you will find him making references to French and Portuguese and even American overseas appetites. But he never criticizes the Soviet Union's grip on Eastern Europe. Why can't we call that colonialism?"

"We should," said Perry. "It's that at least. Why don't you mention it to the P.M., if you'd rather not talk directly to old Westerley?"

Caroline drew closer to Perry. "I wish you were my minister plenipotentiary. I would trust you to do all these things for me, and then if anything at all went wrong, all I would have to do is simply behead you"—she reached over and ran her fingers through his silky red hair.

Perry put his arm about Caroline's neck and, with his other, stroked, ever so lightly, her lashes, which she had closed against the brilliant sun. She raised her hand and laid it on his, and patted it gently.

"I think not, Perry."

"I'm sorry, Caroline. But remember, it will never be too late for me, because there will never be anyone else."

"You're a duck, and I do adore you. I mean *really* adore you. But that is all I want to say right now, except that it would be quite awful, wouldn't it, if the Soviets were to subdivide Windsor Park?"

Blackford knew nothing about the background of the man called Rufus, but it did not require much knowledge to know that Rufus was one of those men of infinite patience in whom displays of impatience are simply patience's tool. "Goddammit, Singer, haven't you got the log from the NSC for last week yet?" didn't mean that Rufus was reproachful of Singer, merely that a shift into the hortatory mood would probably suggest more directly than any other kind of explanation Rufus's impatient desire to see promptly the logs of information passing through from American officials to the Prime Minister, directly and indirectly. Blackford was struck by the relationship between the two men. Callaway's veneration of Rufus was transparent, but a world removed from sycophancy. And Rufus listened carefully to Callaway, rejecting most of his spirited ellipses, but pausing here and again, raising his hand for silence, to suggest that Callaway had come up with something particularly interesting; as when, in the presence of Blackford on that first and very long afternoon, Callaway had suggested that perhaps Blackford should carefully lead a casual conversation, if the Queen should indeed continue to march toward conversational informality, in the direction of nuclear technology, to test whether anyone around the Queen had anything more than a comic-book familiarity with it.

Rufus, leaning back in his chair and studying the cigarette smoke that issued from his respiratory system from reveille to the end of his day as evenly as if through a factory steam pipe, addressed Blackford.

"Did you study nuclear physics at Yale?"

"I had courses in advanced physics," said Black, "and touched on it. I could deliver a layman's lecture on how the A-bomb is made. But I don't know any of the hydrogen-bomb stuff, naturally. I guess the best way to put it"—he smiled happily, and Rufus and Singer quickly found that, like most people, they thawed, and their minds ran more fluently, under Black's uninhibited smiles—"is that I don't in fact know anything about the projected hydrogen bomb I'm not supposed to know."

Rufus spoke. "I have spent a very intensive month in studying the hydrogen bomb. I've talked with Teller and Urey and with their subordinates. I've had scientific training, and I attempted to classify what I have learned into three orders of difficulty. The first could be explained to anyone with a keen mind and a basic aptitude for mechanics. The second and higher order of difficulty would require that the listener had spent time in formal study.

Not a great deal of time—I am not talking about someone who has studied atomic physics for several semesters, but someone who has familiarized himself sufficiently with the great scientific impasses that at various stages in the struggle to achieve the bomb have constituted roadblocks of historical obduracy."

Blackford found himself enjoying Rufus's manifest capacity to speak whole thoughts, and wondered idly whether, during the war, he and Ike had needed an interpreter.

"And—finally—I have studied, and put into the third classification, the keys to those impasses. They number, by the most convenient count, nine. Anyone who chose to do so could reclassify them so as to multiply them to as high a figure as twenty-two, or as low a figure as six, depending on the taxonomic tables you choose. I think of nine as reasonably distinguishing nine problems different in generic kind. It would be possible for someone who was *not* a trained physicist to apprehend those nine solutions and, by rote, pass them along to an atomic engineer who, acting on them, could proceed to crack these impasses. For instance, I could myself, knowing what I now know, put pencil to paper and fill half a standard-sized notebook, turn it over to Sakharov, and the Soviet Union's problems would reduce to mechanics—*provided they could get computer capability.* Granted, mechanical problems are real problems. *But they would know how to proceed.* And it is obvious that this is the category of information that Stalin now needs. And it's just as obvious, however incredible, that some of that information is beginning to filter through to him, thanks less, I should think it safe to assume, to anyone's technical training of the Queen—if she is the source—in the abstruse world of nuclear physics, than to what must be her extraordinary mimetic powers to repeat exactly what the informant, no doubt sweatily, in turn has memorized for her benefit. We need to discover how much of it is being convoyed through to the enemy under the paradoxical protection of someone high up and, above all, to whom."

He went on without interruption, except to light another cigarette, turning to Blackford: "I know about you, your record, and your aptitudes. I propose to teach you secrets I have designated Classification One and Classification Two. You must become *entirely* conversant with them, as if you had picked them up in the course of your studies at Yale and your close association at Yale with a consultant to the Atomic Energy Commission—is there one?"

"I don't know," said Blackford. "If there is, I didn't run into him. But I can find out."

"No—Singer, you find out; and find out something about him.

"You will spend all your time before next Wednesday here, with me, listening to what I explain to you and reading material I have here. Then, in your conversations at Windsor on the general subject of engineering, let the conversation drift toward the miracles of modern engineering, and see what anybody around does with it. We should know, if we can, the level of theoretical and mechanical sophistication of the Queen herself and anybody in her regular or irregular entourage. As far as we *know*, as I say, the Prime Minister doesn't pass along to her any written material, though I frankly can't guess what he would do if she flat-out asked for it. If we *have* to nudge up to him with that question, we'll try to find a plausible excuse for our curiosity—"

"Maybe," Blackford suggested, with the air of the bright-boy at class, observing a positive suggestion, "you could get Senator McCarthy to give a speech demanding an investigation of the passenger pigeons in Buckingham Palace?"

Rufus would not have dealt with anyone whose digressions betrayed a genuinely frivolous concern with grave problems. Already he had accepted Black's interpolations as stylistic; so that he went on with his analysis, serenely confident that the strong current he was discharging would not, in Blackford, dissipate through mindlessness.

"We've laid a bait," Rufus continued. "We've fingered a British radio operator—Foreign Service—guilty as Mata Hari. He's been passing secrets for over a year. We've been feeding him placebos, with every now and then something semi-solid to maintain his interest, and standing with his Soviet bosses. A week ago, referring back to a phony cable from Washington requesting the services of Professor Wintergreen of Oxford to help crack a specific problem, we slipped in a coded cable saying the request was canceled—that the 'Teller-Freeze Bypass' appears to be 'entirely successful.' Just that—the 'Teller-Freeze Bypass.' Now that will go from the radio operator (the Brits will be arresting him in a couple of days) to his contact. We haven't been able to find out who that is, and we wouldn't be surprised if they use the mail—probably someone in London. If it works, Moscow is going to be screaming to the guy *we're* looking for to find out what the hell the Teller-Freeze Bypass is. These things get around quickly, so I give it a couple of weeks, maybe less, to ripen. If this one doesn't work, we'll use another one. But we'll drop the second one through another mole: We can't let our radio operator discover, before he is whisked away, that there isn't any such thing as a Teller-Freeze Bypass outside the imagination of a counterintelligence unit.

". . . Meanwhile," Rufus continued, "I assume you both noticed in the Court Circular that Sir Edmund Hawkins accompanied the P.M. to Buckingham Palace last week—it was made to sound like a ceremonial visit. He's a family friend, but family friends don't usually, *qua* friends, go to the palace in the company of prime ministers on official business."

Rufus paused. One of his long pauses. Singer succeeded, by minimum physical motion, in communicating that during the interval—and, Blackford generalized, others like it—silence was appropriate. Blackford ran his mind over the cliché—Watson, motionless during the ratiocinative convulsions of Sherlock Holmes; Archie Goodwin, silent lest he distract the great Nero Wolfe. But Black, even as a very young man, knew precociously—however amused by them, or even antagonized—that on the whole it was more than social indulgence to give decent berth to the eccentricities of people who commanded his respect, whether because of his knowledge of their attainments or because of his intuitive respect for their capabilities. Rufus, he had very quickly concluded, was an unusual man, of unusual talent and experience, brought in to cope with an unusual problem. Blackford would not mock him; would not treat him like a Dr. Simon, foolishly, dangerously, patronizingly suggesting that the means by which to force one's mind on a problem was some counterpart of THINK LATIN. Blackford didn't interrupt Rufus's silence, or show signs of impatience; or mock it, ever.

"Anyway," Rufus suddenly began to speak again, "the project, at this stage, is perfectly straightforward.

"Blackford, you, insofar as you can do so, are to probe the Queen's proficiency in nuclear scientific talk, and that of anybody who is regularly in her company, her staff in particular. To reca-pitulate"—Rufus liked to do so, but Blackford didn't mind; each time it was clearer—"in order to do this and do it naturally, you must between now and when you next see her learn more about the subject than she knows. If our hypothesis is correct, when she finds you know more than she about hydrogen bombs, and if she concludes that you have secret material she can get from you more lackadaisically than from the Prime Minister, for the pur-pose of satisfying the curiosity of X, whoever he or she is, there is a further reason beyond"—Rufus allowed himself to wink—"the Queen's natural attraction to young Blackford, which apparently germinated quite naturally. Unless"—Rufus, Blackford assumed, was now playing out, with an amusement only faintly detached, the theoretical possibilities, even as, morally, the scientist in him required him to acknowledge scientific possibilities—"the NKVD is not only in cahoots with the Queen, but has penetrated our own counterintelligence operation, and has called on her to cultivate your company."

It was Singer who, at this point, insisted on an interruption. Ap-ropos of nothing at all, he walked to the corner of the room and lit the burner under a kettle, while trying clumsily to recall a ten-sion-releasing, irrelevant, and irreverent limerick about any old queen, the first part of which he abandoned trying to reconstruct, but, finally, produced triumphantly, through his foggy memory, the closing lines,

". . . she said, *'Turn the lights out,*
" '*It's royalty's night out,*
" '*Queens may be had, but not seen!'* "

Black and Rufus laughed, and took the proffered teacups, and, briefly, so very briefly, Singer cackled on about tea and coffee and Ceylon and Brazil, in an animated monotone which, while it en-gaged the interest, did not require antiphonal response, from ei-ther Rufus or Blackford. Singer wound down with a suitable ca-dence, followed by a pause, followed by—Rufus.

"After the visit to Windsor, we'll decide how to go. If things should, for whatever reason, move very rapidly; if, Blackford, you think you may have, suddenly, a once-only opportunity to dis-cover who the Queen is talking to, *use your own judgment.* I pray to God it will prove sound. And remember this about the Queen.

She is quickly attracted to people—and just as quickly put off. The ghettos of London society are crowded with ex-favorites of the Queen. She can be very informal, almost dismayingly informal. And she can be as squatly regal as the Stone of Scone. There has always got to be—that's how I figure it—an *undertone* of deference—

"What the hell, you seem to be doing it all right on your own. Come back tomorrow, 9:03, and be prepared for about four hours. More than six hours of the stuff I'm going to feed you you can't take. Come to think of it, more than four hours *I* can't take."

Eleven

THAT MORNING OVER THE TELEPHONE Boris Andreyvich Bolgin had
been given two numbers and a time. From the time he subtracted
the ritual one hour, according to practice. The first number designated which of the six Catholic churches regularly used by Robinson he had selected for the forthcoming rendezvous. Entering the
designated church through the main door, Boris would begin to
circle it clockwise, and when he had counted twelve—the second
number given over the telephone that morning—he would stop,
turning his back on the priest's compartment, as if pausing to admire the stained-glass window or statuary opposite. Two hands
would reach out and expertly frisk Boris Andreyvich, one half of
whose torso was enveloped by the priest's curtain, invisible to the
gaze of any chance worshiper lingering in the vicinity. Robinson's
hands reached under the jacket sleeves and around to Boris's
front, and when the hands, satisfied that no recording machines
threatened, were withdrawn, Boris would open the penitent's curtain, adjacent, and kneel down. And say, "I don't often hear from
you on Sunday." To which the indicated answer was: "This isn't
Sunday, it's Saturday."

From that point on, it was conventional—convivial, really, because the two men had without any sense of strain evolved a most
cordial relationship over the years. Robinson, moreover, felt
under no time pressure, having satisfied himself respecting security. So Boris gave him a leisurely account, suitably bowdlerized,
of his trip to Moscow, and stressed and restressed the anxiety felt
there (Boris used Stalin's name as infrequently as possible when

talking to Robinson—it was, wherever possible, "Moscow") on the matter of the hydrogen bomb.

"You have been very ingenious, Robinson, in the matter of getting information useful for world peace and the socialist cause, but—"

Robinson interrupted him.

"Boris, old boy, I have told you before. I am entirely committed to the grand historical purposes of our cause, but (a) I despise, as you know, your leader Stalin, though I recognize his strengths and his usefulness; and (b) I find the repetition of the cant phrases of communism altogether depressing. I recognize that they are *necessary*, even as the Baltimore Catechism is necessary, but I would *not* expect in a serious conversation with a cardinal about great affairs that he would punctuate his message with bits and pieces of Christian doxology. You may proceed, Boris."

Boris recomposed himself and told Robinson, frankly, that Boris *had* to come up with more information and that the focus of Stalin's—or, rather, Moscow's—concern, was the hydrogen bomb.

"I've given you a great deal on the subject already."

"I know, I know. But we must have *more, a great deal more.* I need, Robinson, to pass a few pages of paper to you. If it is agreeable, when you leave I'll have the corner of my envelope jutting out, and you can pick it up and pocket it. It is the result of many hours spent with Sakharov and contains the *specific* questions for which they do not have the answers. These may or may not be too difficult for your understanding. But they are not too difficult for the understanding of your contact or contacts who are getting their information, presumably, from America."

"Boris, I have asked you not to speculate about my sources."

"I'm sorry, Robinson. I really wasn't doing that. I mean, I wasn't intending to do that. I say only that the pieces of paper I hand you won't, maybe, be intelligible to you—that's all."

"I shall worry about that, Boris."

Boris found himself wondering, as he had before, several times, whether Robinson was himself an atomic scientist. But he thought it unlikely: Robinson's language was too casual, too makeshift, when passing along to Boris technical information he certainly must have picked up from someone else. Boris was permitted to take notes on what Robinson told him, but, however poetic the formulas sounded on reaching Moscow, they never sounded, from Robinson's lips, quite like a poem of his own devising.

"On the other hand, the second sheaf of papers I will be giving to you are easily understandable. They aren't scientific in any difficult way, Robinson. These are very practical questions. The *eternal* question—about when the first test will be made. Questions about *when*, assuming the test is successful, production will begin. Questions about the weight of the prototype bomb. About the *weight* of the production bombs. The kilotonnage—that is the kind of thing."

Robinson already guessed that Boris was quoting his superior. *Boris's superior* . . . Robinson knew it could not, under the circumstances, be anybody less than the director of the NKVD. He had allowed himself to wonder, when he began passing along secrets of the first magnitude of importance, whether Boris might be reporting directly to the odious Stalin himself, but the reservation was theoretical. When James Peregrine Kirk decided to follow the course he did, he consciously determined to discount these factors, even as Miss Oyen had done, so that his personal loathing of Stalin proved much less an inhibition than—he comforted himself—it had proved to Churchill and Roosevelt, both bourgeois, in their dealings with Stalin during the war.

"Now, Robinson, I cannot begin to tell you how these matters press. Obviously you must not endanger your contacts. But you must not permit them to adopt a . . . bourgeois's timetable. The socialist response to the challenge of the warmongers requires that we have the hydrogen bomb *within months*—not years—of the development by the imperialists."

"There, there, Boris," Robinson said. "I can imagine the pressures you are under. And I will do what I can. And Boris, just as I don't like *you* to repeat things unnecessarily, *I* don't like to repeat things. But I am going to tell you this again, and probably I'll tell it to you again in six months or so, and six months after that. *If I have so much as a suspicion that an effort is being made to fix my identity*, I will do two things. One, I will disappear, as far as you and your principals are concerned, from the face of the earth. And two, an anonymous but highly detailed letter will find its way to the NKVD chronicling our relationship and suggesting that I have grounds for believing that you are a double agent, and that it was for this reason that I finally suspended my meetings with you. I have kept back one or two secrets—not of great objective importance, but the kind of thing Comrade Stalin, pausing from his preoccupation with the historical tides of socialism, likes very much to see—dirty, personal stuff, for instance—which I shall report having passed along to you, along with a professed concern that these critical insights into the minds of Western leaders in fact had gone no further . . . that kind of thing.

"Now, Boris, I have become very fond of you, but although Marx and Lenin did not devote much of their theoretical attention to the abstract need for individual survival by those who help history along toward its final resolution, these are problems that *necessarily* engage the *individual* attention, and, no doubt, have individually absorbed *your attention*. I would not blame you. Indeed, if I were in your shoes, I do not know how I would operate, feeling the insecurity you necessarily feel as an agent not only of a grand historical enterprise, but also, coextensively, of Joseph Stalin."

"Ah, Robinson, how well I understand you. But how poorly you understand poor me. I did not intend to tell you, but it is true in Moscow they asked me to take, ah, steps, to establish your identity. My reply was: Only if I am ordered over my written protests. Ilyich instantly capitulated. Your anonymity is, in fact, the most valuable possession of mine. I would *never* seek to penetrate it. And it is impenetrable *except through me*. I assume, always, that you operate only through me. . . ."

"Your assumption is correct, Boris. And I understand that we have personal interests in common. But you must also understand that from time to time I shall require confirmation that the information I go to such pains to provide you is making its way quickly to the intended source. So far I am satisfied that it is; so the arrangement is sound, and will continue.

"Now, as regards the questions you ask. I shall, as usual, be in touch with you when I have something useful to communicate. In the meantime, let me give you this casual political impression. The leadership of the Labour party in England is increasingly in the hands of the anti-Communists. One or two of them—Herbert Morrison is one—have been apprised of the Prime Minister's surreptitious promises to Harry Truman respecting the use of the atomic bomb to enforce any settlement in Korea. I know that you have been agitating for a mass-member peace party and that the idea of such a thing caused certain popular commotion. But you must not count on it to effect anything more than a very minor influence on the Labour party. So do not report to Moscow that you can count on significant parliamentary strength in England. Not yet. Later. It will come some time after you have developed the hydrogen bomb, my dear Boris; and maybe even some time after you have developed a missile for delivering it. And probably it will have to await the eventual collapse of the American will, than which there is nothing I nor Marx count on more confidently. But although that is sure to happen, its happening is not a vulgar correlation of the development of the hydrogen bomb, a point, Boris, I would not expect you to try to explain to Ilyich, let alone to the great Stalin."

"Thank you, Robinson." Boris always retreated, under this kind of vernacular ideological pressure, to familiarity. *Poor Boris,* Robinson thought; *and to think I am helping his oppressors. But they are *right*—eternally *right*—*

"—I shall pass along your advice, and we will, all of us who desire a great new world, count on you."

Robinson despaired of attempting any further refinements. And anyway, he thought, maybe Boris already understands—completely.

So Robinson pronounced, in public-schoolboy accents, *"Ego te absolvo,* Tovarich Boris, and say a good act of contrition."

He slipped out of the confessional after parting the curtain, cautiously to survey the surrounding area of the church. As he slid by Boris's compartment, he took the envelope, whose tip barely projected, pocketed it, left by the side door of the church, looked at his watch, walked down Brompton Road across to Harrods, took the elevator up to the shirt department, asked by name for a salesman with whom he talked about the necessity of a strategic plan for replenishing his supply of French silk shirts, which were only now, ever so slowly, making their way back to the English market, after the endless period during which they were available only in America, and other porcine countries that had accumulated by military and geopolitical opportunism their squalid surplus of the world's hard currency. Robinson resented the little indignity, even as, after his occasional rendezvous at the Bag of Nails, he resented it that he was expected to leave his little tart, as a tip, a gen-nyu-ine United States five-dollar bill.

Twelve

LATE ON TUESDAY AFTERNOON, having spent three endless days with Rufus probing explosive mysteries he had barely touched on in his theoretical work at Yale, and committing to memory abstruse formulations at a speed that astonished his tutor, Blackford felt tired, restless, and vaguely apprehensive. He wrote a long letter to Sally, full, he thought to himself as he read it, of crap. His letters to her, however keenly he missed her, were becoming inexorably wooden, so that when he finished he was even more restless. The telephone rang. It was his father—jovial as ever, but this time with a little less of the rodomontade, a great deal more of the furtive purpose and quiet authority Blackford had associated with his father many years ago, when there was the Hero, and the Son, and nothing very complicated in between.

The news was *good!* All good! Tom Oakes was so *awfully* sorry he had not been in touch with Blacky for so many months but he hoped Black had received his telegram on his commencement from Yale. (Black hadn't.) He had been traveling, mostly in the Far East, and now he was making a tour of European capitals. He had become the senior salesman and exhibitor for the new Sabre F-86 fighter—"the most magnificent fighting plane in the world, believe me, Blacky, and I don't care what the British say about their Hunter IV. I've been taking up sixty-five-year-old generals and twenty-one-year-old kids and putting it through its paces, and letting them handle the controls. They are smitten by it, they *swear* by it, they want to *make love* to it! . . ."

They met for dinner, the father, from some access of undisclosed insight, having specified the Connaught. He asked about

Blackford's mother and was pleased to learn what he obviously knew, that she was happy.

"She would never have got that dowdy kind of life with me, but that's what she wanted. I've been seeing a very nice girl in Baywater, Long Island, Blacky, not far from the Sabre people. A war widow with a grown-up daughter who is married to a Sabre engineer, and we plan to marry this spring—if I am *one half* as successful as I think I will be!" He pulled his chair closer to his son's, waving away the waiter who had brought an assortment of pastries—he took it for granted that his splendidly proportioned son routinely turned away the pastry dish.

"I'm operating now on a *guarantee—twenty thousand dollars,* plus a commission of twenty-five thousand per airplane, diminishing in five-thousand-dollar leaps to five thousand, minimum, per plane. *I could sell five planes in Paris on Tuesday.* And I'm going from there to Rome, Oslo, Copenhagen, and then all through Latin America. The English, of course, are dogging me, and everywhere I show up, their people are there in five minutes pushing the Hunter and asking for a *mano a mano,* theirs against ours, and I'm disposed to okay it—for next Monday—if I can persuade the home office we'd come out of it the winner." Tom Oakes lifted his wineglass to his incumbent mistress, with whom, for all his talk of the alluring, expectant widow in Long Island, he was utterly engrossed. But right now, he sat happily at the Connaught, his wallet easily capable of paying the expensive bill for the dinner of a son he had so frequently neglected as, for so long, he had neglected his son's mother. The hell with it, his mistakes were in the past. He looked proudly across the table at a creation for which—he often thought of his hero Lindbergh's persistent interest in genetics—he, Tom Oakes, was at least one-half biologically responsible. A fierce love for his son seized him, and hoping that he wasn't just going through the usual, sentimental routine, which he had heard so often at the bar from the middle-aged fly-boys—awful fathers, but usually, after a while, contritely awful fathers—he thought: I would do anything for Blacky. A thought germinated in his mind.

"I'm confident of my model, though the Hunter *does* have a couple of special features. But here is my surprise for you, Blacky. Tomorrow, I'll take you up in the Sabre and you will fly it. After

158

all, you were a certified ace on the previous model. You haven't forgotten how, have you?" Tom Oakes laughed, as if he had asked his son whether he had forgotten how to read.

"Dad, I haven't flown a jet fighter since the summer before last in the reserve. I'd *love* to try this new one. Where do we go, and at what time?"

"Eleven o'clock, Northolt Air Force Base—that's fifteen miles west of London. Go out on Western Avenue. Go to the tower building and ask for your old man. You're in for a ride I think will surprise even you." Tom Oakes had become accustomed to his son's blasé acceptance of gee-whiz experiences, and had never accompanied him to the Café Tipperary.

Blackford made a quick calculation. "Dad, I'll have to leave the base not a minute later than three forty-five."

"Why?" his father asked, clearly crestfallen. He had imagined the entire day with his son.

"I'd change it if I possibly could. But you know I'm here on this foundation project involving a study of engineering techniques. Through a contact, I was able to arrange to examine the library at Windsor Castle, which is the repository of all the old and modern sketches for the famous British buildings, cathedrals, bridges, that sort of thing. The keeper is laid on to begin looking after me at five P.M., and will stay with me through the early evening, and again the next two days. I'm afraid I just can't budge it. But you'll be back in London before going to Latin America? And if the Monday contest goes through, you'd be back for that, wouldn't you?"

"Back for that! I'd probably fly the plane. But if I didn't, I'd be hustling for it with the brass. Whatever happens, Blacky," his father said softly, "I wouldn't leave Europe without seeing you again."

He became more matter-of-fact. "I'm going to leave two Sabrejets at Northolt Base, so that the English aviators can fly them— and weep. We'll leave a couple of American pilots to stand by to take up prospective purchasers. The third plane, I'll fly over myself, with a copilot, to Paris on Thursday. Maybe I'll just go on over late tomorrow afternoon, since you're going to be tied up."

They had a good evening, and Black found his father depending less, than on previous occasions, on booze for animation. But

Black also acknowledged—his objectivity seldom deserted him—that, undoubtedly, he had himself become easier to talk to as he drew away, with apparent success, from the adolescence his father (let alone the faculty at Greyburn) had had such great difficulty in handling. His father, who retained his leathery good looks and happy-go-lucky smile, recalled, with lascivious pleasure, the hours they had spent together, flying every kind of airplane, to the desperation of his mother.

"Do you realize you weren't seven years old when you took the controls of a plane, and that you made your first solo landing at ten? I remember when we arrived home and told your mother you had landed in an airplane by yourself, and she shut the door in our faces and wouldn't speak to me for a week! I told Charlie Lindbergh that story, and he said he had the identical experience when *he* taught Jon to fly. I remember the letter you wrote me after your first week as a flying cadet. The idea that any army instructors could teach Tom Oakes's son how to fly!"

"I didn't get all that much combat flying done in the war, Dad."

"Whoever said aces can't be grounded by hepatitis? You shot down three planes in three missions. The Germans were just lucky hepatitis was on their side."

Tom Oakes called for the bill and paid it, leaving a generous, though not exorbitant, tip.

"Oh, Blacky, I have a delayed commencement present for you. I didn't know what to buy you, because I never know what your mother or . . . Mr. Sharkey . . . is giving you, so I thought the thing to do was to let you decide. I've been saving this from my first big pay check three months ago, and I am really happy for you to have it."

He handed Blacky an envelope.

"Go on, open it."

Black unobtrusively moved it under his napkin, opened the envelope, and counted five one-hundred-dollar bills. He looked up and saw that his father's eyes were moist. Blacky understood. There had never been such an accumulation of cash during his boyhood.

"I did it in dollars, because currency restrictions are tough, and you may want to save this for traveling abroad—I don't know what your arrangements are with the foundation."

Blackford thanked his father, and gripped his hand, and they walked out. Above all, Black didn't want his father to see the apartment, whose opulence would certainly have surprised, and possibly even dismayed, him; and so he volunteered to drive his father home to his hotel.

"I'll tell you what, Dad, I'll pick you up in the morning, and we'll drive together to Northolt Base. What do you say?"

His father, whose thoughts were seldom well concealed, paused . . . and, in the nick of time, Black added conversationally, "I lent my apartment to my roommate to give a friend of his a going-away party, so I'll have to sneak through the kitchen to my own bedroom."

That had the instant, indeed the visible, effect of diminishing his father's curiosity to see his son's quarters; so they drove off together to the father's hotel.

Black, discharging the cargo, whom he embraced with sincere affection, drew a deep breath and drove home, somewhat elated at his rather brilliant prospects, mundane and futuristic. Right now he had *five hundred dollars* in his pocket. Tomorrow morning he would be flying an airplane that was the pride and joy of the American aviation world—sharing the cockpit with his own father. Later that same day he would drive brashly to Windsor Castle, built by William the Conqueror, the burial place of a dozen British monarchs, the repository of perhaps the most famous collection of technical drawings by the old engineering masters; but also—above all—the residence, during the moment he would spend there, of the British sovereign, Queen Caroline. His "mark!"—Blackford struggled, so soon after reading the literature, to retain the terminology. Blackford could not guess what, after a few days' interlude, her attitude toward him would be. Perhaps she had regretted her impetuous invitation. If so, she would clearly find it extremely difficult to undo the invitation, extended through Lady Lunford, to dine with her tomorrow night. But perhaps, though going through with the dinner, she would behave formally, forbiddingly, overbearingly. Perhaps the dinner would prove to be his final personal contact with her. If he sensed this, he would need to trot out his thermonuclear jewelry; and to consider, even, how to question her associates discreetly during the days (as many as he could stretch out perusing the archives) he had liberty to probe, at second hand, the kind of thing Rufus—and Blackford—cared about. Blackford would bring along enough notebooks, and reference books, to persuade a skeptical keeper of the seriousness of his professional concerns. He packed a very full wardrobe, in no sense exhibitionist, but comfortable, resourceful, fine, and self-assured. He decided that very early on he must, somehow, casually reveal his proficiency in atomic physics. As he lay down to sleep, he wondered whether, ever, a young man seeking to catch the eye of the Queen had done so by studying so intensively the elaborate inflections of that horny old equation, $E = mc^2$.

Thirteen

IT HAD BEEN an exhilarating hour and one half. Within ten minutes, Blackford felt he knew the aircraft as perfectly as he had known the old Sabre he had flown in combat, and had previously taught a score of students to fly. His father gradually relinquished the controls, with considerable pride as he saw his son receive them as if by an anointive process, absorbing intuitively the uses of the innovative instruments and features, designed to increase the maneuverability, dependability, and firepower of an airplane that could be throttled up very nearly to the speed of sound.

Flying out over the English Channel, they asked permission of the tower, and received it, to cavort at fifty thousand feet, clear of commercial aviation. Black turned the plane upside down and ran the throttle up to the line of Mach 1 and watched the needle climb, while his father, seated in the rear cockpit, ceased, finally, to give any instructions, electing, instead, to egg his son along through the intercom, promising him that the aircraft would not fail him. . . .

"Go ahead and dive. Set the auto-take to five thousand—that's a safety device, pulls you out in case you black out. I don't have one back here. Remember, Black, back here I would be spending my time navigating, making radar calculations, and positioning your rockets. But even *without* the copilot, you've got an automatic radar circuitry computerized to give you a bull's-eye target for six cannon. And when the sidewinders come around, which is the day after tomorrow, they can perch just under the wings, though they'll slow you up, maximum Mach .8."

Black dove the airplane, from a dizzy height that permitted

him to see simultaneously London and Cherbourg, pulled on the controls, and lazily turned a steady figure eight while aileron rolling the aircraft, bringing a yelp of delight from his father.

"You did that one as good as Charlie Lindbergh could have done it!"

There was no higher compliment, and when they came back ready to land, just for the hell of it Black looped a loop at a nerve-shattering three hundred feet, coming down a dozen feet above the runway, and touching down, like a paper airplane on a wall-to-wall carpet. For a while his loquacious father was silent, and as they climbed out of the plane he said to Black, "It would have been an okay way to go, you and me in the same plane. But whatever you figure the two of us are worth, I think you ought to know the buggy you looped at three hundred feet cost the taxpayers eleven million dollars."

Blacky grinned with pleasure.

"You can tell 'em from me, it's worth it."

They walked slowly to the tower building, where an assistant helped remove their G suits and auxiliary gear. They sauntered off to the officers' lounge, ordered a beer and a roast-beef sandwich, and Black took pleasure from his father's obvious pleasure, and he wished for the first time in many years that he might see him more often. On reaching Black's MG, they hugged each other with feeling, and Black sped off, pulling out the map he had already surveyed, to keep handy on the left-hand seat. He must go west, then a little bit south. He would see Windsor Castle well before he approached the town. He drove through Windsor slowly, past milling Eton boys, freshly returned from their vacation for the Lent term. He noted the obstinate antiquity of their uniforms, the single emancipation he could off-hand think of at Greyburn, where there were no Eton collars required, or top hats. He wondered whether as a schoolboy he had ever looked as young as the young men he passed, and vaguely reminded himself that in a few years, driving through the streets of New Haven, he would no doubt be having identical thoughts.

The moment had come. His car was stopped at Henry VIII's Gateway, at each side of which stood the flamboyantly dressed, immobile sentinels. A policeman approached him. "Visitors' parking is over there, sir," he said, pointing down the cobblestoned hill.

"I am here," Blackford fumbled for a nonpompous way to put it, "at the invitation of Her Majesty."

"What is your name, sir?"

"Blackford Oakes."

"May I see some identification?"

Blackford pulled his passport from his briefcase. The officer, who had memorized the names of all expected guests, handed Blackford his passport. "Go up the road, sir, through that farther arch"—he pointed—"around the tower, into the quadrangle, where you will be met."

An equerry, introducing himself genially, supervised turning the car over to a chauffeur, and Blackford's luggage to a footman, whom Black followed, chatting with the equerry up the stone stairs of Chester Tower. At the third story, the footman unlatched a large door. It opened on a living room of exquisite dimensions, large enough for seven or eight people to sit about it and look out over a great aft-cabin window that followed the contours of the tower and looked over the East Terrace Garden, the sun streaming by it into Blackford's suite. To one side, a page footman opened a second door into a small but warm, heavily carpeted, snug bedroom. To the side, through another door, was a modern bathroom.

Without a word, the footman, who gave his name as Masterson, had begun to unpack Blackford's two suitcases. Blackford let him do so, and busied himself unpacking his briefcase and spreading the papers on the inlaid leather desk that stood by the wall opposite the fireplace.

"Perhaps you will care to look at this schedule, Mr. Oakes"—the equerry handed him a sheet of paper—"and if you have any questions I am at your service. You can ring for Masterson by pushing the bell over there, sir"—he pointed to the side of the fireplace.

While the footman finished with the unpacking, Blackford looked at the typed letter communication.

Windsor Castle
Wednesday, January 16, 1952
Mr. Blackford Oakes
5 P.M. arrival. Mr. Oakes will occupy Suite 3B, Chester Tower.
5:30 P.M. Mr. Claude Squireson, Keeper of the Archives, will escort Mr. Oakes to the library.
7 P.M. Mr. Oakes will return to his suite.

7:45 P.M. Mr. Oakes will be escorted to the King's Drawing Room, where he will be presented to Her Majesty.

8:15 P.M. Dinner

Guests: Her Royal Highness the Duchess of Ogilvie
          The Right Honourable the Viscount Kirk
          Sir Alfred and Lady Schuler
          Mr. and Mrs. George Alex-Hiller
          Mr. Blackford Oakes

The keeper was a little late, quite old, and extremely absent-minded, but good-natured, and what he did, really, was to show Blackford how, with the help of one of the keeper's assistants, he could arrange to bring together anything he wanted. He was assigned a large and comfortable cubicle with powerful overhead lighting, several magnifying glasses, and a stack of clips. "You need only attach a clip to anything you desire to have photocopied, and it will be done for you in just a few hours."

Blackford perused the handwritten indexes and began to compile a long list of sketches, lithographs, instructions, and texts to which, without problem, he could devote several days, if he had to, in pursuit of a plausible purpose.

He returned to his room and rang for Masterson, who appeared instantly.

"Masterson, would you please bring me a whiskey and soda? With ice? And tell me, do I assume that dinner is black tie?" Masterson opened a cupboard where there was already whiskey, gin, sherry, bitters, soda water, and ice. Yes, he said, dinners were black tie.

At exactly 7:40 there was a knock on the door, and a dark-suited butler asked if Mr. Oakes was ready. He was, and followed the butler down the stone steps, across a cold stone corridor, past the chapel, through a massive wooden door opening into St. George's Hall, a room fit, thought Blackford, for W. R. Hearst's San Simeon. The decorations were Tudor, with iron chandeliers, frescoed walls, and flags jutting out over huge but warm brown velvet couches, and dark Flemish-tinted paintings of pallid monarchs of centuries gone by. Eventually they arrived in the ornate drawing room, suppurating with velvet and bric-a-brac.

Blackford was led to the corner of the room where three couples stood, drinks in hand. He was presented first to the Duchess of Ogilvie, whom he knew to be the younger sister of the Queen's mother. Sir Alfred Schuler had just brought out a biography of George V which had been widely admired, and in the preparation of which he had had the full co-operation of the royal family. Lady Schuler was a sculptress of some accomplishment who faintly scandalized the set in which she traveled by a heavy penchant for erotic art, which, however, was so abstractly rendered as to permit the proper viewer to see into it nothing more than an exercise in abstract, sinewy forms. "It would be fun to see Lady Schuler's Rorschach test," the Queen had said that morning to Peregrine Kirk on horseback, as they discussed that night's guest list. Mr. Alex-Hiller was the headmaster of Eton College who had made a number of progressive statements about education which were widely discussed by Old Etonians and anyone who would listen to them, which was not very many people during that busy season. About Viscount Kirk, Blackford knew only that he would one day be Earl of Holly, that he had been an ace during the war and had gone on to try, unsuccessfully, to subdue the Zionist insurrection in 1946, that he had returned to horsemanship, in which he had excelled as a youth, and that he now was completing a protracted but altogether successful recuperation.

He was greeted cordially, and the conversation had most diplomatically turned to the reasons for Blackford's presence in England, when, unobtrusively, the Queen was suddenly there in their company; and, for a moment, everyone stopped talking.

Caroline was carrying a tiny poodle in her left hand, clothed in a gauzy light-blue dress, wearing a small but brilliant diamond-and-turquoise tiara that matched a brooch on her belt and her bracelet. She wore no jewelery in front, but her breasts at the cleavage seemed the color of pearl, and there was no distinct line where the sun had etched a separation between bathing suit and skin. She approached first her aunt, who kissed her, then Lady Schuler, who curtsied, as did Mrs. Alex-Hiller. Then Mr. Alex-Hiller, who took her hand and bowed from the neck, then Blackford, who did the same thing. Then she put her arm around Peregrine's:

"How are you, darling?"

"Splendid, ma'am," he replied formally. She then sat down, and the butler brought her a daiquiri, and her guests sat in a semicircle around her. "I think we'll have the fire," she said, as if to no one at all. Instantly someone lit it, and she turned to Blackford and said, "How did you get on with the keeper, Mr. Oakes? If you succeed in understanding what he has to say, I should greatly appreciate your transcribing it for me one of these days. I know he is a wonderful keeper, because everyone tells me he is, and surely a conspiracy to deceive me on the subject would hardly be worth the time even of a frivolous generation of Englishmen? Speaking of a frivolous generation of Englishmen, how are your students, Mr. Alex-Hiller?"

"They are doing very well on the whole, ma'am, thank you. We have some very gifted boys, a good many of them on scholarships."

"Tell me something, Mr. Alex-Hiller, something I have never understood. Why is it so generally accepted that the sons of rich and titled men will be dull, while the sons of working-class men will be keen? I mean, it is to them, isn't it, that all the scholarships go?"

"Ma'am, it doesn't quite work out that way. The collegers at Eton who are there on scholarships are selected from the poorer classes after very intensive competition. This is not to say that, as a percentage, there are brighter boys among the poor than among the rich."

"No, that doesn't say it, but I warrant it's true. Probably something gets into us that makes our blood sort of etiolated—do you know that word, Perry? Very useful word, and if you are not aware of it, I am sure there are several members of this erudite company, beginning of course with the distinguished Sir Alfred, who will explain it to you. Do you, anywhere in your large book, which I must confess I have not yet read, use the word in connection with my grandfather's speeches?"

Sir Alfred laughed. "I am not sure, ma'am, that diligently though I approached my work, I ever ran into a speech I could confidently assume was written by your grandfather."

"If there had been"—the Queen looked saucily at Blackford—"no doubt it was suppressed, or else there'd have been yet another world war. Shall we go to dinner?"

Two tall vertical doors separated, and the Queen, escorted by

Viscount Kirk, led the way. Blackford quickly took the hesitantly proffered arm of the Duchess of Ogilvie and found himself sitting on the Queen's left, opposite Sir Alfred Schuler. Across the rectangular table from the Queen, Peregrine Kirk was seated, with Mrs. Alex-Hiller on his right. The conversation was desultory during the first course and for most of the second, when Peregrine suddenly addressed Blackford, in a tone that cut peremptorily across other conversations.

"I have been trying to place you, Oakes, and I do believe it all comes back to me. Were you briefly at Greyburn College about ten years ago?"

In the three months he had spent in London not once had this happened to Blackford, which, considering the company he kept, he laid down to extraordinary luck. But now it had happened—and, he reckoned, under the most hazardous circumstances. He wondered whether the young Viscount, seeking to embarrass him before the Queen, would draw the last measure of blood from the incident. He replied casually, "Yes, for a brief period. My mother remarried, to an Englishman. But then there was the attack on Pearl Harbor and as I was an American, not yet useful to the war effort"—his innate sauciness would not permit him a declarative sentence without at least that one retaliatory inflection, intended to communicate to Viscount Kirk, in case he did not know it, that he, Blackford Oakes, American, fought in a war more clearly designed to safeguard the White Cliffs of Dover from Hitler's panzer divisions than the coast of Maine—"the American ambassador sent us packing off to the States."

Peregrine, who had taken note of the Queen's undisguised attraction to the undeniably attractive young American, let it go, and relished the instant's sense of security Blackford was enjoying. But then he spoke again, and the attention of the entire table was given over to him, the normal slouch in his voice having been replaced by something cold and flinty.

"I was head boy when you left—a most remarkable exit. In fact, as no doubt you have forgotten, you shook my hand at the prefects' table on your way out."

He turned to Mr. Alex-Hiller. "Our young American friend could not stand the rigors of a public school. He ran away in protest against a beating by Dr. Chase."

Lady Schuler attempted a laugh of sorts, as did the Duchess of Ogilvie. Mr. Alex-Hiller's nervous chuckle was ho ho hearty, and Blackford thought, looking over at the headmaster's muscular grip of his knife and fork, he was probably reacting with bloody hands.

"Is that true?" Queen Caroline turned to Blackford, who knew that a great deal would depend on his answer.

"No, ma'am, it is not true. But there is no reason for Viscount Kirk to believe it to be anything other than the truth, inasmuch as I never communicated with him from that day until this afternoon, and I do not doubt that, as head boy, he communicated frequently with Dr. Chase, and is a faithful carrier of school legend, as head boys tend to be."

It was an adroit blend, greatly admired by the Queen, of a consistent refusal to validate a historical distortion, a reduction of that distortion to the puerile level of schoolboy lore unfit for the exercise of adult curiosity, and a superbly consummated gesture of condescension toward Viscount Kirk, head boy emeritus. Kirk recognized his disadvantage and instantly retreated when the Queen, abruptly changing the subject, asked Blackford whether his work in England included any effort to compare English and American approaches to atomic research. Blackford knew that as providence had it, he was being tested in the same few minutes on the two subjects he needed, most acutely, to acquit himself well on.

"Well, your Majesty . . . I did work as an assistant, while at Yale, to a consultant in atomic physics for the War Department—"

"Who was that?" Peregrine asked, his voice returned now to the informal drawl, reintegrating himself in the general conviviality.

"His name is Rene Wallack—a colleague of Enrico Fermi when they were at the University of Chicago. He was very active during the entire Manhattan Project part of the nuclear operation. After Hiroshima he pulled formally out of the program, but Edward Teller thinks so highly of him he kept going after him. I was in Wallack's office twice when Teller came in and had long discussions with him about the theoretical problems involved in producing a hydrogen bomb. A lot of the conversation was over my head, but"—Blackford paused, lowered his eyes slightly, and twirled his glass of wine—"not all of it. Teller is the most convincing evangelist I ever met, and by the time he had left, I wanted to go out and volunteer my services in trying to develop a hydrogen bomb."

"Why didn't you?" the Queen asked.

"Because I could tell from their last conversation—that was in May—that by the time I could learn enough to be useful, they'd probably have the problem cracked. Teller actually gave Wallack a day—a target for an actual test. And then he said, 'But vid your help, Rene, dot would be in de sommer, not de vinter, uff negst year.'" The company laughed.

"Teller is a very systematic man, Wallack told me, who has reduced the problems involved into a set of categories, and he apparently knows that Wallack's background qualifies him to crack one, maybe two of these, and he spent a day talking him into the proposition that insight into those two impasses would illuminate the entire problem. Wallack finally succumbed, and agreed to devote full time to the work at the end of the spring semester. So I guess he's been working on it ever since. In fact, he wrote me a couple of months ago and asked if I would go back and carry out some experiments for him. I had already accepted the foundation job here in London, but I knew the kind of thing he wanted— No more, thank you," he said to the wine steward—"so I persuaded a friend of mine from MIT to go see the old gentleman. They hit it off, and my friend is now hired, and for my pains," said Blackford with feigned air of opéra bouffe secretiveness, as if he were privy to the plays to be used in the fall's offensive by the Yale football team, "I get detailed reports about the professor's progress. I have to confess I've developed a curiosity about the hydrogen bomb, but I suppose, ma'am, not even *your* archives at Windsor will give me any insights into *that* problem!"

"I don't know," said the Queen cheerily. "After the next war, when we shall all have exchanged hydrogen bombs, I should think these archives would be tremendously useful, since whoever is left over will be reduced to defending himself by the use of things like moats and machicolations and bows and arrows. . . . Oh dear," the Queen said, rising, thus bringing all in the room to their feet, "why do we need to have things like hydrogen bombs?"

"Because we have things like Communists," said Viscount Kirk.

Blackford thought that exchange could have been written for Lunt and Fontaine, and even wondered, wildly, whether it had been. He wondered whether Kirk's anti-communism was of the dilettante's variety he knew so well from back home. Still, he might ask Singer Callaway to run a routine check on him, if he hadn't done so already.

Queen Caroline walked into a drawing room Blackford could only describe as sort of Jack-and-the-Beanstalk Dresden. There coffee was served, and brandy and champagne. Quite unself-consciously, the Queen having drunk her coffee, approached the piano and went through a creditable version of the first two movements of Bach's C minor partita. There was polite applause when she was done, and of course rapt silence while she played.

"It is a funny thing," she said, turning slightly, and sipping from the champagne that the butler, from habit, had placed on a silver coaster to the right of the music stand. "I played that more competently than I do now when I was a girl of thirteen, but in those days my audiences listened less acutely and applauded less heartily. It is extraordinary how my anointment as Queen has improved the quality of my audiences." There was scattered laughter, as ever, after the Queen drew attention to the enveloping sycophancy.

"I have only a single encore tonight, after which, if you will forgive me, I shall retire, since I simply cannot put off *The Caine Mutiny*. I myself think that Mr. Queeg was bonkers, but I have great sympathy for people who are both bonkers and in a post of authority. Heaven only knows how this kingdom would have fared if there had been a mutiny every time someone had discovered an unstable monarch. Eh, Sir Alfred? Possible theme for your next volume? I shall play the E major prelude from Bach's 'Well-tempered Clavier.' I would also play you the fugue, even though that would bore you, except that I cannot: It is too difficult." She played the quiet, serene prelude with a feeling that belied her derisory approach to her own playing, and the applause was genuine.

She stood, as did the assembly. "Please, do not move." She said this not as a pleasantry but as a command. All stood exactly where they were as, gracefully bowing her head, and reaching up to receive in her right hand the poodle lifted from the couch by a butler, she smiled, turned around, and, followed by a footman, left through the back door.

The Duchess followed her niece presently, and, only a few minutes later, the Alex-Hillers left and the Schulers, leaving only the house guests. It was Peregrine who suggested to Blackford that they move back to the study and have a nightcap. Peregrine, who asked Blackford please so to refer to him, made no further reference to Greyburn. But he was unabashedly interested in the Cold War. The Soviet Union, Perry insisted to Blackford, is *much* more advanced technologically than we think it is, and, besides, there are scientists all over the world, he insisted, including not a few in America, who are passing along secrets as quickly as they are developed. And the concentration of that old fanatic Stalin is such that—Perry gave it as his opinion, after spending several years on a study of the military history of the last war—"there is no doubt in my mind that the Americans are on to the final problems involved in developing a hydrogen bomb. I know this, because I've talked to a lot of American scientists and I've put two and two together. But I can't guess when they will go ahead and detonate a bomb. Probably before the year is out."

"That would sound about right," said Black nonchalantly. "But the working model they have got is a huge cumbersome thing, which you would need one of those guppies to transport. On the other hand, that may be true only of the prototype, and once they go into manufacturing, they will probably come up with something sleeker. I hope to heaven they can devise something that will fit in the B-36."

Peregrine wondered whether NATO would have full authority over the new weapon. "As you know, there are some people in your Congress who believe that new rules should be drafted to cover the H-bomb alone; others think the older rules governing the A-bomb suffice. *My* feeling is that we have got to have total mobility. Stalin is in a crunch, and I should think it terribly unsafe to take any chances with him. My friends tell me some rather bad news, which is that the hydrogen bomb is a hell of a lot easier to build than the atom bomb. That it is, like the other, a construct, really; but that the construct has a certain simple purity to it, which, once you get through the problem of refining the uranium in just the right way, makes the rest of it downhill."

Black knew suddenly that the training taken so painstakingly from Rufus was now glaringly relevant. "It is true," he said, "the construct *is* easy to handle. But it requires a terribly sophisticated computer technology to move toward production. And, too, we have the kind of massive technological reserves the Russians just don't have. Mr. Wallack says that unless the Russians succeed in stealing the entire American model (he is, as you would expect, very sarcastic about what Fuchs got away with, and it *is* true that our people warned that Fuchs was making odd *noises* in the last couple of years), he can't imagine the Soviet Union duplicating ours in less than two years. And to do that, they would have to have a pretty exact copy of our plans—particularly, our electronic computer system."

"Are our chaps working on that, or is that purely American?"

"Purely American, but they have asked one of your labs—Soames—to check out one important part of it, and they're supposed to begin doing that this week, under the supervision of Laszlo Mulner. What do you bet if he succeeds he will be Sir Laszlo Mulner?" Blackford smiled impishly.

Peregrine changed the subject, and asked Blackford about his own experiences during the war. Blackford told him he had come to the European theater as a fighter pilot, had had three engagements "in which I was pretty lucky" but then was grounded, hospitalized with hepatitis.

"Nothing, of course on the scale of what you saw." Blackford was happy to pay Peregrine the compliment of familiarity with his record as an air ace. "But it might interest you that this afternoon I flew the new Sabre. My father is a salesman for the company and he is over here trying to peddle it in Europe. As you probably know, Sabre is in cutthroat competition with Hawker's new Hunter."

"Yes," Peregrine said. "Because of my accident, I went a long time without flying, but a couple of years ago, I began feeling out the jets—God, they *are* lovely, aren't they! No rough stuff. But the doctors only last week told me to go do anything I liked. I like to fly—I've given up competitive jumping—so I notified my unit I am available for test-flying, which I like. Specifically, I told them I'd like to try out the new Hunter, and I received by return mail an invitation to go up in it."

"It would be fun," said Blackford excitedly, "to exchange roles. By the way"—he spoke with spontaneity—"if you would like to fly *our* plane, I think I can arrange it without any problem. Father is in fact in physical charge of the three models we have down here at Northolt."

"I say," Peregrine's voice was equally excited. "Could you really arrange that? I wish I could promise you, in return, that I could arrange for you to take up one of our Hunters, but I have no father with Hunters at his disposal. If you would like to slaughter a thousand pheasants, I have a most useful father. But he has not yet noticed fighter airplanes. Though"—Peregrine paused, as if over a merchandise counter—"I *suppose* I could persuade him to *buy* one. . . ."

Blackford laughed. "Obviously I'd like to do it. But I didn't mean to suggest you would be obliged to reciprocate. Give me your address and telephone, and after I check with my father, I'll be in touch with you. Within the week."

He pocketed Peregrine's card and instinctively gave him one of his own. They finished their whiskey, Peregrine said he would have to be off early, wished Blackford luck with his research, and they walked out together, Peregrine giving Blackford useful instructions on how to retrace his steps to Chester Tower.

Blackford entered his room and felt an unexpected chill; a sense of intensifying risk; of foreboding. The Queen, her wit and beauty apart, was a total enigma. Her detailed interest in the bomb was unfeigned but also, Blackford thought, lacking in any aspect of disingenuousness: She simply *wanted* to know what there was to know that a layman could understand about the hydrogen bomb, and, especially, anything a layman was not permitted to know.

Why?

And how many people did she treat with the familiarity she showed toward Kirk? Black had read in his industrious research—which included the collected works of Crawfie, Caroline's predecessor's nurse—that Caroline and Peregrine were second cousins, and although she was older, he had taken on the job of teaching her the finer points of horsemanship. So perhaps that intimacy was unique. Or were there others whom she befriended thus openly and intimately? What would happen tomorrow? Would he thenceforth eat his meals with the keeper? Served in his room? At what point would someone discreetly inquire how was he coming along with his research, or, perhaps even less discreetly, announce that unfortunately the rooms he was occupying were booked for another guest beginning—when? Friday? Saturday?

At first the Queen's spontaneous receptiveness he had interpreted as a stroke of very good fortune—as if, preparing a laborious expedition to the North Pole, he had suddenly been dropped there by helicopter. But, under the precipitate circumstances, he was not quite sure—sitting on top of the pole—quite what to *do*. If he had become a casual (as distinct from an intimate) member of the court circle, he might have observed Queen Caroline, to be sure from a distance, but over a protracted period, arriving at cautious conclusions about her inclinations, her conversational habits; identifying, perhaps, that awesomely important lead that Rufus and indeed the head of NATO were so desperate to identify. True, his social company might continue to amuse the Queen, and he might quickly, luckily, discover what he was looking for. Perhaps even if his visit to Windsor terminated tomorrow, in another week, or another month, there would be another invitation, and slowly he would cull his observations. But, he thought, he must not needlessly risk any approach to his mission so casually. He had been led to believe that the passage of secrets from the Queen to the Soviet Union needed to be stopped very quickly, and the only alternative to the identification of the intermediary being a wholly implausible interruption in the flow of information from American and British scientists, he would be better to push aggressively any opportunities he might come upon in the next few days, or even hours. He felt he could profitably strike up an acquaintance with Masterson, who, though he was off to a laconic start that afternoon, might, tomorrow, open up, in protective deference to the guest's American innocence. Also there was the keeper. He wondered if there was a publicly available guest book which he could quickly skim to see how many names appeared regularly as guests of the Queen at Windsor.

He lay back in bed, opening the curtains and looking out in the moonlight past the garden over those irenic fields that had bred, according to the famous adage, the flower of British youth. He felt suddenly a return of that rage he had never excreted, rekindled tonight by the smug coarseness of Kirk's reference to Greyburn. So he had been head boy. He remembered him, of course, though he had forgotten his name. He was, to Oakes the third-former, a remote and glamorous athletic and administrative figure, who had never given him, by any word or deed, any indication that he was himself aware of Blackford Oakes. He made a note to himself: He must write to Anthony Trust and ask what impression Trust had of Kirk, who as head boy would have presided over the prefects' meetings. He had always sensed that Dr. Chase would have planted the legend of the Cowardly American running home to his mother rather than endure what every British schoolboy endures as a matter of course, and Anthony had never told him whether, in the few days that Anthony remained at Greyburn before himself shipping out for America, he had made any effort, or met with any success, in modifying the legend Dr. Chase would have worked so hard to propagate. He wondered whether his stepfather's letter to Dr. Chase had been given any surreptitious currency. He wondered at Chase's endurance as headmaster —whom was he beating? Were there any other fresh Americans to whom he could say, after the torture session, "Courtesy of Great Britain, sir"? It was less than the obsession it used to be, but Blackford knew that someday he would need to expunge it from his emotional system, though he could not guess how, or even to let his mind run over hypothetical means of taking condign, if asymmetrical, revenge. Perhaps he had no alternative than one of these days, after completing his present mission, driving his MG down to Greyburn, climbing up those stone steps, walking past Leary-deary's nose, or his successor's, into the inner sanctum, and beating the shit out of the august Dr. Chase. . . . Odd, that after several years of letting that fantasy subside, it revived now in his mind. He knew why. It was Kirk, and what Kirk had said at the dinner table. Black always expected to come up, somewhere, upon it, but he imagined it would be late at night, at a drunken evening at a gentlemen's club. It had happened at a sedate, intimate dinner in the presence of the Queen of England. Black's emotional resentment was bright again, like the fire in the living room, which he had lit on coming in, and at which he was now staring.

In another wing of the castle, Peregrine Kirk lay, also looking out the window and wondering whether communism, really, wouldn't have come easier to people in general if he had come up with an extra-scientific provenance to smooth the pilgrim's way: perhaps in the bowdlerized editions. . . .

He reminisced, thinking now with some excitement about flying the new models, about his long recovery. It wasn't very far from Wembley to St. George's Hospital, but he very nearly did not survive the journey, and it was a week before he grew conscious of his small bedroom, and the constant presence of a nurse, ascetic in appearance and manner, who when she was not massaging him or superintending his leg and arm exercises or bathing his broken body with lotions, sat patiently in the corner of the room, reading. It was several weeks before he had fought his listlessness sufficiently to inquire what it was that engrossed her so. She replied that she was reading, at that moment, *Imperialism, the Highest Stage of Capitalism*. He laughed, which hurt; and then wondered whether he had hurt her, but she was evidently used to it. She never brought up the subject, but did not shrink from it, and in another week she was reading Lenin aloud to him.

The whole of the literature was engrossing to her, not only the theoretical books but the polemical tracts. Miss Oyen was never in search of humor or relaxation, but she was in search of a drastically better world, and so was Peregrine Kirk. She told him about Stalin's response to Lady Astor when that formidable lady had accosted the primate of the Communist world in Moscow at a reception in the thirties and asked, "Comrade Stalin, when are you going to stop killing people?" He had replied: "Your government killed thirty million people in a long war just fifteen years ago. To accomplish what? I may end up responsible for killing one million people—to accomplish a new world." Miss Oyen cherished that reply and asked Kirk if he did not find it apt, and he confessed that he did, allowing his mind to wander over the dull pomposities of his father's set as they belabored the Bolsheviks.

Somewhat to his surprise his interest grew keener, and in the endless days on his back he read through the corpus of the official writings of Marx and Lenin and Stalin. He began then to read the journals, the *New Internationalist Review*, *Mainstream*, and the left organs in America, which he found more passionate than the English journals; probably, he mused, because America is more easy to despise. He felt about his own country that it was headed toward satellitehood to America, a nice historical paradox; that it was bound to be devoured by American money, power, and avarice. Britain he could not hate because Britain had, really, become useless—a vermiform appendix in the world's social organism. Britain had some pleasant institutions, and even some pleasant people in it, but, viewed geopolitically, it was becoming nothing much more than America's Gibraltar off the western flank of Europe.

In another week he would be permitted to go to Aberdeen to begin there his long recuperation at home, under the guidance of a retired therapist his father had retained to live at Holly Manor for three months. When the doctor announced the timetable, after scrutinizing that morning's X rays, he saw Miss Oyen turn away and face the wall, and he knew that his leaving had moved her, however much the professional she was. He could understand why: because his leaving moved him, also. He had never had such an experience, six weeks on his back which grew from a tortured isolation into an invitation to consolidate his complaints against the world and see it whole for the first time—its complex, anomalous, contradictory phenomena, now harmoniously choreographed by a man of unique vision, a true social cosmologist. Miss Oyen—he liked the symbolism—who had washed his feet, had also awakened his mind and his spirit. He yearned to be a conscious part of the revolutionary struggle. He thought about this, with taciturn, lewd delight, as, strapped down on the specially constructed mattress in his father's custom-made Rolls wagon, he headed toward Holly Manor to rejoin the governing class. He had kissed Miss Oyen deftly on the cheek, and she had returned the gesture with an antiseptic kiss on his cheek. He gave her a first edition of *Das Kapital*—he had asked his tutor to secure him a copy, which had cost him seventy-five pounds—and she gave him a copy of Sholokhov's *And Quiet Flows the Don*. "I will write," he said as they wheeled him out; and he did, every week, until, initiating his contact with Boris Andreyvich Bolgin, he thought it prudent to stop, and did so abruptly.

He yawned, but before slipping off to sleep he reminded himself that on his return to London, he would summon Boris and give him a simple assignment. Establish, through an operative in America, whether the American atomic physicist in residence at Yale University, Rene Wallack, ever employed one Blackford Oakes, undergraduate, as an assistant. He should also attempt to establish whether Wallack had recently hired an assistant from MIT.

Fourteen

BLACKFORD WAS NOT LEFT LONG IN DOUBT on the one point. On his breakfast tray, brought in by Masterson, was a sealed envelope. He waited until Masterson had left—

"Shall I draw your bath, sir?"

"No thank you, Masterson, not yet. I'll ring."

He opened it.

"My dear Mr. Oakes," he read in a filigreed but authoritative hand that tilted sharply to the right. "I leave you to your researches during the morning and early afternoon. But the weather being clement, I would suggest that at three o'clock you might be ready for a little sun and exercise. In which event I have a mount ready for you, and would take pleasure in leading you through some of the lovely trails in Windsor Park. The Prime Minister will be calling on me at five-thirty, and leaving, I should judge, at about seven, unless he has details to communicate of the Parliament's incompetence more egregious than usual. There is no other guest in residence, nor have I invited anyone else, for fear that I might be too extensively separated from Mr. Wouk's psychodrama. I should be pleased, then, if you will dine privately with me. But if you would prefer to devote the evening to your work, I should understand your decision, commend it, and very probably profit from it. But pray let me know on the matter of this afternoon. It is inconceivable that you do not know how to ride. But if that should be the case, perhaps, in the interest of orderly priorities, you should forgo the archives during the morning and take lessons? My children's groom is available. Yours truly, Caroline, R."

Blackford gave thought to the exact wording of his reply, and then wrote down:

Your Majesty:

Your thoughtfulness is greater by far than that of the chief of state of my own country, whose hospitality I very briefly experienced a few months ago. I cannot believe that if H.M. George III had been so attentive of the feelings of his colonials, it would all have ended so sadly. I accept with great pleasure your invitation to ride with you. I am a competent horseman, but not in a class with Viscount Kirk, so please do not judge me harshly. And, of course, it would be a great honor to dine with you.

Yours faithfully,
Blackford Oakes

He rang for Masterson, gave him the communication, asked him to deliver it and return, which he did, in a few minutes.

"If you will draw the bath, that *would* be helpful, Masterson," Blackford said, seeking a reason to detain him. "And by the way, Masterson, the Queen has asked me to ride horseback with her this afternoon and I'm afraid I have no proper riding suit. One of my tweed jackets will do, but I have no jodhpurs, breeches, or boots. I wonder: Do you suppose Viscount Kirk would mind if I borrowed a set of his, since we are approximately the same build?"

It worked. "I am certain he would not mind, sir. He keeps an entire closet of clothes here, mostly for riding. Shall I fetch you something appropriate, sir, or do you wish to ring him up first? He left about an hour ago, and should be in his flat very soon now. Though, actually, I don't believe it is necessary, because the Queen once had me go through the closet to outfit a visiting gentleman, and we merely pressed the trousers and replaced them."

Blackford feigned to be going through his shelves in order to take stock of the clothes he had actually brought with him.

"The Queen is certainly thoughtful about the desires of her guests." Blackford decided to attempt a considerable flyer. ". . . Or is it just Viscount Kirk who keeps his riding clothes here?"

Masterson took no notice of any inquisitive inflection.

"Well, sir," he said while testing the temperature of the water, "Viscount Kirk and the Queen used to ride together as children, and when she moved into Windsor Castle she specified that a closet would be kept for her second cousin so that they might ride together as spontaneously as when they rode together in Scotland. But he is the only friend of the Queen's who has these arrangements. Besides, sir, the Duke's wardrobe is very extensive, and there is not so very much room left over. The Queen insists that the guest suites be maintained in perfect order and that no family clothing be stored in any of the recesses here."

"But surely the Duke has regular friends who visit frequently enough to keep a few of their things here—sports equipment, golf clubs?" said Blackford, walking into the bathroom and brushing his teeth.

"The Duke does not regularly invite friends to Windsor, sir, only visitors of state. His friends he invites usually to Sandringham or Balmoral. He feels that Buckingham Palace and Windsor are formal places of residence that belong to the sovereign, as indeed they do. So it is, actually, only Viscount Kirk, who is practically a member of the family."

Masterson left, and Black considered putting in a call to Singer Callaway, but decided against doing so through the palace switchboard. Besides, the following day he would surely know more. Then he could take a stroll through Windsor and use a pay telephone.

He had ridden as a boy, during two summers at a ranch his father sent him to during brief moments of prosperity; and again regularly at camp in Maine. He had never hunted, or shown, and he was more accustomed to a western than to an English saddle. But Blackford found himself strangely comfortable on the mount the groom brought out for him, a stately but docile animal, markedly in contrast to the frisky black stallion the Queen favored, whom she had named after General Eisenhower seven years earlier, at the tail end of her crush on the general, who had subsequently been quoted in the press as saying disparaging things about British contributions to NATO forces—Churchill, Eisenhower's constant defender, had explained to her that generals *never* knew anything about the extra-military economic problems of countries, and tended to think only in terms of military needs, reminding her that Eisenhower, as a young lieutenant, had had to train American soldiers using brooms as facsimiles for rifles, so parsimonious had the American isolationist Congress been toward the army, and that no doubt he was residually bitter on the subject. The Queen's attitude toward Eisenhower did not materially change, even though she predicted to the P.M. (and to Peregrine) that he would be the next President of the United States. But she never changed toward Ike, her stallion, who never gossiped and did not know the secrets of the House of Commons.

They began at a walk, and soon the Queen egged her horse into a trot. Blackford followed her and quickly accommodated to the even gait of his mare, Prissy, and soon they were cantering easily through the apparently endless forest, the Queen stopping here and there, to point out an object or panorama of special natural, historical, or personal interest.

"From here you can see—over there, Blackford—if I may, I shall call you Blackford. After all, it is a rather formidable name, hardly the same thing as suddenly calling you Al, or Butch, or whatever else is a typically American name—Chuck?—over there, you can see the remains of the Windsor Lodge built out of wood by Henry VIII—the stone came later. . . ."

The experience was elating. The weather, by British standards tropical in hue and temperature on this January day, conspired to heighten the experience they were both feeling, a flash of recognition of what lies behind what is seen routinely: the great sinewy trees, the pine needles, the fresh-swept meadows, the modest but adamantly pointed spires, the communicable enthusiasm of the riders for Ike and Prissy, the unencumbered fascination with one another. The conversation was awesomely intimate, but without edge or strain, impulsiveness or opportunism. "I came here alone the afternoon after the funeral. You can imagine the combination of sensations. For *one* thing I actually *liked* her, though we would never have become friends, in a way that Peregrine and I are friends or, even, already, you and I. The journalists of the whole world were here. The press the next morning reported that there were over *five hundred* of them. *Five hundred* photographers and writers from over one hundred countries. I was alone; the Duke was at Buckingham Palace, receiving intensive training in his own new duties, which he learned at disconcerting speed. The guards

did a wonderful job of keeping them away, but it required an entire regiment. I was right over there"—she pointed to a small
glade in the trees—"and I'd stopped for a minute when I heard a
terrible crashing noise, and suddenly, six feet away from me, was
a body. I dismounted, walked over and found a young Japanese,
with his camera and all those fancy lenses, hugged to his bosom—
as he fell, he had thought only to protect them. In a few minutes
he came to, looked at me in a most fearful state, and started, in
not the easiest English to understand, to apologize, and to confess
that he had spent *twenty-four hours* on that tree, just on the
chance that I might go from Westminster Abbey to St. George's to
Windsor Park, and perhaps unbend a little on horseback. He now
expected that my bodyguards would be along any second, to take
him to the Tower of London for summary execution. I told him I
was alone and asked him to show me how to work his camera. At
first he was uncomprehending, but very quickly he forgot his ori-
ental awe, and took great pride in showing me one of the first
Nikons." She laughed with intense pleasure. "Then I told him I
would take a few pictures of *him*, provided he would co-operate
by climbing up to the perch he had sat on all night, from which
he had just now fallen, and that I in turn would trust him to write
down his impressions of the incident. He did exactly as he was
told, and then I submitted to an interview."

She paused pensively, as their horses walked in perfect tandem
along the sunny-wintery trail.

"Actually, it was my very first. All the questions were the obvious ones, and it gave me a chance to formulate some of those
vapid responses that are indispensable to the success of a constitutional monarch.

"'*I shall do everything to live up to the high standards set by
my cousin. . . . I am here as the servant of the people . . .*'—that
kind of thing. Of course I *believe* this, Blackford, but I know that
if I *didn't* believe it, I would be saying exactly the same thing,
and the public would be wanting to hear exactly the same thing.
One can only imagine the reaction to a statement by a freshly
anointed Queen to the effect, 'This is a pretty good job, I have
inherited a lot of money, and a lot of junk, and a lot of perqui-
sites, but there is something in it for *everybody* because of the
presumptive necessity, the people having lowered their idealistic

sights during the past generations, to worship something—somebody—worldly; by biological accident, I am she. I shall see what personal uses I can put this personal veneration to.'"

She laughed in delight at herself.

"Oh dear, oh dear, I pray that the Lord will restrain me, as I am sure he will, but you know, the temptation to say such a thing to one of Lord Beaverbrook's reporters is very nearly overwhelming! Beaverbrook is a very smart man and a tough cookie, as they say in your movies, but he is the world's premier establishmentarian. Do you know the story of Nicholas Murray Butler?"

"All I know about him is that he was forever the president of Columbia University and the soul of propriety."

"Exactly," said Caroline, "and I read somewhere, in one of your uninhibited journals, that it was the ambition of Heywood Broun the journalist to become rich for the sake of indulging himself in only a single pleasure. He proposed to hire the whole of the Metropolitan Opera House and give a benefit concert sending out all the tickets gratis. But he would arrange to send tickets to prominent bald-headed New Yorkers seating them in the orchestra floor so as to describe, for the benefit of the balconies, one huge S H I T—with Nicholas Murray Butler dotting the *i!*" She roared with pleasure. "I am telling you, Blackford, if I had had the keys to the Tower of London I'd have sneaked off in the dead of night and yanked out a ruby or an emerald or something from one of my thrones, and dispatched it anonymously to Mr. Broun. I wish I were as knowledgeable as one day I propose to be about the workings of our own intelligence system. *That's* the way to use secret money." She was combining fancy and fantasy and effortlessly moved from the ribald to the solemn: "Ten or fifteen thousand pounds going through MI-6—they wouldn't notice. Certainly it would not be missed from the money they are supposed to be spending in intelligence and counterintelligence to understand a defense system you Americans seem to confide to us on such an eccentric basis."

They were loping back now, on the hardening trail—the cold pursued the setting sun—toward the castle, and the Queen observed that horses should never be allowed to race home—"it gives them very bad habits."

"Just what do you mean by that business about American intelligence, ma'am?" Blackford would not be deterred. "*My* understanding, both as a reader of the public press and as an engineer with a special knowledge of the whole hydrogen bomb business, is that our orders are to give the stuff along to British scientists as fast as we develop it."

"That is the official line, I know. But I also know, from the confused answers of my own Prime Minister, that there is something funny going on. Either the Americans are running into difficulties they hadn't anticipated and are afraid to let us know what those difficulties are, or some of those Anglophobes in Congress, or some of the people who are afraid of Senator McCarthy, are urging an unnecessary secretiveness, because we simply *aren't* getting consistent information. And I think there is nothing more important for England to know than the answer to the question: *How* reliable is America's nuclear umbrella? How reliable is the general assumption that America will be able to continue to protect Europe, leaving entirely aside whether America, ten years from now, will be disposed to do so?" Her thoughts on the matter were clearly well organized, and she obviously suffered from a shortage of appropriate audiences.

"How well do you know Peregrine? Did you talk to him at any length last night? Or were you put off by that rather silly business he brought up about your time at Greyburn?" Blackford told her, deceitfully, that he hadn't minded the Greyburn business at all—that was old stuff—that in fact he had had a good talk with Peregrine about the new jet fighter planes, and in fact they were going to try to facilitate an exchange in testing out their countries' new models.

The Queen brushed aside the airplane talk. "I wish you would get to know him better. In fact—unless you have some inscrutable, hormonal, male animosity to one another—I shall try to see that it comes about. Peregrine is *very* special to me. Of course, he is one of my oldest friends. But he is much more. He is my most useful friend in analyzing serious matters. A few years ago you could have as easily got him interested in hydrogen bombs as in hybrid corn. Now—no doubt it is the result of his awful accident, which gave him a new perspective on life and caused him to take a more serious view of the strategic problems of the British Isles—he is as highly informed as any man in the kingdom on the subject.

Granted he doesn't write about it, or talk about it publicly, and he says that he is not even sure whether, when his father dies, he will take up the cudgels in the House of Lords. But Perry is not only a great sportsman and flyer, which is how he is known to the public; he is a man intensely interested in important things, and I try to help him in every way by giving him information that fills in the holes in his knowledge. But this means getting that information from the P.M., who is a very decent and a very bright chap, but who, if he were the Connecticut Yankee in King Arthur's Court, would not be able to contribute enough scientific information to construct a sundial. You should hear C. P. Snow on the subject. Do you know C. P. Snow? He fancies that he bridges the two worlds of science and culture, and I fancy he is right, though I would fancy it more enthusiastically if he were to uncover more economical formulations for telling me about it.

"Anyway, here we are, the P.M. will be along in fifteen minutes, and I shall have to put on something a little more regal for him." She dismounted, with the aid of her groom. "I shall send for you when he leaves, and we'll have dinner. A most pleasant ride. Thank you."

"Thank you, ma'am," Blackford smiled. "I must confess I don't feel right now like another hour in the archives. I think I'll walk a bit—I haven't ridden for a long time—maybe to Windsor. I'll be back in an hour, and be ready anytime you send for me."

Blackford, feeling only slightly conspicuous in riding breeches in a town in which little boys went about dressed like fathers of the bride, walked nonchalantly past the guard, exchanged a greeting and informed him he would be back within an hour, past St. George's Chapel, turning left into the commercial district. He inspected one tea room, but the public telephone lay too exposed. So he went to the Castle Inn and was shown into an encloseable cubicle where he secured an operator and gave her a number. He heard the voice of Singer Callaway.

"Singer? This is Black. Do you hear me all right?"

"Yes, indeed."

"On that party you're going to give for me next month, would you mind adding a name?"

"Of course not."

"A very attractive chap, I'd like to know him better. Besides, we both have an interest in aviation. Anyway, be sure to do something about it quickly, as I imagine he has a pretty busy social calendar. He is Peregrine Kirk, the, er, Viscount Kirk; has a flat in London, on Curzon Street."

"I'll take care of it. Everything all right with you?"

"Just fine, but must get back to work."

"Some work."

"It has its moments. I'll call you again when I get back to London."

The dinner, discreetly served in the Queen's Drawing Room, in the candlelight with the crystal boiserie-effect and, always, the family paintings; but also a single early Picasso, lit by a shaft of soft light, its Fauvist colors standing out in the mortuary of regal ancestors. The spell had not been broken by the Prime Minister's visit. Caroline's imitation of him was perfect. "At one point he got as nearly impatient as a Prime Minister is permitted to get with his sovereign, unless he intends to execute her. He said, 'Er, ma'am, really if I knew that m-much about the hydrogen bomb, I do believe I would construct one myself.'"

She laughed, and discussed her usual vexations at failing to get from him exactly the nature and causes of the American delay, though the Prime Minister confided to her that the preceding week, Professor Teller had eliminated what he considered to be the last of the theoretical obstacles, so that the date set for the first explosion—she did not give Blackford this date—was something more than a mere hypothesis. "I do think it is all not only vital, but also exciting. One can imagine the frenzy with which the Soviet scientists are engaged in the similar race, but needless to say we know very little about their activities, although the Prime Minister told me that a week or two ago a defector had come over in Eastern Europe, and the Americans smuggled him away. Apparently he had a pretty accurate idea of the American timetable, though whether this is the result of the fruits of Soviet intelligence, or simply a means elected by Stalin to put on the heat, nobody appears to know."

Caroline glowed as she spoke and elicited from Blackford his views, often disjointed, on the matters, often unrelated, she raised. "Tell me," she said, suddenly, "do you know anything about Cardinal Mindszenty?"

"Oh, the usual things," said Blackford. "And I also know that experts on the subject conclude that in making him perform as he did during the public trial, the Communists have done a good bit in advancing their knowledge of the show trial. Mindszenty is a hell of a tough character, and they had to use everything on him: torture, threats against his family, drugs, a phony defense attorney, and, even, at the end, a couple of scientists who worked out an unbeatable way of forging anyone's handwriting, to write out incriminating evidence."

"Explain that," the Queen said, intrigued.

"They defected only a few months ago," Blackford said. "There was an article about it in an American magazine. This couple—he-she scientific types—developed a way of forging a person's handwriting through a photographic mechanism in a way so accurate, no expert can detect the imposture. They do this after a scientific study of material written by the target. All this they did in the spirit of science, but when the Rakosi people heard about them, they were brought in and forced to forge extensive confessions by Cardinal Mindszenty, his disavowal of which during the trial seemed halfhearted and unconvincing."

"Fascinating," said Caroline. "I suppose they could concoct an authentic instrument of abdication for me, right? . . . I, Caroline, do hereby abdicate as Queen of England, and relinquish all titles, deeds, and appurtenances that go with the office of the sovereign. Caroline, Regina."

"I should think that logically you would have to sign that, 'Caroline, ex-Regina.'" Blackford smiled, accepting a glass of port from the anonymous butler, who was then waved out of the room by the Queen and did not reappear.

"That is a problem of metaphysics," Caroline said. "After all, only the Queen can give up being Queen, but in the instrument in which she gives up being Queen, she must necessarily assert Queenly authority, and this she can only do by signing her name, Blankety-blank, Regina. What do you have to say to that, Mr. Oakes? Why don't you stick to bridges?" Suddenly her voice became a little husky. "By the way, how do you build a bridge?"

"From where to where?" Blackford asked.

"Well, say from America to England."

"You wait for England to take the initiative," Blackford said.

190

"Why?"

"Because," said Blackford, his heart beating, "if America took the initiative, it would appear an act of aggression, because America is so strong nowadays."

"England is not exactly defenseless."

"Certainly not at Windsor Castle," Blackford smiled.

"Windsor Castle has not been impregnable for four hundred years," Caroline countered.

"I should think then that Windsor Castle's reputation for hospitality would long since have outweighed its reputation for impregnability."

"But so far, it hasn't."

Caroline looked at him, sitting on the sofa next to her, the man-boy American, loose, bright, shining with desire and desirability, his port and coffee at his side, and she felt something she had never felt before—this she knew. What she didn't know was whether, in other days, in other circumstances, she would automatically have checked such an impulse before it possessed her. It could be that her assumption of office had encouraged her not to bridle her passions, as—she had read—persons of great power customarily do, or at least are supposed to do; but, instead, to give them freer rein. But this was all the thought she would give it at the moment.

"Blackford"—her voice quivered now, and she had to clear her throat to restore her authoritative accents—"I shall ring, and a footman will come in. Bid me good night after he comes in. I shall be with you within the hour." She pressed a bell twice.

"Ah. Jason, Mr. Oakes is retiring. Please lead him to his chambers. He is not yet familiar enough with the castle to make his own way."

Blackford stood. "Good night, Your Majesty, and thank you for a very pleasant dinner and of course for the ride. I hope you find the last chapters of *The Caine Mutiny* as exciting as I did. I shan't let on as to the verdict."

"I think I can guess it. Good night, and if you need anything, just ring. Masterson will bring you your breakfast in the morning."

Blackford filed after Jason, his mind reeling with excitement and apprehension, his body aching. He did not say a word to

Jason, in his absorption with the moments that lay ahead of him, until, suddenly, Jason stopped.

"Here you are, sir," he said, opening the door for Blackford.

"Thank you. Thank you very much, Jason. Thank you. Good night."

He opened the door, shut it, and leaned back against it, his head raised as if for air. My God, he said, the fucking Queen of England. I mean, I'm—somewhere in the back of his memory, in one of those disorderly trunks of unfiled information, he fished out the law that specified the remaining crimes for which hanging was stipulated and recalled something dating back to the Treason Act in the fourteenth century about "violating" a royal figure. Great God, thought Blackford. What about when you—he could not bring himself even to think of the word under the circumstances—do it with . . . the goddamn Queen herself!

He sat down and, briefly, began to laugh.

> OAKES, Blackford. Foundation official. Born, Yellow Springs, Ohio, December 7, 1925. Schools: Scarsdale H.S., Yale ('51). Executed, 1952, for viol. fornication provisions of Treason Act of 1351.

He thought, suddenly, of Dr. Chase. The piquancy was more than he could bear. Dr. Chase! And Rufus. "Well, Rufus, sir, I got in about as far as I could get, and . . ." He started to laugh again but stopped himself and became briskly efficient. He drew the curtain. He stripped, took a shower, and put on a dressing gown. He lit the light in the bedroom, left the door slightly ajar, and turned out all but one light in the living room. He reached into the ice bucket always left out for him and pulled out a bottle of champagne, which he decorked, taking two glasses from the cabinet just as he heard the faintest knock. He moved swiftly to the door, which was unlocked, opened it, and Caroline, fragrant, walked by, wheeled about, and kissed him passionately as, with his right hand, he slid the safety latch on the door. They went hand in hand to the sofa at the end of the room. "Light the fire," she said, and he did so, and came back to her with the glass of champagne, which she took, looking him always in the eyes, and sipped at it until it was half empty, when she put it down and said, "England has taken the initiative."

He rose, extended his hand, and brought her silently into the bedroom. She pulled away the covers, dropped her yellow gown, and lay on her back as with her left hand she turned off the bedlight. The flames from the fireplace lit her body with a faint, flickering glow. She arched back her neck and pointed her firm breasts up at the ceiling, and he was on her, kissing her softly, saying nothing. Her thighs began to heave, and she said in a whisper, "Now." He entered her smoothly, and suddenly a wild but irresistible thought struck him, fusing pleasure and elation—and satisfaction. He moved in deeply, and came back, and whispered to her, teasingly, tenderly, "One."

And a second,

And third,

Fourth,

Fifth,

Sixth—her excitement was now explicit, demanding, but he exercised superhuman restraint—

Seven . . .

Eight—she was moaning now with pain—

And, triumphantly, *nine!*

And they collapsed into each other's arms in silence, with animated sobs coming from deep in Caroline's throat. Blackford drew out, and in a voice kind, but gently stern and mocking, he whispered to her:

"Courtesy of the United States, ma'am."

They lay together in silence, but Caroline kept her eyes on Black, and when the fire began to die down she told him to put in another log. Getting out of bed, Black reached instinctively for his dressing gown.

"No," she said, "go as you are." He did, and her eyes shone with pleasure as she watched his lithe body walking into the living room, lifting a log, inserting it deftly, and stirring the embers —his rhythms, Caroline thought, were never disharmonious, in talking, in walking, in bed. He turned around to come back to her. She opened her arms to him again and, this time wordlessly, took over, and guided his erection; after which Blackford, excited, but also amused, remarked to her softly, "England has recovered the initiative."

"Britannia, Blackford, still rules the waves."

They lay there, studying the changing shapes of the fire-shadows on their bodies, when she said to him, "Blackford?"

"Yes." He could not, then, call her ma'am; to call her Caroline could, just could, ruin it all.

"Blackford, you know all about this hydrogen bomb business you were talking about yesterday. What is the Teller-Freeze Bypass?"

Blackford's heart stopped beating. Suddenly his fondling of her breasts and haunches was mechanical, and he had to force himself to put life into his fingers.

"Whoever asked you about that?" he asked teasingly.

"I asked the P.M., and he said he had never heard of it, that he would ask Sir Edmund Hawkins, but he told me today that Sir Edmund never heard of it. I think it's one of those secrets the Americans are keeping from us."

"How *did* you hear about it?" Blackford worked hard to make the words sound casual, accompanying them with a flirtatious pinch on her buttocks.

"Oh," Caroline replied quite openly, "from Perry, a week ago. He tells me he hears that it is the final breakthrough they're looking for. And you know Perry—well, you don't really—but Perry always wants to know things firsthand, so he asked me to find out specifically what it was: What does it actually accomplish? Of course, the P.M. never asks me how I find out about these things— he's constantly being surprised. He would be less surprised if he would start reading something besides the *Times,* the *Telegraph,* and the *New Statesman.* I have been reading the *Bulletin of the Atomic Scientists,*" Caroline said proudly, "and Perry has got so he can explain to me passages in it I am curious about but don't understand, and of course sometimes I ask Sir Edmund, though, poor dear, he is becoming vague, and I don't see him so often."

The words filtered through Blackford's mind and in the daze of the experience he could only come up with vaguely plausible acknowledgments. If Rufus was right, then Blackford's mission was completed. He stared back at Caroline, whose eyes were closed now, and said finally, languorously, "Never heard of it. Must be something brand-new." Caroline's interest apparently lapsed, and now she was talking about how she wished she didn't have to return to London in the morning, and how much longer would Blackford be staying at Windsor?

"I should be through the first part of my work by midday," he said; "but I would love to come back later, to catch what I missed."

"You can come back anytime, whether to study bridges or to build them," Caroline said, rising, and kissing him lightly on the lips.

The telephone rang in his bedroom while he was having breakfast. It was his father, calling from Brussels.

"Thanks for calling back, Dad."

"Good to talk to you, Blacky. Anyway, I've got news for you, so I was about to call your mother to track you down when I got your cable. I didn't know you were taking up permanent residence at Windsor Castle!"

"Dad, there's an Englishman here, a close friend and a second cousin of the Queen. I made him something like a promise, and maybe I shouldn't have, but I hope you'll help me out. He was a terrific flyer during the war, and I told him about the new Sabre—and found myself saying I could get permission for him to fly it."

"You don't mean Peregrine Kirk?"

"Well, yes! What made you think of him?"

"Well, he's probably the best fighter pilot who survived the war, and the English have decided tentatively they want him to demonstrate their new Hunter. He had an accident and has been out of commission, but they want him to go up on Sunday, and if he's in good shape, to fly the Hunter at the big deal on Monday. Half the generals in Europe will be there, and probably half the civilian spectators will be Russian agents. Now, *my* news is this: The Sabre people want the very best out of our ship. There's a billion dollars riding on this one, Blacky, and I was pretty bucked up when they got me yesterday and told me *I* had been selected to fly the plane, against Kirk in the Hunter."

"Gee, Dad, that's great! Life begins at fifty!"

"Hell, Lindbergh's five years older, and he could fly the pants off me or anybody else. But now listen, Blacky, I called up Averill Hubbard—do you know who he is?"

"No."

"At Sabrejet he is (one) chairman of the board, (two) chief executive officer, (three) largest single stockholder; and he is (four) brother-in-law of the chairman of the joint chiefs. He's flying over for the Monday contest. And here's what I told him—that you would do a better job of flying the plane than I would."

Black whistled.

"I'm not saying this on account of paternal pride, and Hubbard knows me well enough to know that. I want that plane *sold*, and that means I want the *best* demonstration of it, especially up against the Hunter, I can get. I saw you do things with that plane the other day after an hour that are as good as and better than what I can do with it. Put three or four hours in between now and Monday, and you'll handle that plane as if you designed it."

Black was excited. "Okay! . . . But what does that do to the invitation to Kirk?"

"Tell him this: that I have okayed the invitation. But that for reasons he would be the first to understand, we couldn't let him fly the plane until after the air match on Monday. Anytime after that—Tuesday, if he wants."

"When will you be back, and when will we start working out?"

"I'll be back tomorrow, late. But I've already spoken to Ace Simpson, and Hubbard has confirmed by cable. The plane is yours—exclusively—from now until Monday. Simpson or one of his engineers will ride with you and take notes. On Sunday afternoon, Hubbard will be here, you'll take it up, and Hubbard and his people will watch. If they like what they see, you're on. Otherwise it's agreed I'll take it up on Monday myself."

"Okay, Dad. I'll be leaving here this morning, and you can get me at my flat, or by leaving a message there. It's a deal." He slapped down the receiver animatedly, then picked it up again and asked the switchboard operator to get him Viscount Kirk.

"Peregrine, good morning."

"Good morning, old chap. How are the bridges?"

"The bridges are coming along fine, thank you, but I've got

news for you. My father called me just now and told me about the big deal on Monday."

"Did he tell you who is slated to pilot the Hunter?"

"Well, yes, he did."

"I hope you know, Blackford, that I wasn't aware of this when we spoke the night before last. The selection was made yesterday —I think rather impulsively. They pushed me through the doctor yesterday morning and he okayed me. I'm to go up this afternoon and work out over the weekend. As it stands, I'm slated to go if my reflexes are up to snuff."

"Well, here is *my* news, Perry. *I'm* slated to go on the Sabre if *I* check out successfully. Otherwise, you will be flying against my father."

"Your father!"

"Yes," said Blackford, a little defensively. "He is considered one of the finest test pilots in America."

"Indeed." Peregrine's voice was thoughtful. . . .

Blackford took advantage of the pause. "Now, Dad says sure, you can have the Sabre and fly it to your heart's content. But not before Monday. I think I'll quote him exactly: 'Viscount Kirk would be the first to understand the reasons why it will have to wait until after Monday.'"

"I bet he didn't refer to me as 'Viscount Kirk.'"

"Well," said Blackford, "as a matter of fact, I did contribute that." And, to himself he said: *At least he didn't call you that Communist son of a bitch who has been stealing secrets that could jeopardize the safety of your family, your countrymen, and your . . . Queen.* Blackford shifted gears and wondered, idly, whether Kirk would be capable of turning in an inferior performance if it happened that the Hunter *was* the superior plane: It would after all be ideologically consistent, since fighter planes were being designed for use only against one conceivable enemy. . . . But this was fantasy and he checked himself. Could Chaliapin, taking pity on an aging Martinelli, fumble his end of the quartet in *Rigoletto?* Blackford simply didn't know Peregrine, could not guess what was the mysterious dislocation that had prompted him to this dizzying treachery—what an old-fashioned word, Black thought, in the cosmopolitan world of summit conferences, where the American President, the British Prime Minister, and the Soviet despot make dispositions involving hundreds of thousands of people—millions of people, actually—committing them, for the sake of temporary geopolitical comity, to any convenient fate—these men go back to receive the great acclaim, to be gartered by the Queen (Blackford thought it would be interesting to be around for one of these). But at another level, there was still something like consensus: What Peregrine Kirk was doing was a capital offense, which, really, was the least of it. England, so tolerant of eccentricity, has hated two species: traitors, and people unkind to animals. Peregrine's ultimate audacity: *to use the Queen!* He thought: The British are by and large a calm people. But for this, he thought, they would gladly tear a man limb from limb. He made a wry deduction. Would they, as gustily—lustily?— tear apart an American patriot who, in an effort to detect the violation of the Queen, violated the Queen? But Blackford, who thought quickly, had only split seconds for these meditations. He was, on the telephone with Peregrine Kirk, required to give as much attention to what he was saying, and to what he must answer in return, as he would give, during a dive in a fighter plane, to replying to the concatenated demands of the instruments on the dashboard.

Peregrine laughed. "Of course I understand. And we'll meet at the zone of combat on Monday at two P.M. After it's over, we can compare notes at our leisure. And I'll make it a condition with our people that you can have a run in the Hunter after Monday. Okay?"

"Okay," said Blackford.

"I'll see you, old chap. My compliments to the Queen, if you see her before you go—are you, by the way, coming soon to London?"

Blackford's instincts, cultivated by his Washington training, guided his reply.

"I expect to, but I'm not absolutely sure. One of the foundation people is in Paris and wants to see me, either there or in Brussels. Fortunately, my dad has a Sabre in several European cities, so I can work out and spend time with my project director wherever I am."

Peregrine was gently persistent. "You mean, you may go abroad directly from Windsor?"

"No, I'll certainly go to London today to arrange my things."

"Very well. Good luck, old chap. And don't take it too hard on Monday."

Blackford put down the telephone and felt cold, from one end of his body to another. He closed his eyes to help organize his thoughts. It was nine-fifteen. The Queen would be leaving, she had said, at ten. He must, for appearance's sake, put in at least an hour in the archives. But above all he must be in touch with Callaway and, this time, with Rufus. He knew he had to move fast, and that therefore he had, consciously, to slow down his physical movements. He forced himself to take a studiedly prolonged bath, during which he thought back, meticulously, on every word he had uttered in the presence of Peregrine Kirk.

The Queen left Windsor after dispatching a number of communications, to the Lord Chamberlain, to the groom, to the head gardener—and to Blackford Oakes, Esq., which last she dictated to Mabs, one member of the fourteen-man royal caravan readying for the discreet departure.

Dear Mr. Oakes: I have advised the Lord Chamberlain
that you expect to leave some time around midday. I have
also instructed him to give you lunch should you desire to
have it here in the castle. I repeat that you are most welcome
to return to complete your researches. And I hope you
will, some time in the weeks ahead, come to Buckingham
Palace and have dinner, perhaps with your charming friend
Miss Hanks. With all good wishes, Caroline, R.

Ten minutes after the Queen's departure, Blackford got up from his desk at the library and told the receptionist he would be taking a little walk and be back in a few minutes. He walked down to the same telephone he had used the afternoon before. Callaway answered.

Blackford used the emergency code.

"Singer, this is Black. I'm going to be busy next week. I wonder if we could go over the list for the party today? But it would be a lot easier if we could do it while Nancy was there; otherwise there'd be a lot of duplicated effort."

Singer answered: "Hang on a moment, and let me look at my schedule."

Two minutes later, Singer having communicated with Rufus over a different line, his voice came back.

"Fine. Two o'clock at Nancy's."

"I'll be there," said Blackford.

He forced himself to spend another full hour at the archives. He had to concentrate even to manage to set the plans laid before him right side up. Finally he pulled a mass of papers together and put them into two large briefcases. He walked to the keeper's office and thanked him most cordially, and from there to his room, where he rang for Masterson, to whom he slipped two quid in an envelope, and asked to have his car brought up front.

Masterson came to help him pack, but the job was already done.

Blackford shook hands cordially and went out again into the cold muggy air, January having returned to the British Isles. He had memorized, that being his way, the simple, unmistakable road instructions for returning to London. He drove to his flat and unloaded his briefcases, but kept his large traveling bag in the back of the car, for reasons not entirely thought out. He drove then to a garage several blocks away from the garage he usually patronized, left the car, and walked down Brompton Road, checking the time. He was early. He dropped into the same Lyons Tea Room his stepfather had taken him to eleven years earlier. He thought to amuse himself by asking for hot chocolate, but settled for coffee and a meat pie. At five minutes before two he paid the bill, walked down Beauchamp Place, turned the corner to No. 28, Walton, and rang the bell. The door was opened by Singer Callaway, who wordlessly moved him in to Rufus's study.

"A cup of tea?" Rufus looked at him.

"No thanks," Blackford shook his head, betraying an unwillingness to speak. Rufus detected it.

"You are safe here," he said. "We sweep every morning. Go ahead."

"Your man is James Peregrine, Viscount Kirk," said Blackford.

"How do you know?"

"One. He is an intimate friend of Queen Caroline, sees her regularly. He has got her greatly exercised over the state of England's atomic defenses, and most particularly about the imprecise knowledge England has of America's progress with the hydrogen bomb.

"Two. The Queen asked me if I knew what progress our people were making with the hydrogen bomb. Why did she ask me? Because she thought I might know the answer. Why did she think I might know the answer? Because at dinner the first night, when there were six guests including Viscount Kirk, I told a very tall tale about my apprenticing at Yale under the retired atomic scientist Rene Wallack, and about having been present on at least two occasions when Edward Teller himself came down to try to persuade Wallack to come back from retirement and help crack the remaining problems of the hydrogen bomb. In the course of it all —I told them debonairly—Professor Wallack asked me to stay on as an assistant, but I was already committed to the foundation job. But I added—goddammit, I know, I know I overdid it—that I had suggested a friend of mine from MIT, who had taken the job, and this friend keeps me pretty well posted on the kind of progress we're making on the bomb."

Rufus was the perfect audience for so orderly a presentation. As long as it proceeded thus systematically, he would not have shown any signs of impatience, let alone have interrupted, if it had gone on for hours.

"Three. Needless to say, when I spun all of that out, I had no idea Kirk was our guy. But I felt I had to say something that would make me interesting to the Queen. Remember, it was altogether probable that my luck had run its course—having got into the castle and been incorporated into one official meal, I might never lay eyes on her again and would have to pursue the identity of our man through questions directed at stray cooks, valets, and curators.

"Four. I was lucky. The Queen continued to show an interest in me—which might well have been stimulated by my horseshit about my closeness to Wallack, Teller, et al. A day later, the Queen asked me, some time after we had ridden horseback together, if I knew what the Teller-Freeze Bypass was. I said, sort of casually, 'Who wants to know?' and she said 'Peregrine—he's very much concerned about national security.' Of course, I told her that unfortunately I had never heard of the Teller-Freeze

Bypass, though I could have rattled on, giving her one of those formulas Rufus gave me last weekend.

"And that's the whole story."

Blackford, having spent the better part of the morning searching his conscience, could not see that it was any concern of his employers, of the republic he served, from sea to shining sea, to report on what clothes he and the Queen were wearing when they discussed the Teller-Freeze Bypass, or by how many centimeters, if measurable, their bodies were separated.

Singer looked at Rufus. Rufus looked like a man smoking a pipe without a pipe. He was the most infuriatingly deliberate man, Allen Dulles had once complained, in the history of thought, and it was all the more infuriating that he was utterly unconscious of any imposition on the people who waited on him. He could act very quickly, but never did so when there was an alternative. He was that way with Dulles, and had been that way once with Churchill, who finally stormed out of the room and asked to be summoned "when Socrates comes out of his trance."

During all this Singer and Blackford exchanged not a word. Blackford's eyes had begun to roam about the room, looking at the book titles and thinking that old Tom in Washington would be proud of Black's capacity, at an instant's notice, to reproduce on sketch paper the exact contents of this room.

Suddenly the silence was broken—by Blackford.

"I forgot something that may prove important."

He told them in detail about his conversation that morning with his father, and his subsequent conversation with Peregrine, and about the match set for the following Monday.

Rufus returned to his thinking.

Finally he said:

"I would suppose that NKVD-London has got hold of Professor Wallack by now, though it is just possible they found reasons for delaying a bit—we must find out. Singer, it's worth the risk. Get someone to approach Professor Wallack *immediately* to ask whether he has been questioned about Oakes; and to ask him, if the answer is no, to agree to dissimulate when he is approached, as he certainly will be."

Blackford interrupted. "Excuse me. But I know the right man to do that. The man who recruited me, Anthony Trust, who is in

New York, graduated from Yale two years ago. He knows every-body there, and he is smooth, very smooth."

"Excellent. Singer, get that done *now*, and"—he looked at his watch—"ask for an answer within four hours. Trust should locate Professor Wallack over the telephone and ask him to dodge *any* telephone call, or *any* visitor, until Trust himself drives over to see him. Tell Trust he can use Teller's name, and get word to Teller that if he gets a call from Wallack asking whether he should co-operate with a man called Anthony Trust, the answer is emphat-ically affirmative."

Singer left the room, opened a door apparently to give instruc-tions to a technician in the adjoining room, and was back in a minute or two.

Exactly five minutes later a bell rang, and, answering the sum-mons, Singer returned to the cryptographer's quarters. The mes-sage, in all its apparent complexity, had been received by Trust, who would act instantly and report, in a matter of minutes, on his conversation with Wallack. But before doing anything, Trust had said, he would take the precaution of telephoning Teller.

In another ten minutes Singer was summoned again, and came back with a roll of butcher paper, a message from Trust, through the decoder. He read it out loud:

REACHED TELLER WHO INSTANTLY CALLED WALLACK WHO
AGREED TO ACCEPT A CALL FROM ME. I ASKED WALLACK WHETHER
HE HAD HAD INQUIRY RE B. OAKES. HE REPLIED NEGATIVE
BUT SAID MAN CALLED HIS OFFICE TWICE THIS MORNING
WHILE HE WAS AT SEMINAR DECLINING TO LEAVE NUMBER.
SAID HE WOULD CALL AGAIN THIS AFTERNOON. I DECIDED TO
RISK DIRECT TELEPHONE ORIENTATION WITH WALLACK RATHER
THAN TWO-HOUR-DRIVE TIME DELAY AND RUN RISK MORNING
CALLER SUSPECTS WALLACK IS EVADING HIM. TOLD HIM IF
CALLER ASKS HE SHOULD REPLY YES BLACKFORD OAKES WORKED
FOR HIM AS PART-TIME ASSISTANT FINE YOUNG MAN VERY
BRILLIANT YOUNG THEORETICAL PHYSICIST TURNED ENGINEER
IN FACT TRIED TO HIRE HIM TO STAY ON FOR SPECIAL PROJECTS,
DETAILS UNSPECIFIABLE. WALLACK AGREED AND WILL TELEPHONE
ME WHEN CONTACT IS MADE.

The relief in the room was celebrated by a concerted silence. Rufus then said, "Singer, we must put a tail on Kirk, and try to bug his flat. But use only your top man, or nobody. It would be better, at this point, if we lost him than if he caught on that we are on to him. Get that started right away." Rufus's intensest emotions, like J. S. Bach's, were rendered pianissimo. Again Singer left the room.

Rufus, though looking at Blackford, was actually talking to himself.

"So far, they don't know we've got our man. But there's something *we* don't know, and that is: What precautions has Kirk taken?"

"You mean to get away?"

"That's one kind of precaution. Another is to neutralize us. He has a hell of a lever: the reputation of the Queen of England. The unity of the West is a fragile thing as it is. Institutional stability, in Europe, is practically a monopoly of Great Britain, West Germany, and Monaco. The demoralization that would follow from the exposure of the Queen as inadvertent agent of the Soviet Union is something Europe would have a hell of a time adjusting to. You can imagine what it would do to the British. Abdication. A huge, iconoclastic assault on the monarchy, general hell. The problem now is less Kirk—he has to be disposed of, of course— than saving the Queen—I repeat, and we don't know what precautions, if any, Kirk has taken. And we don't know how deep the NKVD's knowledge is of the relationship between Kirk and the Queen. . . ."

"Isn't it safe to assume they know everything?" Blackford asked.

"Has it occurred to you, Blackford," Rufus stared into space, "that the NKVD *may not even know who Kirk is?* That, really, is the principal purpose of our tailing him—to try to establish if there *is* any face-to-face contact with any of the known NKVD agents."

The bell rang in the next room, and Singer came back with a fresh communication from Trust.

"It sure is moving fast today," he said excitedly. "Here's the latest."

WALLACK JUST CALLED BACK. MAN IDENTIFYING HIMSELF AS
FBI AGENT SAID HE WAS DOING ROUTINE INQUIRY ABOUT B. OAKES

WHO IS BEING CONSIDERED FOR SECURITY ASSIGNMENT AND
LISTED WALLACK AS A FORMER EMPLOYER. WALLACK GAVE
PRESCRIBED ANSWERS AND AGENT, WHO GAVE HIS NAME AS
WILLIAM FURCOLO, SAID THANKS. AND SIGNED OFF. QUERY:
DO I NEED TO GO TO NEW HAVEN AND GIVE WALLACK MORE
INFORMATION?

"Tell him no," Rufus said, "but ask him to have Wallack telephone in any other inquiries relating to Oakes and tell him whoever his current assistant is, Wallack's impression is he trained at
MIT and was recommended by Oakes; and to report any inquiries on that front also."

Rufus resumed his thinking, silently. He turned again to Blackford, this time with instructions.

"You must go ahead with the training on the Sabre airplane. It
is, I assume, too late to fly it this afternoon. Go to your flat, and
telephone your father's people and tell them you will fly it tomorrow morning, tomorrow afternoon, and Sunday morning before
you exhibit for the Sabre officials on Sunday afternoon. Let me
have the key to your flat." Black handed it to Singer, wordlessly,
and Singer walked into the code room and, a few minutes later,
returned with quadruplicated keys.

Rufus handed the original and two duplicates to Blackford.
"Two young men will have dinner with you tonight—'old college
pals.' You'll put them up for the weekend. They are plausible-
looking and acting young men, but also very highly trained. The
two of them together could blow up the Tower of London and
make it look like an earthquake. Certainly they can look after
your own safety. One of them—because, so the story will go, he
has nothing else to do, is avocationally interested in flying, and
would prefer staying with you to going to Madame Tussaud's or
Westminster Abbey—will accompany you to Northolt tomorrow
while you fly the Sabre. The second will stay in your flat, and answer, and record on tape, all calls. Introduce them to the doorman
as old college chums who will be staying with you a few days. If I
need to see you before Monday morning, Singer will get word to
you. If not, come here at *nine P.M. on Sunday* for a briefing. If the
Sabre committee rules against you on Sunday afternoon, advise
Singer, and stand by at your flat between five and seven. If there

is *any* unlikely action—anything at all that makes you feel you are being followed—go to the second rendezvous in the list you already have, and travel from there to the airfield for the next practice session. You will ostensibly be taking your companion to Stratford for a little Shakespeare. There will be a standing reservation at the inn in your friend's name—Joseph Amundson. The appropriate room will be assigned to you. Now: If there is an unambiguous effort to interfere with your movements—that, Blackford, is Company talk for anything from blackmail through mayhem to attempted assassination—*leave the country,* following the prescribed route."

Blackford rose, tipped his hand in mock salute, which, before his fingers reached his eyebrow in the old-time fly-boy casualness, had suddenly transformed into a salute suggesting something between respect and reverence. Rufus had been his appointed superior. He had become his leader.

Blackford, after the routine cautionary look through the side window, walked out of 28 Walton Street.

Rufus sat with Singer, the door to the cryptograph room—following a nudge by Rufus—tightly closed.

"What I am trying to do is obvious to you, Singer. What is not so obvious is that I am also trying to figure out a way to come away from it without disposing of young Blackford Oakes. He has performed for us at least faithfully, at best brilliantly. I suspect he has not told us everything, but I am confident he has told us everything he conscientiously believes we need to know in order to do our part of the job. But he is too inexperienced to know, fully, what our strategic responsibilities are. I want to reason my way through to a solution that leaves Oakes alive. So far I haven't discovered a way. I hope to find one.

"Meanwhile, get me a top-security Sabrejet weapons engineer. Fly him in from the States, if there isn't one of them around already. And have him arrive with a *full inventory* of all the weapons the new Sabre is designed to use. I will need him here by Sunday afternoon. Let's say five P.M. unless you tell me it can't be done, in which case please resign and go work in some university."

Singer rather liked it that way. It was how it was seven years ago; and he knew that Rufus would try very hard to save Blackford, but that saving him could not stand in the way of the successful operation. "Too much is at stake" was the way Rufus would put it. Singer appreciated it that Rufus never tried for fancy formulations of terribly basic statements. A cliché, used by Rufus, had crawled back into aphorism.

Blackford told Joe Amundson and Victor Luckey—who had silently and systematically swept the apartment and, finding it clean, authorized direct conversation—that they were free to carouse, either ostensibly or in fact; that a great many of his visiting friends did—there was the bar, there the record player, there the magazine rack, there the telly, but that he, Blackford, would be going to sleep. He must be in shape tomorrow for his flying. Joe told him he and Victor would be alternating watches. They examined Blackford's bedroom, and after looking out the bedroom window, slightly rearranged the position of his bed. He was told to lock the door from the inside and open it only on hearing a prescribed signal.

Blackford called his mother on the telephone, told her briefly his plans for Monday ("provided I persuade the Sabrejet people I'm a better flier than Dad!"). His mother was not at all pleased, but said that he must understand if Alec, who had been invited to the trials, rooted for the Hunter—"After all, Alec's bank is heavily involved." Blackford said that would be okay, and he simulated a kiss over the telephone, and hung up. He turned off the lights, and daydreamed about a bedroom not thirty miles away, in Windsor Castle, empty at the moment; and of another bedroom, not two miles away, in Buckingham Palace, whose design he did not know, could not guess at—here Crawfie had let him down— where, he agonized with longing, he might find himself, this moment, stark naked, his staff at stiff attention, prepared to build yet one more Anglo-American bridge, however urgent his need for sleep.

Kirk cursed himself for having forgotten that at the Immaculate Conception Church on Farm Street the priests regularly heard confessions between five and six on Fridays. He had given five forty-five to Boris as the time for their meeting. But, of course, there were contingency arrangements. On discovering that there was a queue of the faithful, or, even without a queue, if it happened that, entering the penitent's compartment, Boris discovered that it wasn't Robinson who slid open the opaque screen, but a priest, Boris would simply leave the church and proceed directly to the next numbered church on the carefully memorized list, reporting to the equivalent confessional box *exactly* one half hour later—having, at the original rendezvous, confessed his sins or not, according as he found himself stuck, speaking to a live priest, or in a position, having observed the queue, to abort the engagement in advance. On leaving the church, Boris knew to take the nearest church exit, keeping his eyes down, under no circumstances looking about him, lest his eyes fall on the intangible, impalpable Robinson. Kirk, who had arrived at the Farm Street church only to discover the priest pre-empting Kirk's compartment, moved diagonally across the dimly lit church and knelt down, to await Boris's arrival, and observe, while he had the opportunity, whether Boris would follow his instructions exactly. He had no complaint—the queue having disappeared, Boris did, as it happened, step confidently into the compartment expecting to speak to Robinson, and Kirk amused himself wondering what he might appropriately be saying now to the priest.

"*Forgive me, Father, for I have sinned. I last went to confession before the Revolution. Since then, I have killed directly four hundred and seventy-two men, ordered the execution of approximately twelve hundred others, and participated in a corporate effort to kill somewhere between four and seven million more. I have also been lacking in charity, and missed my morning prayers. For these and other sins, I beg forgiveness.*" In a minute or two, Boris emerged, and walked, head dutifully bent down, out the Farm Street entrance. One or two other men, and two young girls, sauntered into the church and queued up outside the confessional, three on each side, while Kirk reflected. He might as well stay where he was for another five minutes, which would leave him exactly enough time to walk to St. James's on Spanish Place, to arrive there at six-ten, five minutes ahead of Boris. With five minutes to kill, he found himself, suddenly, wondering whether, if Miss Oyen had, during those long intervals in the hospital, been reading, alternatively, the Bible, and the Confessions of St. Augustine, and St. John of the Cross, and even the moderns —Newman, Chesterton, C. S. Lewis, Merton, Belloc—he, Peregrine, might have found himself in this quiet chapel not, in his search for a better world, frustrated by the queue of penitents, but lining up along with them, confessing to a priest a microcosmic, rather than a macrocosmic responsibility for the troubles of this troublesome world. Peregrine was imaginative enough to consider the alternative without emotion, but he was decisive by character, and five minutes proved ample to reinforce his determination. Shit, he said, the Christians have had it for two thousand years. The Communists have had less than fifty years. As a confirmed redistributionist, I'll call time on St. Mark, and give St. Marx equal time.

He strained to read his watch in the light, and presently rose, and walked out briskly. He followed the far perimeter of Hyde Park, loped off into Manchester Square, slowed his pace a little, and walked into the main entrance of St. James's, which was dark except for candles on both sides of the sanctuary, the four dim lights overhead for tracing the aisles and the pews, the lights inadequate for reading one's missal or breviary unless you knelt directly below them. There was no one in sight and, counting clockwise from the left, he slipped into the priest's compartment in the second confessional, and waited. In exactly five minutes, he felt the weight of a penitent and slid open the partition, which allows the ear to hear, but not the eye to see. After establishing that it was Boris, Boris stepped out and submitted to the routine frisk. The formalities disposed of, Boris, back in the penitent's box, said, "You are talking, Robinson, to someone who has just received absolution."

"God is more forgiving than Stalin, Boris Andreyvich."

Boris's voice changed quickly, pursuant to his role: no participation in any jocularities involving Stalin.

"You have a message for me?"

"No, but *you* should have a message for *me*."

"I do. And it comes exactly ten minutes before I come out to meet you. Your friend Blackford Oakes, whoever he is, did not, it seems, lie to you. He worked for Professor Wallack, and we discovered even that Professor Wallack asks him to stay on."

Peregrine felt greatly relieved. Inordinately relieved, from which he deduced that his suspicions about Oakes had been more than perfunctory.

"Good show, Boris; bloody good show. Did you find the answer to whether Wallack's current assistant is an MIT man?"

"No, but in good time, Robinson, in good time . . . Now, Robinson, you were going to try especially hard to get for me a description of the Teller-Freeze Bypass. You have succeeded?"

"I have not. I have made inquiries which would ordinarily bring results, and I am now wondering whether it is possible that you have the term right. Or perhaps it is a recently coined scientific nickname? Or a fresh code word for a process we have already investigated?"

"I don't think it is any one of these things. There is much excitement over the Bypass and the easy solution it has provided for serious problems."

"I think," said Robinson thoughtfully, "that provided you are correct—that there is such a thing—I can probably get you the answer in a week."

He had, after all, asked the Queen to demand of the Prime Minister that he consult his top scientific advisers. And if *they* did not know what the Teller-Freeze Bypass was, they were in a position to demand of their American counterparts that they be duly informed, according to the terms of the compact between the P.M. and President Truman. All that should flush out before next Thursday's meeting between the Queen and the Prime Minister. He himself could arrange to see the Queen the following weekend.

"I figure approximately ten days, Boris, and I will call you in the usual way. Now, is there anything else?"

"Only the usual: big, big pressures from Moscow. The feeling that the American scientists are moving faster and faster while we are seemingly . . . stuck."

"I'll see what I can do to unstick the revolution, old boy. And remember, Marxist dogma will see us over this crisis in due course."

Boris did permit himself to say, under the cloistered circumstances, "Marxist dogma will not come down and save my head if I don't have the answers for Moscow very soon."

"Pending Marxist dogma's assuming the role of protector, I, Robinson, will look after you, Boris Andreyvich. I have not failed you yet."

"No, Robinson, you have not. Your ways are very unusual, but you have never failed us, and have never deceived us, and one day, when you are ready for it, you will be given appropriate recognition."

"I am perfectly happy, my dear Boris, to make my contributions anonymously. Besides, if I were to accept a medal from your friend Stalin, it would probably make me sick. I need constantly to remind myself how many evil popes there have been when I consider that Stalin was selected by history to guide us through to a socialist paradise. Ah, well, Boris Andreyvich, enough of that. It is late. About ten days, as I say."

"Good evening, Robinson."

Fifteen

RUFUS STUDIED THE REPORT and said to Singer, "Hard to understand why they went into the Farm Street church first. Did anybody check on the priest who was in the confessional with Boris Bolgin?"

"No," Singer said. "We had only two men on the job; one of them tailed Kirk, the other Bolgin—your hunch about him was right. But Kirk did stay in the church seven or eight minutes, and during that period other people came in and went right into the confessionals, so my guess is the priest was genuine, and Boris walked in there looking for Robinson and had to play out a penitent's role. Probably it was an unscheduled confessional hour, or maybe Kirk just forgot, and they went automatically to the alternative rendezvous."

"So," said Rufus, "what do we know?"

"One, Oakes is right, and we have our man.

"Two, Kirk is dealing with the top NKVD man in England—rather surprising, really. But less so—

"Three—if my hunch is correct that Kirk *hasn't permitted Bolgin to discover his identity.* Sure, Bolgin could arrange to have Kirk tailed, but chances of exposure multiply geometrically. . . . It could mean, also, that Kirk is taking great precautions to protect the Queen. Why? Because it's less messy that way? With only himself knowing she is the source of the leaks? Perhaps. But also, maybe, for—sentimental reasons . . . We need not assume that his hostility to the West is also a hostility to the person of his second cousin, the Queen. . . .

"Get me everything you can from the newspaper morgues

about Kirk and the Queen, how often they see each other—Oakes tells us he is the *only* nonfamily man who actually keeps riding clothes at Windsor Castle. I'd like to know more about him, including any hint of any irregular romantic"—Rufus would, whenever possible, reach for the tushery—"relations. I'm not *sure* what I am looking for, but I need the information fast. Tell you what: Get someone you know to call the foreign office and say that Viscount Kirk has been nominated for a VIP invitation to the United States under the auspices of the State Department, but that because of the McCarran Act—they're used to this—we are required to have a look at the security portfolio, which we are loath to insist formally on doing, given his eminence and his closeness to the Queen—and would they either let us have it or else look it over themselves, and we will gladly take their word for it—just see if there is anything there that catches the eye—anything at all."

Singer was taking notes.

"And the Sabre man?" Rufus continued, drawing parallel lines on a piece of yellow paper with a sharpened pencil.

"He'll be here on schedule. The army had to be brought in on that one, because the hardware you want isn't just sitting around at Macy's basement."

"Good night, Singer."

Singer knew when he was being dismissed, and he never tarried.

"Good night, Rufus." And yawned—it was after midnight.

Rufus turned down the light, popped a pill in his mouth, which would keep drowsiness at bay for two hours at least. Taking the key from his wall safe, he entered the deserted cryptograph room and sat down at the operator's chair. He opened now the interior safe and brought out a code register, and a second volume, from which he extracted a code number. He turned on the machine and carefully tapped out a message which, under the gravity of the indicated rubric, was decoded in a room in Washington, inserted on a roll of paper a quarter inch wide which, unseen by human eyes, was wound under spring pressure through a slit, on to a spool in a steel box protected by a marsupial envelope within the decoding machine itself. When the clattering stopped, and a bell rang signifying that the dispatcher was finished, a clerk opened a steel door, as if to check the fire within a furnace. Then with a pair of scissors he severed the inch of exposed tape reaching umbilically from the decoding machine to the box's narrow, coin-box aperture, thus leaving the message inside the box unviewable except to the man with the key to open it.

The clerk, carrying the box and followed by an armed guard, proceeded according to regulation down the hall to an elevator, and then into a waiting car, preceded by one car with two armed men and a radio and followed by another car with identical equipment. The caravan drove out and, a half hour later, drew up outside an inconspicuous house in the Virginia countryside. The clerk and his bodyguard, the accompanying men carefully watching their movements, one of them talking into the radio with the guard inside the farmhouse, watched. Two guards let them through a gate opposite the main entrance. As they reached the front door, it opened, and the clerk, always with his escort, was guided to a study. He turned the box over to the occupant of the study, who asked them both to wait outside.

He looked at the number on the steel box and, opening his own safe, tabulated the corresponding code and applied the appropriate combination to open the box. He pulled out the spool of paper, unwinding it and laying it neatly across his desk, dabbing down the ends with Scotch tape. He lowered the desk light and read:

WE HAVE OUR MAN AND I HAVE EVOLVED A SATISFACTORY PLAN. BUT THERE IS A RESIDUAL RISK IN ALLOWING THE SURVIVAL OF OUR YOUNG MAN. I CAN AT THIS POINT VERY EASILY ARRANGE FOR HIS ALTOGETHER LOGICAL ELIMINATION. BUT ON THIS ONE, CHIEF, YOU'VE GOT TO GIVE ME THE WORD, AND I'M USING THIS QUOTE WORD UNQUOTE IN CASE YOU DIDN'T NOTICE, AS A DELICATE SUBSTITUTE FOR ORDER. I KNOW IT'S IRRELEVANT TO SAY SO, BUT I LIKE HIM AND TRUST HIM. BUT YOU KNOW MY RULE: NEVER RELY ON YOUR OWN JUDGMENT WHEN THE DOING SO IS TO TAKE A CHANCE WITH THE NATIONAL INTEREST. TELL ME NOW—I AM WAITING AND WILL WAIT THROUGH THE NIGHT IF NECESSARY—"YES," AND HE GOES TOO; "NO," HE LIVES TO FIGHT AGAIN. OH YES, HAVE A GOOD SLEEP, BOSS. RUFUS.

He sat down in his armchair and set fire to the crumpled ball of paper. Then he picked out a book from the shelf, an advance copy, sent him by a friend in the publishing business who knew his tastes, which inclined heavily to books about history in which he had himself been involved—*The Diary of a Young Girl*, by Anne Frank. He was halfway through it, and found that his pencil had marked a passage he wanted now to reread. It was from the girl's notes when she was hiding in the attic from the Gestapo, who by concentric deductions were coming closer and closer every day to discovering her. "I wonder," the little girl had written, "why they let people like them grow so powerful?" He paused and his eyes blurred. People like *them*. People like *whom?* He reached again for his directory, scratched down a code number, and after it wrote out a single word, dropped it into the box, and rang for an aide. "Have the operator waiting outside dispatch the message instantly." He handed him the locked box, called his wife on the intercom, and said he was ready for cocktails.

Most of Saturday morning Blackford spent on the ground, briefed by the chief engineer on the aircraft and on the agreed-upon drill for the following Monday. The two airplanes would perform a total of six exercises each, three of them in tandem, three individually. The contest would to some extent be judged impressionistically, but also there were instruments, both in the aircraft and on the ground, that would record precise scientific data—obvious things like speed and angle of climb, less obvious things like pressures on the pilot, oil viscosity changes, fuel consumption, and a hundred other metabolic arcana of vital interest to generals, economists, and aircraft specialists. The exercise would begin by a tandem sweep past the reviewing stand at an elevation of fifteen feet, to begin ten miles west and terminate ten miles east of the stand—"Later on we'll fly over to Farnborough and you can look at the actual lay of the land." This was really pyrotechnical stuff, since the two aircraft would fly at a prearranged six hundred miles per hour, or Mach .89. In the individual exercises, the Hunter and the Sabre would take turns beginning. The odd-numbered exercises were to be done, like the first, in tandem. The final exercise would have the two airplanes approach the field, loop as narrow a diameter as the pilots dared, and land side by side.

"When do Kirk and I get to practice the duets? We can't walk into that kind of stuff cold."

"Well, you can, actually, since they're all standard maneuvers, and the radio contact between the two of you is perfect—no outside interference on this one. We're trying out the new closed-circuit radio communication system. But we'll do that on Monday morning. The reason we're putting it off until then is that it won't be until Sunday afternoon that either of you is finally selected."

"What if we're both turned down?"

"Your father has trained with a Hunter counterpart, and they can go over it again on Monday morning if they want to, or your father with Kirk, or another Hunter man with you—whatever."

"Well," said Blackford, examining the reports on the expected performance he was to get out of the Sabrejet, "I'm sure glad that swimming coach at Yale talked me out of four years of booze and tobacco. . . . On the other hand"—he smiled and looked up—"they don't seem to have hurt my father."

He spent two hours in the morning and three in the afternoon going through the maneuvers. He mastered the airplane, as his father had predicted, with considerable ease. It was like his old Sabre, except that everything was better, smoother; dozens of adjustments required the use of fingertips instead of clenched fists, and quickly Blackford learned to play these as a pianist learns to reduce the finger pressure on a clavichord. Far from ending the afternoon tired, he was exhilarated, and he wondered how any other flying machine could begin to match the versatility of the new Sabre.

As they set out for London, Blackford said impulsively to Joe: "Ever been to Stratford-on-Avon?"

"No."

"Well, let's go," said Blackford, smiling at the thought that his first visit to Stratford was prompted by fear of the NKVD. They got tickets for *Othello,* and at an early dinner Blackford gave Joe the plot, but not the denouement, and as they were driving home Joe expressed himself as genuinely indignant at Iago, and Blackford told him that was really a good sign, because jealousy was no longer so strong a human passion, in part because people loved others less, loving themselves more, so that jealousy was therefore more a form of idolatry, or so it was held by people who scorned patriotism. Joe said that was very interesting, and they reached their flat before midnight, Joe having meanwhile telephoned Vic Luckey to learn that there had been no messages for Blackford during the day except a call from his father telling him he would meet him at the field at 9 A.M.

It was at this session that Blackford was told that for the critical Exercise Six, which called for a mock dogfight between the Hunter and the Sabre, each aircraft was equipped with six simulated cannon from one of which a light beam of sorts shot out in response to the pilot's trigger, the trajectory registering instantly at a console in the reviewing stand, indicating whether a hit had been scored. The two fliers could fire their six rounds at will during the dogfight that must end exactly 120 seconds after it started. The results of their marksmanship would not be known to the pilots until after they landed, at which point the winner would be announced. His father hastened to add that one could easily lose Exercise Six and even so impress the generals as having the better airplane, since the winner of the exercise was showing off not only his airplane but his own prowess. "And there's always luck. . . . Still, you should try to win them all."

His father then flew with him for an hour, through the run of the exercises, and pronounced himself totally satisfied.

"We won't do any more. You're going to have to do it all again at two for Averell and the boys. Let's stay fresh." So they went to a roadside restaurant, Joe having tactfully excused himself, and had fish and chips—and one beer, for Dad, who simultaneously ordered a Coca-Cola for Blackford, and looked, talked, and acted as excited as if Blackford were about to win a Nobel Prize for stunt flying.

Tom Oakes told Blackford he thought it would be more tactful not to introduce his son to the North American brass until *after* the exhibition.

"There's always the chance they'll turn you down—you just can't tell. It's a lot harder on them if they've just finished socializing with you. Did you know I was a judge once at a Miss America contest? I'm telling you, poking Miss Alabama on Friday night, and disqualifying her on Saturday night, was one of the toughest things I ever had to do."

"Dad, I take it the moral of that story is that we're supposed to feel sorry for you, not for Miss Alabama?"

"I never went to Yale, Blacky, so I can't answer those high colonic ethical questions." He grinned at his son, left the tip, and they walked, *High Noon* style, to the hangar.

It went well. Very well. And when he had finished the final loop and brought the plane within feet of the brass, there was spontaneous applause. Blackford looked not unlike Lindbergh emerging from *The Spirit of St. Louis,* his father thought, only maybe even handsomer. Black shook everyone's hands, and they sauntered off to a reception, followed by a showing of an extensive documentary on the design, manufacture, versatility, and prospects of the F-86 Sabre. At six, Blackford whispered to his father: "Dad, I've got a date at eight I can't break, so I'll just slip away. I'm going to be tied up tonight, but I'll be here tomorrow." They were interrupted by a North American engineer who informed them that the Hawker-Hunter Committee had just designated Viscount Kirk to fly their flagship. "Chap said over the phone his performance was unbelievable, *unbelievable.*" Blackford said good, he was pleased it would be someone he knew. "I'll be here tomorrow at ten for the tandem work with Kirk."

"Make it nine-thirty, son."

"Okay, Dad."

His father pressed his son's hand with that special pressure he felt Blacky earned for turning in a performance that did justice to the supership, and credit to his father.

There was just time for a bath at home, and a change of clothes, and a scribbled, long-overdue paragraph to Sally.

Blackford, ready to leave, said, "Joe, I assume I'm to go where I'm going without you."

Joe looked unhappy—professionally unhappy. "I don't know, Black. My orders were to stick with you."

It was only four forty-five, so Black suggested Joe use the telephone and ring whatever number it was he took his orders from and ask.

He did so, and Blackford could hear the grunts. "I'm to go with you as far as Brompton Road and Beauchamp, southwest corner, then you're on your own. When they're through with you, they'll call me and I'll go back and meet you at that corner at the time they say."

They hailed a cab, and Blackford, about to deposit the letter in a postbox, suddenly found Joe's iron grip on his wrist. The voice was tender, but firm.

"Sorry, Blackford, orders."

He took the envelope gently from him. "No letters mailed till after tomorrow."

Blackford, fighting to subdue resentment, barely succeeded in doing so. In the cab he said, "You bastards are primarily watching me, not guarding me." Joe shrugged his shoulders.

So, in effect, did Black.

"See you, Joe," said Blackford, waving his hands when they had reached Brompton Road at the specified corner. He was mildly surprised to see Singer Callaway there, whom he knew better than to greet, walking instead by himself to Walton Street and turning the corner. The door opened for him, stayed open a few seconds, and Singer followed him in.

"You people are making me feel creepy," Blackford said, taking off a blazer and dropping it on the sofa. "It makes me feel good you're not sure I can get from Brompton Road to Walton Street without armed surveillance. And that I can't post a letter to my girl until Rufus or President Truman or whoever allows it."

Singer smiled. "It's just that animal magnetism of yours, Blacky —we can't leave you alone."

Rufus's solemnity brought Blackford, wordless, to the same sofa he had sat on for so long on Friday.

"Good evening," Rufus said.

"Good evening," Blackford said.

Rufus looked at Blackford and said, "Do you know anything about me?"

"No, sir, not much."

"There is no reason why you should. There is every reason why you should not. I don't talk about myself, but I am going to do so to you, very briefly. I was in general charge, during World War II, of keeping hidden from the Germans the knowledge that we had broken their most secret code. I was in specific charge of misleading the Germans into believing that the invasion of Europe would occur in the Calais area. In order to discharge these duties, I made every day a decision that I knew would cost at least one man his life. On one occasion I made a decision that cost many men their lives. I retired from this work, gratefully, after the war was over. I soon realized it wasn't really over. I was called back by General Eisenhower and Allen Dulles because in their estimation the problem in which you are involved is the most delicate diplomatic-security problem they have ever run into; certainly it is the worst I have ever run into. It is, quite simply, unique: because the Queen of England is about all that is left of this diminishing empire, and the destruction of her reputation could mean something very like the dissolution of the Commonwealth. The damage already done is staggering. The information the Queen has given to the Soviet Union via Viscount Kirk cannot mean less than a five-year acceleration in the Soviet hydrogen-bomb program, and that acceleration means that the history of the last part of this decade, and of the next, will be changed, to the disadvantage of millions of people. We know now how to staunch the lesion—we have only to get rid of Kirk, and that is done easily. What cannot be done easily is to protect the Queen from any possibility that the story of what she did will ever become known—even to her own Prime Minister."

"What do you want me to do?" Blackford asked, with just a trace of impatience.

"I want you, tomorrow, to effect the death of Kirk even if, in order to do it, you have to end your own life."

Blackford stood up, pale. Rufus watched him with a searing intensity. The next few words would govern Rufus's instructions to the Sabre weapons expert waiting, alone, at the hangar at Barrington.

"Would I have a *chance?*" Blackford asked. "Or are you talking kamikaze stuff?"

"You would have a chance."

Rufus gave his plan.

Blackford, lying flat now on the couch, his eyes fixed on the ceiling, paused when Rufus was done, and then, after a long interval, said almost listlessly, "Okay."

Rufus got up, walked over to Blackford, and shook his hand.

"You understand, I can't let you out of our sight from this moment on. I don't need to explain. You'll sleep upstairs, and dinner will be brought in."

Black was out of wind, and, catching Singer's gesture, followed him out, and up the stairs to a bedroom-sitting room. Singer said, "There isn't any reason not to have a bottle of wine, so I've ordered it. All I want to know is: Do you want me here for a while, or gone?"

"I'd like you here," Blackford said, and so for an hour, sharing a bottle of wine, they spoke about matters grave and trivial. Blackford came desperately near to telling Singer, whom he liked and trusted, that his willingness to sacrifice for the Queen was motivated by something more even than his willingness to protect her kingdom. He almost smiled as he wondered what *that* variable, entered into the complex mind of Rufus, would do to affect the morning's plans?

The morning papers carried extensive descriptions of the forthcoming duel. There were reports and features on the military, the economic, and the psychological impact of a clear victory by one or the other plane. Commentators warned that such a clear victory was unlikely, that all that the experts would probably be left with would be merely suggestive. Still there was much excitement, and though the feature story on Peregrine Kirk was extensive and included several pictures of him taken during the war, and during the celebrated 1948 Olympics, the offsetting feature on the American pilot was necessarily spare. It had even proved necessary to wirephoto a picture of him from New Haven, Connecticut, where he had recently graduated from Yale as an engineer, because he could not be located at his flat in London, and it was assumed that he was away from the city, resting.

The big social news was that the Queen had announced, in plenty of time to record her decision in the Court Circular, that she would be going out to Farnborough to view the exhibition (she cautiously declined to call it a contest), and that although of course she was very pleased that her second cousin and old friend Viscount Kirk was flying the Hunter, she had in fact met Mr.

Oakes, the American, and wished him good luck with his own country's airplane.

Although air shows in England are popular pastimes, they do not occur in the month of January, but suddenly the thirty-mile trip to Farnborough became the thing to do, and by noon the traffic on the southwest highway was clogged. The police estimated that, whereas not more than a few hundred people, most of them official guests, had been expected, now there would probably be as many as ten thousand spectators.

The weather was in part responsible. It was like midweek the week before, an equable temperature, with a yellow snap in the air that made you, if you were sitting in one place, wish to rise in order to sit somewhere else; and vice versa. The fledgling television industry was there in force, and of course BBC radio. Both the pilots had agreed, while dressing in the morning, to speak to no one, but the radio and television were busy, beginning at one o'clock, reporting. Kirk, veteran of a hundred equestrian contests, was altogether natural, quietly confident. Blackford, he noted, was nervous; but why should he not be? He was flying, so to speak, in hostile air. And it had already been rumored that his selection was nepotistically contrived. But when they were in the air together, and after they had gone through the first maneuver, Kirk noticed the utter mastery with which Blackford handled his ship. The signals between them were orthodox, following the rules of the same handbook that had governed some of the cheek-to-cheek dancing of the little biplanes at the county fairs a generation earlier. It was the individual exercises, and the mock battle, that would test the men and the planes. The balletic parts were for the visual satisfaction of the spectators.

Forty-five minutes later they were down on the ground, shook hands, and went their separate ways, Kirk to his quarters and the hangar set apart for him, where Hunter officials buzzed about him; Blackford to his own room, where he asked his father if he might be left alone. But he caught the look on Singer's face, Singer having been introduced as a young engineering professor on sabbatical in London, and amended his request to say that he would like Singer to stay with him.

An hour later there was a knock on the door. Her Majesty the Queen would be pleased if Mr. Oakes would join her and Viscount Kirk for a light lunch at the hastily improvised royal quarters, vacated that morning by the division group commander, and dominated now by Queen Caroline as though it had always been her favorite doll house.

"Blackford, what a pleasure. I do hope you are well. But not too well. Are you aware, Blackford, of the dollar drain we poor English are sustaining as a result of your vulgar commercial successes?" She munched on a cucumber sandwich and sipped her tea.

"Well, ma'am," Blackford said, reviving slightly, "I am aware that the Industrial Revolution that began here germinated quite nicely on American soil."

Queen Caroline smiled. "Yes, indeed, indeed. Thanks in large part, would you not agree, Mr. Oakes, to the irenic circumstances your industrial gardens enjoyed due to the protection of the British fleet?"

"No doubt about it, ma'am." Blackford smiled in turn, munching *his* sandwich. "Indeed I had always thought of the British fleet as invincible and was accordingly all the more surprised when, during the early days of the war, it all but disappeared."

Caroline, though enjoying the exchange, was enjoying it a little less in the presence of a half dozen of her aides, including a gruff retired admiral who was visibly prepared to make Blackford Oakes disappear on the spot. She noticed, also, that Perry was not pleased by the young American's incapacity to be awed by the British sovereign. Caroline broke the tension by saying:

"Was that, after all, the *British* fleet that disappeared at Pearl Harbor?" Her courtiers laughed, and Blackford smiled, and thought back on the haggard state of England on the day of Pearl Harbor, and was thereupon taken in conversation by a general who began to explain to him something about how Pearl Harbor might have been saved which Blackford was prepared to listen to indefinitely, just so long as he didn't have to comment intelligibly. It occurred to him that the finger sandwich he was nibbling might be the last food he would consume on earth, and that made him not only profoundly sad, but suddenly so weak in the knees that he excused himself as if he needed to visit the lavatory, which in fact he did, noticing that the identical impulse had seized Singer who, somehow, from outside the royal parquetry, knew to move toward where Blackford was headed.

A huge loudspeaker had been rigged, and someone was outlining to the crowd the forthcoming events. The voice announced that the pilots and the supporting ground personnel should report to their stations. Blackford returned to the royal enclosure, bowed to the Queen and thanked her for her hospitality, shook hands yet again with Kirk, this time in front of the cameras, and left to put on his flight suit again. And, as he did so, he repeated to himself, for the thousandth time, exactly what he was to say to Kirk, word for word. He thought primly of Mr. Simon and his recommended means for memorizing irregular Latin verbs, running them through the mind on every occasion. Word for word, Black had thought them through, and for every conceivable answer from Kirk, the most appropriate response. Stepping into the airplane, his eyes turned instantly to the red fire-button, immobilized by seals unbreakable by human hands.

A loose card hung over the radio control knobs. It was arranged, again as usual, that the pilots could talk to each other, and the tower could talk to them. But they could not talk to the tower, nor could the tower monitor the pilot-to-pilot conversation. The objective was to use a closed-communication system for combat mission secrecy, and incidentally to minimize the need for dial manipulation—indeed there was none of it to do. When the tower needed to speak, it would only be to give the countdown to the beginning of each succeeding exercise. Otherwise the only necessary talk was between the two pilots. It was not as if they were flying with two men aboard, when an extra set of hands would be available for radio controls.

The announcer could be heard through the closed cockpits.

"Having drawn lots, Viscount Kirk's Hunter will be the first craft to be airborne."

The tower gave the clearance, and Kirk roared down the runway and, halfway down it, appeared to rise vertically like a rocket.

The tower motioned Blackford on, and he did the same thing— the differences between the airplanes were not yet discernible.

Kirk spoke. "All right, old chap, let's get on with the review.

We'll meet as planned at Point Shelter, I'll come from the north, you from the south, make contact at 2:08, and we'll go through our paces to Point Escape."

"Roger."

It was perfectly executed. They came like mating birds flopping about until they espied each other and then proceeded with umbilical closeness, zooming over the rooftops, down over the field, fifteen feet above the ground, one hundred from the reviewing stand, disappearing to the east to the roar of unheard applause.

Exercise Two called for each plane to fly down to the field, and then proceed as vertically as possible while aileron rolling at least thirty times in one minute, and to do this for two minutes. The higher the plane reached at the end of the second minute, and the nearest to the point vertical from the field, the better.

"This one is mine," Kirk spoke. "I better warn you, I did almost 8,000 feet at an angle of fifteen degrees yesterday. Here I go."

Down he went, and then up in a steady roll. The radars flashed the information to the announcer, who said excitedly, "8,159 feet, angle fourteen degrees!"

Blackford said, "Nice going."

And went down to do it himself. The announcer boomed, not without satisfaction: "And for the Sabre, 8,025 feet at fourteen and a half degrees." The partisan crowd cheered.

"Too bad, old chap," Kirk said, watching his competitor as if in a sailplane—the off-duty aircraft, to conserve fuel, lazed out of the way, at 150 mph.

"Rendezvous Point Shelter at 15,000 feet," Kirk said, "at . . . 2:21." From there, they went in tandem into a screeching forty-five-degree dive toward the reviewing stand, lifting up just short of it at an angle of ten degrees. The crowd went wild with terror and delight.

And the moment had come. They were back up to ten thousand feet.

Black's heart was beating like a drum roll. "Listen, Kirk, we have to talk, so let's make a continuing, Lufbery circle, keeping at opposite sides of a diameter approximately a mile wide. The delay shouldn't be long, and the spectators won't fidget, not for a few minutes."

"What's the matter, Oakes?" Perry spoke perfunctorily, with just a touch of impatience. "Something wrong with your aircraft?"

"No. But listen carefully, Kirk. Hear me. I am an agent of a very exclusive two-man team composed of the head of MI-6 and the director of the CIA. We are aware of your activities. A technician was able, through the curtain, to pick up and record your conversation with Boris Bolgin at the confessional at St. James's on Friday. In other words, you're through.

"Now my orders are to see to it that you do not return to earth alive, and there are two ways of doing this."

The planes, describing a perfect circle like contented seagulls, were objects of admiration by the crowd below.

"One way is, during Exercise Six, for you to fail to come out of your dive in time. There would be great national mourning, and the case would be closed.

"The other way is for me to shoot you down during the next exercise. I have two live cannon with me, and you know I wouldn't miss."

"They're bonded and sealed, Oakes."

"Right. And the seals on this one are rigged to peel off like Band-Aids. I'd fire them during the dogfight, and put the blame on the engineer who failed to apply the seal on the bands and on my reaching accidentally for the traditional trigger. But that would of course mean an investigation and would be a great deal messier and not in any way that would help you personally, or the Soviet Union. What it might do is hurt the Queen. Now if you give me your word that on your dive down you will not pull out, which is after all only an alternative to the gallows a few months from now and after public disgrace—the machinery is prepared for your arrest and indictment within seconds of your landing anywhere in England, and you don't have the fuel to get away—if you give me your word, I will give you mine that I won't use the ammunition on you during the dogfight. And—my word of honor, in behalf of MI-6 and CIA—that no one—ever—will know of your use of Queen Caroline."

Kirk's voice was ghostly clear.

"Now *you* listen, Oakes. *I* also have a tape recording—of the Queen giving me information about atomic installations. Unless I pick up that package, at the end of the month, it will be forwarded automatically to a prominent publicist. Unless I get away —safe descent, twenty-four hours to get out of England, handy excuse why I left—the *whole world* will know, on February 1, what the Queen did."

Blackford felt the coils of death fastening about him, as concretely as though they were an executioner's electrodes. If he could talk Kirk into the suicidal dive, he, Blackford, would be spared. If he had to shoot him down, his own airplane—Rufus had been altogether honest on the point, and Rufus could not be doubted—was synchronized to explode with the firing of the cannon, so that the destruction of the Hunter would appear to have been an accidental result of the explosion of the Sabre, instantly deflecting any suspicion of foul play. Blackford wondered if— knowing now that Kirk had proof that the Queen's conversations would survive him—he could in good conscience take matters into his own hands—abort the entire operation, let them both land safely, tell Rufus that under the altered circumstances he did not feel he was authorized to proceed with the original plan. . . .

Before knowing how, finally, he would answer the question, he started to talk: "Kirk, I can believe you want communism to triumph. I can't believe you want Caroline destroyed. You are certainly in a position to hurt her. But doing so won't advance communism by a single step—and I can give you only thirty seconds to reflect on a fact so obvious that only cowardice would prevent you from acknowledging it. Cowardice and a total indifference to Queen Caroline's feelings, and future. In thirty seconds I'll take the initiative in the dogfight, as scheduled. And unless you give me your assurance by then I'll blast you out of the sky."

With this, Blackford arced his plane back, to assume an attack position, and watched the seconds go by on the dashboard timer. Five seconds were left when Kirk's voice, metallic, now hollow, came in:

"You have my word."

Blackford thereupon dove, resuming the scheduled exercise, pressed the radar triggers and zoomed in, scoring a hit; whereupon Kirk, in one of the flashiest maneuvers ever seen by the witnesses below, contorted his plane, doing an Immelmann, arriving almost miraculously at a position perfectly situated to blast the Sabre out of the sky. Blackford, even from that altitude, thought he could almost hear the crowd cheering this feat of virtuosity: and found himself saying into the intercom, "Nicely done, Kirk." Blackford then all but stalled his plane in order to edge it fitfully down for a retaliatory shot, which he squeezed out of his radar beam into the barely visible helmet of Kirk, who made no acknowledgment, the tower having pronounced the time up; and decreed that they should proceed to fifteen thousand feet for the next exercise, the final dive. . . .

It was the Hunter's turn. Black's strategy was not to wait the prescribed one minute, but instead to trail Kirk down fifteen seconds after he started his dive. If he changed his mind, it would then become necessary, after all, for Black to fire his cannon. But as Kirk slowed, in preparation for the dive, his voice came over:

"Okay. You chaps won this one, and you're right, you Yankee cocksucker, there isn't any point in doing her in for the hell of it. So check Box 1305 in Chelsea Station. Do you have that?"

"Got it, Peregrine."

The dive began which, that night, would be repeated endlessly over television in Britain; and, indeed, all over the world, as soon as the films could be flown out. The Queen for the first recorded time lost her composure and fell, and was carried quickly to her car, and to the palace, and three hours after the accident was reported still in shock. The press surrounded the young American, but he would only shake his head. A friend pulled him into a limousine—someone from the engineering faculty at Yale, the *Daily Express* reported. He was pale and, as one radio commentator said, "looked as if he might be sick." Zooming down the highway, he told Singer to stop the car. The driver was given instructions through the glass. Blackford opened the door, and was utterly, writhingly sick. Back inside, the color slowly returning, he leaned his head back, eyes closed, and said to Singer:

"Gee, that was fun. What's my next assignment?"

Sixteen

THE NEXT MORNING Caroline woke early and, on spotting her, immediately dismissed the nurse who had been discreetly insinuated into the royal bedchamber after the Queen was given sedation by her physician. She was entirely restored, she said to Lady Mabel, for whom she had rung even as she called for breakfast. It remained only to make appropriate arrangements for the funeral of her old friend who, really—she explained to Mabs—had died a hero's death in trying to advance the cause of British aviation. She did not, Caroline said, distinguish in her mind between Peregrine's death, under the circumstances, and death in the field of battle.

Sipping her tea as though it were a doctor's prescription, she instructed Mabel to get the Earl of Holly on the telephone. The call having been placed, she told Mabel to ascertain, by inquiry in her name to the Prime Minister, what was the highest posthumous honor that might be paid to a Britisher dying under such circumstances as Viscount Kirk's; and to get word back to her before noon, "even if I have to listen to some Duke giving me a half hour's heraldic lore." The telephone rang. Mabs took it, and handed it to the Queen.

"The Earl of Holly, ma'am."

"Uncle Archibald, let us agree not to discuss the obvious things that are on your mind, and on mine. I would like your approval of a memorial service for Peregrine at St. George's Chapel at Windsor."

The Queen, chewing at her sausage, permitted the sputtering at the other end of the line for a reasonable period of time.

"There, there, Uncle Archibald, you needn't express gratitude—except to Peregrine. That we shall all do. The service will be at eleven A.M. on Thursday. Kindly telephone to Lady Lunford of my office, or to one of her assistants, a list, not to exceed a hundred fifty persons, of those you would like invited. Telegrams will go out to them this afternoon. I shall personally direct the memorial services. Any suggestions you have, please make to Lady Mabel." In a rather forceful disengagement, the Queen nevertheless diplomatically terminated the conversation.

"Now," she said, "get me Blackford Oakes."

The palace switchboard rang Blackford's flat. Blackford and Singer were having coffee, silently. Singer, having insisted on spending the night, wore pants and a T-shirt, Blackford a dressing gown. The maid had gone out for the morning papers which, Singer said, he wished to study meticulously before "slipping out of Blackford's life." Blackford, looking across now at someone no less, by now, than an old friend, muttered something about the pertinacity of the press. Singer reflected that, even now, Rufus was going over the papers and that his directives would prevail.

Singer, assuming that the call was yet another inquiry from the press, answered the telephone. When the operator said, in answer to his question, that it was Buckingham Palace calling, Singer, wise to the artifice of deadline journalism, asked, "Who in Buckingham Palace?"

"The call is from the royal apartments," the operator said, that being the closest an operator is permitted to go in such circumstances to announcing the august identity of the caller.

Though still slightly skeptical, Singer turned to Blackford and said, "You'd better take this. If it's on the level, it's the Queen."

"Hello?"

"Is this Mr. Blackford Oakes?"

"Yes."

"Hold on, sir, for Her Majesty."

"Blackford? I want you to know that I do not think you are in the least responsible for the tragedy of yesterday. There is no reason why you, or anyone else, should entertain even the thought of it, but some people are given to irrational self-reproach, and though I don't think you're that type, I wanted to say that much to you."

230

"I am most grateful, ma'am."

"But I do think that a gesture of sorts would be appropriate, and I'm going to suggest it to you."

"Anything you say, ma'am."

"I am sponsoring a memorial service for Peregrine at St. George's Chapel on Thursday morning at eleven. There will be the usual liturgical business and a short eulogy. I wish you to deliver the eulogy."

Blackford, receiver in hand, rose to his feet, his face flushed. He looked across at Singer in desperation, and said, "But—but, Your Majesty, I hardly *knew* Peregrine!"

"I don't believe that matters. You knew that he gave his life for his country. You know more keenly than anyone else what chances he took in order to excel, so as to maintain British pride and British morale."

Blackford paused, and said, "I guess that is true, ma'am; I guess I do know better than anybody else."

"Thank you, Blackford. You will be notified by the Duke of Norfolk exactly what the arrangements will be. After the service, come to the palace for lunch. And give my secretary a list of anyone you wish included at the ceremony and at the lunch. Keep your lunch list down to four, please. Good-by, Blackford." She hung up.

"Christ, Singer, I'm the official eulogist for Kirk! I thought the war was over!"

Singer tried to disguise it, and though he turned his head slightly to be out of Blackford's view, Blackford rose, suspecting as much, wrenched Singer's face around and saw that he was suppressing something near to hilarity. The phone's ringing interrupted what might have turned to mayhem. Singer lurched to the phone and forced himself to answer soberly. It was a code message, the meaning of which was that he and Blackford should go instantly to Walton Street, which they did, taking the usual precautions.

Rufus sat as though he had not moved since the Sunday evening Blackford had last seen him. He looked up at Black and said, "You are a good man."

Blackford bowed his head slightly in acknowledgment.

"I think I should tell you," Rufus said, with the nearest intimation of a smile since Blackford had known him, "that if you had declined to volunteer your own life in the event of having to use the cannon, I'd have regretfully made a different estimate of you and would have taken steps. But you convinced me you were willing to give your life, and that has always weighed heavily with me in assessing the risk of letting a man stay alive."

"Taken steps? Blown up my plane, I take it? When did you plan to detonate? And how?"

"It was remotely controlled by a Sabre engineer. It would have appeared as an apparently sympathetic detonation. Either on the heels of Kirk's fatal dive or after you shot Kirk down, or during your own dive."

"I thought you had it set to go off automatically?"

"Not quite. It required that I give the ground operator the word, which I'd have done if you had had to shoot Kirk out of the sky."

"Remind me to go back to engineering," Blackford said, sitting down and wondering why Rufus had told him all this. He wondered for only an instant.

"I know that you will never reveal our secret. But you must know that if you were ever tempted to do so, the order I did not give yesterday would, mutatis mutandis, automatically be reissued, and the republic would lose not only you, which I say sincerely would be a real loss, but my reputation, which rests on a professional record of: taking no risks."

Blackford looked at Rufus's deeply set eyes.

"I understand," he said.

"Several details. We have the package from 1305 Chelsea Station. It was, in fact, everything Kirk represented. The voices were clear and frighteningly unmistakable. The recording was apparently done at Windsor Castle, in one of the Queen's drawing rooms, I take it, while she was having tea with Kirk.

"As for the morning papers, there is a tremendous hue and cry from the Hunter people, which was to be expected. They are urging the conclusion that Kirk died of a heart attack a second before his ostensible death. They have this going for them: Slow-motion movies do not reveal any suggestion that he attempted to bring the aircraft up from the dive at the final moment. Clearly the Hunter people are concerned to bring their new model back to life, not Viscount Kirk. Since it is unseemly to suggest that he was guilty of bad judgment, they urge the medical conclusions. An autopsy, however, will prove impossible, given the fragmentation of the corpse. Management has announced that on Monday next, allowing a week's mourning for the lost pilot, they will demonstrate the Hunter in a nose dive attaining a speed identical to Kirk's, and will recover beginning only at five hundred feet from the ground. The names of the three pilots who will perform the exercise three times running have already been released.

"Now, there has been absolutely no suggestion, anywhere, of anything, over on our side, except personal dismay, and a certain professional disappointment that in one or two of the exercises, the Hunter showed itself to be narrowly superior to our Sabre. But these are conceded to be inconclusive, so it is safe to say that yesterday's events have not significantly advanced the answer to the question which of the two is the plane of the future for NATO. That is not our concern."

"It's sure as hell my dad's concern," Blackford felt constrained to say, and wondered, for the first time, whether his preoccupations had caused him to perform, as test pilot, less well than he might have. . . .

"On the other hand, the press has shown an enormous interest in you, Blackford, more than I'd have anticipated, and more than I welcome. Obviously their correspondents in America have done a lot to poke into your background."

He pulled out the *Express*. "'AMERICAN ACE SCHOOLED AT GREY-BURN / QUIT AFTER FLOGGING.' Another story pokes around London and your job here for the American foundation, identifying it, and calling you something of a social lion. That fellow discovered that you spent two and a half days at Windsor Castle at the invitation of the Queen, and there is even an interview, not unfriendly, with the keeper, who pronounced you a serious student of engineering.

"Now, there isn't anything in all this that we need to worry about. However, I think it would be a good idea for you to leave this afternoon. Go back to New York, and spend a couple of months preparing some reports for the foundation. Your presence in England while the story is hot is a magnet to the press."

"Rufus, my dear, omnipotent friend . . ." Blackford hadn't remembered enjoying himself so much since the nightmare's begin-

233

ning. "I bring you the news that Her Majesty the Queen has commanded me to deliver the principal eulogy over the corpse, or rather the memory of it, of the late Peregrine, Viscount Kirk, at St. George's Chapel, Windsor, the day after tomorrow at eleven A.M., thereafter joining her and, I am sure, a most august assembly, at lunch, where no doubt I shall be fought over between that half of the company that holds me responsible for Kirk's death, and that other half that will be appalled at my presumption in showing up at all, let alone in delivering the eulogy. But wait a minute, Rufus —I've got a terrific idea! Why don't you kidnap the Queen, hypnotize her, then send her back and have her rescind her invitation to me to do the eulogy?"

Rufus's eyes widened, and he fell, as expected, into one of his silences. He began to put his thoughts into expressionless words, addressed, primarily, to himself. . . . "You could simply take off, and leave the Queen a nice letter . . . you couldn't face it . . . that kind of thing. . . . But that would be uncharacteristic . . . and the Queen must be unaffected . . . nothing must shake her self-confidence. . . . *You will have to go through with it.*"

"Will you write the eulogy for me, Rufus?"

"That can be arranged."

"Never mind, I'll do it."

"I shall have to see it. No irony, Blackford. *Absolutely no irony.*"

He turned to Singer. "I still think we should get Blackford away from the press. Take him to Paris and come back late tomorrow. Keep Joe in the flat, answering the telephone, in case any of the questions suggest they are on to something. If so, get word to me. Blackford, my boy, look me in the eye right now and tell me: We did a thorough security check on you. But is there *anything* the press is likely to uncover that we haven't?"

Blackford paused, and then said nonchalantly, "The press has less to discover about me than about the Queen of England—and I haven't scared her off. . . . I suppose if they went over George Washington U's records for last summer they would find I hadn't actually spent much time in the engineering school. But I can't imagine they would go that far, or that if they did, there would be any sensational inferences to be drawn. After all, I *didn't* shoot

Kirk down. I just invited him, in the most genteel way, to commit suicide, or else I'd kill him."

"Is there anything in the Greyburn story I ought to know?"

"Yes," said Blackford. "Up until about a week ago if anybody had accused me of being a coward at Greyburn I'd have punched him in the nose."

"What happened a week ago?"

"I got it out of my system."

"How?"

"Suddenly . . . it just came . . . steaming out. I don't care anymore. However, if, while I am in Paris, you think my manhood at age sixteen was endangered, contrive to get somebody in the press to telephone Sir Alec Sharkey, at 50 Portland Place. He is my stepfather, and he examined the damaged goods after I came home. He can answer, as an Old Greyburn Boy, whether I was the coward or Dr. Chase the sadist. The only other witness to the event I doubt you would want to summon, since his name is Anthony Trust, and he is a trusted agent of our thoughtful, energetic, easygoing, but obstinately anonymous employer, the Central Intelligence Agency."

Boris Bolgin was not expected to stay late at the Soviet Embassy for routine diplomatic business, so he was usually home, in his little flat, by six o'clock, and on Monday had already poured himself his first vodka. He followed a procedure here which he found not only prudent, but quaint, and in a sense protective. In his apartment he kept six goblets ranging in size from the miniature one-shot glasses the pubs liked to use—for no other reason, Boris of course understood, relapsing by habit into a class explanation for so labor-consuming an object, than to exploit the masses by requiring them constantly to refill a glass that would hold only a single ounce at one time. Still, he always began with one of these and graduated to a port-sized glass, then to a Bordeaux glass, finally to a white-wine glass, though he seldom totally emptied it—Boris, he liked to tell himself, was a fan of vodka, not a slave of it. He had usually downed the first glass and begun to sip the second by the time the national news came on, and it was then that he saw the graphic record of what he had heard about the exciting events of the early afternoon. But BBC, exercising great ingenuity, had pieced together a considerable retrospective on the short but dramatic life of Viscount Kirk. Most of it was given over to old clips of Kirk talking about his horses during the Olympics, though there were in fact still earlier shots, including one that reproduced a minute's worth of a patriotic speech given by Kirk after he had been acknowledged as one of England's outstanding aces, and even a schoolboy shot as captain of the Greyburn eleven when they defeated Eton. Boris's glass was untouched throughout the television special. For all the precautions he had taken, Peregrine Kirk had not attempted to disguise his speaking voice, which after all was never these days broadcast on radio or television. So that for the first time outside the confessionals of a cluster of Catholic churches in London, Boris Andreyvitch Bolgin heard the voice of Robinson, while staring at his face.

It did not take long for him—the vodka glass was now entirely forgotten—to understand the potential consequences of the death of Robinson. For the Soviet Union, of course. But, most particularly, for himself. He did not instantly decide what would be his own course of action, but he reasoned that he must take what measures he could to explore the possibility that the enemy had got on to Robinson. And this was easily reduced to the single question: Was the American, Oakes, aware of Kirk's double life? If so, did Oakes have a hand in Kirk's death? If so (very important), how would he, Boris, account for the loss of his most productive contact? Stalin did not have that part of the normal man's brain that understands that certain things happen without the acquiescence of his nearest agent. The death of Robinson would translate, to Stalin, as the dereliction of Boris.

But one step at a time, the old warrior said, as he turned the safety key in his apartment, relocked it on the outside, and trudged back the four blocks to the Soviet Embassy where the guard instantly admitted him, forgoing the formality of an identification card for someone as indelibly conspicuous as Boris Karloff.

He went directly to the radio room and roused the operator, who was studying English by translating British comic strips. Boris had become autocratic by habit not so much as a matter of nature—as a young man, he was elaborate in his courtesies to subordinates—as of training. A generation of Soviet bureaucrats responded in one way to barked commands, in an entirely different way to whispered velleities.

"Take this communication instantly. Address it to" —Boris consulted his note pad and, mentally, effected the necessary transpositions; no one else, coming upon his note pad, would be able to decipher it— "Hilton Jones, NTX-NTX-NTX SovEmbassy, Newyork. IMPERATIVE WITHOUT ANY DELAY YOU ESTABLISH WHETHER ASSISTANT TO PROFESSOR RENE WALLACK AT YALE UNIVERSITY (A) PREPARED AT MIT, (B) WAS RECOMMENDED TO PRESENT EMPLOYER BY BLACKFORD OAKES YALE CLASS OF 1951, (C) WRITES REGULARLY TO OAKES IN LONDON GIVING REPORTS ON PROGRESS EFFECTED BY WALLACK IN LIAISON WITH TELLER RE HYDROGEN BOMB RESEARCH. IMPERATIVE I HAVE REPLY WITHIN HOURS. I AUTHORIZE YOU" —Boris paused to find another page in his notebook, and once again he made the verbal transposition— "UNDER PRIORITY SCHELL-YUCIN GIVE THIS TOTAL ATTENTION."

It worked. At six in the morning his number rang. Boris quickly put on his clothes and coat, and trundled back to the embassy. He knew not to expect any explanation of how the mission had been accomplished—these romantic appoggiaturas on the mechanics of the spy business were peculiarly the anxiety of the Americans and the British. He was pleased by the directness of the message handed to him. "EXTENSIVE RESEARCH CONCENTRATED IN FEW HOURS PENETRATED FLIMSY STORY WALLACK ASSISTANT. SUBJECT WAS IN FACT TRAINED IN BERKELEY, HAS NEVER WRITTEN OAKES, BUT WAS INSTRUCTED TO INDICATE OTHERWISE LAST FRIDAY."

Boris walked home slowly.

Blackford Oakes, then, knew about Robinson. How? He could not imagine. But on the other hand he could not imagine, either, that Robinson's operation could go forever undetected. But where had Robinson gotten *his* information? This Boris had never been able to imagine, and his failure to conceive what were Robinson's sources had contributed to his decision to permit Robinson to remain anonymous. Now he had no alternative. He would need to inform Ilyich that Robinson was dead, and that by voice identification, he, Boris, had identified him as Viscount Kirk. Would he then be expected to conduct an investigation into the contacts of Viscount Kirk? He was one of those English royal blades who move everywhere. How could Boris divine from whom he got the vital information? He would need to try and would concentrate on Robinson's friends within the nuclear scientific community. Was there someone there who, passing along the secrets to Robinson, knew what was their ultimate destination? Was it possible that Boris could approach that person, once his identity was deduced?

But something else was more likely. Blackford Oakes having discovered and exposed Robinson, wasn't it likely that the CIA, or MI-6, had done the work necessary to demolish Robinson's scaffolding? In the next few days, could Boris expect to read in the paper or—more probably—hear through the grapevine, the news that scientist Jones, or cryptographer Wren, had been silently arrested and was being held incommunicado?

It occurred to Boris that the young American was as close as he was likely to come to identifying the source of the great leak. But perhaps Blackford was only the mechanic—had he actually *killed* Robinson? If so, how? How in the world had he persuaded that cocky young man who occupied the priest's compartment in the confessional with such assurance to commit suicide? . . . In fact, Boris meditated, he was left with only this: Oakes was a fraud. He was a secret intelligence operative of the United States. Whether he had personally contrived the death of Robinson, Boris simply did not have the necessary information to conclude.

Boris liked to write notes to himself, when in tight situations. He did so now. A course of action, together with variables.

"1. I can notify Moscow that Peregrine, Viscount Kirk, turns out to be the invaluable Robinson. That I have arrived at that undeniable conclusion. But that I cannot know how many of the enemy are similarly aware of Kirk's double role.

"2. I can notify Moscow that I have ascertained that Blackford Oakes is most probably an agent of the CIA, and possibly had a hand in the death of Robinson.

"3. I can recommend to Moscow that we take steps either to abduct Oakes or to neutralize him by letting him know obliquely that we are on to him.

"4. I can do none of the above, save (2), which the embassy cryptographer will pass along in any case. Moscow is bound to

238

learn that Oakes is a fraud. But Moscow doesn't know that Kirk was Robinson. And doesn't know that Oakes might have had a hand in killing Robinson.

"5. [Here Boris's handwriting became less emphatic. In fact the script became almost flimsy, demure, as it shifted into English, deserting the intractable Cyrillic.] I can defect, and have a useful conversation with Oakes and the CIA. I could give them useful information and get a big-big settlement. Question: Would they all be able to protect me? . . . All very confused . . . Maybe I am better off putting the noose on the head of the American 'flier.' . . ."

He had, by this time, very nearly drained the large goblet, and his thought was getting foggy, and anyway there was time to come to a conclusion in the next few days. He knew one thing, and—again in English, whose vernacular constructions appealed to him—he repeated to himself, as he drained the goblet and turned the light off, "Well, Mr. Oakes, you son of a bitch, sir." Boris's old habits, earthiness and deference, accepted the rhetorical incompatibility. "I know who you are, you don't know it, and you shall pay for it."

Boris was quite right about one thing. Blackford had no idea he hadn't got clean away. And Wallack's young assistant, in turn, had no idea that the inquisitive and alluring graduate student who had enticed and then yielded to his advances had been moved by anything more than, at the margin, his irresistible charms, or that she had got from him anything more than a good dinner and a splendid tumble in his quiet little apartment with the computer print-outs on the desk, and the large technical drawing on the wall of a nuclear device, spilling out its aphrodisiac charms.

They were in Paris at five, began dinner at seven, and at nine they were drinking champagne with Mme. Pensaud, Michelle, and Doucette, and at nine-thirty, notwithstanding Doucette's ever-loving attentions, Blackford's eyes riveted on the portrait across the room, the coronation portrait of Queen Caroline. He sighed deeply, closing his eyes and trying to fancy a tiara on Doucette's head. She smiled maternally, through her rapture, and

Blackford smiled back. Doucette, eyes only partly closed now, knees raised, hands working, asked finally, more inquisitively than wistfully, why Blackford stared at the picture of the Queen. *"C'est encore question de symbiose?"* She laughed, and Black laughed back, forgetting for these few extravagantly carnal moments the consuming nostalgic fantasy. In fact he was asleep when, at eleven, Singer nudged him, held out a glass of champagne, and told him to get dressed.

"Would you believe it, our girls are going to give themselves to another pair of gentlemen? Make cuckolds out of us? Hurry up, Black, they're downstairs already. We are to leave the back way. I've settled the account."

"Aw, go settle your own fornicating account," Blackford said sleepily, belligerently; then, cheered by the accidental pun, he said resignedly, "Take me home, Uncle Sam, I've got an Inaugural Address to write." Singer took him to the hotel, guided him to his bedroom, looked at him as he slumped down, still dressed, on the bed, left and came back with a sedative, which he coaxed Black into taking, declining to be provoked into responding to Black's monologuist interrogation, which sprang from a blend of fatigue, alcohol, and tension, and seemed to revolve around the theme of the continuing necessity of looking after the safety and happiness of the Queen, to which duty Blackford Oakes should perhaps be assigned. . . .

Seventeen

Dressed in a mourning coat, Blackford Oakes drove in a palace limousine to Portland Place to pick up his mother and stepfather. His own father, always deft at getting out of the way, was conveniently off in Rome, preparing for the next Sabre exhibition and suavely superintending the defense against the British offensive, aimed at profiteering from the great Monday duel. At Windsor, Sir Alec and Lady Sharkey were detached from Blackford, and led to a pew in the center of the chapel, while Blackford was led to the forwardmost pew on the left, and directed to the lefthandmost seat, whence he could unobtrusively rise and walk to the lectern when the moment came for the eulogy. The Queen entered the chapel a minute before the ceremony began, and everyone rose. She was wearing black, and sat down at the opposite end of the same pew as Blackford. Between them were assorted royal cousins, aunts, and uncles, whose names were written out in the program Blackford discreetly leafed through, while apparently turning the pages of the hymn book.

The Archbishop of Canterbury read from the Book of Common Prayer. Then the choir sang "Komm' Süsser Tod" and a Scottish ballad that, the program noted, had been one of Viscount Kirk's favorites. Blackford wondered whether the choir would finish with the "Internationale," a less widely known enthusiasm of the late Viscount. Then another reading from the Archbishop, tailored to the occasion and ending with the words:

"No one in this company knows this more keenly than the young man who shared with Peregrine Kirk his last moments of life, high in the skies over England, both in their separate instru-

241

ments, striving to develop mechanisms of peace, whose deathly potential is designed to prolong life: life in freedom, life as citizens of sovereign nations, allied against any worldly conspiracy against human liberty. Her Majesty the Queen [Black had *insisted* on this, and Queen Caroline, when finally reached, understood and readily agreed] has asked Mr. Blackford Oakes to say a few words."

Blackford rose, walked gravely to the lectern, and bowed with that faintly wooden truncation that becomes those ill at ease with the filigreed lengths of native obeisances, first to the Queen, then to the Archbishop.

"Your Majesty; lords and ladies; family, friends, and admirers of the late Peregrine, Viscount Kirk. You know, most of you better than I do, the background of the man whose death we are gathered here to mourn. In everything he excelled. As a horseman, he was supreme; briefly, even, he was a competitive champion. As a war ace, he was unrivaled by anyone so unfortunate as to cross his path. Those of you who know anything about his inner life must know that he strove after perfection in disciplines you cannot even guess at. He showed at the very end his love for his country, and whatever misjudgment caused his death, there was surely no misjudgment in the unswerving strategy that, from his earliest years, brought him to his death: the determination that his will should prevail. We cannot know all the mysteries of this world, let alone those of individual human hearts, but I give it as my own judgment, whatever it's worth, that Peregrine Kirk's will did indeed prevail, that in his final moments on earth his mind was fastened, as the minds of all Englishmen, everywhere, should be, on the sublime imperative of their civil lives: saving the Queen. This, in his own way, he sought to do by his heroic exertions. As an American, I can only honor his singular act of self-abnegation, and suggest to you that he would have found it most appropriate if we should reiterate now the full meaning of the words he would most clearly have wished us to meditate, as surely he did at the end: God save the Queen."

There was a murmur of appreciation as Blackford returned to his pew. Another hymn, the final prayer, and, the organ launching into the recessional, the Queen rose, as did the congregation. Grave, beautiful, and blond, she was escorted out by the Duke of Gloucester, their pace slow—majestic. The royal party and their luncheon guests walked silently up the courtyard, past frozen sentries, observed by all Englishmen with a television set.

As Blackford filed gravely out of the chapel, he felt the warmth of the mourners who brushed up against him, ostensibly under the pressure of the moving crowd, actually so as to come close enough to whisper, "*Such a fine eulogy, Mr. Oakes,*" or somehow, tactfully, to communicate that sentiment. Blackford smiled and made what forward progress he could until, suddenly, he realized that only a few yards ahead, whom he would overtake, at the rate he was going, in a matter of seconds, was a grim figure, the back of whose head he instantly recognized—he'd have recognized him at any angle. The last angle at which he had in fact seen him was oblique: Blackford's head down on a couch, Dr. Chase's head four feet away, staring intently, his right hand upraised, at Blackford's protruding backside.

Blackford slowed his pace, notwithstanding that this meant more quietly exchanged hypocrisies with the mourners. Why, he wondered, should he have been surprised? As he thought about it, the monarchy is an elaborate venture in the ongoing validation of the Establishment. Of *course* Dr. Chase had to be invited. In England the headmaster of a boys' school is a major figure in his life, and Peregrine had not only been at Greyburn nine years, he had been Head Boy. The question Blackford now considered was whether he could escape into Windsor Castle without having to exchange amenities with the monster. If not, what would he say?

The enterprising British tabloid press took the choice away from him. Although Dr. Chase emerged from the chapel a full half minute ahead of Blackford, he was promptly arrested by the correspondent for the *Daily Express,* who held him immobile until Blackford spilled out, at which point the photographer of the *Express* propelled the two together.

Dr. Chase, having no reasonable alternative, turned to Blackford, arm extended, as the photographer flashed a picture, and the reporter started to take notes.

"Awful tragedy, Oakes. Quite awful. A fine young man, he was. Your remarks were altogether . . . apropos."

Blackford had from the beginning sensed that—somehow—he could not live forever in England without running into Dr. Chase. Yet he had never given thought to composing a phrase suitable to a reunion. He had read in an essay of the contempt George Orwell felt on coming upon his sadistic headmaster years later, a contempt unanimated by hostility or vindictiveness. Yet a week earlier it would have been different, because unlike Orwell's, Black's disdain had been undissipated. But that had now happened—only a hundred yards away, he smiled inwardly. He could hardly communicate to the headmaster of Greyburn School the great social achievement of this Old Boy—he wondered, had any graduate of Greyburn got as far as he, the one-term American, with a British sovereign?

He knew now that he was the center of attention not only of the team from the *Express* but of the many others who, coming out of the church, came upon the paralyzed piquancy; the stern headmaster and the chastened schoolboy, dramatized in the press, face to face under unimaginable circumstances.

"Yes, indeed, Dr. Chase. Kirk was an exemplary graduate of Greyburn. I cannot think of anything you failed to teach him."

The crowd cooed. The reporter from the *Express* sensed there was something in Oakes's words worth probing, and sought an elucidation, but the instincts of both men were similar. Dr. Chase turned to his left to greet the Earl of Holly, and Blackford turned to his right prepared to greet anybody at all, and gratefully recognized the groom who had for so many years mounted Peregrine's horses, and the Queen's, and only last week had done as much for Blackford. Black then set out for the gates of Windsor Castle.

The police, check lists in hand, had politely tabulated the guests, admitting fifty-odd persons before resuming their casual posture as human substitutes for the old portcullis. The very last to approach them, invitation in hand, was Blackford Oakes, and before the gates closed between him and his companion, a man named Callaway, he was heard to say to him:

"So long, Singer. Do please let me hear from you if there is anything, anything at all I can do to help you out in the future. You have my number."

Epilogue

BLACKFORD OAKES WAS ALONE. *It was never suggested that witnesses should have a lawyer sitting alongside, or even that they should be accompanied by another member of the Agency. The hearings were to be utterly confidential, and in a way—that was how Rockefeller had described them—"informal"—a meeting between a few of the most prominent men of the Central Intelligence Agency, and the presidential panel instructed to interrogate them, to discover just exactly what the CIA did, what limits it observed, and what mechanisms, if any, were needed to perfect the dominion of it by a self-governing public.*

So that Blackford was quite literally unaccompanied when the clerk, and the recorder, rose, as the august panel filed in. Blackford rose too, and the chairman, settled in his seat, looked down over the elevated desk-table to the clerk, and said matter-of-factly, "Proceed to swear in the witness."

The clerk turned to Blackford and said, "Please stand, and raise your right hand." Blackford did so.

The clerk, his glasses lazing over the bridge of his nose during the formality, uttered the workaday incantation in the humdrum cadences of the professional waterboy at court. The procedure is everywhere the same. The speed must be routinized, and accelerated, like liturgical responses, the phrases agglutinated, yet somehow audible. The inflection at the very end requires a note touching gravity.

"Do-you-Blackford-Oakes-solemnly-swear-to-tell-the-truth-the-whole-truth-and-nothing-but-the-truth so help you God?"

"No, sir," Blackford said.

The clerk stared at him dumbly. He was frozen by the irregularity. Eighty per cent of the people he had sworn in to tell the truth during the thirty years he had served as clerk had proceeded quite regularly to lie, and this upset the clerk not at all, that being someone else's problem. But he had always assumed that the imperious demands of his summons to the oath-taking were undeniable and had never experienced—or even heard about—someone who had reacted the way this . . . kook . . . this blond, trim, blue-eyed movie-star type in his young middle age, showing no sign at all of nervousness or panic or neurosis—who had gone to the deceptive length of actually raising his right hand, only to . . .

The clerk looked helplessly to the chairman.

Mr. Rockefeller's composure, though temporarily adrift, quickly kedged up in that splendid self-assurance of investigating panel chairmen.

"Please sit down, Mr. Oakes."

Blackford did as he was told.

"Why do you decline to swear to tell the truth?"

"Because, Mr. Vice-president, I am involved in a conflict of interest."

"Will you elaborate on this, Mr. Oakes?"

"To the extent I can, sir. If I swear to tell the truth, I am bound to answer truthfully questions you might put to me which, if I answered them truthfully, would jeopardize those interests of the United States which I have been trained to concern myself with as primary."

"I appreciate very much your devotion to duty, Mr. Oakes. But the fact of the matter is that this panel was appointed by the President of the United States, precisely to inquire into questions raised publicly about the Central Intelligence Agency, for instance, is it always engaged in matters that enhance the national interest, and, if so, by the use of methods that are compatible with American ethics? Now, it ought to be clear to you that the authority of the President of the United States exceeds the authority of the director of the Central Intelligence Agency, let alone any of his

*subordinates. So that by telling us the truth, you are in fact
upholding the integrity of the democratic chain of command."*
   *"Mr. Vice-president, I understand your theoretical argu-
ments. I reach different conclusions on concrete questions.
I would most willingly give you the reasons why I reach
these conclusions if you desire me to do so. But if you feel
that merely to listen to me give my reasoning is somehow
a waste of your valuable time, and that of your distinguished
colleagues, then it would save time—all the way around—for
me to say nothing at all beyond what I have already said.
I am of course aware of the penalties you are in a position
to impose on me for failing to co-operate by your definition
of co-operation."*
   *Rockefeller looked hard at Blackford Oakes, and the
political reflexes that had taken him where he was itched with
apprehension. He paused a moment, and then moved.*
   *"Will the clerk please escort the witness out of the room?
The panel will caucus in privacy."*
   *Oakes was led out to an anteroom. He tried to con-
centrate on the* Congressional Record *for the day before,
but found he could not even remember, in his current
distractions, whether Earl Butz, the subject of the longest
speech delivered the previous afternoon at the House of
Representatives, was the American, or the Soviet, Agricultural
Minister, and he was not able to infer from his actions, as
reported, which of the two posts he served.*
   *Next door the talk was animated. One member said, as
the chairman expected at least one member to say:*
   *"I say let's get Van Johnson back in here and tell that
prick to take that oath or—"*
   *"Or what?" the Vice-president said—a question he was,
really, asking himself.*
   *"Or"—the senator looked, as if for help from a legal aide,
first to his right, then to his left; but lacking help, said, a
little less resonantly—"send him to jail for contempt. . . .
At least we can get him fired. . . . Can't we order the
director to order him to take the oath?"*
   *"I actually don't know," the chairman mused. "I really
don't. Sure, we can get him fired—we can get anybody fired.*

If we can't do that"—he grinned jovially at his colleagues—
"we ought to quit. . . . And"—he was thinking it through—
"we could theoretically get him jailed for failure to co-
operate. But contempt citations, as you gentlemen know
from many recent experiences with the, ah, dissident American
elements, are not easy to get through Congress and the
courts. . . ."

The panel discussed the matter for forty minutes, coming
finally, grudgingly, to a conclusion. Decorum required that
it should not be humiliatingly announced in the presence
of the witness. So the clerk was called in.

The chairman addressed him:

"Inform the witness, Oakes, that he is excused."

The clerk, palpably disappointed, slurred his way into
the antechamber. He used the indirect address.

"Mr. Oakes is excused."

Blackford put down his reading matter, rose, thanked
the clerk, and picked up his briefcase. He left the room for
the corridor and waited there for the elevator, a grin
almost forcing its way through the facial anonymity he
cultivated in all public situations, though he could not refrain,
as he went down the eighteen floors to the lobby, from
whistling, softly, "God Save the Queen."

248